ALSO BY DAN FESPERMAN

PARIAH

PARIAH

Dan Fesperman

Alfred A. Knopf | New York | 2025

A BORZOI BOOK
FIRST HARDCOVER EDITION
PUBLISHED BY ALFRED A. KNOPF 2025

Published by Alfred A. Knopf, a division of Penguin Random House LLC,
1745 Broadway, New York, NY 10019.

Knopf, Borzoi Books, and the colophon are registered trademarks of
Penguin Random House LLC.

Library of Congress Cataloging-in-Publication Data
Names: Fesperman, Dan, [date]- author.
Title: Pariah / Dan Fesperman.
Description: First edition. | New York : Alfred A. Knopf, 2025.
Identifiers: LCCN 2024045923 | ISBN 9780593802236 (hardcover) |
ISBN 9780593802243 (ebook)
Subjects: LCGFT: Spy fiction. | Novels.
Classification: LCC PS3556.E778 P37 2025 |
DDC 813/.54—dc23/eng/20241004

penguinrandomhouse.com   aaknopf.com

Printed in the United States of America
2 4 6 8 9 7 5 3 1

The authorized representative in the EU for product safety and compliance
is Penguin Random House Ireland, Morrison Chambers, 32 Nassau Street,
Dublin D02 YH68, Ireland, https://eu-contact.penguin.ie.

To all allies, near and far,

in the fight against disinformation.

Don't give up.

PARIAH

Chapter 1

SEPTEMBER 2023

Her team had watched him for three days now—in the town, on the beaches, and in the breezy oceanfront bar and grill where he now sat alone in a booth for four, a nightly regular with his dirty martinis and the Philip Roth paperback he never opened.

He kept to himself, an introvert who had been an extrovert, a nobody who'd been a somebody, hiding in plain sight on this tiny Caribbean island of Vieques, where visiting Americans liked to pretend they were abroad even though it was U.S. soil. Yet, even in eclipse, he sat before a backdrop that might as well have been staged by his former handlers and publicists—butterscotch sun melting into a darkening sea, palm trees in silhouette, perky waitress delivering his latest refill with a smile.

The drink was his third, which told Lauren Witt that his reflexes were suitably impaired for what they had in mind. In addition, the usual evening crowd of drunks and ne'er-do-wells would soon begin to gather, a complication she'd rather avoid. So, when Malone glanced in her direction from over by the entrance, Lauren nodded. It was time.

Malone set out for the target. Their other colleague, Quint, who'd also been awaiting Lauren's cue, slid off a bar stool and dropped a few bills to cover his tab. The two men converged, pincers of a carefully planned offensive.

The Agency had offered Lauren up to five people for this part of the job, but she preferred simplicity, especially when dealing with a dolt. And that was her assessment of the target, even though he'd been educated at an Ivy and, until recently, had been considered one of the brighter lights of both Hollywood and Congress.

She doubted he'd make a fuss. He wasn't the type, or not anymore. Her greater worry was more existential: Recruit a scoundrel to take down a scoundrel, and maybe you'll wind up as one yourself, stained indelibly.

Malone slid into the booth, sealing the target in place just as Quint occupied the facing bench. They immediately had his full attention. He set his martini aside, eyes suddenly alert, face more animated than at any time in the previous few days. And, oh, that face! Even on a crowded street, Lauren would have instantly recognized it—handsome but haunted, lively eyes framed by laugh lines that now seemed obsolete. In his late forties, his profile was a near-miss for the classic lines of a fading sports hero—a former quarterback or ace pitcher—marred only by a bump on the bridge of his nose. But the man's signature feature was his mouth, appropriate considering all the catastrophic utterances that had crashed his career. It was wide and expressive, flexible, as if specifically engineered to mug for cameras and deliver outrageous punch lines. Although here on Vieques it had generally been as rigid as a death mask.

A little over two months earlier, this face—that of comedian, actor, filmmaker, and former U.S. Representative Harold C. "Hal" Knight, Democrat of California—had popped up almost continuously for several days running on Twitter, Instagram, Facebook, Fox, CNN, and the websites of every major American newspaper.

It began with the emergence of a video, shot with a phone, of a profane, sexist, demeaning (and possibly inebriated) verbal tirade by Hal on a film set. The clip was shocking enough for its language, but it went viral partly due to a brief moment of, well, indecent exposure. Or that was the most popular interpretation. Others weren't so sure.

By itself, the episode might not have sunk him, but its instant popularity had elicited further disclosures from half a dozen female co-stars and crew members from his recent professional past, who came forward in rapid succession with their own tales of unseemly things Knight had said or done. On a spectrum of bad male behavior that ran from, say, Al Franken at its tamest to Harvey Weinstein at its vilest extreme, Hal's transgressions fell well toward the lower end, yet still within the vast middle ground where final judgment often depended on who was doing the judging. While none of his actions would ever land him on a criminal docket, they had been more than sufficient to immediately convict him in the court of public opinion.

So, for several days he'd been a sensation, a story, a fable of instant infamy. Then, almost as quickly, he'd vanished from public view, presumably to either sink into obscurity or quietly plot a comeback. Ten days ago he had alighted here, walking ashore from the rocking deck of a ferry with only a roller bag and a fraying backpack, and now, in a seaside bar and grill in the village of Esperanza, he was within their grasp.

As Lauren watched, Malone began to speak while Quint leaned closer across the table. Knight's features twitched and tightened. He'd been cornered by two strong and capable strangers, and his eyes darted back and forth between them. His tongue emerged fleetingly to wet his upper lip, in the manner of a small reptile. He nodded rapidly at whatever Malone was saying, as if eager to please. His third martini remained untouched.

Lauren supposed that, for some people, Knight's predicament might inspire pity. Not from her. Never from her. And that's when it occurred to her why they must've picked her for this job. Her lack of empathy. Because even at this crucial moment she perceived a hint of accommodation in the calming gestures of Malone and Quint. And while that was certainly reasonable, perhaps even necessary—*We're on your side, so you should be on ours*—she also knew from her colleagues' recent words and actions that both men felt a little sorry for Knight, particularly with regard to the pathetic way he had sought refuge in this tropical bolt hole, cowering in a small, stuffy room with a view of a chicken coop and a littered dirt lot, when obviously he could have afforded far better digs.

Quint had already referred to him several times as "the miserable bastard." Malone, the previous night over dinner, had fondly recalled a favorite scene from one of Knight's movies, a crude gag which still made him laugh.

"He wrote his own stuff, you know," Malone had added, as if the blunt material in question had been the work of a sophisticated comedic genius.

Both her colleagues were professionals, of course, trained to not let their emotions get in the way of whatever needed to be done. Yet, to her mind, their recent behavior carried an undercurrent of fellow feeling, of "there but for the grace of God go I." Enough so to make her wonder if prolonged exposure would further rally them to his cause, to the point of undermining the op. Go soft on an agent or asset and you lost control. You gave them license to hedge, procrastinate, shrink away from the objective, and even lie. Which brought her back to the reason they were here: Get Knight on board with the Agency's plan—and do it fast, because the window was closing.

It was also imperative that Quint and Malone be as fuzzy as possible about the inherent dangers that lay ahead if Knight accepted—death and dismemberment among them, she supposed—because their proposed destination was a country in Eastern Europe in which the security apparatus was even more unforgiving than social media. Compared to those goons, the bogeyman of cancel culture was a prankster with a whoopie cushion.

Lauren and her colleagues would also be at risk, of course. Weren't they always? Although at this point her greater worry was professional disgrace, especially if this op ever became public. And if it ever came down to a choice between saving Knight's skin or her own reputation, she wasn't yet sure which one she'd pick. Did that make her a bad person? Certainly no worse than Knight, although that was setting the bar low. A bad employee? Possibly, but it wouldn't be the first time.

Then a second reason occurred to Lauren for why she'd gotten this assignment. Maybe her superiors thought the whole setup was a little too loopy, risky, and unstable—not to mention a rush job by their usual standards—to foist onto one of their favorites. So, hey, give it to Lauren.

There was always the chance Knight would say no. Her team had discussed the possibility that morning over an early breakfast on her terrace while roosters crowed and sunlight crept down the hillside.

"What if he won't do it?" Quint had asked.

"Why give him a choice?" This from Malone, hardly surprising given his expertise in more forceful techniques.

"He's not that kind of target," Lauren said.

"Besides," Quint added, "an unwilling agent is a worthless agent."

"Well, sure, but there are other forms of persuasion besides talk."

"Don't touch him, Malone. Not in any way that inflicts pain . . . Or not too much pain."

They'd all laughed, but they'd never really answered the initial question. If Hal Knight refused, she supposed she might even be relieved. Her superiors would deem it a failure, but would that be so bad? A week ago she'd fielded an offer from the outside with shorter hours and better pay. It was still on the table.

But for now she was solid with the Agency, even if that meant betting her future on someone who had idiotically squandered his own. She frowned and raised her glass—a shot of single-malt Scotch, neat. She'd been holding it in reserve until everyone was in place, so she finally allowed herself an exploratory sip. Tasteless. That happened sometimes when she was focusing hard on a job, a sensory embargo that endured until the task was done. She set down the glass and watched as Knight reared back his head and, for a moment, looked poised to laugh, a sound she knew from far too many hours of watching his movies in preparation for this op. But the brief noise that emerged fell well short of his capabilities. Not a bang, but a whimper. He lowered his head while his mouth formed words she couldn't hear.

Malone nodded reassuringly while Quint leaned closer and spoke in a confiding manner. She knew firsthand the soothing effects of Quint's baritone, so she wasn't at all surprised to see Knight respond with a nod and a wry smile. So, yes, it was working. They were softening him up, wooing him gently, winning him over. Perhaps he was even easing toward submission.

But don't lay it on too thick, boys. Keep it professional, maintain your distance. He's our instrument, not our colleague, and not our friend. Never our friend.

Lauren pushed aside her drink. Bad idea to have even ordered it.

Chapter 2

———≈———

Hal Knight's first thought was that they had come to beat him up, or spit in his face, or film some sort of humiliating video that they'd post immediately for the entertainment of millions. Yet another viral sensation at his expense.

In that case he'd pack his bag tonight and hop the next ferry out of here. By sunrise tomorrow he'd be in San Juan, scouting maps and travel sites for his next possible hideaway. Or, if things got bad enough, he supposed there was always what he had begun calling Plan Z, an escape option of last resort involving the contents of a pill canister zipped into the smallest compartment of his backpack. But first he needed to deal with this intrusion as quickly as possible. Endure it and move on—the new mantra of his fucked-up life.

"Who are you? What do you want?"

He spoke sidelong to the beefy fellow who had popped into the booth to his right. Hal didn't even want to look him in the eye. The guy smelled like cheap aftershave and wore an Omega watch as big as a sand dollar. The second fellow, staring from across the table, was even taller but not as muscular, although his hands were huge. He was black, but not as threatening as the white guy. And as soon as that thought crossed Hal's mind, he realized it was the very sort of observation that would only bring deeper embarrassment if it ever went public, which made him want to groan in despair. Maybe he was incurable.

"Actually, we're here to help, long as you've got a few seconds to listen."

The beefy white guy had spoken first. Then, in a pattern they would repeat throughout the conversation, they spoke in turns.

"We're here to present you with a modest proposal," the second guy said.

"With no obligation to buy."

"Not that we're selling anything."

"Other than the possibility of a brighter future."

"With you in charge of it."

That made him laugh, something he must have needed because he instantly felt better, although the strangled bark that emerged sounded rusty and unfamiliar, the rasp of a tool long abandoned in an outdoor shed.

"As if that were even possible," he said.

This time the second guy began the verbal tag-teaming.

"Hey, man. Everyone's entitled to a second chance."

"Or should be, if they only had the opportunity."

"And that's what we're here to give you."

Hal shook his head. Maybe they were pitching a bogus investment scheme, or cryptocurrency, or some idiotic product they wanted him to endorse. Late one night on cable he'd seen a disgraced televangelist promoting two-gallon buckets of coffee for riding out the End Times, and he'd be damned if he'd ever stooped to anything like that. The most encouraging sign so far was that neither of them had yet gotten out a phone. Nor did anyone else here seem to be paying him the slightest bit of attention, because at this point he'd rather take a punch to the gut than be subjected to yet another round of mass abuse by a faceless, ravening public. Although as he scanned the room he suspected that the woman over at the bar, the slender one with a stern cast to her eyes, probably at least knew who he was, even though she was pretending she didn't. He'd already encountered quite a few like her on his road to perdition.

Hal's main hope in coming to this small island had been that, at the very least, the herd of potential predators would be thinner, the opportunities for humiliation less frequent. The day before, he had stepped onto a half-mile-long beach populated by only two other people. Paradise, if only for a few hours, and he was apparently the lone lodger at the three-bedroom guesthouse where he was paying a mere eighty a night—understandable, given the mildewed shower stall and the occasional lizard, but still, it was genuine privacy. Besides, it wasn't the bargain rate that had attracted him; it was his need for camouflage. Or maybe a lousy room was a form of self-punishment, like those religious nuts who flogged themselves with chains.

Now the woman at the bar was gazing down at her drink, so maybe he'd imagined her interest. It certainly wouldn't be the first time he'd made that mistake.

"Okay, then. If you two have got some sort of pitch, go ahead. Make it."

He squeezed himself more tightly into the corner of the booth while he darted a glance at the beefy guy, who was now smiling. Hal considered taking a fortifying sip of his dirty martini, then decided against it. He was already tipsy, and had a feeling he'd need his clearest judgment in the moments ahead. Because whatever vibe these guys were trying to convey, the one they were projecting was of a trained, easy confidence. None of the barely disguised desperation that your typical sales jerks tended to emit. These two were almost military in their bearing, guys who wanted you to know they had all the time in the world to exploit their advantages, so you might as well settle in for the duration. *Professionals.* At first that was comforting, but then it was worrisome. Professionals at what, exactly?

They again spoke in turns, as if from a script, although their delivery was assured and convincing.

"I'm Sal," the first guy said.

"And I'm Chris."

"We work for the U.S. government."

"But not the IRS."

A brief moment of shared laughter ensued, but in Hal's case it never quite bubbled to the surface.

"And not the FBI," Sal resumed.

"In fact," Chris said, "since this is U.S. territory, we're technically not supposed to be operational here. So consider this entire conversation to be informal."

"Strictly unofficial."

"And off the record."

"I see."

And he really did, because for a while Hal had served on the House Intelligence Committee, and he knew from his briefings there, plus a few classified background papers, that just about any government employees who made it a point to say they weren't with the FBI and weren't supposed to be working on U.S. soil probably worked for the CIA. He also knew they weren't likely to ever admit that, but he decided to test them anyway.

"You fellas got any IDs to show me?" He addressed the question to Chris because he seemed more approachable, although they again took it in turns to answer.

"Doesn't work that way, my man."

"You probably knew that, too, right?"

"From your days on the committee?"

"Yeah, well . . ."

Hal was momentarily at a loss, but for the first time he was also a little interested, and as a comedian, or ex-comedian—because, of all his past roles, that was the one he still identified with the most closely—he couldn't help but appreciate the inherent absurdity of this dynamic: Anyone who says he's CIA is almost certainly an impostor. Only someone who cagily avoids mentioning CIA can really be an Agency employee.

Unless, of course, this was an elaborate practical joke, a brilliantly planned setup in which they would later spring the jaws of a trap and humiliate him even more grandly than he had humiliated himself to date. By nightfall this whole scene might be streaming online, with Hal starring once again in a role he'd never wanted. He again checked the room for any sign of someone filming with a phone. Still nothing, and this place didn't seem to have any security cameras. Although the woman at the bar *did* glance away when he looked in her direction.

Hal inhaled slowly to steady himself, then he finally reached for his drink. Dirty martini. Why had he ever decided that would be his regular tipple on Vieques? He really wasn't fond of that splash of olive brine, and he suspected that this joint used a cheaper gin than the one on the label. Plus, whenever he drank more than two, he always woke up the next day with a headache that lasted till noon. Still, as remedies go, he supposed it was preferable to Plan Z, and certainly less final, so his sip turned into a full gulp, then another, before he set the glass down. Having decided he might as well try to relax and enjoy this—and, boy, did that ever sound like the beginning of a crudely tasteless remark that would only sink him deeper into trouble—he wiped a sleeve across his mouth in the manner of a cowpoke in a saloon.

"Do your worst, then. Long as I'm really free to go whenever I please."

Sal looked at Chris, as if checking to see if he did. Or maybe they were both surprised that things were going so smoothly. Had they really thought he might resist? Or lecture them, or make a scene? Understandable, he supposed. Making a scene was pretty much how he'd made a living for a couple of decades.

Chris spoke first.

"You ever heard of Nikolai Horvatz?"

"Sure. The guy who's, what, premier or something? Of Bolrovia, in Eastern Europe. The one all the Republicans love."

"President is his official title. Has been for seven years now."

"And, well, turns out he's quite a fan of yours."

"Has all your movies, all your stand-up routines."

"And apparently watches 'em all the time."

"Like, he's almost obsessive about it."

"Why am I not surprised?" Hal said. "One dick to another, right?"

Another interlude of laughter, but this time it was Sal and Chris who were forcing it. Chris lowered his head as if embarrassed for him.

"Freely elected, I seem to remember. But hasn't he turned into kind of a tinpot dictator?"

"Some people think so," Chris said.

"And others don't."

"But, yeah, he's tightened the screws on dissent, the media, universities. On foreigners and asylum seekers, gays, that kind of thing."

"So of course he'd be a fan of mine, is that what you're saying? Yet another crypto-fascist bro looking for cheap laughs at anybody's expense other than his own?"

Sal and Chris exchanged uncertain glances, which for Hal was unaccountably pleasing.

"What? Are you actually surprised I'd hold my core audience in contempt? So does he look like them, too? A geeky, pimply white guy who feels naturally entitled to the girl of his dreams? Frankly, I wouldn't know him if he bit me in the ass."

"Well, uh . . ."

Sal looked mildly disappointed, but Chris seemed to be suppressing a laugh.

"I also doubt he'd be a big fan of my foreign policy positions," Hal added, although it felt like a desperate stab at virtue almost the moment the words left his mouth.

"I doubt he knows about those," Sal said, which began another round of tag-teaming.

"Even if he did, you never really took a public policy position on Bolrovia. We checked."

"And now that you're out of office, well . . ."

"Right. No, you're absolutely right. Completely irrelevant. Which tends to be the case when you only hold office for six months. Shit, I've had scripts in development longer than that gig lasted."

"But those comedy videos of yours," Chris said, "and your movies. He's all over those, man. Can't get enough of 'em."

"And those will outlive us all, alas. Not that I won't keep cashing the residuals."

"Well, for him that seems to be a good thing. Like Sal said, he's a fan."

"A big one," Sal added.

"Which you'd already know if you followed him on Twitter."

"Afraid I'm not much of a follower of anyone on social media these days. Don't even have an account anymore, for which I plead self-defense."

"Totally understandable, man," Sal said.

"Yeah, brutal place."

"Except for on Nikolai Horvatz's feed. Tell him, Chris."

"He tweeted out a thread a couple weeks ago where he was saying how much he'd love to have you over to his country."

"It was an open invitation. Said he thought you'd been greatly wronged in your own country, so why not come visit his for a while, as his personal guest."

"A place where he could guarantee that your work is still appreciated."

"Oh, yeah? Great. The Jerry Lewis of Bolrovia."

"He offered full hospitality. All expenses paid, for as long as you cared to stay."

"Provided you performed some of your old routines for him."

"A private show, for him and his buddies. A few of his favorites."

This time Hal's laughter came easier, and felt almost therapeutic, like when you flexed a stiff knee a second time. Or maybe it was that the whole idea was genuinely funny, far better than the premise of some of his movies. And wasn't it just his luck that the one prominent fellow advocating for his redemption was a would-be dictator, a leader well on his way to becoming an international pariah.

"Yeah, well, I'm out of that business now. Comedy, acting, screenplays, all of it. And truthfully? I have zero interest in getting close to somebody as retrograde as Nikolai Horvatz. Or Nicky. Okay if I call him Nicky, since we're practically best buds?"

Sal frowned and looked to Chris.

"You can call him Nick the Prick far as I care, but your interest isn't really what counts. Because *our* interest, for a variety of reasons, is in placing somebody close to the man. Right, Sal?"

"Absolutely, Chris."

And that's when it finally dawned on Hal what they really wanted, the whole reason for their pitch. Provided, of course, that this wasn't an elaborate prank—a possibility that still seemed quite plausible.

"Oh, I see. You're *recruiting* me. Our man in Bolrovia. Your break-through source to the Horvatz inner circle."

"See, Chris. Told you he's a quick one."

"You nailed it, man. Picked up on it right away."

"No, no. No way, guys. Because, well, you see the score here. Look at where you found me. Out of sight and, hopefully, out of mind, and that's how I'd like to keep it. Even if I did want to step back out into the open, the last place would be in some benighted capital in Eastern Europe, as court jester to a wannabe dictator."

"Except he's okay with keeping it all on the down-low," Sal said, setting off another double-teamed pitch.

"Or so he's letting it be known. Outside of Twitter, of course."

"Meaning, if you wanted, you could keep the whole thing hushed up."

"Completely under wraps."

"And, trust us, he's got the security capability to pull that off."

"And if you were willing to go over there—for us, we mean—we'd also want to keep everything under wraps."

"Especially our role in it."

"Completely so. Out of his sight, out of the public's sight, and, most important for you, out of sight of his security people."

"Which would free you up to, well, give him whatever sort of private audience he wanted."

"With no cameras, no publicity."

A brief pause followed. Hal had the idea that they had just expended their most important rounds of ammunition, the part they must have rehearsed the most. Both men looked a little anxious and out of breath.

"C'mon, guys, you know how this kind of shit works, even in a country like his. Word would still get out. And with an ego like Horvatz's, he'd probably be the first one to leak it."

Sal frowned and looked at Chris, who'd obviously been designated to handle this line of resistance.

"Maybe. You might have a point there. But even if word did get out, that would cause, what, a few days of further embarrassment? But eventually, well. Tell him, Sal."

"Eventually, after you were back home, safe and sound, the *real* story would come out. It might take a year, maybe longer. But it could be sooner, too."

"About how you'd done your country a real service."

"With no small amount of sacrifice."

"It's not like we'd be in a position to officially confirm or deny anything, but we have ways of leaking these things so that the right people in media know it and publicize it. And they'd say that you'd been in on this operation of ours from the very beginning."

"And, hey, once that happened?"

"It would be worth a book deal at the very least, right?"

"Maybe even film rights. With you doing the script."

Now they were pissing him off, because now they were sounding as insincere and overpromising as every hack rep and studio executive he had ever met in Hollywood, especially early in his career, when the pitch meetings had almost always worked this way, and had almost always failed to deliver afterward. In those godawful sessions, just as with this one, you were always the most important person in the room, maybe even in the world—hell, the universe!—until the moment you departed. Afterward, if you'd happened to bump into any of them out on the street a half hour later, or even in the elevator on the way down, it's doubtful they would have given you a second look.

He held up a hand to halt the flow of words.

"You guys are full of shit."

Sal's mouth dropped open, and nothing further came out.

"Maybe," Chris said, with a smile that this time looked genuine. "You know that world better than we ever will, so, yeah, maybe you're right.

But we're totally for real about this Horvatz thing, and from everything we've picked up on the ground over there, so is he."

"And we're totally for real about our interest in him. Which you could really help us with."

"Especially if you could put us closer to his team. His inner circle, like you said. Even in ways that might seem totally insignificant to you, you could really do us a solid. Then, even if all this public vindication bullshit never went down, well, *you'd* know, wouldn't you? And you'd always have that, right?"

And that, when Hal thought about it much later, after it was far too late to back out, much less go home, was the line that hooked him. It was convincing partly because Chris seemed to have come up with it spontaneously, but more so for its ring of truth. Because, while the whole world had become a tough audience for Hal Knight, in some ways he had become his own harshest critic, the least forgiving of them all. Even after three or four drinks every night, and after reading and rereading the highlighted passages in his Roth paperback before bed, he was still the person who most needed to be sold on any possibility of redemption.

And if doing what these fellows were asking offered a slim—okay, *very* slim—chance for that, well, didn't he owe it to himself to at least consider their offer? Not to mention that, if things worked out even remotely like they said, there was one other person who might yet be convinced of his value. And that possibility, however small, was also a great motivator, because up to now he had harbored zero hope on that front.

Hal sighed—a bit theatrically, perhaps, as if he were already slipping into a scripted role. He picked up his drink, then set it back down. He looked first at Sal—the Boxer, as Hal now thought of him—and then at Chris, who he already thought of as the Luther Vandross Dude, partly for the calm wisdom radiating from his eyes, but more for the silky voice that had just talked him to the precipice of yes.

"Okay, then. I'm willing to keep listening. Lay out your pitch for me. Tell me what would be involved, and tonight I'll think it over. You've got fifteen minutes."

He looked at his wrist to check the time, only to be reminded that he no longer wore a watch. But they did, so just as well.

Sal nodded at Chris, who spoke next.

"For the real pitch we've got to go somewhere more secure."

"But it's right around the corner."

"And somebody else will be doing the pitching."

"And I'll tell you right now," Sal said, smiling and shaking his head as if marveling at the whole idea, "she doesn't like you one bit."

"But she's good, and she runs a tight op."

"And for you, that's the most important thing."

"Because she'll keep you safe, and will get the most out of you. And we'll be there, too. Even though you probably won't see us."

"Yeah, every step of the way, wherever this leads."

"Just don't expect her to sweet-talk you. And you *sure* as hell better not try to sweet-talk her."

Sal chuckled and slid out of the booth. Chris joined him.

Hal, who hadn't yet budged, watched for a few seconds, wondering again if he should just bring this to an end, here and now. Walk back up the hill to his room. Read a little, make an early night of it.

Then, that tiny glimmer of hope flickered again, dim but unmistakable, so he pushed himself to the end of the booth and stood, feeling all three of the martinis as he waited for the floor to stop rolling like the deck of the ferry. He saw that the woman from the bar had left her seat and was halfway to the exit.

Deep breath. Last chance. Go home or keep going?

"Okay, then. Lead the way."

Chapter 3

———◈———

Pavel Lukov stood from his desk, cracked his knuckles, and stepped to the window of his fifth-floor office in the Presidential Palace. It was already midmorning in the capital city of Blatsk, yet all he'd managed to accomplish was stare at a phone for nearly two hours, waiting in vain for it to ring. The phone was encrypted, and had been delivered overnight by the Interior Ministry. It sat on his desk like a grenade with the pin removed.

Pavel checked his watch and again calculated the time difference between here and the island of . . . what was it called? Vikos? Keevis? No, Vieques. Barely four a.m. there, the dead of night. But shouldn't he have heard *something* by now? Maybe the silence was a snub, Branko Sarič's way of keeping him out of the loop, yet again, while initiating some reckless action which, if it failed, Pavel would be blamed for.

His two predecessors—both fired after only a few months on the job—had been no match for Sarič, and Pavel wasn't at all certain that he was. One needed only to glance at the organizational chart of the presidential staff to see that his position as chief administrative aide was a natural choke point for blame, disinformation, and thankless drudgery. But if, at age twenty-eight, he was now perched in the most precarious spot of his professional life, it was also by far the loftiest, and after barely more than a month on the job he was still getting used to the heady feeling of being there at all.

Pavel again glanced back toward the phone on his desk. Just beyond it was a framed photo of his wife, Jana, their five-year-old son, Tomas, and infant daughter, Ava. Their pleasant smiles now seemed forced, as if they were holding their breath over how badly Dad might screw things up. He turned back toward the window and drummed his fingers on the sill.

He needed a distraction to make time move faster, so he looked out at the view that, so far, had never failed to transport him. Stretching off to the right, just beyond the palace grounds, was a wide cobbled alley that angled away for a hundred yards toward the city center. Its far end opened onto the main square like the eyepiece of a telescope. For Pavel, it was like gazing back through history—his country's and his own.

In the foreground this morning were the alley's usual food vendors, steaming carts all in a row. Old Rudi was already hard at work at the third one down, preparing his chimney cakes. Pavel watched him wrap a strip of yeasty dough around an iron cylinder, then roll it in sugar before placing the cylinder on a spit to rotate above charcoal embers. He would baste it with butter until the pastry turned a flaky golden brown and the sugar caramelized into a sweet crust. Pavel's mouth watered.

Rudi had worked that spot for ages, and if Pavel squinted he could easily imagine his grandfather down there with him, hands on the shoulders of a younger, skinnier Pavel as the old man, his Poppy, placed their order.

"One for me with walnuts, Rudi. And one for the boy, with cinnamon."

And, just like that, Pavel might as well have had a warm pastry in his right hand as Poppy led him toward the square, where people were crossing in all directions on a beautiful Monday in late September, headed to work, to school, to market. There were pigeons, too, of course, a few of them breaking from the flock to stalk the young Pavel in case he dropped even a crumb of the chimney cake, while the rest took wing in a fluttery orbit of the vast cobblestoned plaza.

It was a grand and glorious space, bordered by a gilded town hall, a massive cathedral, an imposing clock tower that rang out the time every quarter hour, and, along every side, neat rows of charming timbered buildings with sloping tile rooftops—enough hotels, restaurants, bars, and souvenir shops to house, feed, water, and bilk more than three million tourists a year, all of whom came to gape at one of Europe's best-preserved medieval squares.

Tour groups large and small would already be on the prowl this morning, casting their eyes up to the saints and gargoyles that presided over the space from pedestals and rooftops. Pavel could recite the guides' patter from memory, having heard it in passing a zillion times since he'd tasted his first chimney cake.

"King Viktor Square is a showcase of beautifully preserved Gothic and

Romanesque architecture from the thirteenth through the eighteenth centuries."

What the guides never mentioned was that all of this Old World charm had survived the ravages of the twentieth century only because local leaders had twice capitulated to murderous tyrants without firing a shot—first to Hitler in 1939, then to Stalin in 1945.

At some point the guides always herded their wards to the center of the plaza, where Bolrovia's very own murderous tyrant—and the square's namesake—King Viktor IV, reared up on a bronze horse atop a huge block of marble. Viktor eternally held aloft the legendary sword that had cleaved the skulls of Mongol invaders and, less celebrated, brained quite a few of his fellow Bolrovians, including the entire family of his rebellious eldest son, Rogov. Yet, without Viktor IV, perhaps no one else ever would have united the region's warring fiefdoms into a single country, back in a wobbly era when colorful rivals like Frederick the Quarrelsome and Boleslaw the Chaste might otherwise have held on to their own slices of land and power.

The square's other dirty little secret was its scattered array of sewer grates, which exhaled a sour stench of rot from below, as if the ghosts of all the previous centuries still lurked down in the slime of those dripping, brick-walled tunnels.

But it was history of a more recent vintage that Pavel had in mind as he gazed up the alley, and he again thought of his grandfather, remembering the day Poppy had gestured toward an opening on the opposite side of the square—the entry to Prince Boromir Boulevard, which led to the splendor of the Saint Astrik Bridge across the turbid River Volty.

"That, my boy, is where the Russian tanks rolled in, guns firing at all of us, in 1958, not long after your father was born. We'd tasted freedom for three glorious days up to then. It was a peaceful uprising, with flowers, leaflets, and high-minded proclamations. But they answered us with bullets, of course, just like they'd done in Hungary. That was the way it worked in those days. Life behind the Iron Curtain. They fired without discretion, without a care in the world for anyone who might have simply come out to watch on a fine afternoon. Your grandmother had come with me and, well . . ."

At that point Poppy's voice had faltered, and when Pavel turned to see why, he'd been shocked to see tears streaming down the creases of the old man's face.

Years later, in almost exactly the same spot, Pavel's mother and father had showed him where they'd stood on a sunny day in 1989, when the Russian soldiers of a later generation had merely lolled and milled, guns slung lazily over their shoulders, benign witnesses to yet another crowd of restive Bolrovians as it toppled a statue of Lenin. Those actions had ushered in a new era of freedom, of governance by and for Bolrovians, and they had climaxed with an afternoon of stirring speeches in which a young firebrand named Nikolai Horvatz had especially impressed everyone with his impassioned but reasoned eloquence. As in 1939 and 1945, no one had fired a shot.

Pavel supposed that he had now climbed aboard the lead car of this lurching train of Bolrovian history, even if he still felt like a stowaway. Just over five weeks ago he had been working as the press spokesman for a parliamentary nobody. Now, thanks to a chance acquaintance, a few valuable connections, a couple of firings, and a whole lot of luck, he was working just down the hall from the president, and he spoke personally with Nikolai Horvatz nearly every day. It was thrilling, yet daunting. And all of it still felt fragile, a scaffolding of chimney cakes that could crumble with the merest flick of a presidential wrist. Unlike Viktor IV, Horvatz did not wield a sword, but he did have Branko Sarič, whose security service within the Interior Ministry grew more ruthlessly efficient by the day.

Pavel again glanced at his watch. The radio silence had lasted far too long, even by Sarič's standards. He stepped toward his open doorway and called out to his secretary in the anteroom.

"Marika?"

"Yes?"

She was out of sight but within earshot, because he had positioned her desk so it would not block his view of the hallway beyond. His most recent predecessor had been blindsided by an office coup, which he might have foreseen simply by monitoring the comings and goings of the aides who'd plotted to dump him. All visitors to Horvatz passed in this corridor, and when Pavel couldn't watch the traffic, he had instructed Marika to do so. He eased into her line of sight.

"Has, um, *he* been in touch yet this morning?"

Marika arched her heavily penciled eyebrows.

"The president?"

"No. I was referring to, um, well . . ."

"Mr. Sarič?"

"Yes."

"Not a word."

"And no sign of him in the corridor?"

"No, sir. Only two people have passed in the last two hours." She consulted a pad. "The Minister for Trade. And Wally." Wally was Hugo "Wally" Wallek, chief political adviser and all-around fixer. His presence could mean just about anything.

"Did you remember to switch on the special phone?" she asked. "Is it online and fully charged?"

The special phone. She made it sound like a device for communicating with a superhero. Pavel's bat phone. Then, as if her words had summoned it to life, the damn thing began to ring back on his desk before he could even reply.

In addition to the shrill ringtone, it was vibrating as vigorously as an electric shaver, making it shimmy and slide toward the edge of the desk. Pavel stepped quickly toward it, grabbing it just as it was about to plunge to its death. He fumbled for the right button as the ringtone shrieked again, and was nearly out of breath by the time he answered.

"Yes?"

"We have confirmed and isolated the location of the target, and my men are in place. They await your authorization."

Pavel hated the way Sarič talked. The man could make a stroll on the beach sound like an amphibious assault.

"Authorization to do what, exactly?"

He also hated what his own voice did whenever he spoke to Sarič. It rose like that of a choirboy soprano, making him sound much younger and a little timid, probably because Sarič reminded him of those bigger boys at school who'd shoved him up against walls and lockers, usually after they'd been caught smoking weed or had flunked a math test that he had passed. And if, like them, Sarič wasn't particularly book smart, he was, also like them, quite sophisticated in the arts of sensing and exploiting weakness. His additional skill was in knowing how to massage and manipulate power. He had a knack for detecting hidden pools of influence, like one of those old fellows with a dowsing stick who told farmers where to dig their wells.

"Authorization to launch the action that will achieve our objective."

"At this hour? Shouldn't we at least wait until sunrise, or until the man is up and about?"

"Of course. I said nothing about immediate movement. But we might as well give my team the go-ahead in case unforeseen circumstances arise."

"You make it sound like a snatch-and-grab. I thought this was going to be a friendly approach. We want to make him like us, not scare him to death."

"Obviously. But there is always value in the element of surprise. And who's to say he'll accept if we aren't at least somewhat . . . *emphatic* in our approach."

"There's emphatic, then there's overkill."

"I discussed all this with the president. He is in agreement."

Did Pavel believe that? Not really, but he had no basis for rebuttal, so he didn't argue the point. He heard a slurping noise—Sarič, sipping from his hundred-euro water bottle, a brand that supposedly filtered out every known pathogen, because, well, that was also his nature, ever alert to all possible threats, including ones that existed only in his head. But the most infuriating thing about the man was the way he almost always managed to gain the upper hand, even when he was supposedly reporting to you.

"Okay, then. Just tell them to keep their actions within reason."

"Is that your authorization?"

Covering his ass, like always.

"Yes. But keep me updated."

"I always do."

Another lie, this one provable, but not worth disputing. Sarič disconnected before Pavel could say anything further. The phone went dead in his hand like a small bird shot from the sky.

Pavel put it back on the desk and again looked out toward the square. He had just set something in motion, but wasn't exactly sure what it was. State resources of no small consequence were being expended over a matter that, to him, felt like a vanity project, an elaborate stroking of the president's ego. But it had been approved at the highest level, so he could hardly say no.

And if something went wrong? Pavel shook his head. Maybe one of Rudi's chimney cakes would set his mind at ease. He grabbed his jacket, dropped the fucking bat phone into his pocket, and breezed out the door.

"Back in an hour," he said over his shoulder.

"Yes, sir," Marika answered, with a knowing tone that told Pavel he should have shut his door before speaking to Sarič.

By the time he reached the elevators, he had changed his mind. A chimney cake would not suffice. Midmorning or not, what Pavel needed now was a drink.

Chapter 4

Spies do not sleep like you and me. Even as they dream, their minds creep along deeper channels of awareness—probing the darker corners of their rooms, perhaps, or assessing noises from the corridor. If all is quiet, maybe they review the details of their latest cover identity, once more for good measure. In this kind of existence, arising refreshed can feel like an operational failure, as if they'd squandered an opportunity to get ahead while the rest of the world slumbered.

Lauren Witt had no such qualms when her phone awakened her an hour before sunrise, mostly because, somehow, she'd already sensed that events were moving beyond her control out there on the quiet streets of Esperanza.

Reaching across the bedside table, she grabbed the phone, hit the right button on the first try, and answered before it could ring a second time. It was Quint. He was whispering.

"Something's about to go down over here, and it's not good."

She sat up, already alert. There was a skittering noise from the far corner of her room, but it was only a lizard. This goddamned island.

"They're here?"

"Four of them. Must have come in on the last ferry while we were pitching him. Three are in tactical gear, so not exactly a welcoming committee."

"Jesus, they're going to *kidnap* him?"

"No idea. But everyone's in place and they're ready to rock and roll. Two in the hall, two downstairs."

"Armed?"

"Oh, yeah."

"Is he awake?"

"Doubtful. His lights are off and I can hear his breathing on the mikes. Slow and steady."

"Good thing we told him they might make an approach."

"We also told him they weren't here yet. We should've sent Malone to check the last boat."

"Nothing we can do about that now. Hopefully he'll keep his head. I'll wake Malone. We'll see you in ten."

"Travel on foot. Come in from the east."

"Got it. Putting my phone on silent for any updates."

They ended the call. Lauren swung her feet to the floor and reached for her clothes.

"Fuck!"

Quint had pissed her off a little by second-guessing the way she'd deployed them last night, but it rankled mostly because he was right. She should've sent Malone to the ferry port in Isabel to watch the day's last arrivals. They'd been tracking incoming air passengers by monitoring a video feed from a security cam at the tiny local airport, but the cameras at the ferry terminal were unreliable, so they'd had to watch those unloadings in person and had missed a few incoming boats. Maybe the Agency had been right to offer her five people. The kicker was that, based on signals intel from Blatsk, they'd had no reason to expect anyone to get here so soon. Even so, she had underestimated the opposition, always a dangerous mistake. Or had she, perhaps, *wanted* this to fail, out of a subconscious desire to sabotage either Knight or her job?

Worrisome, but a moot point now. She banged on the wall three times, a prearranged signal to Malone next door. The walls were so thin that she heard him groan in response. He then answered with a double knock and the thud of his feet on the floor. As she dressed, the lizard scurried into the bathroom. She slipped on her shoes, ran her fingers through her hair, then followed the lizard into the bathroom for a pee and a splash of water on her face.

She grabbed her phone, then stepped into the corridor. Malone emerged from his room a few seconds later, looking bleary and out of sorts.

"Trouble?"

"Four of them. Armed. Must have come in late. Quint said to approach from the east."

Malone nodded and followed her downstairs. They were already moving stealthily, like nocturnal hunters—an owl and a puma. It was nearly four thirty a.m. First light was only half an hour away, but for now even the roosters were quiet. She supposed that by the time they got there the whole thing might be over, so she picked up the pace, and Malone followed. Three more blocks—or, no, make that five, since they'd be taking a roundabout route to avoid detection.

Lauren again cursed beneath her breath, already second-guessing everything about herself and this op.

Chapter 5

At the epicenter of all this movement in the dark, Hal Knight lay awake in bed, restless and unaware as he stared up at the rotating blades of a ceiling fan. The moon had risen, and the shadows of palm fronds played across the far wall. Having just been recruited only a few hours earlier for a clandestine mission abroad, Hal supposed that he should be feeling like a man of action, a Humphrey Bogart in a languid noir universe of exotic cocktails and slow-moving fans. Why, then, did he instead feel like Peter Lorre, weaselly and cornered, doomed to be erased before the end of the script?

He got up to shut off the fan. Maybe now he could fall back to sleep. The martinis had dragged him beneath the waves for several hours, as they always did, but a few minutes ago a vivid dream had floated him back to the surface. The subject had been the usual one, except this time she had been happy, approving. They were coexisting peacefully, even lovingly, in a rosy world where he hadn't yet done anything horrible. Or not publicly horrible, anyway. He'd awakened with a lightness in his chest that he hadn't felt in ages, only to immediately realize where he was, and why.

Bad dreams were so much easier to deal with. When you woke up, you got to feel happy just to be alive and unharmed. All he felt now was regret, yearning, a desire to curl back up inside his pleasing fantasy like a wet dog on a warm hearth. A day earlier and this sort of comedown might have triggered further contemplation of Plan Z—that tiny pill bottle, beckoning from inside his backpack in the darkest corner of this sad little room. Fast-acting, mostly painless. And virtually untraceable in an autopsy, or so he'd been assured by a friend with enough experience in exotic pharmaceuticals to qualify as an expert. Although Hal supposed that to really baffle the paparazzi with that kind of exit, he'd first need to dispose of the canister.

Instead, because of what had happened last night, he contemplated what might lie ahead for him in Bolrovia. Not his first choice for international travel, or even top ten. And surely his presence would quickly go public, a prospect that made his stomach rumble. It also sounded, well, a little iffy, maybe even dangerous. Had he actually said yes? Apparently so, although that entire scene still felt subject to revision, or to being slashed from the script altogether.

From the bar they had taken him to a rental car parked around the corner, a four-door Jeep Wrangler. Sal and Chris sat up front while he climbed into the back with the woman, Susan. None of their names were real, he supposed. Spying already seemed a little bit like Hollywood—a world of constant fakery where you could never afford to be yourself.

"This isn't the kind of car I think of you guys as driving."

"Pretty much the only wheels available on the island," Chris said. "Unless you want to ride around in a golf cart."

That's what Hal had been driving here, like many tourists on Vieques, a flimsy open-air crate that topped out at twenty-five miles per hour and always verged on calamity when careening down steep hills. Throw in the island's wandering population of wild horses, which sometimes clopped alongside you or, more often, grazed on the shoulder, and it made driving here feel like a thrill ride at a shabby amusement park, a liability lawsuit waiting to happen. The Jeep was luxurious by comparison, with air-conditioning and the reassuring glow of a dashboard display.

Susan pitched him while they drove along the shoreline and up into the darkening hills. He immediately sensed a greater distance in her manner than he had with either Chris or Sal. At first, he attributed it to heightened professionalism. She was the team leader, the closer. But gradually, as he watched the flash of her eyes, the set of her mouth, he realized it was hostility. He found it easy to imagine her seated before a laptop several months earlier, seething as she read the various accounts of his misdeeds. Maybe she was one of those millions who had eagerly clicked "like" on tweet after tweet that had skewered him to the wall.

Or were the CIA's covert employees even allowed to participate in such things? If he'd still been on the committee, it would have been a decent question to ask.

She nonetheless exuded capability and was quite efficient in laying out the task at hand. It took only about ten minutes before she began wrapping things up.

"It's pretty simple, really. Just accept Horvath's hospitality and do your shtick, or whatever else he wants from you. Entertain the man and make nice with his friends. All you have to do on our behalf is keep your eyes and ears open."

"That's it? Just look and listen?"

"While reporting to us, of course."

"How?"

"We'll set up a channel of communications. Rudimentary stuff, mostly. Everything analog. Minimal risk."

"How small is minimal?"

"Well, if anything feels too hazardous, you can just bag it and wait to tell us after you're out of the country. Is that minimal enough for you?"

While her disdain was hardly unexpected, it was a little unnerving. If he got into trouble, how hard would she work to extract him? Or maybe that would be up to Sal and Chris, which made him feel better. Still, he felt a need to defend himself.

"I'm not saying I'm unwilling to take risks. Especially if, well, this is important enough. Is it?"

The three of them exchanged a look. Sal, who was driving, looked at Susan in the mirror. Chris turned for a glance.

"It is. But there isn't much more we can tell you, for your own protection. We know the stakes, and they're high. We know what we're after, and, yes, it's important."

"But what if I don't really find out much, or get close to anyone?"

"Anything you get from the inside will be a plus, even if it's only general impressions," Chris said, "even if you're only there a few days."

"Sometimes even the most seemingly insignificant stuff can help us leverage information from other places," Susan said. "And there are some other considerations, which aren't anything you need to know. Nor do you want to, if you know what's good for you."

"Yeah, I can see the logic in that. Still . . ."

Sal braked suddenly on a curve. The Jeep swerved sharply, tossing everyone from side to side. Some horses had loomed up in the darkness, and he'd barely avoided a collision. The car crept along until it cleared the last one, and then Sal accelerated smoothly. The roads here at night were pretty spooky.

"When would you show me how to get in touch and all that stuff?"

"Tomorrow. It'll only take a few hours. But first we have to know you're in."

Was he? If not, then what the hell else was he going to do for the next few months, other than keep wandering from one isolated stopover to the next while drinking himself to sleep every night. Was a lack of options a good enough reason to say yes?

His lengthening silence seemed to make the others restless. Chris glanced back over his shoulder. Susan stared from her corner. Their salesmanship—and their professed confidence in managing any possible problems he might face—reminded him with some irritation of his final meeting with his agent and publicist, who had converged on his house in Malibu only a few hours after the dam had burst on social media. A "crisis meeting," as Jill, his publicist, had called it. Lisa, his agent, had nodded emphatically in agreement while watching him over the edge of her iPad, an item that was as much a part of her as her fingers and toes.

Jill and Lisa had appeared on his doorstep as if summoned by a 9-1-1 dispatcher, their black BMWs arriving in tandem, like the vanguard of a motorcade. As if to convey their urgency, they had entered talking, immediately spouting phrases like "crafting an appropriate response" and "your need to get out in front of the information curve."

He'd seated them on the couch and offered coffee, which they had declined. Both had brought their own bottles of overpriced mineral water. Then, just as Chris and Sal had done earlier that evening at the bar, the two women had tag-teamed their pitch, with Jill leading off.

"The first thing we need to do is seize control of the narrative."

"But with humility, of course."

"And the appropriate amount of contrition."

"And remorse."

"Yes, but without overdoing it."

"Absolutely. No need to give away the store."

"Not when the real need here is for you, in your own subtle way . . ."

"Or not so subtle."

"Okay, no. Maybe not subtle, that's not your style. But with skill."

"Of course. And sophistication."

"Exactly."

They'd paused for a moment, having lost the thread, so he'd prompted Jill.

"You were about to tell me the real need."

"Right."

"The real need here, Hal, is to begin resetting the narrative."

Before Jill could speak next, Hal had raised both hands to halt the flow of words. Or maybe just to surrender.

"First off, both of you should know that, right before you got here, I posted a public apology."

The two women exchanged horrified glances.

"Posted where?" Jill asked.

"On Twitter. Then I closed my account. And if it makes you feel any better, I also didn't consult anyone on my congressional staff before doing this. This was my action, and mine alone."

Lisa was already hunting it down on her iPad. She found it within seconds. Jill sidled up to view her screen, and he watched their lips move as they read. The glow of his words on the screen reflected on their reading glasses, although he could have recited them by heart.

My words and actions, as described so well by so many in recent revelations, were reprehensible and wrong. I apologize unconditionally. I also announce that, effective immediately, I am resigning from Congress and, not to be redundant, from the entertainment industry as well. Henceforth I will absent myself from public life. No follow-up questions, please, and no interviews.

Their snap assessments, like their BMWs, arrived in tandem: "Oh, shit."

Jill was the first one to get back on track.

"We can still salvage this."

"Salvage? What's left to salvage?"

"Your career."

"Finished. Done."

"Okay, then. I understand why you'd feel that way at the moment. Especially about Washington. But nothing is ever final in this town—you should know that by now. So maybe if we all took a breather . . ."

"A *breather?*"

Lisa joined in.

"Sure. And then we could all reassess in a few days. Or even a few weeks. Start off slowly, but with a positive statement."

"I've made my statement. You just read it."

"A statement you'd make with your actions, I mean."

Jill took up the thread.

"Lisa's right. You could check into a rehab clinic. Go for that whole nine-step thing."

"I think it's twelve," Hal said wearily.

"Whatever. Just get into a program. We've drawn up a list of options."

Lisa reached into her purse.

"Stop. I'm a drinker, not a drunk. This isn't a substance-abuse problem. The problem is me. The person I've become."

"Maybe you're right. But Jill's right, too, okay? Because we're talking about public perception. There are *always* mitigating circumstances, and your fans will want to hear them."

Jill nodded rapidly and doubled down.

"Absolutely. In fact, most of your fans are probably far more upset by the idea you won't be making any more movies than by anything you said or did to those women."

"Exactly," Hal said. "You've outlined the problem perfectly, the whole goddamn syndrome of codependence and my willingness to make a buck from it, which is yet another reason for me to quit. Who needs twelve steps when you can fix it with one? So go. Now. Both of you. Your services are no longer needed, although you'll of course be paid through the duration of your contracts."

Their mouths had dropped open in unison. If Hal had still been making movies, he would have wanted to capture the moment on camera, for its perfect comic synchronicity.

Neither of them was accustomed to being ordered from a room, especially not by a client with such an obvious and urgent need for their services. Yet, when Hal stood, they stood. When he walked to the door, they followed in lockstep, and they remained dumbstruck as he waved them through. Although Lisa did pause just beyond the threshold, where she turned to make a final plea, waving her iPad like a preacher with a well-thumped Bible.

"Hal, really. Seriously. This doesn't have to be the end of things. The whole MeToo thing is losing momentum, anyway. Everyone is aware of that, and we can do better for you. *You* can do better for you. And it's not about the money."

"It's always about the money, Lisa."

Then he shut the door in their faces.

Disentangling himself from his seat in Congress had been more cumbersome, mostly because other people's livelihoods and interests were at stake—the jobs of his staff, the leftover contributions of donors, the pressing needs of constituents. Fortunately, most of his staffers were holdovers from the previous member, rather than his own hires—hell, they pretty much ran the place anyway; not just his office but all of Congress—but the paperwork and other chores needed to cut himself loose had required him to duck in and out of places where cameras always seemed to be waiting in ambush. Thankfully, California law required the governor to act within two weeks to set a date for a special election to fill his seat, an action which had instantly diverted attention to the seven men and women who had eagerly lined up to replace him. Four were Democrats, and each had furtively approached him to request that he *not* endorse them, which had been good for a few private laughs.

And here he was now, enduring another pitch, only this time as a more interested and engaged listener, and maybe the only thing still holding him back from saying yes was knowing that it was definitely what Lisa and Jill would want him to do. An extreme version of career rehab, and by working for a shadowy organization which, when he was younger, he had deeply mistrusted. The CIA had always seemed to Hal to be an unchecked instigator of all sorts of undemocratic activities. Although, in his brief time on the Intelligence Committee, he had developed a grudging respect for the Agency's rank and file, if only for the way they'd stood up to the whims and "Deep State" bluster of the recent ex-president.

As he hesitated further, it also hit him that in Bolrovia he would once again be performing for people who would be predisposed to laugh at anything he said, a debilitating syndrome that had cheapened each successive triumph in the arc of his comedy career. He supposed that the venture might be dangerous, too. Although how risky could a little spying be when the alternatives still included Plan Z, which for weeks had hovered at his periphery like a black helicopter awaiting orders to open fire? This spy scheme, no matter how foolhardy, might be his last, best opportunity to shoot that chopper down.

Why not say yes, then? Maybe because his vanity—or what was left of it—was enjoying the idea of being courted again, even though he knew Susan would never have accepted that characterization. So he put them off one more time.

"I dunno," he said at last. "I've still got a few questions."

Up front, Sal sighed and mashed the accelerator a little harder. Chris kept his eyes on the road. Susan just nodded.

"Okay," she said. "Ask away."

"Apart from the watching and listening, will you be making any special requests of me?"

Sal and Chris exchanged another glance up front.

"What do you mean?"

"Well, like maybe, 'Here's a pill, we want you to drop it in the president's coffee.'"

"You're an asset, not an assassin."

"Okay, then. How 'bout something you guys would think of as really easy, but I might not. Like, 'Next time you're in his office, grab a few items out of the trash can.' Isn't that how these assignments work? Once somebody's comfortable doing one kind of thing, you start upping the ante?"

For a moment the only sound was the thrum of the tires on the road, so Hal pressed the point.

"Well? Am I right or not, guys? And gal."

Even in the dark he could tell that she hadn't liked the "And gal" part, and in retrospect he realized that was half the reason he'd said it—to provoke her, to piss her off. But it bothered him that they already seemed to be holding out on him. Because once he was "in place," as they kept saying, he was almost certain that a CIA version of mission creep would occur, and he'd feel obligated to go along with every increment if he ever wanted to return home.

Susan, to her credit, had tried to address his concern.

"Look. There will never be a moment where we won't be able to extract you, if that's what it comes to. We'll see to that from the beginning. If you ever feel like we're pushing too hard or you're getting in over your head, just say so. And that will be your call, not mine or anyone else's."

Did he believe that? He wasn't sure. But he also doubted that even a fairly unpopular world leader like Nikolai Horvatz would want to have the killing of an American comedian—even a disgraced one—on his international résumé. Although he supposed they could always make those kinds of deaths look accidental, a thought that kept him quiet for a few seconds longer.

"Anything else?"

"How, uh . . . how would you, or we, initiate this thing? Would I just fly over there unannounced, or should I send some kind of email, maybe even a letter, to tell them I'd like to come?"

"No need. They'll come to you."

That had surprised him.

"Here?"

"If you stay long enough. Tell him, Chris."

"The wheels are already in motion. Apparently, they've figured out that you no longer look at Twitter, which, by the way, isn't even called Twitter anymore."

"It's not?"

"It's called X. Happened not long after your fuckup."

"X what?"

"Just X."

Hal snorted. It was stupider than any of his jokes.

"Anyway, their plan is to recruit you personally. Kind of like we're doing now, which is why we wanted to talk to you first."

"Shit. So they're really serious about this."

"Oh, yeah. Horvatz is the kind of guy that, when he really wants something, his people tend to get it for him."

"Are any of you based there? In Blatsk?"

Chris looked at Susan, as if seeking permission to answer. She nodded.

"Sal and me both."

"Going on two years now," Sal said.

"Three for me," Chris said.

"They're both NOCs," Susan said.

"Nonofficial cover operatives," Chris added.

"It means they're working under commercial cover, not embassy postings. Sal's a supervisor in an office for an American construction firm, Chris is a musician working his way through Europe."

"Keyboards," Chris said.

"And you?" Hal asked Susan.

"Based in Langley, but I spend a lot of time abroad. I'll also be there under commercial cover, to manage the logistics."

"How soon before they get in touch? Ballpark."

"It could be any day now. But we've seen no sign of them here, or not yet. Soon as we do, we'll give you a heads-up. We'll coach you on how to respond."

He digested everything for a few seconds more. By then they'd topped a rise and were headed back downhill toward the lights of Esperanza.

"How 'bout this," Susan said, with a note of exasperation. "Our need on this is pretty urgent, but if you'd like to sleep on it—"

"No, no. I'd rather decide tonight. Still . . ."

Was he in or out? And even if he was out, it was now apparent that he'd soon have to deal with visitors from Bolrovia. Unless, of course, he hopped a ferry first thing in the morning and again went on the lam. But to where? And to what purpose, other than hearing the rattle of that pill container every time he unpacked?

"Still?" she prodded.

"Part of me says what the fuck, do it. Part of me would like to see something in writing."

"We can accommodate that request."

Susan had immediately reached down between her feet and clicked open a briefcase, from which she'd withdrawn a sheaf of pages that she handed to Hal, along with a pen.

"Standard boilerplate, basically saying that you're doing this of your own free will, et cetera. All you need to do is sign and date the last page." She flipped to the final page. "Right here."

"Does this include anything about disavowing any knowledge of me if I happen to be caught or killed—the whole Mission Impossible disclaimer?"

He'd been hoping for a laugh but didn't get one, so he turned back to the first page, figuring he should at least scan *some* of the fine print.

"Could somebody maybe turn on the dome light?"

Sal flipped a switch, and Hal began to read.

"Guess I can't run this by my agent, huh?"

Silence to that as well. He'd worked better rooms in Omaha.

Hal made a show of scrutiny while turning the pages slowly, but in truth he barely glanced at most of the wording, maybe because he was afraid to see what it really said. The only contract language that had ever mattered in his previous life were the parts about money and control—how much, who got it, when, and for what reasons. But with this job no one had said anything about getting paid, meaning the only negotiable item of value was his life. And the net worth of that commodity was at its all-time low, no matter what these numbered paragraphs said.

He signed his name, dated it, then handed over the pages and the pen.

"Okay, then. I'm officially in. All yours."

Sal and Chris said nothing. Not even a nod, much less a high five, which would've been nice. It was all a bit deflating. He had hoped for at least a few words of encouragement, or some camaraderie, like, maybe, *"Welcome aboard, you're one of us now!"* He had even thought they might buy him dinner. Unless, of course, they were as skeptical of this operation as he already was. It felt a little bit like his earliest days in stand-up, lean times when he'd been desperate for any and all bookings but had still cringed at some of the backwater venues procured by his agent. Few things were deadlier than the wrong audience, and, apart from Horvatz, he had no idea of what sort of crowd awaited him in Bolrovia.

Susan dropped the document back into the briefcase, snapped it shut, and settled back into her seat. Sal switched off the dome light. Everyone was quiet.

Hal tried to think of an appropriate one-liner to mark the occasion, then gave up. It was a dead crowd. Let the next act give it a try. He turned to look out the window, but the darkness left him staring at his own reflection.

And now, back in bed, the room was suddenly flooded with sunlight and someone was knocking loudly on his door. Hal, realizing he must have fallen back to sleep, scrambled unsteadily to his feet. He was wearing only his boxers. His head hurt, his mouth was dry, and his voice croaked as he answered.

"Coming! Hang on!"

Christ, but these CIA people started early. Maybe this was part of his training, to get him ready for whatever lay ahead in Bolrovia.

Then he opened the door.

Chapter 6

For Lauren, headphones on, the helpless dread she felt as she listened to Knight step toward the door was like watching one of those horror movies where a hidden slasher awaits an unsuspecting victim, and everyone in the theater, you included, wants to shout out in warning, "No! Don't do it!"

Because she knew it would be a disaster. Knight would be expecting to see one of them, of course, and in his grogginess and confusion he'd say all the wrong things, and would blow the entire op. In reaction, the thugs from Bolrovia would either back off or, worse, rough him up, question him, sweat him for every last detail of who'd gotten to him first, and why. End of op. End of career.

But it was too late for any warnings, so she braced for the worst. Quint, seated to her right and wearing his own set of headphones, grimly did the same. They were upstairs in the guesthouse across the street from Knight's, where they'd been waiting for more than three hours. Malone was outdoors and out of sight, awaiting a summons in case things got out of hand. She leaned forward, concentrating, intent on every sound.

The knocking stopped. The doorknob turned, the latch clicked, and a hinge creaked. There was a quick, startled intake of breath. Knight spoke first, his tone uncertain, his voice raspy. In her mind's eye, Lauren saw him standing barefoot at the threshold, dressed only in his boxers, an image she immediately tried to erase.

"Who the hell are you?"

The voice that answered was brisk, chipper, with an accent like something from a cheap vampire movie.

"Good morning to you, sir! My apologies if I have awakened you."

Good god, was this really the best they could do?

"Come later," Hal answered. "All I need is fresh towels."

The hinges creaked. Was he closing the door?

"Wait, sir. Please!"

The creaking stopped.

"You are Mr. Hal Knight, correct? I have your picture here, and it is a match."

"Give me that."

There was a snatching sound, a pause, a rustle of paper.

"This is me, all right. And . . . hey, is this my fucking cell number? What are you, some kind of stalker? And . . . what the fuck! Who's that other guy down the stairs? Does he have a *gun*? What the hell is he even wearing?"

There were creaks and thuds and grunts of effort as Knight must have tried to shut the door. His visitor, who had probably jammed a foot in to stop him, spoke in a frantic rush.

"He is security, sir, in case we were stopped or interrupted! It is okay, he works for me!"

There was some further grunting and creaking as the door seesawed. The envoy's next words were breathless, staccato.

"Please, sir, you misunderstand! I am here as a goodwill ambassador of the President of Bolrovia!"

The shoving stopped. Surely this was where things would begin to fall apart. Lauren could hear the two men breathing rapidly.

"You're joking, right?"

"No, sir. And I have brought you a valuable and important invitation."

A pause, two beats of relative silence as the two men caught their breath.

"Look, pal. I have no idea what you want, but I didn't come here to receive visitors, from fans or anybody else, even if one of them is . . . did you say *president*? And even if you did, I'm out of that racket. So if you've got something to give me, make it quick, 'cause I'm going back to bed."

The man's voice took on an edge of desperation. His words again came in a rush.

"You have heard of our president, yes? The President of Bolrovia?"

Knight waited for a full beat.

"Horvatz, right? Nino Horvatz?"

"Nikolai. Nikolai Horvatz."

"Yeah, well, it's a little early for global trivia."

"*Trivia?*"

For the first time, the envoy sounded a little affronted.

"In fact, what time *is* it?"

"Eight fourteen, sir." His tone was brusque now. "And if you could kindly—"

"Look, how 'bout this. If you'll just take your goddamn foot out of my door, I'll go get dressed, and in a little while, if you're still interested in talking to me, I can meet you somewhere in town for coffee, or to sign an autograph for your president, or whatever the fuck you really came here for."

"To extend an invitation, as I said."

"Fine, then. Maybe by the time I've had some coffee I'll even be able to give you an RSVP. But don't bring the goon with you, okay? None of that shit. Unless you want me to call the cops first."

"No, no. Please! That will not be necessary. But perhaps it would be easier if—"

"Move. Step back. You're not coming in. I'll be at Trade Winds. It's a little restaurant upstairs from a guesthouse, right on the Malecón. Get a table on the terrace and I'll see you there in . . . let's say fifteen minutes. No, better make it twenty."

"But if you would just—"

"Take it or leave it, dude."

"Okay, then. Yes. I will—"

The door shut before the envoy could finish. Lauren heard the snick of the lock, followed by emphatic whispering in the hallway in a language she didn't understand. There were thumps of descending footsteps, then more whispering as the envoy must have encountered his "security" on the way downstairs, followed, at last, by the opening and shutting of the door at ground level.

Lauren slipped off her headphones and exhaled in relief. Quint did the same.

"Damn," Quint said, in that pleasing baritone of his. He was smiling. "The guy's a natural. Handled that like a goddamn pro."

She was momentarily too surprised to answer, but Quint had nailed it.

"I mean, I know you don't like his ass, but . . ."

"No, you're right. We couldn't have scripted it better if we'd planned it out last night. In fact, that was a better performance than *anything* in one of his movies."

This drew a belly laugh from Quint. The sense of relief in the room seemed to almost call for a drink, and she thought longingly of that Scotch she'd shoved aside the night before. Not that anything but coffee was a realistic option at this hour.

And even that would have to wait. Because now it was her turn to scramble, to improvise, and she found herself oddly energized by the idea, especially after the performance they'd just heard. Yes, the man was an idiot, and her deeper doubts about the op, and his judgment, remained. But at least he was quick on his feet, a crafty dissembler— skills that she might actually be able to put to good use. And if things didn't run off the rails in the next hour—a possibility that still seemed quite plausible—they might yet make this arrangement work in their favor.

"Call Malone," she said. "Those guys are bound to be redeploying. Tell him about the scheduled meetup. He needs to stay out of sight but set up somewhere he can keep an eye on them. I've got to make a quick wardrobe change so I can grab a front-row seat."

"At Trade Winds?"

She nodded. "Those guys have never seen me, and Knight needs to at least know we haven't deserted him."

"Want me down there with Malone?"

"No. They're already a step ahead of us, and we have to turn that around. I need you to set up our next move before they've finished breakfast."

He raised his eyebrows. She crossed the room to her dresser, where she picked up a splashy tourist map. It had colorful ads with names and photos of the town's various bars, restaurants, and outdoor attractions. She spotted the item she was looking for, handed the map to Quint, and pointed to a picture of a gleaming motorboat cruising majestically across a turquoise lagoon.

"Here's what I want you to do."

He listened as she quickly outlined his marching orders. A moment later, they were both out the door, off on their separate missions.

Chapter 7

———≈———

Hal managed only a couple of steps before collapsing onto the bed. His legs were quivering. Another thirty seconds and he would've fallen apart, told them everything, agreed to whatever they wanted. And, Jesus Christ, that guy with a gun! In a flak vest, too! Hal wondered how many more of them had been lurking in the building, or outside. He considered looking out the window, then decided he didn't want his forehead showing up in the middle of a gun sight.

And where the fuck were his so-called friends from the CIA? He should've kept a copy of that agreement he'd signed, to see if he had any legal recourse in case of negligence or professional malpractice. Not that he'd be around to collect damages if worse came to worst.

He sat up and exhaled loudly. Then he laughed, probably out of nervous release, although it instantly made him feel better. He swiveled his bare feet to the floor, still a little shaky but beginning to regroup as he tried to pin down the last time he'd experienced such a bracing mixture of relief, fear, elation, and near-disaster.

Then it hit him: improv, during his earliest days as a comedian. Those wonderful but harrowing sessions in which he and two or three like-minded fools had stepped onto a stage, a floor, or into a clearing in a park and then spent an hour or so trying to create laughs out of random prompts for an audience of a few dozen skeptics. When it clicked, it was a thing of beauty, loose and exhilarating. When it didn't—which happened more often than not—it quickly regressed into a form of public execution, a slow, excruciating death by awkward silence. But what a rush it had been to try it, every time out of the box. And that was how he felt now, like he had just managed to tap-dance his way across a balance beam above a yawning gorge of eternal peril.

Because he'd killed it, he really had. And it had started with his very first line, even as he had absorbed the shock of the man's unfamiliar face, and the sight of a gun barrel peeping from around the corner of the stairwell on the landing below.

"Who the hell are you?" he'd said, even though he had known almost right away that the fellow was probably from Bolrovia. Then the man's accent and greeting had sealed the deal, and Hal's brain had gone into overdrive.

The first thing he'd had to do was shunt aside an onrush of fearful questions:

Why are you here now? Why wasn't I warned? Where are my buddies from the Agency? What can I say that will make it look like I'm entirely ignorant of why you've come?

Out of this momentary panic had come his second line, the one he was now proudest of, because it had changed the course of the entire exchange.

"Come later. All I need is fresh towels."

As if the guy had been some flunky from housekeeping. It had immediately thrown the fellow off balance, just enough for Hal to gain the upper hand, an advantage he had then built on by snatching the piece of paper out of his hands. Everything afterward had seemed to come almost naturally.

The night before, Hal had convinced himself that spying was all about acting, about learning your lines and playing a role. Now he adjusted that view. It really was more like improv, except it was 24/7 improv, and with a less forgiving audience. Blow a line or muff your timing and, instead of groans and stony looks and people departing in droves, you got a private session with an armed guy in a flak vest. Or worse.

Had his edgy performance managed to put him on safe footing, at least for now? He began going back over everything he'd said, just in case, to check for any false notes.

Perhaps, for instance, he had gone a little overboard by referring to Horvatz as "Nino."

No, the line had worked. Because it, too, had thrown the envoy off his game, although it now felt like an oversight that Hal hadn't bothered to ask the fellow's name, something he needed to correct when they met again. But it did amuse him now to recall the way the guy had seemed to take offense at his "global trivia" reference.

And that accent, how perfect had that been? *Good morning, sir, I am from Bolrovia!* Hal, a gifted mimic, thought about trying to recreate it in front of the bathroom mirror, then composing a line or two for further comic relief, but he quickly thought better of it. If they were still in the corridor, they might hear him, and that wouldn't be cool. Maybe they had even wired up his room.

But, yeah, where the hell were Susan and Sal and Chris? Or whatever their damn names really were. The only consolation was that at least they'd told him that an approach was coming, and that it might be soon, or else he almost certainly would have panicked and blown the whole performance. Although he now wondered if any chance for training had just gone by the board. Especially if the people from Bolrovia insisted on whisking him away as soon as possible.

How had they managed to take everyone by surprise? Had they flown in on a private jet? Or maybe even come ashore overnight on inflatables with outboard motors, like a commando team? Were those the kinds of people he'd be dealing with from here on out?

The whole experience of the past few days—being approached by one group of spies, and then another—drove home to him what a frightening lack of privacy he had. Even when you thought you'd gone into hiding, even when you'd shut down one phone number and two email accounts to halt the last pleading communications from former aides, hangers-on, and other staffers in studios and on Capitol Hill, to these kinds of people in the secret world you would always be as visible as a prisoner caught in a spotlight, snagged on the razor wire. Try to run from them and the sirens would never stop, even if you never heard them.

Hal checked his phone for the correct time. Five minutes had already slipped away, meaning he only had fifteen more to get dressed and make it down the hill to Trade Winds, which, with its breezy terrace and ocean view, had become his go-to spot for breakfast.

Or maybe it would be a nice touch to show up a few minutes late, to keep them off balance. And, whatever they said next, he should definitely try to hold them off on his departure time for at least another day. Anything to give Susan and her team a chance to reestablish contact.

Hal stood. He felt better now, more confident, even though it was still unsettling to think that the American side in this competition already seemed a bit overmatched. Should he shower? Shave? No. Play it sloppy.

He sniffed an armpit. Okay, maybe a quick shower, but no shave.

That took another five minutes. Then, as he stared into his open closet, wondering what to wear, he imagined the voice of his longtime wardrobe manager, Shirley Halston (no relation to the designer), nattering away at his side, just as she had always done on the set.

"No, no. Not the T-shirt, the collar's frayed. You want to say, 'Sell me on this,' not 'Fuck off.' Go with the orange polo, which at least is clean. And for god's sake run a comb through your hair and use some deodorant. Jeans? Are you kidding? It's already 80 degrees. They'll be soaked through before you're halfway down the hill. The khaki shorts, yes. And sandals."

He complied, as he always had with Shirley's orders. But she wasn't done.

"Oh, and wear your shades. Make it look like you're hiding a hangover, they'll expect that. Order your coffee black, even though you prefer it with milk. And, for at least a few minutes, let them do all the talking. Be noncommittal for as long as you can."

"Thank you, Shirley."

Hal had always had a knack for these imaginary conversations. It was the real ones he tended to fuck up. He stepped in front of the bathroom mirror. Shirley hovered over his shoulder.

"Okay, good. The look is perfect. Are you ready?"

"Ready as I'll ever be."

Was he really? Oddly enough, yes, even though his need for coffee was beginning to split open the center of his forehead. So he grabbed his phone, wallet, and keys, slipped on his sunglasses, and headed for the door. He decided to drive the golf cart down the hill instead of walking, because they'd expect that, too. The lazy, entitled American, always willing to burn gas instead of calories.

But Shirley had a last bit of advice.

"Whatever you do, don't look around for your CIA buddies. Not even on the drive down the hill. They'd pick up on that right away. From here on out, always assume someone is watching. Oh, and let them pick up the check. Don't even offer."

"Right. Cheapskate to the bitter end."

Hal nodded, smiled to himself, and stepped into the corridor. To his immense relief, the stairway was empty.

Chapter 8

———— ≈ ————

Lauren was pretty sure Knight spotted her as he passed her table, even though he scarcely glanced her way. He headed for a sunny spot out on the terrace, where the Bolrovian envoy was already seated and waiting.

Malone, stationed on the sidewalk downstairs, then texted Lauren to say that the envoy's three goons had departed in a Jeep Wrangler almost identical to the one the Agency was renting. They'd already changed out of their tactical gear into Hawaiian print shirts still creased from the box.

Lauren set her phone aside as she flashed on an absurd image of a column of Wranglers and golf carts weaving down a narrow seaside road as they dodged horses and each other in surveillance of an oblivious Hal Knight. She didn't know whether to laugh or start drafting a letter of resignation, but the air smelled of the sea and her view was spectacular, so she sipped her coffee and sat back to enjoy the show.

The envoy had reached the restaurant before her. Lauren watched as he nervously wiped his hands on his trousers before standing to greet Knight, who reluctantly accepted the moist handshake. She couldn't make out their words, but Knight must have asked to see some identification, because the envoy reached into a pocket and produced a passport.

Knight snatched it away from him, then flipped through its pages. He looked long and hard at the photo before handing it back. Once again, he had seized the advantage, but she worried he might be laying it on too thick—a worry that dissipated when she saw the envoy's face, abashed and embarrassed. My god, was he, too, a fan? Or maybe he was so eager to succeed that he'd stoop to anything. Either way, it gave her a glimpse of how Knight must have gone through life before his fall from grace—appeased and catered to at every turn by people who either worshipped him or wanted something from him.

Once the two men sat back down, Knight seemed to be on his best behavior. He nodded intently and paid close attention, as the envoy leaned forward and spoke in a low voice. With no idea of what they were saying, Lauren's thoughts wandered to Quint, who she hoped was making progress on his little mission. For all she knew, Knight was already agreeing to terms that would render her plan useless.

Or maybe not. Because at that moment her phone vibrated and a text popped up indicating that Quint had completed his assignment, meaning that at almost any moment Knight's phone should buzz as well—but only if he'd bothered to turn it on. Given the way he'd been living here, he might even have left it in his room. If so, lights out.

She watched closely, peering at an angle through sunglasses as she pretended to gaze straight ahead, toward the ocean. The envoy put something on the table between them, a blue sheaf of paper. Oh, shit. Airline tickets? If Knight assented to whatever the envoy proposed, then he might be flying out of here within a few hours, before they got a chance to prepare him.

Hal was then distracted by something. He glanced down to his left, reached into his pocket, pulled out his phone, and gave it an irritating glance. The fruit of Quint's labors, she was sure of it. Hal then squinted in seeming consternation. The wrong reaction now could scuttle everything or, at the very least, delay any valuable intelligence for days, perhaps weeks.

She inhaled deeply, took another sip of coffee, and tried to seem as disinterested as possible. Resigned to the worst, she again looked out at the tranquil sea.

All in all, not a bad spot for watching your career come to an end.

Chapter 9

———≋———

Hal's first impulse was to delete the text. Obviously, it was junk, some bit of promotional garbage from a local vendor. Maybe the kid who'd rented him the golf cart sold customers' phone numbers to other local merchants.

But just as he was about to consign it to oblivion, he noticed it was a *confirmation* text, not a come-on, a verification of his supposed reservation for an excursion tomorrow morning with an outfit called Buccaneer Bob's Bio Bay and Snorkeling Tours. The text said he should arrive at the dock, located just down the street, no later than eight forty-five tomorrow morning.

Even then, if he hadn't just seen Susan over at that nearby table, acting cool as you please in her shades, a blond wig, a floppy straw hat, and a white cotton sundress, he might well have dismissed the text as a mistake, or a scam. But now he got it. They had redeployed. And this was their reaction to his capture, or to whatever else you'd call this awkward courtship by Bodi Orovan, whose name Hal had just learned by looking at the man's passport.

So, instead of deleting the text, he sighed—not too theatrically, he hoped—and turned the screen so that Bodi could see it as well.

"See? This is what I mean. If I leave right away, I'll miss half of what I came here for."

Bodi leaned closer to read it.

"A snorkeling trip?"

"It was the only opening they had the rest of the week. It's one of the main things I wanted to do while I was here, and supposedly these guys are the best. And, well, you know what I've been through. The whole parade of public humiliation. And if I just jump right on a plane without at least another day to decompress, then I won't be half as funny as I'm sure your man Nick would want me to be. Right?"

Bodi winced, either at the idea of a delay or at Hal's flippant use of "Nick." He sagged and stared down at his plate of uneaten eggs, then laced his fingers in a prayerful pose.

"Please, sir. Or Hal. May I call you Hal?"

"Certainly. It's my name."

"Hal, I can assure you that in our country there are also many places where you can, as you say, decompress. We have the famous mineral springs of Dravas. Or the cool mountain air of the Kotras Range, the hiking trails of the Javorska Forest. Even in Blatsk there are spas and places for Turkish massage. Very reputable, I assure you. And it is not as if you will be performing at all times. Our president's whole intent is to make you feel welcome again. And valued. That was the word he uses many times. *Valued.*"

"Yes, and I'm glad to hear it. But I need to make this one last little trip. For snorkeling. In that beautiful, clear water. I mean, really, look at it."

Bodi dutifully turned and squinted out at the sea. He nodded but looked quite forlorn.

"Besides, I've already put down a deposit, and if—"

Bodi brightened, seizing upon this opening.

"Oh, but we will be happy to reimburse you for that, and if—"

"No, no, Bodi. I need this, okay? It's a reset for me, this whole trip. And going snorkeling is the final button of the reset. In fact, maybe I should delay departure by at least a couple of days, so I can swing by my house in LA first. If only to get the right kind of clothes for Europe in September."

This matter also proved to be right in Bodi's wheelhouse.

"There is no need! We have already procured a complete wardrobe for the entirety of your visit! And in all the correct sizes!"

Hal swallowed with difficulty.

"You know my sizes?"

"My employer is very thorough. But only in order to serve you, of course."

It was a little disturbing, the idea of some minion who'd been assigned to ferret out all his sizes and measurements so that some other minion, with god knows what sort of taste, had gone out to buy an entire wardrobe for his stay. He pictured himself dressed in blocky brown shoes and a lot of leisure wear made of synthetic fabrics in hideous tones. Maybe they would also style his hair, give him a Slavic pompadour. It was potentially funny, this riff, something he could easily develop into a full routine. Then he realized he needed to shut it down and get back to the business at hand.

"Look, this airline ticket. Didn't you say it's flexible?"

"You can redeem it for any flight to Blatsk, as long as you use it within a week."

"Then why the rush? Did they give you some kind of deadline or something? Will you be taking the blame if I miss it?"

"Not from the president, no. As long as he knows you're coming, I think he would even be okay with you waiting a few weeks."

"So it's your boss that's the problem, right?"

Bodi looked at him closely, as if assessing whether to trust him. Then he looked away, out toward the water. Hal felt a twinge of pity for him.

"Yeah, I've worked with assholes like that. Every 'i' has to be dotted the way they want it, even if it doesn't really matter. Control freaks, leaning over your shoulder on every detail. Like sending that guy with the gun up my stairwell. I'll bet that wasn't your idea, either, right?"

Bodi grinned sheepishly.

"He told me we had to show how *emphatic* we were. That was the word he uses many times. He also wanted us to show our strength, in case others were watching."

"Others?"

"Competitors. The opposition." Bodi then waved away the thought, as if he wished he'd never mentioned it. "It is not important." Then his brow furrowed in apparent concern, and he leaned forward. "Unless, of course, there *have* been others. Is that possible?"

For the first time in the conversation, Hal felt a little off balance. Bodi was looking him in the eye, so he needed to get this exactly right, to play it cool and aloof without giving anything away. To lie, in other words, and to do it well. Fortunately, his six months in Congress had offered even better training than Hollywood for this kind of moment. He tilted his head and furrowed his brow while never taking his eyes off Bodi's.

"Seeing as how I'm still not quite sure what you mean by 'others,' I'll say the answer is no. Other people like you, you mean? People in your business, except from some other country?"

"Or from your own country."

"No. There have been no others. Just you guys."

Bodi watched him for a second longer, then nodded as if satisfied.

"But pleasing your boss is important, right?" Hal said. "So how 'bout this. When I arrive in your country, whether it's two days from now, or three, or whatever, I'll say I almost didn't come at all because of the guy with the gun, but then you talked me into it. Even then I wanted to wait at least a week, but we settled on a few days because you were so convincing."

Bodi seemed to like the idea at first. Then his face clouded over.

"No. It is best if you say nothing about any of that."

"This guy can't handle criticism, huh?"

Bodi shifted in his chair. He glanced from side to side, as if checking for eavesdroppers.

"Please. The less we talk about him, the better. You will see."

"I'll be meeting him?"

"As I said. You will see."

"Look, if it makes you feel better, I can take a flight out of here as early as late tomorrow afternoon. Provided that all the connections work."

It was a reckless promise, but Hal was almost certain the connections *wouldn't* work, not between San Juan and Blatsk, especially after having to reach San Juan on a puddle jumper so late in the day. This would mean he'd have at least two more days to prepare. And with a window like that, he might even be able to slip back home, provided that no one alerted the *paparazzi*, if only to clear the decks on a few personal matters.

Bodi frowned and mulled it over. He got out his phone, put his reading glasses back on, then pecked in a few commands as he eyed the screen. He suddenly sat up straighter.

"You can promise me that? That you will leave tomorrow?"

"Like I said, only if the flights work."

"Oh, but they do! Look!"

Smiling broadly, he turned his phone around. And there it was, the whole damn itinerary, beginning with a hop from Vieques to San Juan at three thirty in the afternoon, followed by an overnight flight to Frankfurt that almost seamlessly connected to a final leg to Blatsk, landing at around noon local time.

Hal's heart sank. He'd just fallen into that old trap that trial lawyers always cautioned against before an important cross-examination: Never ask a question that you don't already know the answer to.

"Shall I book it for you, then?"

Hal had an urge to look over at Susan, as if to seek her advice, but checked it. Instead, he nodded in assent.

"Yeah. Sure."

"Super! Hand me that airline voucher. I need the numbers on it to complete the arrangement."

So there it was, then. In roughly another fifty hours—or more like forty-four, once you accounted for the difference in the time zones— he'd be on the ground in Blatsk, jet-lagged and groggy, prepared or not, as a newly minted agent of the Central Intelligence Agency. An actor once again, except this time he didn't know whether the script called for farce or tragedy, or if he'd still be standing by the final scene.

"Now," Bodi said, looking as happy and relieved as he had all morning, "we can begin going over some of the other details. Then I must go somewhere more secure, to call my boss with the good news."

Yes, his boss. That lovely fellow who liked for his men to be fully armed and dangerous, even when wooing a comedian on an island paradise. Emphatic, indeed. And also the boss who, apparently, already suspected that a competing intelligence agency might be part of the mix. Now where could he have gotten that idea?

A bubble of anxiety swelled in his chest as Hal contemplated what he had just agreed to do. In the past twelve hours he had made irrevocable commitments to two competing groups of spies. For one he had even put it in writing. Such were the dangers of applying the skills of improv to the business of espionage. Just when you thought you were about to get a big laugh, you realized that instead you'd walked into a crowd where no one was in the mood for joking around. Except, maybe, Nikolai Horvatz.

"Ah, here is the confirmation email. Your arrangements are complete!"

"Lovely," Hal said, not even trying to sound convincing. "Just lovely."

Chapter 10

A house—any house, really—lives and breathes. It's an organism that, if you listen closely, will tell you what it's up to, how it's feeling. Especially at night, after nearly everyone and everything else have settled into slumber. Because houses never sleep.

Pavel Lukov, always a careful listener, had long been acquainted with his home's moods and complaints—its creaks and groans of effort whenever a strong wind blew, or whenever heaving trams passed on the street outside; its gentle sighs of relief at the easing of winter; the labored exhalations of its heating and cooling system.

Having lived in a grand, three-story townhouse in one of the city's most desirable neighborhoods for the past six years (ever since Jana's wealthy and domineering father had insisted on buying it for them, shortly after their marriage), Pavel could tell you within a few minutes of walking in the door every evening whether the furnace was running smoothly or the water pipes were flowing free and clear. If something was amiss, the house told him right away.

But his closest readings always occurred in the deepest hours of the night, when he would often lie awake by his sleeping wife, alone with his worries as the house whispered only to him. And that was how he picked up a disturbing bit of intel only a few hours after he had finally gotten some good news from Vieques.

Their house was on narrow Jalovna Street, at the corner of the much busier Boulevard of Heroes, where trams rumbled and cars passed. It was in the Prospekt Quarter, less than a mile's walk from the Presidential Palace, a storied neighborhood that had endured centuries of empire and upheaval. At many times in the past, the street's cobbles had been pried loose by rioters, strikers, and revolutionaries for throwing at police, soldiers, and various other armed authoritarians.

In the years leading up to the Second World War it had been home to many of the city's most prosperous Jews. Look closely at some of the door frames and you could still detect the ghostly remnants of tiny scars, long since filled and painted over, from where mezuzahs had once been attached to the woodwork, only to be gouged out during the German occupation.

During the Iron Curtain era most of the houses were clumsily subdivided into apartments. But in the early 1990s, not long after Bolrovia again became a free nation, some were converted back into single-family homes, a trend that accelerated after Bolrovia joined the European Union in 2004 and grant money began to flow. That was the case with Pavel's house. The previous owner had restored the original floor plan by removing the flimsier newer walls and doorways. He had also modernized the wiring, plumbing, and heating. Instead of an old boiler with steam pipes and radiators, the house now had an electric furnace with forced-air ducts. All of this had vastly changed the way in which the house communicated with its residents—no more clanks and whooshes, but plenty of sighs and heavings, accompanied by the thumps of dampers and vents.

In any event, when Pavel arrived home that evening, he was somewhat distracted due to the news he'd just gotten from Branko Sarič, or else he might have noticed what the house was already trying to tell him. The news had arrived via the special encrypted phone, shortly after six o'clock, and just as Pavel had been preparing to leave his office. Marika had already gone home, and he was alone at his desk. Sarič began speaking without even saying hello.

"The target is secure."

"Could you put that into plain Bolrovian, please?"

Pavel later wondered what had emboldened him to be so impertinent. Maybe it was because Marika wasn't there to listen. Or perhaps he had still been feeling the aftereffects of the stiff drink he had enjoyed earlier in the day, which had led to a long lunch followed by a second drink. Whatever the reason, his tone convinced Sarič to actually oblige his request.

"He has agreed to come. He did so with no resistance."

"Wonderful. When?"

"He will arrive two days from now, around noon after an overnight flight. I will text you the full details, and you can begin planning for his welcome. The president will expect you to be there to greet him, and we will of course waive any sort of entry impediments, such as customs, although you should arrange for photos to be taken as he receives the visa stamp in his passport. For publicity purposes."

"Publicity? I thought we were keeping this under wraps. Weren't we going to promise him that?"

"Yes, but we all know this will not stay secret for long. And when that happens, we'll need to have documentation of all the highlights, for public release. To show the world the benevolence and goodwill of our president."

"I see."

"You are to handle these matters personally. Do not delegate any of them to your secretary or the protocol office. Understood?"

Pavel frowned but withheld his complaint. Turning him into an errand boy was another habit of Sarič's, designed to keep him too busy to keep track of what Sarič might be up to.

"Yes."

"After his arrival, you will escort him directly to his hotel. Use an official car and driver."

"Will he be staying at the Esplanade?" It was the city's grandest and most luxurious hotel and was less than half a mile from Pavel's house.

"Of course. Oh, and a masseuse has been secured for his arrival, by arrangement with my ministry. We want him to be as rested and relaxed as possible for his initial meeting with the president that evening, when there will be a small welcome dinner, as we discussed earlier. It will be held in the ballroom of the Presidential Palace. I will text you the guest list, which the president has already approved."

"Did you say a masseuse? Will she be a, um, well . . ."

"Yes?"

If the mere word "yes" could be said to have a leering tone, then Sarič had just managed it. Or maybe Pavel only thought that because he'd been about to ask if the masseuse would be a prostitute. He then decided that he didn't really want to know.

"Never mind."

"Fewer questions are often better. You have plenty to do already."

Sarič had disconnected before Pavel could ask anything more. Still, it was good news, and an immense relief, because he knew it would please President Horvatz. Pavel had rarely seen anyone, male or female, who was as smitten by an entertainer as much as Horvatz was by Hal Knight. The president had supposedly used videos of Knight's movies and stand-up shows to build and bolster his excellent English, and he would sometimes recite favorite lines at staff meetings and official events, even though they often left his listeners baffled.

The idea of inviting Knight for an official visit had originated before Pavel was hired, and also before Knight's public downfall. But the president's political adviser, Wally Wallek, had nixed it, figuring that, since Horvatz was a favorite of American Republicans, a Democratic lawmaker like Knight might turn down the invitation just to score a few political points.

Then Knight's moment of public disgrace had occurred. For Wallek, that had closed the book on the idea. Horvatz, however, saw it as grounds for hope, and on the week Pavel came aboard the president made his case anew at a staff meeting.

"This is perfect, don't you see? All those assholes in America who never give me a chance are the same ones who've turned on him."

"You may be right, sir," Wallek had responded. "Invite a pariah like Knight, and everyone over there who already dislikes you will only hate you more, of course. But the ones who like you, well, now they'll *love* you. And that's something we can build on. Those other people are a lost cause anyway. But our friends? They'll appreciate the boldness of it. Yes, let's do it."

So, after further careful deliberations, Horvatz had used his official Twitter account to extend an official invitation to Hal Knight, which, up until only a few hours ago, had not yielded even the slightest response.

In the meantime, Pavel had brought himself up to speed on the matter by taking home a DVD of Knight's most popular movie, *Barefoot and Pregnant*, for further study. Jana, initially excited by the idea that she might soon be rubbing elbows with a famous American entertainer, had been unimpressed.

"He thinks like a thirteen-year-old with too many hormones. And your boss actually likes this shit?"

"Loves it. And, yes, my boss, but our president."

She had rolled her eyes at that, just as she had when Pavel had been offered his new job.

And now, it seemed, Knight had not only accepted, but he would be arriving the day after tomorrow. If Pavel could manage this visit without a hitch, he might be able to stay employed far longer than either of his predecessors.

Thus, he had arrived home in a mood to celebrate. So instead of being alert to any coded messages from his house, he had burst through the door and immediately called out to his wife.

"Jana! Where are you?"

He found her in the kitchen, scrolling through a takeout menu on her phone.

"Those assholes kept me an extra hour to prepare for that stupid lawsuit from Petrotek, so there's no dinner. What do you think, kebabs or pizza?"

"Forget all that, I'm taking you out."

In the few seconds it had taken him to reach the kitchen, Pavel had come up with a plan for a wonderful evening. It featured a quiet, relaxing candlelit dinner with Jana and a bottle of wine. He'd call their babysitter, Zoé, a teen who lived on their block, and then secure a reservation at one of their favorite restaurants. If the place was swanky enough, Jana might even be convinced to slip into that slinky black number that he always loved to touch—and loved even more to unzip. And if they returned home late enough, preferably after both children were asleep, maybe they'd head immediately upstairs for an amorous conclusion to the evening—a rare privilege on any night in the eight months since the birth of their second child, Ava. Rarer still for a Monday.

His hopes on that front ratcheted up another notch as Jana looked up eagerly from her phone.

"Tonight? That would be lovely. What's the occasion? Don't tell me you were actually able to land that stupid comedian for a visit?"

"Yes! So let's celebrate. I was thinking maybe even The Forge. I'll call Zoé."

"Oh, but she's never available on weeknights, not with that school she goes to and all the work they give her. And after the day I've had, even an ounce of wine would have me nodding off into my plate. Besides,

Tomas has been so good lately, he's entitled to a treat. And he loves that place where they always give him crayons and chocolate ice cream."

So the four of them had instead trooped off to Gertmann's, a place around the corner that was known for reasonable family prices and rustic local fare. In lieu of wine, Pavel had celebrated with a single bottle of pils, and instead of unzipping that slinky black dress, he had repeatedly retied Ava's bib after she kept pulling it off, while Jana wiped melted ice cream off Tomas's chin. They had returned home at the sane and sober hour of eight p.m., with sane and sober Jana almost immediately crashing into bed, where, shortly after three a.m., Pavel suddenly awakened into a swirl of barely coherent thoughts about airport timetables and dinner invitations. At the office he would soon have to be checking and double-checking a lot of arrangements, all in preparation for heading to the airport the following morning in time to meet Hal Knight's incoming flight at noon.

The house at that hour was speaking its usual language for a cool night in September. The furnace was running, so the blowers were exhaling with the sound of a distant cheering crowd. Nothing abnormal there, so Pavel's mind moved on to other concerns, such as how many people would be coming to this introductory dinner for Hal Knight? At least a few dozen, he was pretty sure. But what would he do if there were any last-minute cancellations? Not that any were likely. The odds of anyone saying no to a presidential dinner invitation, especially for such an intimate gathering, were pretty low, even though the guest of honor was an American of somewhat damaged reputation. He then wondered how Sarič's people had gone about choosing a masseuse, a move which still struck him as a little tawdry. Unless of course it was just a masseuse and nothing more.

Down in the cellar, the furnace switched off as the house reached the thermostat's setting of 68 degrees. Pavel knew instinctively what would come next. Inside the walls, the flaps of three separate dampers would shut in a familiar sequence—two rapid thumps, followed by a pause, and then a third thump of a damper on the floor below.

And there it was, like clockwork, the double thump of those first two dampers. Then came the pause, and then . . . something new happened. Something unexpected. There was a thump, yes, but far less crisp and emphatic than what Pavel was accustomed to hearing. What's more, it was preceded by a sort of stutter, as if the damper, in shutting, had brushed against an obstruction that had nearly kept it from closing.

The house was trying to tell him something. But what?

Was this a nascent malfunction which would grow worse over time? If so, then he needed to phone the heating company first thing in the morning. Maybe he should check it himself, right after he got up for work. He would have to haul up the stepladder from the cellar, plus a screwdriver and flashlight so he could remove the vent grate in the hallway and peer into the duct. Although, in thinking further, even as the house sighed and groaned as it inevitably began to cool, he wondered what in the hell could possibly be obstructing one of those dampers?

The first possibility that occurred to him was a little horrifying. Maybe a mouse had died inside the duct and the flap was brushing against it while shutting. If so, the tiny, furry corpse would quickly begin to rot and smell, especially with all that warm air blowing on it. The odor would then waft throughout the house. Yuck. So, yes, he'd better take a look first thing in the morning. Which meant he'd better get out of bed at least twenty minutes earlier than usual, to allow time for inspection and possible mouse removal.

Pavel's unsettled mind then moved on to other matters as the next day's agenda began unspooling in his head. A Chinese trade delegation was visiting the president midmorning and would need special care and handling. Wally had asked for a meeting at midafternoon, topic unknown. Marika wanted a decision on whether she could take two weeks off at Christmas. A television crew from an obscure right-wing cable network in the United States had asked for an interview with the president, and Pavel was supposed to coordinate with Juri, the press secretary. And at some point during the day he wanted to grab a chimney cake from Rudi's. He'd been craving one since the previous morning, when he'd decided to get a drink instead.

After fifteen or so minutes of this, and just as Pavel was dropping back to sleep, the thermostat ticked down by a single degree, triggering the furnace to rumble back to life. Fifteen minutes after that, having done its job, it again shut down. Pavel, as if alerted by the sudden stopping of the noise, opened his eyes in anticipation just as the dampers began to shut.

And there it was again—that stuttering noise leading into the third thump.

Obviously, this was going to awaken him over and over, so he decided to deal with it now.

He pulled back the sheets, taking care not to wake Jana. It was chilly, so he grabbed a robe, slid his feet into a pair of wool slippers, and stepped quietly into the hall.

The cellar was dark and spooky, as it tended to be at all hours. So much dust had accumulated on the stepladder that he sneezed on his way back upstairs. He carried it to the hallway and opened it just beneath the grate. He climbed up a few steps, then steadied himself as he unscrewed the two bolts which secured the grate. After setting the grate onto the floor, he climbed back up, switched on the flashlight, and peered inside.

There was an obstruction, all right, but it was no mouse. It was a small black box, about four by five inches, and an inch thick. It stood endwise over to one side of the duct. On its top edge was a pinprick of green light. To Pavel's untechnical eye, it looked like some sort of router. Or, at least, that was what it most closely resembled from all the computer gear they had in the house. There was no wire attached, so it must be powered by a battery, and it was close enough to the damper that it was obviously the item causing the flap to hitch as it opened and shut.

Pavel felt a chill just looking at it. Who had put it there? When? And why? Was it intercepting every wireless signal in the house? He switched off the flashlight, climbed down the ladder, and pulled his robe tighter.

He tried to recall if Jana had recently mentioned scheduling any sort of maintenance visit, and came up empty. Had the nanny who looked after their children during the day perhaps let a repair person into the house? Would a telltale invoice or bill be lying on the console table by the door, where letters and flyers sometimes piled up? In Pavel's haste to entice Jana out to dinner earlier that evening, he hadn't bothered to check the mail.

But even if any of those questions could be answered in the affirmative, what could that little black box possibly have to do with the heating system? No. It was an infiltrator, a foreign object, some sort of router or signal box. And if that was the case, it might well be intercepting every electronic communication in the house—from the desktop computer in their home office, from both their laptops, and maybe even from their phones.

Pavel didn't have to wonder for long about who might be responsible for something like that.

His first impulse was to yank it out of there and remove the battery. But then whoever had put it in place would know it had been disabled.

His next thought was that he should immediately shut down his desktop computer and turn off his phone. But those actions might also arouse suspicion, and he'd also have to explain everything to Jana, who would be alarmed.

He climbed back up the ladder for another look. He decided he had better restore everything to its normal appearance or Jana would ask unwanted questions in the morning. Although he also didn't want her to use her phone and laptop too freely if every signal was being intercepted.

Shit.

First things first. He reached into the duct to pull the box forward just an inch or two, so that the damper would no longer be obstructed. Then he reached below, grabbed the vent cover, and raised it into position. With his other hand he took the first screw out of the pocket of his robe and threaded it back into its opening. By the time he'd reattached the grate, his back was stiff, and returning the ladder to the cellar only made it worse. He then had to swallow a cry of pain after stepping on a small wooden train car that Tomas had left in the hallway.

On his way back upstairs, he thought of Maksim Polikon, a geeky friend from university days who knew all about these sorts of gadgets. Maksim wrote code, crunched data, and could prattle on for hours about various communications systems and how they might be corrupted or compromised, phished, or infiltrated. He'd know exactly what the black box was, and exactly what Pavel should do about it.

Pavel crept back into the bedroom, retrieved his phone from the bedside table, and took it into the hall to check his contact list. Yes, Maksim was on it. Pavel was on the verge of texting Maksim when it occurred to him that this, too, might show up as a blip on the radar of whoever was tuning in to their Wi-Fi signals. So instead he went back to the bedroom, picked up his discarded clothes and shoes, and carried them downstairs. The night was turning into an ordeal, and tomorrow was already looming as one of the more stressful days he was yet to have in his new job.

He narrowly avoided stepping again on Tomas's train car. Then he dressed in the kitchen, pocketed his phone, grabbed his keys, and slipped out the front door onto the darkened street. At this hour the trams were no longer running, and there was almost no traffic on the boulevard. Pavel looked in all directions. The sidewalks were empty, silent. He set off. A streetlamp buzzed overhead as he rounded the corner and walked for two blocks, his footsteps sounding loudly. He then stopped beneath another streetlamp and got out his phone.

He paused to consider exactly how to word this, then he typed in a text to Maksim.

Can you come to my house first thing a.m. to look at something? Will be there till 8. Do not answer this txt. If you can't come, call me later at this number. Delete txt after reading. Thx

Pavel waited as his phone beeped and whooshed. Then he deleted the message. He walked back to the house, where he managed to lock up, change out of his clothes, and climb back into bed, still without waking a soul—which was a little alarming, given the circumstances.

Just as he was beginning to warm up beneath the sheets, the furnace shut off, having again warmed the house to the set temperature.

He waited, listening closely, eyes open. This time, the sequence of noises proceeded normally—the double thump of the first two dampers, following by a brief pause before the third one. But Pavel would never be able to hear that sound again without thinking of the little black box with its diabolical green light.

He rolled over onto his stomach, shut his eyes, and pulled his pillow over his head to cover his ears. But he did not go back to sleep.

Chapter 11

⸺≈⸺

That same night, in a nearby hotel not nearly as grand as the Esplanade, an American man, tanned and fit, early forties, punched a number into his cell phone. Someone in a faraway office answered on the first ring.

"We have a complication. Nothing major, but I wanted to give you a heads-up."

"Okay."

"That comedian, the ex-congressman who fucked up?"

"Hal Knight?"

"Yeah. He's on his way here, as an official guest of the president."

"You're fucking kidding me."

"No. Didn't you see those Horvatz tweets?"

"Who didn't? Still. When's he coming?"

"Day after tomorrow. They sent their security people to some island to round him up. They're personally escorting him here."

"You're fucking joking."

"My source is as solid as it gets."

The other man exhaled loudly, thinking it over.

"You think he'll cross paths with our clients?"

"Bound to. He'll even be staying at the same hotel."

"Should I advise them to steer clear?"

"No. They'd ignore it anyway. They probably think of him as one of them now."

"But he's not."

"They'll figure that out for themselves. But it wouldn't look good if it was clear they already knew he was coming. So keep this quiet. The good news is that Knight supposedly wants it that way as well. So maybe *he'll* steer clear of them."

"Maybe. Shit." A pause while he thought it over, followed by a sigh. "You assured me the decks were all clear over there."

"They are. Like I said, it's minor. But if push comes to shove, our people will know where to find me, right?"

"They will. But you seem to be saying it won't come to that."

"I'm saying it isn't likely."

"Well, don't wait for a distress signal. If you sense trouble, act preemptively."

"Like in Managua?"

Another exhalation, followed by a pause.

"That's your call."

He smiled, a little disappointed but not at all surprised. None of these guys ever wanted accountability, which was half the reason they hired him. It was also why he made a lot more money now than he ever had on the inside. Better pay, looser rules of engagement, and, on jobs like this one, zero goddamned paperwork. He should've switched years earlier. But even with slippery people who wanted to keep everything at arm's length, it never hurt to make them state things a little more explicitly, in case troublesome questions arose later.

"So do I still have your assurance of full freedom of action here?"

A pause. A reflective sigh. He could almost feel the man squirm.

"Our operations there are in total disarray. It's a momentary vacuum, you know that."

"Is that a yes?"

"Take it however you need to take it."

"I'll take it as a yes."

Silence, which was chickenshit, but better than a no.

He ended the call without a further word, then stepped to the window and pulled aside the curtain to look out onto the night streets, eight stories below. All quiet. His thoughts turned to the man in question, Hal Knight, whose face came easily to mind. A washed-up comic, a fuckup who had barely lasted six months in Congress. How bad could it be, no matter what his politics were? And if he had now stooped to accepting the invitation of a leader he once would've snubbed, then it was pretty doubtful he'd make any trouble for their clients.

Especially if he was already seeking a backdoor route to resurrect his career.

But if, by chance, Knight *did* become a problem? Contingencies like that were one of the reasons he was here, holed up in a second-rate hotel where no one cared who you were or what you were doing.

He shut the curtain and stepped toward the bed. No immediate action was necessary, but he should at least begin plotting out a few worst-case options. He checked his watch. Late, so maybe he would sleep on it. By morning a few possibilities would already be percolating in his head. He was good at that, solving problems while he slept. Some of the solutions were likely to be unpleasant, even harsh—for others, not for him. He climbed into bed.

Long ago, something like this might have kept him tossing and turning for an hour or more, but over the years he had gained quite a bit of experience in having to break a few things after someone else's best-laid plans changed or began falling apart.

He was asleep within seconds.

Chapter 12

Hal awakened alert and refreshed early the next morning. For the first time since arriving in Vieques he had gone to bed sober and had set an alarm. The appointment at the dock might be his only chance for further instructions before he reached Bolrovia.

He had also looked up the website for Buccaneer Bob's. The company's most popular offering was its nightly paddle tour of the bioluminescent Mosquito Bay, a few miles outside of town, where, on a good night, glowing swarms of phytoplankton lit up the water in response to every splash, ripple, and paddle stroke.

Their snorkeling trip went to an offshore reef on a gleaming white cabin cruiser. It was a three-hour tour.

The moment Hal read those words, he repeated them aloud.

"A three-hour tour."

Then, because, like millions of other Americans, Hal had been raised on far too many hours of TV sitcoms that had survived for decades in the afterlife of syndication, he began humming the theme song of *Gilligan's Island* while readying himself for bed.

Further, because this was the way his brain operated, he had then recalled an item he'd read years ago which pointed out that just about any poem written by Emily Dickinson, due to its characteristic rhyme and meter, could easily be set to that tune. So, instead of just humming, Hal had broken into song.

Because I could not stop for Death, he kindly stopped for me.
The carriage held but just ourselves—And Immortality.
And Immortality.

It made him smile. Maybe this spying gig agreed with him. And if anyone had wired up his room while he was out yesterday—the Bolrovians, or his purported friends from CIA; either seemed possible—he hoped they had just been mildly entertained. On second thought, he doubted Bodi would have gotten the joke. No great loss.

Now, having showered, shaved, and put on his swimming trunks, a T-shirt, shades, and sunscreen, Hal set off down the hill. He walked instead of taking the golf cart, and he had enough extra time to pick up a coffee and a sweet roll at a bakery along the way. Even then, he was the first customer to arrive at the dock, where a Buccaneer Bob's sign was posted on one of the pilings next to the cabin cruiser that he'd seen on the website. It bobbed gently in the turquoise water. A school of silvery fish flashed and undulated below the hull before disappearing into the shadows.

The next to arrive was Sal, wearing aviator shades, a New York Yankees cap, and a Derek Jeter jersey above bright red trunks. Sal established the etiquette for the morning by acting as if Hal was a total stranger.

"You here for the snorkel trip?"

"Yeah. How many people usually go on these things?"

"No idea."

They both turned toward the shore at the sound of approaching footsteps and saw Chris coming up the dock. He, too, was dressed for swimming.

"I'm Sal, by the way," Sal said, offering his meaty hand. "From New York."

"Yeah, I kinda guessed that. Hal. LA."

Chris introduced himself, too, but didn't offer a home city.

Hal took the opportunity to scan the Malecón, which at this hour was still kind of sleepy. An old fellow with a newspaper sat on a bench in front of a closed-up bar. Further down the way, strolling in their direction, was a guy in shades who, judging from his black slacks and baggy Hawaiian shirt, just might have been Eastern European. One of Bodi's minions, probably, keeping an eye on their new asset.

Then, down at the end of the dock, one of the beat-up white vans that passed for taxis on Vieques pulled to the curb. Out stepped Susan. No wig today, but she wore sandals, loose cotton pants with a drawstring, and an unbuttoned cotton shirt that billowed in the breeze to reveal a snug and surprisingly scanty purple bikini top.

Sal, playing up to his role of brash New Yorker—or maybe that's what he really was—gave a low whistle and said, "Well, this is mighty fine. Hope she's shipping out with our group."

Chris looked down at his flip-flops while swallowing his laughter. Nothing like taking advantage of your cover to spoof the boss, Hal supposed, although there was no damn way he was going to say a word, or even let his gaze linger for more than a fleeting second. He cleared his throat as Susan approached.

"I'm Susan," she said, nodding curtly but keeping a polite distance.

The men responded in kind.

"And how long will each of you gentlemen be staying here on sunny Vieques?"

"Another week, maybe," Sal said, "depending on the weather and the fishing."

"Same," Chris said.

All eyes then turned to Hal, who suddenly realized this had been the whole point of her question—to find out when he and the Bolrovians were leaving.

"Last day on the island for me. Taking off this afternoon. Three-thirty flight."

"Then I guess you better make the most of this little boat ride," Susan said.

"That's the plan."

Up the dock bounded a hale and hearty young man in shorts and a white polo with a Buccaneer Bob's logo on the front pocket. More like a kid, really. Deeply tanned, with dark hair and engaging brown eyes.

"Right on time, all four of you! Perfect. I'm Carlos. Grew up here and also in Ohio, which is where I'll be going to college next year, and I'll be your guide today out on the reef."

He turned at the approach of a salty-looking older fellow, mid-fifties, in a polo, cargo shorts, deck shoes, and one of those fishing hats with an overly long bill and an apron in the back to shade your neck.

"And this is our skipper, Nate, who knows where all the best spots on the reef are."

Nate merely grunted and weaved past them as everyone made way. He stepped aboard the boat, where it took him only seconds to get out a pack of smokes, light one, and switch on the engines with an eruption of smoke from the twin outboard motors.

"One last bit of business before we shove off," Carlos said. He stooped down to a strongbox on the dock, unlatched it, and threw open the lid. "This is strictly voluntary, but we highly recommend that everybody put their phones, keys, wallets, and anything else that you don't want to get wet or lose overboard into this lockbox while we're out on the water."

He then turned toward a young woman, about his age, who was walking up the dock toward them.

"Rosa here will keep everything in our office while we're gone. And when we get back, she'll be waiting for you at that shack down at the end, where you'll drop off your life jackets and snorkeling equipment, which are on board. Like I said, strictly voluntary, but we've had some people lose things in the water, while our recovery rate from the lockbox is a hundred percent."

"Sounds smart to me," Susan said. She handed over her phone, wallet, and keys, which Hal took as his cue to do the same. Sal and Chris followed suit. Carlos closed up the box and Rosa hauled it away.

"All aboard, then," Carlos said. "And the first thing I'll want everyone to do is put on a life vest, which I'll be handing out right away. I'll give a little safety talk and get everyone equipped on our way out to the reef."

The four of them stepped onto the boat, walking a little unsteadily at first. They sat toward the stern, facing each other from bench seating along the sides. Carlos went into the cabin and returned with life vests for all of them.

Rosa undid the lines from the cleats on the dock, and the boat grumbled out of the slip. After clearing the end of the dock, they soon moved into deeper waters. The skipper eased the throttle forward as they rounded the point, and the bow rose as they gathered speed.

Glancing back over his shoulder, Hal saw Bodi's man standing on the Malecón, arms folded as he watched their progress. Sunlight glinted off his shades. He and the rest of Esperanza soon disappeared behind a green hill as the boat headed east along the island's south coast. Hal immediately felt better. Chris gave him a nod. Perhaps he, too, had been keeping an eye on the guy. Maybe they all had.

Carlos squatted between them for his safety talk, proceeding in the quick, boilerplate manner of a flight attendant who had done this a zillion times. He then opened a compartment and began pulling out masks, snorkels, and swim fins, which he handed out to each of them.

"Okay, then. First question. How many of you have been snorkeling before?"

All four of them raised their hands.

"Great! You guys are making it easy on me. But once you're all set with the gear, I'll give you a few tips and refreshers, just in case."

Susan spoke up.

"Actually, can I talk with you up front for a second?"

Her assured tone instantly commanded his attention. It also didn't hurt that she was holding a folded pair of twenties in her right hand. Carlos glanced at the others. Chris and Sal nodded, as if to say it was cool with them, so Carlos followed Susan along the port-side railing past the cabin to the bow, where they turned to face each other, each of them holding the rail as the boat bounced against a light chop. Susan leaned closer to speak as he nodded, their hair blowing in the breeze.

Hal guessed that, when she returned, Carlos would remain at the bow and the lessons in spycraft would begin. While that was reassuring, he found himself hoping they'd still have enough time left over to do some snorkeling, if only because his brief lifespan as a little-noticed island tourist was rapidly approaching its end.

And that's when it hit him. In only six hours he'd be boarding a flight with Bodi. And in fewer than twenty-four hours he'd be landing in Blatsk, where it was probably already chilly and gray, and there would be far too many people, and he would again be the center of attention. Scrutinized. Evaluated. And performing on demand, not only for a president, but also for these new colleagues of his. Trusting them with his life even though they hadn't even trusted him with their real names.

The boat crested a rolling swell, and then another, and for the first time in his life Hal felt a little seasick. And then a lot. He queasily looked toward the shore, trying to ground himself, but all he could think about now was the spying assignment—and the potentially unforgiving audience—that awaited him overseas in a city where he had never been before.

He stood shakily, turned toward the rail, heaved violently, and watched as the jumbled contents of his breakfast spattered colorfully upon the crystalline sea.

Chapter 13

Lauren was never quite sure how much money to pay to keep someone quiet in situations like these. Pay too little and they would blab just to spite you. Pay too much and they might decide that the information you were protecting must be so hot that they simply *had* to tell their friends and family all about it, especially after a few drinks. In other words, money alone was never sufficient, which is why she handled the job with Carlos like this:

First, she handed him the folded twenties.

Carlos nodded his thanks and glanced over his shoulder at the skipper, who had no doubt witnessed the transaction and would demand a share. There was then a slight delay as Carlos spotted Hal vomiting from the stern.

"Hey, is that guy okay? Maybe I should—"

"Just nerves. He'll be fine. And neither he nor the rest of us will be going into the water, or not for at least an hour or two, anyway. In the meantime, what we'll mostly want from you and the captain is some privacy."

She reached into her right pocket, where she'd stuffed a wad of bills, and handed Carlos another five twenties.

"Sure. Okay. So you guys are working together on something?"

"Let's just say we wanted to get away from prying eyes for a while. We happen to be involved in a very large but very delicate real estate transaction, and it has reached a critical stage in negotiations. Which is why I'm going to ask you to remain here at the bow until we've concluded our discussions. We also ask that, until then, your captain should keep the engine running. If there's extra fuel usage as a result, naturally we'll take care of that as well."

She peeled off another five twenties.

"I see."

"I thought you would."

"So you won't be going in the water?"

"Oh, I suppose we will toward the end. Probably wouldn't look good for your business or ours if we arrived back at the dock bone-dry, right?"

"Sure. And, uh, just out of curiosity, because my lips are sealed, of course"—he waved his wad of bills, as if to display the value of his sincerity—"but does this have anything to do with the Mendoza estate, over on Culebra?"

"As I said, it's confidential. But you might want to think closer to the main island."

"Like around Fajardo, maybe?"

She handed him another pair of twenties.

"No more questions, Carlos. I'll let you know when we're ready to jump in. Until then, keep your distance, and keep those motors running."

She made her way back down the port side toward the stern, figuring that she now had several things working in her favor. Yes, Carlos, and probably the skipper as well, would both start blabbing about this before they had time to order their second round of drinks at day's end. But first they'd be running a second snorkel tour at one p.m., and by the time they came ashore from that one, at four p.m., Hal and the Bolrovian entourage would have departed on their three-thirty flight. And while a rumor of an impending real estate deal might make a few wavelets on Vieques, they weren't likely to make it all the way across the Atlantic, and certainly not to Eastern Europe. It also helped that Carlos apparently hadn't recognized Hal Knight, or surely he would have said something earlier.

She reached the rear of the boat and sat back down. By then, Hal was again seated, and had opened a water bottle from a cooler on the deck, although he still looked a little green around the gills. Lauren leaned forward, her signal that it was time to get to work. The others did the same. Hal nodded dutifully and set aside the water bottle.

The boat increased speed, making the engines roar. Spray from the wake rose up in a fantail to either side of them. Carlos, who had briefly ducked into the cabin for a word with the skipper, was now back at the bow, studiously avoiding any glance in their direction. Their heads were only inches apart, but Lauren had to raise her voice to be heard.

"All right, then. Spy school is in session."

Chapter 14

Hal, happy for any distraction from the sight of the bobbing waves, listened closely as Susan spent the first few minutes warning him about the capabilities of the Bolrovian security services. She said that the guy who ran it, Branko Sarič, would be obsessive about monitoring him at all times, sometimes with personnel, but more often with a dazzling array of gadgets for snooping and eavesdropping. Apparently this Sarič fellow was addicted to all forms of electronic surveillance.

"Technological stuff, that's his strong suit."

"And his weakness," Chris added.

"Are you saying he's not very good with people?"

Susan deferred to Chris and Sal, who tag-teamed the response, just as they'd done in the bar, with Chris going first.

"Oh, he cultivates plenty of human sources, too. He just doesn't trust any of them."

"Or treat them worth a shit."

"And when he took over, he cleaned out a lot of the old hands. Some of it was deadwood, but . . ."

"Some of it was guys who knew their shit, down at street level."

"So, as you might guess, his humint networks, well . . ."

"They're a little frayed at the edges."

"And not all of his people really trust *him*."

"Yeah," Hal said. "I kind of got that vibe from Bodi. He seems more in fear of the guy than anything."

"Which makes the human side of his outfit a little shaky sometimes— a little, well . . ."

"Subject to penetration?" Hal asked.

"Not that we've had much luck yet."

"And that," Susan jumped back in, "is where you come in."

"But how am I supposed to get around all of the, well, gadgets and stuff?"

"One way is to just be careful," Susan said. "You'll learn by exposure and repetition to know when it's safe and when it's not."

"That's not very convincing."

"Which is why we arranged this little trip. Chris and Sal will give you a few tips, techniques, some ways of communicating with us outside of normal channels. And all of them will be analog, so you'll at least go into this feeling a little steadier on your feet."

"But no devices?"

"Sarič's people would detect something like that before you even reached your hotel," Chris said.

"I'll have an encrypted phone," Susan said. "Because it fits with my business cover. But for you it would look suspicious, especially if you were to switch models on the eve of your trip. For the same reason, none of our people will be sweeping for bugs in your hotel room."

"So don't even think of using your own cell phone or laptop over there," Sal said. "Or not for anything that you want to keep private."

"Okay."

"Speaking of which," Susan said, "this morning at breakfast I saw you hand your phone over to their guy—Bodi, you said?—right before he paid the bill."

"Yeah. He wanted to put a few names into my contact list."

"Shit," Sal said. "Maybe you *should* have brought your phone along, and then lost it overboard."

"That bad?"

"He almost certainly put something on it to give them access to everything. And if your phone is synced to your laptop, well, they'll have that shit, too. But they probably would've hacked their way into both of them anyway."

"Well, damn."

"What's done is done. Did he at least really put some names in your contacts?"

"Yeah. Three of them. His own, for starters. Bodi Orovan—or at least that's the name in his passport. Plus, the guy you've already been talking about . . ."

"Sarič?"

"Yeah."

"We'll want that number for sure. Who's the third guy?"

"Some presidential aide, the guy who supposedly will be meeting me at the airport. Pavel something."

"Lukov, maybe?"

"That sounds right."

The three of them exchanged glances. Hal couldn't tell if this was good news or bad.

"He's Horvatz's chief administrative aide," Susan said.

"A new guy. You could do worse," Sal said. Chris nodded in affirmation. "Not that you should trust any of them."

"Will you want his number, too?"

"We'll want all three of them," Susan said. "For now, let's start with a few hard-and-fast rules to live by from the moment you hit the ground."

Hal nodded. Susan glanced again toward the front of the boat. The captain was still at the wheel. He had turned on some music. Carlos remained at the bow, staring off into the sea. She looked back at Hal, her eyes intent, alert, all business. This time he didn't detect any hostility, which somehow made him feel a little safer.

"Always leave your phone behind in your hotel room whenever you go out for a walk, or for a drink, or for dinner. And you need to establish that habit right from the start, from your very first evening in Blatsk. If anyone asks, tell them it's been a habit of yours ever since, well, the whole downfall thing. They'll get it. They might even sympathize. It'll be one less way they'll have to track your movements."

"Got it."

"Rule two. Carry a pencil and a small notebook wherever you go. This one."

Susan reached into her left pocket—not the one with all the twenties—and pulled out a pencil and a small black A6 kraft notebook, a refillable model about four by six inches, with binding screws that let you open it to remove or add pages, plus an elastic band to hold it shut or mark your place. She handed them to Hal. He opened the notebook and flipped through the pages, as if looking for signs of secret ink.

"It's nothing gimmicky or special. Just a notebook."

"I used to carry one of these all the time, same model even. Back when I was writing a lot but before, well . . ."

"I know. I read about it in a profile in *Variety*. Figured that now would be as good a time as any for you to get back into the habit. You can tell them the visit has rekindled your creative urges."

"Better still," Chris said, "tell 'em that Horvatz has inspired you."

"You don't think maybe that would be laying it on too thick?"

"The thicker the better, man. In terms of having his ego stroked, our man Horvatz is not unlike a certain American politician we've all come to know and love."

"Oh, fuck. Not another T—"

"Whoa, now. Don't even say his name. As certified members of the Deep State, we could all get in trouble just for joking about him."

"But that's a joke, too, right?"

"Hey, man, what did I just say?"

Susan and Sal both laughed, but Hal still got the message. And in his brief stint on the Intel Committee he had heard enough scuttlebutt to know that, by the time the Former Guy had left office, he had been dismissive enough of the CIA's work to earn the scorn of much of its rank and file.

"Okay, then, back on topic," Susan said. "The notebook. Use it early and often, whether you're actually inspired or not, even if all you're doing is taking notes about your meals. But use a light hand. Press too hard and, even if you tear out a page, they'll be able to figure out what you wrote from the impressions on the next one. Because the notebook is how you're going to send us messages."

"In writing?"

"Yes. Sarič is all about the gadgets, and maybe the only way to beat that is to go old-school. So you'll compose your reports on those pages, remove them, and deliver them personally to our local contact—your designated mailman—who will give you replacement pages. That way, if anybody checks the notebook, nobody will wonder where all the missing pages have gone."

"And how will I find this mailman guy?"

"All that comes next. After rule number three."

"Okay."

"From the moment you get there, they may start showering you with little gifts. Leave them all in your hotel room, maybe all in the same drawer, and don't ever take any of them with you. Not even if it's something you like, or something functional."

"*Especially* if it's something functional," Sal said.

"If anyone asks why you're not using the stuff they give you, tell them it's what you always do with gifts, for sentimental reasons. You're saving them for the trip home."

"Sounds kinda lame."

"Would a conviction on espionage charges in Bolrovia sound less lame?"

"I take your point."

"And feel free to come up with a better excuse—just don't take any of those items out of the room with you."

"Got it."

"Now for your homework, which you'll do here, on the boat."

She got another item out of her left pocket—three pages of printed instructions, single spaced, which she unfolded and handed to him.

"You've had a lot of practice in memorizing things, right? Scripts, comedy routines, all that kind of stuff?"

"Not for a while, but yeah. I soak up material pretty fast."

"Good. Spend the next hour going over all these pages, and finish before we get in the water, because, for obvious reasons, we can't let you keep them. They cover the procedure for how you'll deliver your messages, how we'll send you any replies or instructions. Although it's highly probable you won't hear from us at all, especially if things are going well. These instructions have about twenty code words—for names, procedures, plus other stuff that you might need to mention in your messages. That way, even if they're intercepted, they'll still look as harmless as possible. In the unlikely event we *do* send you a message, you'll dispose of it as fast as possible. There are instructions for that as well."

"What if they catch me with any of them?"

"Our messages will also be in pencil, written on the same kinds of pages. We'll mimic your handwriting and use the same code words. We'll do everything we can to make it seem harmless, like something you took out of the notebook earlier."

"Okay."

"And now we'll wait while you study. Don't worry about Carlos or the captain. If they see you poring over something, they'll probably think it's a real estate contract."

"Got it."

Chris spoke.

"Maybe now's a good time to give him the number."

"The number?" Hal said.

"For my encrypted phone," Susan said. "But only in the case of the most extreme emergency. And I cannot emphasize those last two words enough. Extreme—"

"Emergency." Hal finished it for her. "I get it."

Judging from her skeptical expression, she wasn't convinced. Nonetheless, she told him, repeating it three times until he could repeat it back to her. With any luck, he'd never need it.

"One last thing. They're probably going to insist on having someone with you at almost all times, but even if you manage to get some time on your own, always assume that it's an illusion, a mirage. You will never be able to go anywhere without another set of eyes on you, even when you're delivering our messages. Which is why you'll need to pay special attention to the protocols on those pages that tell you how to deal with that."

Hal nodded. His mouth was dry. He wished he was within reach of the water bottle, but it had rolled across the deck.

"And what if, well, in a pinch, there's something I really need to do but without, as you said, having anyone's eyes on me?"

"Like I said, there are some tips for that in the instructions. Although, since you're not trained in this—or not like his people are, or ours—I wouldn't count on them working, not a hundred percent. Or not without our help, anyway."

"Your help?"

"Sal's. Chris's. Mine. That's all in there, too."

"Then I guess I better start cramming for the exam."

"Sal, grab that water bottle for him. Looks like he could use a drink."

She had that right. Hal settled back into the seat, which wasn't especially comfortable. He took a long swig of water and got to work as the boat rolled beneath him, his departure now only five hours away.

Chapter 15

Jumping into the clear, beautiful water was bliss. Putting on the mask and snorkel, and then shutting out the rest of the world by immersing himself in the colorful silence of the reef, was better still. It was calming, exhilarating, like submerging into a sensory-deprivation tank alongside psychedelic beings that flashed and flowed through filtered sunlight. Hal reached out to touch some orange fan coral, then gawked at a passing angelfish in iridescent blue and yellow. Massive schools of tiny silvery fish flickered like neon confetti, and if you held still long enough they surrounded you, a cloud of life.

The study session had gone quite well, and he felt good about that, too. There had been only one glitch, when he had a question about one of the code words.

"Hey, guys?" he'd said, looking up from the notes. And this time he'd had the presence of mind to not add, "And gal." They turned toward him in unison.

"Yes?" Susan asked.

"I see that I'm supposed to use the word 'family' whenever I mean 'CIA,' but I'm not sure that's a good idea. Or not if they know very much about me."

"Why's that?"

"Well, and not to blame you or anything, because this wasn't in the *Variety* piece, or any other story, but I don't really have a family. Not anymore."

There was an awkward silence, so he explained.

"My mom and dad died years ago, and I'm an only child. We moved around a lot, so I never really saw any cousins or aunts or uncles. I was pretty close to getting married up until a short while ago, but then, well . . ."

"Right."

"So I guess what I'm saying is, if they ever intercept one of these pages and see me using the word 'family' a lot . . ."

"Yes. I see the problem."

The three of them exchanged glances. Clearly, none of their training had prepared them for a moment like this. Susan looked to Chris as if hoping he could fix it, but he shook his head. She turned back toward Hal.

"You said you were close to being married. You were talking about Jessamyn Miller, right? The screenwriter?"

The name hit him in the chest like a boulder and took the air out of his lungs. He had to inhale before he could answer.

"Yeah. Jess."

"Did she, or *does* she, I guess, have family? And were you at all close to them?"

"I am. Or was, yeah. Pretty close." He needed another deep breath.

"Could you maybe use 'Jess's family,' then? Or 'her family'? Either way, we'll know what you mean."

"Sure. That could work. Thanks."

They quickly looked away, as if to give him as much space as possible. But for Hal the moment had actually made it easier to focus, by reminding him of his top goal in taking on this assignment. So, by the time he jumped into the water—after Carlos told them they still had twenty minutes to explore the reef—he had mastered the material. And now, among the fish and the coral, Hal experienced that rare sensation that he had momentarily regained control of his life again. So why not enjoy it.

Another school of small fish enfolded him as he drifted in the water, legs dangling. There were hundreds of them, maybe thousands, turning in unison, first one way, then another. A few were close enough to look him in the eye—their gazes fixed—until suddenly it all felt a little claustrophobic, like being ambushed by a horde of autograph seekers or paparazzi, so many eyes on him that he couldn't move. Seized by panic, he kicked his flippers, dispersing them in an instant. He raised his face above the water and tore off the mask, gasping for air as he thrashed his arms.

Chris, swimming nearby, surfaced to his left.

"You okay, man?"

"Yeah. Fine. But I think I'm done with this."

"Time's about up, anyway. We should get back in the boat."

Hal nodded and swam toward the stern.

When they reached the dock, Bodi's man was gone, but Bodi himself was at a sidewalk table at a restaurant on the Malecón, where he seemed to be having lunch. Now that they were back under observation, the three CIA people again acted like strangers. Susan departed in an apparent hurry, carrying her snorkeling gear quickly up the dock toward the Buccaneer Bob's equipment shed, where they were supposed to meet Rosa to reclaim their phones and wallets. Sal was close in her wake.

By the time Hal reached the shed, still dripping, Rosa was waiting by the strongbox.

"Enjoy it?"

"Absolutely. The perfect end to my week."

"Great. Just drop your gear on the table over there so we can rinse it off."

The shed offered some privacy. Bodi's view was blocked, so Hal took a moment to collect himself before heading out. Chris entered and dumped his mask and snorkel.

"Everything okay now?"

He spoke with a note of concern. It was reassuring to know that the three of them would always be nearby throughout his stay in Bolrovia.

"Guess I had a little panic attack out there. Probably overthinking it."

"It happens. But you've got a knack for this, I can tell."

"You really think so?"

"Yeah, man. I do."

"Aren't you guys worried that Bodi's people have seen you now. I mean, I know they don't know who you are, but—"

Chris shook his head.

"This crew here is one of Sarič's outreach teams. They don't operate in Blatsk, and they haven't been shooting any pictures or video. It's all cool."

"Mind if I ask a personal question?"

"Try me."

"It's just that, well, I get the impression Bolrovia's kind of white. And you're in the clandestine biz, so . . ."

"Yeah, I had the same thought when they posted me there. I mean, what the fuck, right? They might as well have sent me to an igloo or some country club in Alabama."

"An igloo. That's good. Then why send you there?"

What Chris—or Quint, of course—could have said, maybe even wanted to say, was that the assignment had been a sort of punishment after he'd lectured a placement officer about all the countries he didn't want to go to, most of them in Africa or the Caribbean, because at the time those were the default destinations for every black field operative and he wanted to be the guy who broke the mold by going someplace where people who looked like him would be part of the mix but maybe not the main event. Instead, to teach him a lesson, they'd placed him in Bolrovia.

But all he said to Hal was, "It's not important. The funny part is, it's kind of worked out. I mean, I stick out for sure. But there's a small community there, in Blatsk anyway. Mostly West African expats—guest workers, asylum seekers—and all of them are so marginalized that most Bolrovians don't even *want* to see them. Meaning nobody does, or not really."

"So it's like you're invisible?"

"Goddamn right. Whole new form of cover."

"But it can't be easy. Personally, I mean."

Chris shrugged.

"Hey, one more year and I'm out of there. Now I got a question for you. What's with that book of yours?"

"The Roth?"

"Yeah. You've always got it, but you're never reading it."

"Two things, I guess. One, it never hurts to have a prop. Something you can open in case you need for somebody, or a whole lot of some-bodies, to leave you the fuck alone. Plus, well . . ." He looked out at the sea. "There's stuff in it that's instructive for me. It's basically about a guy who thinks with his dick. Hell, all his books are."

"You mean like ninety percent of us? Shit, you don't need a book to tell you that."

"I guess. But it's helped me figure out some things about myself."

"Whatever works, man."

Obviously, Chris thought the whole idea was nuts. Maybe it was. But he'd be taking the book with him to Bolrovia.

"You go first," Chris said, nodding toward the Malecón.

"Right. See you in Blatsk." He paused. "Or will I?"

"I'll be seeing you, for sure. Doubt you'll see me. And if you do, I'll just be part of the scenery, a face in the crowd. But good luck, man."

"Yeah. Same. Thanks."

Hal stepped back out into the sunlight, squinting in the brightness. He strolled off to look for Bodi.

Chapter 16

———≈———

High above the clouds over Europe, in the bright blue yonder of a September sky, Hal convinced himself that everything would be fine. First-class seating probably had something to do with that. He had slept reasonably well during the overnight crossing, and he was also in the front cabin for this flight, out of Frankfurt. Better still, Bodi and his minions had been banished to steerage, and had departed after watching him board for the final leg, which had given Hal time to further memorize his marching orders and start scribbling in the black notebook. The more he thought about it, the more he felt certain that this gig would not last more than a week. Meaning that soon enough he'd be flying in the opposite direction, his duty fulfilled. By then he might even be ready to go home. This trip might be the reset he'd been needing all along.

His election to Congress was supposed to have been the event that set his life on a new and better course, his way of no longer playing the role of a somewhat boorish buffoon, a creative type who had let popularity steer his work into a rut. But being a candidate, and then a U.S. Representative, had only been a change in roles and wardrobes, a job in which he had quickly begun playing to a different crowd, with different wants and needs. So maybe it was just as well he'd left that behind, too. It was time to be more hopeful, perhaps, especially now that both his former audiences would be thousands of miles away.

Then the plane dropped into the clouds and began its descent into Blatsk, bumping through the turbulence. The sunlight dimmed, then disappeared—and with it, his fragile optimism. Out the window, the countryside below materialized faintly through a layer of mist. Farmsteads, brown fields, clumps of forest. Dotted here and there were villages where small homes and businesses huddled closely, as if for warmth and protection.

A network of highways passed below as the outer reaches of Blatsk came into view. The slabs of gray apartment towers covered the ground like spiky mold. They must have been built while Stalin was alive, and even from up here they seemed to be crumbling at the edges. He'd bet that half the elevators were out of order and that every stairwell smelled of cigarettes and boiled cabbage.

Or maybe not, because Hal was not exactly a man of the world. For all his wealth and celebrity, his only previous travel to Europe had been to Paris, Rome, and London, and he had spent most of those trips in the company of studio executives and people who'd been paid to move him from place to place without bother or discomfort. All of his escorts had spoken perfect English—unless you counted the Scotsman whose accent had been as impenetrable as Arabic.

And now, here was central Blatsk, laid out like a toytown of medieval disarray. Twisting narrow lanes fed into big squares flanked by spires and steeples. Snaking through it all was a brown river spanned by impressive-looking bridges from another era. Who did he know down there? No one. The three Americans had assured him they'd be nearby, but if he never saw them, how would he know for sure? He sat back and waited for the wheels to touch down. By the time they reached the gate, he was enveloped in gloom.

Only an hour later he got his first lesson in the dynamics of local power, which began with a knock on the door of his hotel room just as he was about to unpack. Having been forewarned of a visit by a masseuse, that's who he expected to see when he opened the door. Would she be young and pretty, or built like one of those East German swimmers, with shoulders strong enough to knead his muscles into pudding? The whole idea had struck him as kind of weird, but he had figured it would be ungrateful to say no.

Instead, the visitor was a man of about Hal's size and build. He wore black pants and a gray wool blazer over a black turtleneck, but had managed to ruin the austere effect of his wardrobe by clipping an orange water bottle to one side of his belt, like a holstered gun. He had a five-o'clock shadow even though it was noon, and his dark eyes were alert and on the make. He was not smiling.

"Oh. Hello."

"Greetings, Mr. Knight. I am Branko Sarič. I am here as a representative of the Interior Ministry, which will be responsible for your safety and security throughout your stay."

"I see."

So here he was, then: Bodi's boss and, according to everything the CIA people had told him, the goon of all goons, the single greatest threat to his health and well-being. Hal was surprised to be meeting him so soon. From all the earlier descriptions, Hal had figured him for the type who would prefer to lurk at the margins, revealing himself only if necessary. Was this a good sign or a bad one?

Sarič extended his right hand, more in the manner of a challenge than a welcome, although his next words were pleasant enough.

"Welcome to Bolrovia, sir."

His English was far more polished than Bodi's, with only the slightest trace of an accent.

"Thank you. Would you, uh, like to come in?"

"No, no. I have not come to invade your privacy. In the interests of assuring you of our competence, I thought that I might do you the courtesy of a brief tour."

"Oh. Well, I really have no worries about anyone's competence. But I was told a little while ago to expect a visit from a masseuse, so, uh . . ."

"Yes. I arranged that appointment. But this morning I decided this might be a more productive use of your time. You may reschedule the masseuse at your convenience."

"Okay. Sure."

"Shall we, then?"

Well, this was sudden, but he supposed it would be foolish, maybe even dangerous, to say no.

"Sure. Let me get my things."

Should he leave behind his phone, as instructed? No, that was only supposed to be his habit when he went out for a walk or an evening on the town. But he wanted his notebook, so he retrieved it from the bedside table and stuffed it in his rear pocket. Sarič, who despite his earlier assurance had followed him back into the room like a wisp of smoke, tilted his head as he watched, as if logging every movement for future reference. Hal felt scrutinized in a way that made him need to explain himself. He tapped the pocket with the notebook.

"It's a creative thing. I always like to keep it handy when I'm working on something."

Was he saying too much? Yes, for sure. He wondered if Sarič had this effect on everyone.

"And what is it that you're working on now? Or is it rude of me to ask an artist that sort of question?"

Sarič made the word "artist" almost sound like an insult.

"I'm more at the point where I'm looking for inspiration."

"I see."

Sarič smiled without humor, as if he knew the whole notebook thing was bullshit. It was clear to Hal that this session of improv was not going to go as smoothly as the one outside his room in Vieques. Maybe he was letting all the warnings get to him. His throat felt constricted, his fingertips tingled. Henceforth he would say as little as possible. Let Sarič do the talking.

———◆———

They rode the elevator in awkward silence—awkward for Hal, anyway. A few men in the lobby turned as they passed, and it wasn't Hal they were watching. Sarič's crossing was like the passing of a shadow from a solar eclipse.

A black Mercedes with several extra antennae waited out front. It was blocking the prime space reserved for the Esplanade's courtesy van, but not a single doorman was protesting, or even acting as if anything was amiss. Hal climbed into the back. Sarič joined him from the other side, then knocked twice on a panel of smoked glass that separated them from the driver. The car slipped into traffic like an eel into a school of prey. Presumably the driver knew their destination.

"I hope that everything was in order for your arrival at the airport. Was Mr. Lukov there to greet you and smooth the formalities?"

Sarič's tone was skeptical, implying a low opinion of Pavel Lukov, the amiable young man who had indeed been waiting for Hal at the arrivals gate, just as Bodi had said.

"He was. He was quite helpful."

Although Hal had admittedly been a little perturbed when Lukov had asked him to pose for a photographer while having his passport stamped.

"It's not for publicity," Lukov had reassured him. "It's for, well, President Horvatz. He wanted to make sure the moment was recorded for the historical record."

The *historical record*? Hal hadn't known whether to laugh or cringe. He'd then stolen a sidelong glance at Lukov, who, to his credit, had looked a little sheepish. When Hal caught his eye, they'd both laughed, which had helped break the ice.

"Look, I'm grateful to be here as your country's guest," Hal had told him. "I wouldn't be getting this kind of welcome anywhere else, so, believe me, I'm not complaining. But, well, doesn't this whole setup feel just a little bit ridiculous?"

Lukov had nodded, cheeks reddening.

"It does. But I'm new to the job, and this is what the boss wants."

"Then let's give him a nice smile for the camera."

Hal had turned to face the lens as he opened his passport for the stamp. He smiled goofily, in the manner of the dim-witted leading role he'd played in *Barefoot and Pregnant,* knowing instinctively that, as a superfan, Horvatz would recognize it right away.

Lukov had nodded approvingly. Hal decided he might actually like this fellow.

"C'mon over here," Hal said. "Let's get a shot of the two of us, to impress the boss."

Hal threw his arm around Lukov's shoulders as they mugged for the camera.

"Will this help get you a raise?"

"Right now I'd settle for job security."

Only later did it occur to Hal that, if his true role ever became known, the chummy photo might become a liability. It made him hope Lukov didn't have a family to support. And now, here was this grim fellow Sarič, offering the flip side of Bolrovian hospitality.

"Did Lukov present you with your welcome gift?"

"What? Oh, the music player, yes. Thank you."

Hal blushed, because he was thinking of the warning that the CIA people had given him about accepting gifts, especially electronic devices. Lukov had given him wireless earbuds and an MP3 music player—quite a nice one, actually, even though Hal put all his music on his phone— that was supposedly filled with all sorts of Bolrovian favorites, from classical to folk to rock. He had shoved it into a dresser drawer the moment he'd reached his hotel room.

"And did Lukov remember to brief you on your schedule for this evening?"

"Fully. Cocktails at six at the Presidential Palace, followed by a state dinner. He'll be picking me up at the hotel a half hour beforehand for early delivery to the palace."

Sarič nodded, seemingly mollified.

"Will you be there?" Hal asked.

"Perhaps. Although my schedule allows little time for frivolity."

Hal let that pass without comment, then decided to change the subject.

"I've been pleasantly surprised by the number of people here who speak such good English."

"Why surprised? We are part of the European Union, not some backwater. And linguistically, English is now the coin of the realm, yes?"

"I guess. Sure."

"Probably twenty percent of us are fluent. The rate is higher among the well educated. And in government, too, of course." Then he frowned, as if all this fluency was yet another security headache for his ministry to keep track of.

"Forty years ago, you know, the most prevalent second language was Russian. Very little English then, unless you were an academic." He spoke the latter word with the same distaste he had shown for "artist."

"That is a major reason our president became such a fan of yours. He was of that previous generation which had to learn English late in life. It was not easy, but he is a man who handles such struggles with strength, with fortitude. He came to rely on your work as one of his favorite ways of practicing."

"That would take some fortitude, all right," Hal said, trying to loosen things up. Sarič frowned, not getting the joke. Maybe Hal should have added a rim shot. This was one of the hazards of being known as a comedian. People almost always expected you to be funny, and in Hal's case they often came away disappointed. He was not the sort of fellow who always lighted up a room, who always tried to be "on." Even if he had been, Hal suspected that Sarič would not have been an easy audience.

"He liked using your films not just for words and pronunciation, but as a way of mastering slang, popular culture."

"That's nice to know."

And it was, although Hal had to repress a smile as he imagined the president dropping items like "beer me," "bropocalypse," and "booty call" into his remarks at some important international gathering.

"But maybe now," Sarič said, grinning, "Russian is ready for its comeback, yes?"

"Or maybe not, with the war in Ukraine."

"Oh, that?" Sarič waved it away. "That is their own matter. Not ours. And not America's."

Hal knew better than to pursue that further. Sarič was almost certainly familiar with the anti-Putin statements that Hal had made on the floor of the U.S. House of Representatives, but there was no way he was going there now, or at any time while he was here.

"What about your own language skills?" Sarič asked. "Do you speak any Bolrovian?"

"None."

With Lukov he might have apologized for that, but Sarič seemed like the kind of guy who'd see any apology as a sign of weakness.

Sarič nodded. Then he pulled out his phone.

"Excuse me. I must make a call."

He launched into a rapid stream of Bolrovian. It felt pointedly like a demonstration of Hal's ignorance and reminded him that, no matter who he was with in the days to come, there would often be moments like this, when he would be missing out on practically everything that was transpiring unless someone was willing to translate.

"Da, da," Sarič said, nodding vigorously, which even Hal knew was an emphatic yes. Sarič then laughed and glanced over at Hal, as if to say, *We could be talking about you, but you will never know as long as I avoid mentioning your name.*

It was chilly in the car, and the radio was off, meaning the only sound apart from the muffled noise of the traffic was Sarič's voice, drumming rapidly along as they turned a corner. Now that he had a chance to look around, it was clear to him that this was no ordinary limo. And while he'd certainly been in hired cars with better amenities—TV screens, hideaway cocktail bars—this one had the feel of a mobile command center. Its signature feature was a screen for some sort of GPS system, which at the moment displayed not only their own location but four other moving dots. Hal wondered who else Sarič was tracking, and how many other targets he could follow at any one time while riding in this car.

They were in the heart of the city, heading down one of those twisty lanes he'd spotted from the plane. They'd made several turns, each street narrower than the one before it, which made it feel like they had entered a maze. If they dropped him off now, he'd be completely lost, although he supposed he could use his phone to find his way back to the hotel.

Then, like a plane emerging from clouds, they turned onto a wide boulevard that quickly opened onto a plaza, where a large granite building—five stories, with neat rows of blank windows—loomed just ahead behind a wrought-iron fence. The architecture was monolithic, early '80s. It looked completely out of place here, although the national flag of Bolrovia hung from a pole out front. The rooftop was a nest of antennae and satellite dishes.

Sarič stopped talking, pocketed his phone, then unclipped his orange water bottle from his belt and took a long swig.

"We have arrived."

They drove to the right side of the building, where a steel security gate rolled open. An armed sentry emerged from a guardhouse and nodded as Sarič's car passed through. They rounded the corner of the building toward the back, rumbling across cobbles and then onto smooth pavement as they disappeared from view for anyone who might have been watching from the plaza.

"I thought I would spare you the bother of the main entrance, with all its bells and whistles for security. No need to subject you to all that. You're our guest."

"Where are we?"

"The Interior Ministry, where I work."

"I see."

Why had they come here? Why not instead a trip to the Presidential Palace, or to one of the city's more popular destinations? Hadn't Sarič said this was a tour?

They entered through a rear door that was a few steps below ground level. Another armed guard nodded at Sarič and waved them through a metal detector that beeped as they passed. The guard's flak vest reminded Hal unpleasantly of the goon who had lurked in the stairwell of his guesthouse on Vieques. He wondered where Bodi and his minions were now. Already dispatched to some other locale, perhaps, to haul in someone else, this time a bit more forcefully.

Sarič held open the door of a narrow elevator as Hal stepped aboard.

There were buttons for all the upper floors and for three basement levels. Sarič hit the one marked B3, and the row of lights overhead showed the progress of their descent. They stopped at the bottom. By then even the air pressure felt different, like on a submarine or in a tunnel.

They stepped into a dim hallway where the air was damp. Hal hesitated, waiting for Sarič to show the way.

"Go left, down to the end. You will see the open door."

This was a cellblock, for god's sake. He passed five cells on each side of the corridor as he walked to the end. Each had a heavy iron door with a small window of thick glass reinforced by metal mesh. All the doors except the one at the end were shut, and all the windows were dark, although Hal heard the muffled sound of coughing coming from behind one of them. Conceivably, every cell but this last one may have been occupied. It was certainly an odd choice for a tour.

"Is there a point to all this?" he asked, a little surprised by the boldness of his question.

"Of course. Please. Keep moving."

Hal felt like he needed to keep asking questions before entering the open doorway.

"What, uh, what is this place?"

"It is where we will bring anyone who tries to make things unpleasant or unwelcoming for you. I wanted to show you in order to demonstrate my personal commitment to not letting anyone disrupt your stay."

"Do you think anyone is even likely to try that?"

"Almost certainly not. And this is one of the reasons why, of course."

Hal paused at the threshold of the open cell, figuring that a glance inside was all he needed.

The cell was about six by eight feet, with a ten-foot ceiling. On the left was a low concrete ledge, presumably for sleeping, although there was no mattress. In the middle was a small square table, bolted to the floor. It was flanked by a metal stool, backless, and, on the opposite side, a swivel chair that looked fairly comfortable. Hanging from overhead was a bare bulb of low wattage.

"Please," Sarič said, gesturing toward the stool. "Be seated."

Hal sat, the steel uncomfortable against his buttocks, his back immediately stiff from having to maintain his balance by planting both feet on the floor at an awkward angle. Sarič, still standing, reached outside the room to throw a switch. The overhead bulb went out, and a green light mounted behind a protective cage near the ceiling flickered on, casting the room in a dim and ghastly glow that made it feel like they were at the bottom of the ocean.

Sarič stepped fully inside and shut the door behind him. Did it lock automatically? If so, how were they going to get out, and when?

Hal saw now that a pair of handcuffs dangled from his side of the table. He considered making a joke about them, then thought better of it. Sarič slid into the swivel chair, which creaked. The seat was several inches higher than the stool. Hal's balance felt precarious, and he didn't know where to put his hands, so he folded them in his lap.

"Why are we here?"

"I thought this might be an appropriate place for us to talk."

"About what?"

"A warning. For your own protection. To put you on notice that some of your countrymen may try to contact you while you are here in Blatsk."

"Americans?"

"Ones working for your government."

"From the State Department?"

"No. And not anyone who will have your best interests—or ours—in mind."

Sarič leaned forward, put a hand on Hal's shoulder, and gave it a firm squeeze. It was not at all a companionable gesture. It felt more like the way you'd grip a piece of meat with tongs when you were about to toss it on a grill. In the green lighting, the glow of Sarič's eyes was diabolical. If Hal had ever written such an exaggerated moment into one of his scripts, he would've had to pause for a chuckle, because it was so overly dramatic. No one had told him Sarič was a subtle man, but this was over the top by anyone's standards. Effective, however. Hal would readily vouch for that. And the cell was clammy, spooky, claustrophobic. He wanted out of there now, but he didn't dare show that he was worried or panicked, so he strived instead for annoyed.

"Is this how your ministry always shows its hospitality? By bringing your honored guests to a cell block for political prisoners?"

"Most of our guests are not such ripe targets for recruitment as you."

"Recruitment for what?"

"Your assistance in undermining our president. They will be in touch. I am nearly a hundred percent certain of that. And when they do contact you, you will tell me. Immediately. Me personally—not someone like Lukov, or anyone else. Do you understand?"

"What if they don't?"

"Answer my question."

"Yes, I will. Now answer mine, please."

"They will. You will see. In fact, I would not be at all surprised if they had already laid eyes on you, perhaps even while you were sunbathing on the beaches of that island, Vieques."

Hal sensed that a reaction was called for, so he raised his eyebrows and said, "Well, that's kind of spooky."

The line drew an appreciative grin, the first time Hal felt like he had handled Sarič well—unless the man was grinning because he already knew about the CIA trio.

"Yes, spooky. That is how they often operate. Here they are likely to be bolder still. My only question is whether they will reveal their true identity or even admit they are working for your government. Because they may also try to contact you through an intermediary, a Bolrovian. Perhaps even someone who works for our government."

"Okay."

"So, then. Do I have your assurance that you will notify me of any such contact?"

He squeezed Hal's shoulder again, as if it were time to flip the meat on the grill.

"Sure. Yeah."

"Do not take this request lightly. I certainly will not."

"Nor will I."

Sarič studied him for a few seconds, then nodded.

"I believe you. Do you know why?"

Hal shook his head.

"Because I know that you are soft. The worlds you come from—the American Congress, Hollywood—they are places of softness. Places where you are always taken care of by others. Deferred to. All that it took to drive you into hiding was a lot of people saying silly things online."

"It was a bit more than that."

"Perhaps. But the main damage, it seems to me, was that your feelings were hurt. Tell me, does this look like a room where people are brought in order to hurt their feelings?"

Hal decided not to answer that. Sarič released his shoulder and stood.

Hal tried to do the same, but his awkward position on the low stool made him a little wobbly as he rose to his feet. A bead of sweat began its long journey from the nape of his neck to the small of his back, even though it was cold in here. Sarič knocked once on the door. It was opened almost immediately by a guard outside.

"My driver will return you to the hotel."

He gave Hal's shoulder another squeeze and led him to the elevators. When they reached the ground floor, the driver was waiting just outside, smoking a cigarette.

"Think carefully about all that I have told you," Sarič said. "Go for a walk, perhaps. Take your little notebook with you. Who knows, maybe you will even have some news for me as early as tomorrow morning."

Half an hour later Hal was back in his hotel room, still feeling a little shaky, so he stripped off his damp clothes and stepped into the shower. He turned the water to as hot as he could stand it and let it blast his shoulders, his face, his back. The chill went out of his bones, but his worries multiplied.

He wished he hadn't come here. He wished he'd read the fine print on all those forms he'd signed. He wished he hadn't smiled for the camera while getting his passport stamped. But mostly he wished he hadn't fucked up so badly a few months ago—and all those times before—or else this trip, this role, would never have been even a remote possibility.

Did his regrets make him soft? Maybe. Sarič had certainly been right about one thing. Hollywood and Congress were places that made you feel protected, coddled, entitled to gripe about anything and everything. And even though he had taken great financial and artistic risks to climb his way into those realms, and had done so in the glare of public scrutiny, his *life* had never been part of the wager, as it seemed to be here.

That was the main drawback to deciding that your life might again be worthwhile, he supposed. Suddenly you were again determined not to lose it, which magnified every risk. He turned the heat of the water up another notch. The stall filled with steam, and as his muscles relaxed his fear at last began to melt into something that felt more like anger and, finally, resolve.

Hal switched off the water. He dripped on the tiles as the steam cleared, gathering his thoughts in the sudden silence. Was having only his life left to lose so intolerable, especially given his other current circumstances? Sarič was a bully. Anyone could see that, but maybe Hal saw it more acutely because for a while he had been one, too—on the set, before the mike, in the writers' room, whenever he was debating a dull-witted opponent during a committee hearing. And if experience had taught him anything, it was that bullies could be beaten, even bullies who seemed to hold all the cards.

He dried off, wrapped himself in a towel, then walked to the chair by the window, where his trousers were folded neatly. He removed the small black notebook from the rear pocket, grabbed a pencil, then sat at the foot of the bed to begin writing his first secret dispatch.

It felt good. It even felt a little bit like vengeance, and for a few moments he wrote without pause—two pages, then three. The correct code words effortlessly sprang to mind, and he poured his anger into the message, describing what had happened, the place he'd been taken, those cold cells with their dim lighting. Then, as if someone had shut off a faucet, he ran out of words, ran out of anger, and suddenly felt cold sitting there in only a towel.

He stood, rubbing goose bumps on his arms. He should get dressed, but what should he wear? Then he remembered Bodi's assurance that a full wardrobe would be provided for him. Fat chance, probably, but he stepped to the closet, opened the door, and gasped in surprise at what he saw.

Every hanger was full and, what's more, every shirt, jacket, and pair of trousers looked oddly familiar, as if he had picked them out himself. It was creepy, so much so that he found himself wishing that everything had turned out to be as tasteless and tacky as he'd feared. He checked the size on one of the jackets—42 Regular, right on the money. All the colors, patterns, and fabrics were to his liking. He walked over to dresser drawers and pulled them open, one by one. Same story. They'd even gotten his favorite brand of underwear, his preferred style of socks.

Hal imagined some minion in the Interior Ministry hunched over a screen a few floors up from those dreary interrogation cells as he spent hours poring over footage and photos of Hal at various public events and appearances, or candid shots that had been snapped at trendy clubs and restaurants, at a Lakers game, at Dodger Stadium, or on the waterfront at Marina Del Rey. But what was even more disturbing than this easy intrusion into his personal preferences was that he had been so easy to read, to duplicate.

As if to double-check what this might all mean, he went to the bedside table where his constant companion of the past month, the Roth paperback, awaited. He flipped it open to one of the pages he had folded at the corner, where his eyes were drawn to a passage he had bracketed in ink. He read it, yet again.

What was astonishing to him was how people seemed to run out of their own being, run out of whatever the stuff was that made them who they were and, drained of themselves, turn into the sort of people they would once have felt sorry for. It was as though while their lives were rich and full they were secretly sick of themselves and couldn't wait to dispose of their sanity and their health and all sense of proportion so as to get down to that other self, the true *self, who was a wholly deluded fuckup.*

Wholly deluded fuckup. Yes, indeed.

Hal set aside the book. Then he looked to the foot of the bed, where the black notebook was still splayed open, showing his handwriting. The words which a few minutes ago had felt like an act of urgency, of inspiration, now seemed like an impulsive mistake.

Who was he kidding? He wasn't cut out for this. More to the point, why would the CIA care at all about his trip to the Interior Ministry? It revealed nothing about Horvatz, or anyone else in the man's inner circle. It only told them what they doubtless already knew—that Sarič was a bullying thug who would stop at nothing to intimidate you, to beat you.

He picked up the notebook, tore out each of the three pages, crumpled them, and tossed them to the floor. Then, thinking better of it, he picked them up and carried them to the bathroom toilet, where, standing over the bowl, he tore each page into tiny strips and dropped them into the water. He watched for a moment as they floated, the letters darkening as the paper absorbed the water and slowly began to sink.

He pushed the handle.

With a rushing swirl and a final gurgle, everything was gone in an instant.

Just as he was starting to feel good about that, the spirit of Shirley Halston spoke up from over his shoulder.

"Really? You're throwing in the towel already? Just 'cause some B-movie hood in a black turtleneck said 'boo'?"

"Yeah, well, I guess you had to be there. It's my first day, Shirley, go easy on me. Give me a chance to get my sea legs."

He walked back to the closet, feeling a little steadier. Then he changed his mind and headed for the minibar.

Chapter 17

The deeper secret of Lauren's assignment—one which even Malone and Quint were not privy to—was that she had far more to manage in Blatsk than the care and feeding of Hal Knight. She was there to build a network. Or rebuild, actually, because in the past few months Branko Sarič's counterintelligence people had rolled up at least six of the CIA's agents and assets.

They had also ID'd every Agency employee currently serving under diplomatic cover at the embassy in Blatsk. Only a handful of NOCs—Malone and Quint among them—had managed to stay off his radar. If not for a fortuitous signal intercept by the National Security Agency, the Agency also wouldn't have known that Sarič had dispatched a team to lure Hal Knight to Blatsk, and, as Lauren had learned the hard way, even that warning had been belated.

The larger truth was that the CIA had gone dark in Bolrovia, just as Horvatz had begun publicly cozying up to Russia, China, and other disturbing players. And if he was willing to do that out in the open, far worse behavior might be occurring in secrecy. Why would Sarič have gone to such lengths to blind them unless he was about to orchestrate something he wanted to remain unseen?

The Agency's recent debacle here had largely been the fault of the Blatsk chief of station, Leo Garvin. He had turned out to be a bit of a drunk, and in becoming obsessively careful about hiding his habit he'd become correspondingly careless in his tradecraft. This explained Langley's willingness to take a hasty gamble on a disgraced comedian and, further, trust its rebuilding efforts to an out-of-country operative who wasn't exactly an exemplary employee.

What Lauren *did* have going for her was a preestablished cover which made her suitable for immediate deployment. More to the point, her greatest strength had always been starting from scratch on unfamiliar territory. Look past the low marks for attitude and team play on her annual performance evaluations and you'd find comments like "quick study," "adaptable," and "always hits the ground running." A deputy chief of station in Zagreb had praised her skills as "rare and invaluable." He had also vowed to slit his throat if he ever had to work with her again. Then again, he hadn't much liked working with anybody.

When stepping onto new ground, Lauren had a knack for quickly absorbing the habits and tics of the locals. In spite of the language barrier, she took in a lot of little things at once—the way people drank their coffee, the way they formed lines, or behaved on trams, or interacted with cops, with waiters, with bartenders, with strangers. She noted what they read, what they watched, what they wore. At times she wondered if this skill was also a sign of weakness—an aversion to any job, relationship, or living arrangement that required deeper roots and a more enduring focus.

For all that, she was under no illusion about the difficulties ahead. Some higher-ups had already written off this op as an act of desperation—a Hail Mary or, to the more cynically inclined, a human sacrifice. Branko Sarič, intent on consolidating his victory, was already on the lookout for American reinforcements, meaning that any and all new arrivals would come under immediate scrutiny.

The usual way of dealing with this sort of heightened risk was to double down on tradecraft and careful behavior. But Lauren's instincts told her Sarič would be especially suspicious of newcomers who played everything by the book, the quiet ones who immediately headed for the shadows. So she'd decided on a counterintuitive approach: Deflect attention by attracting it. Not through sloppiness; that was Garvin's mistake. More like a slouching disregard for privacy, a tendency even to minor flamboyance. She'd dare to show a personality, an outgoing nature. And, yes, it was mildly disconcerting to her that the warmest, friendliest version of Lauren Witt was the one that was playing a role. Maybe the happiest version, too—lately, anyway. Being someone who was livelier and more effervescent could make you feel, well, livelier and more effervescent. It was also a better fit with her cover identity as an international public relations consultant. Because if you couldn't create a little buzz for yourself, how could your clients possibly expect you to be able to create it for them?

With all that in mind, she paid close attention to the clerk at the head of her line as she waited in passport control. She watched carefully as he dealt with each arrival—the alert flick of his eyes, the tilt of his head as he examined faces and photos, the care with which he flipped the pages in search of visa stamps from unsavory places. And the way that, for every female arrival, his appraising glances lingered a bit too long.

She smiled as she approached him. He smiled back, scanning her from stem to stern. He opened her passport, gazed for a moment at the photo, and began turning the pages with his gloved hands.

"Cheryl Tucker," he announced. "Miss or Missus?"

"Miss."

"And where are you arriving from today, Miss Tucker?"

"New York. LaGuardia." She had taken the long way to avoid attracting suspicion by flying directly from San Juan.

"Are you here for business or for pleasure?"

"Both, I hope. But mostly for business."

"And what is your business here?"

"I'm an international public relations consultant, hoping to spread the good word about all the exciting things happening in your country."

As if to show she was already on task, she handed him a business card with the name of her company—Ellington, Buncombe Associates, Washington DC. It was a real and even prominent player in lobbying and public relations. If anyone there were asked, they would instantly confirm her employment. He glanced at it briefly. Then, instead of handing it back, he tucked it away—not into a folder or drawer, but straight into his pants pocket.

Playing fast and loose with business cards wasn't something that her colleagues tended to do, especially not when dealing with a government employee so far down the food chain, but Lauren again sensed a possible value in going off script. Besides, the number for her encrypted phone was not on the card.

"And where will you be staying, Miss Tucker?"

She knew this question was not part of the usual drill, even though some countries asked for a local address. He might even try to phone her at the Esplanade. It would be a pain to deal with it, but it could work in her favor if anyone happened to be listening in. Giving a low-level civil servant enough access to hit on you would certainly run counter to the sort of behavior Sarič's people would be looking for. Plus, if she were to tell him now that it was none of his business, he'd almost certainly hassle her further.

"The Esplanade."

His eyebrows arched. For a moment she thought he might actually lick his lips.

"Excellent choice. Very big beds." He stamped her passport, and his smile widened as he handed it back to her. "Enjoy your stay."

"I plan to."

She felt his gaze follow her into baggage claim.

Lauren's minor superpower in international assignments was an immunity to jet lag. A single cup of coffee was all it took to reset her biological clock, as long as she managed to avoid caffeinating while en route. So, after clearing customs, she stopped at an airport café for an espresso. Moments later she emerged into the taxi rank as fresh as if she'd just showered, and by the time the cab reached the Esplanade she had drawn up a mental checklist of items needing immediate attention: First, text Ellington, Buncombe in Washington to let them know she was here and on the clock. Nearly everyone there knew her as a contract employee who often traveled abroad and occasionally landed a new account. Only the firm's two principals—Marie Ellington, a Democrat, and Al Buncombe, a Republican—were in on the actual nature of her work, an arrangement that the Agency repaid with inside information and the occasional supportive word to other departments of the federal government.

Second, review the location and surroundings of her upcoming appointments and meetings.

Third, find out whether Hal Knight, whose plane was scheduled to arrive shortly before hers, had made it here safely.

Last on her list was her most important piece of today's business— a late afternoon meeting with a potential source. Such small beginnings were the stuff of new networks. Unless, of course, the contact was a freshly baited trap set by Sarič.

She had little experience in Bolrovia, but this was not her first time here. A year ago she had laid the groundwork for her cover identity by touring Warsaw, Prague, Vienna, Budapest, Zagreb, Belgrade, and Blatsk on behalf of Ellington, Buncombe. She had spent four days here, sitting in on meetings, touching base with clients, and chatting her way through several diplomatic cocktail receptions.

The man she would see this afternoon was Sandor Matas, the deputy secretary of commerce, a fast riser who had purportedly become disillusioned with Horvatz's style of governance, mostly because he saw it as a threat to free markets, business development, and the kickbacks which had made him a wealthy man. If Horvatz's repressive tendencies also bothered him, he wasn't saying. But that was fine with Lauren, because assets were always safer when they didn't wear their hearts on their sleeves.

The Agency had learned of Matas's disaffection after he'd confided it to a U.S. commercial attaché while downing his fourth drink at a reception held by Kampfer Vogel, a German investment firm that had just opened a branch office. The attaché had passed along Matas's name to Leo Garvin, who, by then, was under orders to relay all such items to Langley without acting on them or putting anything into a file, and on that particular day he had fortunately been sober enough to follow orders to the letter. Garvin remained officially in charge of Blatsk station, as part of a feeble effort to fool Sarič, but neither he nor any of his top people knew of Lauren's arrival or of Hal's recruitment. Garvin also didn't know about the participation of Malone and Quint, who, as far as he knew, were both on leave and slated for redeployment.

Lauren, using her cover, had phoned Matas the day before from New York to set their appointment. She had framed it as a pitch for her firm's services in tourism development. Matas told her his ministry already had a vendor.

"I'm painfully aware of that. But I'm hoping to lay groundwork for the next time the contract comes up for bid," she told him. "Plus, I know that smaller jobs arise from time to time, special campaigns which might call for a fresh voice. More to the point, I'm buying."

Matas had chuckled agreeably.

"All right, then. Thursday, you said?"

"Yes. How about four p.m.? Does the Green Devil sound okay?"

"So you *do* know the city. The place to see and be seen. If Dimitri is in, I'll introduce you."

Dimitri Kolch, he meant, proprietor of the bar in question. Lauren already had his name on her list of people who she needed to be aware of.

"That would be worth the price of drinks all by itself."

Her main plan for the meeting was to never once mention the Agency. It was hardly an unusual tactic. Some assets passed along information for years without knowing who they were really reporting to. Or maybe they didn't want to know. Matas might eventually figure it out for himself, but hopefully by then he'd be too entwined to cut himself loose. In the meantime, she'd be better protected against Sarič.

Lauren's cover offered no pretext for meeting up with Hal Knight. But it *would* allow her to fraternize in the same circles, drink in the same bars, eat in the same restaurants, and stay in the same hotel, meaning she could at least enter his orbit. If an emergency arose, she'd be well positioned to act quickly. The only others who were privy to all these details were Lauren's immediate supervisor, Dickson Fordyce, and his boss, Tina Merritt, deputy director for operations in Eastern Europe. It was a tight and, hopefully, closed circle.

Chapter 18

———≋———

Mere blocks away, on the opposite side of King Viktor Square, Pavel Lukov was also keeping close track of the time as he walked toward the food carts near the Presidential Palace. The smells alone were enough to make him hungry—a heady blend that had become more exotic in recent years as Blatsk, despite every effort of the Horvatz administration, had been more deeply infiltrated by the wider world.

There were seven carts in all. Old Rudi with his chimney cakes had been there the longest, but the two most recent additions belonged to Lan, a Vietnamese woman who sold banh mi sandwiches on split baguettes, and to Khalil, a Palestinian selling falafel and shawarma beneath a sign assuring that everything was halal. And, as an indignant Rudi would readily tell you, even the cart offering local sausages and pickled cabbage was now operated by Adnan, an asylum seeker from Syria.

Pavel was heading home to shower and change before summoning the official car which would take him and Hal Knight to tonight's presidential dinner. By his own careful reckoning, he had at least twenty minutes to spare, so he decided to stop for a brief chat with Rudi, whose crumbs of gossip were sometimes as tasty as his chimney cakes. Then his phone began to buzz.

He saw that it was his father, and for a few uncharitable moments he considered ignoring it, before deciding better now than later.

"Hi, Dad."

"How do you always know it's me?"

"You're in my contact list, so your name comes up on the screen."

"Well, no wonder I can't get you half the damn time. I need your help."

Pavel's father, Lucien, always shouted into his mobile phone, as if he had to compensate for the tiny size of the device with a corresponding increase in volume.

"Yes, Jana gave me your message. I'm sorry I haven't had a chance to get back to you, but work has been kind of crazy."

"Oh, I know all about how busy you are, Mr. Indispensable with his big new promotion. But at least now you're working for someone who actually gets things done, instead of that layabout assemblyman."

Pavel's father then launched into a tirade about the latest crisis at the southern border, where incoming refugees had been herded into camps, generating bad publicity worldwide. Lucien was a fan of Nikolai Horvatz, especially his policies on immigration, and his views had hardened since the death of Pavel's mother six years earlier. Like his president, he didn't stint on using blunt language.

"They are an infestation, all across Europe, and now all the more permissive countries that created the problem want it to be our problem as well."

Pavel turned away from the food carts so that none of the vendors could overhear. At least he wasn't sitting in his office, where Marika would've eavesdropped on the whole thing. This, in turn, reminded him of the black box that now lurked in the heating duct at his house. Even home was no longer a safe place for an intemperate call, or so his geeky friend Maksim Polikon had advised him the day before. A signal interceptor, that had been Maksim's diagnosis, and he had initially been puzzled when Pavel had turned down his offer to disable it. Then the truth of the matter must have dawned on him.

"Oh, I see. You think this must be the work of . . ."

At that point, Pavel had shushed him with a finger to his lips.

"Yes. I understand," Maksim had said. "In that case, you should act as if everything you say or write on any device will be seen by someone else. Tell Jana to be careful as well. Speaking of which, don't contact me again at that number you used this morning. I'm deleting that account pretty soon."

"Send me your new number, then."

"When I can. I've taken a new job, and they're kind of antsy about these things."

"A government job?" For a moment he wondered if Maksim might have even gone to work for Sarič.

"No, no. But it's new, a start-up, and like all tech assholes they're obsessively secretive, and the pay is too good to blow it by doing something stupid. In a few months everything will probably be fine. Then we can have a beer, especially since you're practically a big shot now."

"Yes, a big shot with a black box in his heating duct. But sure."

Maksim had suggested a few technological work-arounds that Pavel could use without arousing too much suspicion, although Pavel hadn't yet had the time or energy to try them. Nor had he yet worked up the nerve to tell Jana about the black box.

Now the problem was his father, who was still rambling on about all the money wasted on people who didn't belong in this country. It was conversations like these that made Pavel wonder if he should even have taken the job. The pay was great, but Jana and most of her friends hated what his boss stood for, and his dad was now reminding him of why.

"Maybe the only way to fix it is to dig a deep hole and push all of them into it. If the others see that, they'll all stop coming."

"Dad, can we not do this over the phone?"

"My feelings as well! You need to come see me. Would a visit be so hard? Bring Jana and the kids. I'll make those dumplings Tomas likes. You could come tonight."

"Tonight's impossible. How 'bout next week?"

"Yes, it's always the next week, until it's the end of the next week and you still haven't come."

"I'll call you, Dad. I promise. But I really have to go now."

"Wait! I haven't even mentioned the reason I called. It's about your grandfather."

Hal had been poised to hang up. Now he stopped, genuinely worried.

"Poppy? Has something happened?"

"Nothing terrible. Or not yet. But that neighbor of his out in the woods . . . Oh, hell, I can never remember his name . . ."

"Petaro?"

"Yes, him! He called me this morning to tell me your Poppy was up on a ladder trying to fix the roof of his dacha, and then the whole damn thing fell apart."

"His *dacha*?"

"The ladder. He was too cheap to buy one, so he'd built his own."

"My god, is he okay?"

"Just a few bruises, but he walked over to this neighbor's place to get some bandages, and so the neighbor—"

"Petaro."

"Yes, whatever, but he thought we should know. He's planning to stay out there for the winter again, you know. With no electricity, no running water, no heat."

"He has his stove."

"As long as he doesn't run out of firewood. And if it snows too much, he'll have to dig his way out to his well. It's too much for him."

"We've been over this before, Dad."

"Yes, because he never listens to me, but he will listen to you. You have to talk him out of staying there again. One day we're simply going to hear that he has frozen to death. Or died of starvation. Or has been killed by a wild boar."

"I know. I worry, too. But how can I talk to him when he doesn't even have a phone?"

"Because sometime in the next few days he's going to be driving that beat-up old truck of his into the city, to buy his winter supplies."

"Petaro told you that, too?"

"He said your Poppy asked to borrow a quart of oil, so his truck can make it into Blatsk. And if it's like every other year, he'll stop by to see you without a word of warning."

"Maybe he won't come by this year, not if he has heard who I'm working for now."

"Of course. The smartest thing you've ever done, so naturally he will hate it, him and his stupid communist politics."

"He didn't like the Russians, either, Dad."

"You're right. He's an anarchist, he doesn't like anybody. But when you see him, talk some sense into him. If anyone can convince him to go back to his old apartment, even if just for the winter, it's you."

"One of the reasons he still talks to me is that I don't tell him how to live his life."

"Fine, then. Leave him to the wolves."

"There are no more wolves in the Javorska Forest."

"The boars, then. And the cold."

"I'll do what I can."

"And come and see me. Please. All of you."

"I'll call next Monday. I promise. Oh, and Tomas loves the toy train, so thank you again."

It was the same train that Pavel had stepped on so painfully the night before last, but, yes, his boy loved it. Then he stopped talking, because his father had hung up.

For Pavel, learning to be a dad hadn't been easy, but learning to be the son of a father who, in his mid-sixties, expected him to mediate all family squabbles, especially those between his father and grandfather, had been even harder. Both of the older men had become unreasonably demanding and more stubborn than ever, especially when dealing with each other.

His father had been a plumber, a practical man who believed there was always a fix for something that was broken. Poppy, on the other hand, preferred the idea that there was never just one correct answer. He had been a campus intellectual and then had taught history. He had seen his son's choice of livelihood as a plumber as an act of rebellion, and had insisted on a university education for Pavel even as Pavel's father had tried to convince Pavel to take over his plumbing business or learn some other trade.

Pavel sometimes wondered if this was why he always tried to be so accommodating, occasionally to a fault, in his jobs and relationships—as a reaction against their longtime tug-of-war, pulling at him from opposite directions. He pocketed his phone, then turned to see Rudi staring at him through the smoke of his brazier.

"What can I get you today, young Pavel?" Rudi had called him that since he'd been old enough to walk. Pavel now realized that, thanks to the call, he had lost his appetite.

"Nothing today, thank you. Just passing by."

"You look troubled. Everything okay?"

"Oh, not bad. Just busy."

"Well, sure. A big new job brings big new responsibilities, yes?"

That was another thing about Rudi. He knew things. Rudi had heard about Pavel's promotion before Pavel even told him. It was partly because Rudi was an inveterate schmoozer, an expert at getting his customers to talk, and when your cart was this close to the Presidential Palace, your clientele tended to talk about some interesting stuff.

Rudi also saw things. His vantage point offered a commanding view not only of the palace's front entrance, but also of the narrow sidewalk that led toward the back, to the freight entrance, which was the preferred point of entry for guests who wished to keep a lower profile. Every visitor who came in through the front was logged into a big book.

There was no such record for the ones allowed in through the back. Unless, of course, Rudi had spotted them, and then it might as well have been printed in a newspaper. It was another reason Pavel liked to stop for a chat even when he wasn't hungry.

"How's business, Rudi? Anything new?"

Rudi shrugged and glanced sidelong at the food carts to his left.

"That woman selling ice cream is still trying to get me to make warm chimney cones to help boost her sales."

"Not a bad idea."

"For her, maybe. If she didn't waste so much time talking to that new guy who sells the haluski, they'd both make more money. But talking seems to be mostly what they do, to each other and to that Syrian, who really knows nothing at all about sausages, unless it's Arab sausages, and ragheads don't even eat pork."

Rudi said all of this loud enough to be overheard by all six of the other vendors, although by now they were probably used to him. He had never been shy about letting you know his politics, and he, too, was a fan of President Horvatz. Rudi had been especially grumpy lately about the vendor selling haluski—a local dish of egg noodles sauteed with cabbage, ham, onions, and goat cheese. The cart had recently been taken over by a twenty-something Bolrovian named Egon. The problem was that Egon's predecessor, an older fellow who had recently retired, had been one of Rudi's best pals. They had often talked throughout the day while shunning the newcomers in solidarity. But Egon talked mostly to the foreign vendors, which left Rudi feeling abandoned and outnumbered.

"And did you see what little Egon has already done?" Rudi said, pointing with his grill tongs. "First that stupid yellow umbrella. And now a tip jar."

"Don't you take tips, Rudi?"

"Sure, but I don't put a jar out to make people feel guilty." Then Rudi broke into a smile. "But you're the one who knows all the juicy stuff today, yes? Is it true that you'll be squiring around that American funnyman, Hal Knight?"

"Not so loud, Rudi. His name's supposed to be a secret."

Rudi shrugged.

"Everyone knows the president likes him."

"His jokes, yes. And his movies. But hardly anyone knows that, well . . ."

"That he is in town? C'mon. Stand here long enough and you can find out almost anything."

Then, as if to prove his point, he nodded and pointed his tongs toward something over Pavel's right shoulder.

"Like those two fellows. What do you think they're up to, and who's the tall one?"

Pavel turned and was surprised to see, about fifty yards away, Branko Sarič in his customary black turtleneck and gray blazer, orange water bottle holstered like a six-shooter in an American western, heading briskly up the sidewalk toward the rear entrance of the Presidential Palace with a fellow who was at least a head taller. The bigger man had a blond buzz cut and wore an expensive-looking charcoal suit, which fit him perfectly. There was something athletic and alert about the way he carried himself, a sense of readiness—especially in contrast to Sarič, who, for all his ability to exude power and control, walked somewhat stiffly, more like a bureaucrat, a man who spent far too much time staring at a screen.

"That's Branko Sarič," Pavel said.

"Well, of course. But who's the American?"

"How can you tell he's American?"

"How can you not?"

"But you don't know his name?"

"Not yet, no."

Pavel wasn't as certain as Rudi about the man's nationality. Russian seemed like a possibility as well. A few decades ago, his well-cut suit and stylish shoes would have ruled that out, but not anymore. Whatever the case, the two men were headed toward the rear entrance. Sarič gave a furtive glance over his shoulder just before they disappeared from view. If they were headed to Horvatz's office, maybe Marika would see them pass and log it in her notebook—as long as she wasn't too busy painting her nails. Pavel decided that Rudi's eagle eye deserved a reward, or maybe he had regained his appetite.

"Changed my mind, Rudi. I'll have a nice warm one to tide me over to dinner."

"The usual?"

"Yes, with cinnamon."

Rudi nodded and got to work.

Pavel looked back again toward the Presidential Palace, wondering about the man with Sarič—someone important enough to merit a personal visit with the president, perhaps, yet shady enough for Sarič to use the back entrance.

No sooner had Rudi handed him a warm chimney cake than his phone began to ring—not his personal one in his left pocket, but the encrypted phone in his right pocket. He shifted the chimney cake to his left hand and, with a shower of crumbs and sugar, reached for the vibrating bat phone. For whatever reason, the man he'd just seen made him uneasy about taking the call, and he certainly didn't feel comfortable answering in front of Rudi. So, even after taking it out of his pocket, he let it ring again. And then again.

"Aren't you going to answer that?" Rudi asked.

Pavel then noted with satisfaction that the battery charge was nearly at zero. The phone would go dead in a matter of minutes, and that would take care of the matter—for the moment, anyway. Now that Hal Knight was safely in town, the whole idea of needing a special phone just for communicating with Sarič seemed excessive, even intrusive, and the dead battery would give him a built-in excuse if Sarič complained later.

"No need," he said. "Junk call."

"Interesting-looking phone, though. What model is that?"

Pavel dropped it back into his pocket before Rudi could scrutinize it further. He got out his wallet to pay, but Rudi waved it off.

"May I ask a small favor from you instead?"

"How small?"

Rudi sometimes needed help with obtaining a permit or license for his business. Pavel just hoped it didn't involve sabotaging any of his competitors, especially not Adnan, Khalil, or the Vietnamese woman, Lan, who were already vulnerable enough these days.

"I'd like you to get me an autograph. From tonight's dinner for Hal Knight. He's a favorite of my grandson's."

Now how in the hell had Rudi found out about the dinner?

"Sure. I can do that."

"And if it isn't too much trouble, could you ask him to write, 'For Kirov, my biggest fan'?"

"Consider it done. In the meantime, maybe you can find out who that man with Branko Sarič was."

Rudi grinned.

"I'm on it! And keep up the good work for our president. I'm sure your father is so proud of you, Pavel. Your Poppy as well."

Pavel didn't have the heart to break it to him about Poppy, maybe because Poppy had once been a faithful customer. He then checked his watch and saw that his twenty-minute cushion was nearly gone. No longer time for a shower, but he would change his shirt, maybe his socks. Eating a chimney cake suddenly seemed like a foolish idea, especially with the mess it would make. But it would be unthinkable to toss it in the trash in front of Rudi, so he took an obligatory bite, smiled to show how tasty it was, and headed off toward the main square.

Halfway across it, and safely out of sight, he tossed the pastry to the ground at the foot of King Viktor's statue, where pigeons immediately tore it to pieces.

Chapter 19

———≋———

Lauren arrived early at the Green Devil. It was only a block off the main square and had been a fixture of central Blatsk for nearly two centuries. Originally it was an absinthe bar—thus the name—but its decades behind the Iron Curtain had taken their toll, and by 1989 it had devolved into a dreary refuge for drunks and low-wattage dissidents, malcontents too ineffective to even merit an arrest. By then it was known mostly for its surly waitstaff, its poor selection of watered-down spirits, and the damp sawdust that no one ever seemed to sweep from its floors.

But in the early '90s, as Bolrovia reawakened to the joys and headaches of commercialism, the enterprising Dimitri Kolch, a playwright turned real estate developer, bought the place with a windfall from his investments in Western tech firms. He cleaned and modernized the place, stripped the plaster from the interior brickwork, restocked the bar, hired a new staff, opened up the cellar, and came up with several innovative ways to curate a new clientele. In doing so, he transformed it into that rarest of attractions—a gathering place that appealed to locals of all stripes and also to the city's most prominent visitors yet, so far, had avoided being overrun by tourists.

Up-and-comers in business and government liked it because, as Matas had noted over the phone to Lauren, it was a great place to see and be seen. Out-of-towners seeking local connections were attracted for the same reason. Despite the prosperity of much of its clientele, its prices were reasonable. For customers willing to wait a bit longer than they would at a restaurant, its small kitchen turned out local specialties at all hours, whether your need was a hangover breakfast or a midnight bowl of stew.

Its waiters and bartenders were finely attuned to the art of stroking egos and coddling the finicky, but their most valuable skill was their ability to discourage the quick-drink urges of package tourists who, as a result, tended to avoid the place. Some locals were convinced that Kolch had paid the authors of tourist guidebooks to *not* mention his establishment or, if they did mention it, to describe it as snooty and unwelcoming. All of which made it the perfect spot for Lauren's meetup. As a bonus, she knew that Hal Knight, because of its location and the company he'd be keeping, would probably end up spending time there as well.

She approached on foot from King Viktor Square, dodging a flock of low-flying pigeons and sidestepping the leavings of one of those annoying horse-drawn carriages that clopped along so many of these cobbled lanes, ferrying tourists.

The only holdover from the bar's era of decline was a faded green awning, which sheltered a dozen outdoor tables in the manner of a Paris bistro. Any arrival carrying a guidebook was automatically seated out there, rain or shine, hot or cold. At the moment the only outdoor customers were a bewildered-looking husband and wife from the UK, with a camera sitting on the table between them. Lauren waltzed past them through the door, nodded smartly to the barman, and headed straight for an empty table in a far corner.

This, the main room of the Green Devil, was its showpiece. A vaulted brick ceiling made it feel like you'd entered a massive ceramic barrel. To the right was a stylish bar where four ascending rows of booze were lined up along the wall, backed by a mirror and illuminated by emerald lighting. There were roughly two dozen tables of various sizes. Customers seeking more privacy had further choices—descend a narrow staircase to the beer cellar (although it, too, had a fully stocked bar) or continue through a vaulted passage into the back, where a quieter and even more spacious room awaited. By day this bigger chamber was usually dark and deserted. At night, depending on the day of the week and the whims of management, it either remained dark or became a lively spot where a musician or even a full band might be performing as waiters carried in trays of food from the kitchen.

Every few weeks, on no particular schedule, there was even karaoke, an event which was never advertised in advance. If you happened to be present on one of those nights, you might be lucky enough to catch a hammy bit of crooning by Largo Fonseck, the city's top divorce lawyer; Gisela Margol, Bolrovia's hottest film director; or even, on one particularly memorable occasion, the Minister of Defense, Kamron Bartz, who, with tie loosened and pinned medals swaying to the beat, had led a raucous full house in a boozy rendition of Gloria Gaynor's "I Will Survive." When he was fired a week later, no one knew whether the performance was to blame or if it had instead been a sign that he'd known what was coming.

On this particular afternoon, the front room was nearly full. Lauren's corner perch gave her the best possible vantage point. She'd already recognized a press spokesman from the Foreign Ministry over to her right. To the left was a table of three men in suits speaking German. At the near end of the bar, nodding and loudly holding court, was a lively fellow, early forties, in a crisp tan business suit whose easy and familiar manner made it look as if he knew everyone. He spoke English in a British accent, eliciting smiles from the bartender and those around him, and his face was oddly familiar, although Lauren couldn't yet come up with a name.

The waiter arrived with a curt nod. She ordered a shot of Békési, a Hungarian single-malt Scotch that she knew was popular here. It had just arrived when the front door opened to reveal Sandor Matas, a paunchy fellow in his early fifties, in a charcoal gray suit and gold tie. He squinted, scanning the tables. She thought he looked a little nervous, like a boy on a blind date who was already wondering if he'd made a mistake.

He turned abruptly as someone called out to him from the bar—the loud Brit in the tan suit.

"Sandor! Come have a drink with me."

Matas smiled—it looked genuine—and then he replied.

"Thank you, Ian, but I'm meeting someone."

Then he scanned the room. When his eyes found her, Lauren switched on a smile that she hoped was welcoming without promising too much. Although to judge by the way he beamed back, maybe she had miscalculated. She greeted him with a prim handshake, then nodded to the waiter, who had efficiently returned.

"I've already started," she said to Matas, "so what's your pleasure? My treat, of course."

He ordered a Manhattan, which struck her as a potentially pro-American gesture, unless it was his usual.

"How are you finding it here?" he asked.

"I've only just arrived this morning, so we'll see."

"Remarkable. You look as rested as if you've been here all week."

"Blatsk is an easy place to get comfortable."

She used that as a lead-in to begin telling him about the wonderful things that Ellington, Buncombe could do for his ministry and for Bolrovia's image abroad. Such a direct approach wasn't the preferred way of doing business here, but Matas nodded politely, finished his Manhattan, ordered a second one, and reminded her that his ministry already had a vendor, another Washington PR firm which also handled their lobbying.

"And that contract is good for another year and a half, correct?"

"Yes." He was beginning to look bored.

"Well, here's my thinking on that. During that time frame I'll be coming here regularly to build up our base of clients. While doing so it would help to have access from time to time to people with your sort of expertise, your knowledge. If our consultations were regular enough, my employer could pay a fairly handsome retainer."

Matas sat up a little straighter. He glanced to either side, as if checking to see if anyone had overheard them. He leaned forward.

"How handsome?"

She quoted him a number in dollars. He nodded.

"Then, when the time *did* arrive for bids and proposals on a new contract, both of us would be better positioned to expand our business together. And I can already assure you that our fee would be at least ten percent below what your ministry is currently paying, but with the same or better level of service. And we'll of course continue the payment of what I believe is known as the 'service charge,' in reimbursement of your own costs, a total which would be adjusted upward annually for inflation."

He smiled and cleared his throat. For a moment he looked a little uncomfortable.

"You, um, know about that arrangement? The service charge?"

"I'm hardly the only one."

"I see."

In making these sorts of offers, Lauren had no worries about overstepping the bounds of her cover employment with Ellington, Buncombe. The Agency would make up the difference for any discounts and additional fees by paying the company from a discretionary account that even the House Intelligence Committee wasn't aware of. In return, Ellington, Buncombe would happily accept any and all new clients while logging the full cost into its books, which certainly helped at tax time. Ellington, Buncombe had also been given a supply of ultra-secure cell phones, like Lauren's, for all its employees abroad, a generosity which allowed Lauren to carry one without attracting undue suspicion. Nor would the firm bat an eye at wiring payments for Matas's "retainer" to a numbered Swiss account, one which Lauren knew he had set up two years earlier. It was the perfect arrangement for all parties, as long as neither side ran afoul of either Branko Sarič or some overly intrusive government auditor.

Matas leaned back in his chair. He still seemed a little taken aback that Lauren knew so much about him.

"How did you happen to settle on me for an offer of this kind? Not that I'm objecting, but, given the current political climate here, well . . ." His words trailed off.

So he, too, had sensed the tightening of internal security that was underway, which was hardly surprising.

"Yes, I've heard talk about some of the recent . . . purges? Would that be the correct term?"

"Perhaps. It's this fellow at Interior who's behind it."

Sarič, he meant, although Matas seemed reluctant to say the name. That was also Lauren's preference.

"I heard about you from Barry Bullard, cultural attaché at the U.S. embassy. He said he'd run into you recently at some reception and that you'd had an interesting conversation."

Matas frowned. He began tearing at the damp napkin beneath his drink.

"Well, you know how it goes at those things, especially when the waiters keep coming at you with trays full of drinks and everyone is a little bored. Sometimes you say things that, later, you wish maybe you hadn't. Please tell Barry that."

He again glanced from side to side, his eyes hooded. If Lauren had said "boo" or made a sudden movement, he probably would have fallen back in his chair.

"You can rest easy. Barry happens to be an old friend. He only told me after I promised it would go no further. No one else knows."

"I hope that is true. In recent weeks there have been several, well, abrupt departures from the government. Some were people who I thought were untouchable."

"Such as?" she asked, even though she already knew the names, because all three had been assets of Leo Garvin's.

"Well, Gurganus, for one. The economic adviser. He's now in prison, or maybe just some cell at Interior, right around the corner from here. Then there's Kelenič, the president's chief administrative aide. He simply didn't show up for work one day, and now they've hired some young nobody, Lukov, to replace him. Plus Arzhanov, at Defense. He was hauled off to a rehab facility to dry out, way over by the eastern border, even though no one could ever remember seeing him take a single drink. So, yes, I am a little *on the edge*, if that is the right term. We all are."

"Except that your behavior and service are beyond reproach. I heard that not only from Barry, but from everyone else I've spoken to. And anything that you and I talk about today, or going forward, will always remain between us. Your words will be for my ears only."

He seemed to like the implications of that, but not necessarily in the way she'd intended, because he responded by leaning forward until their foreheads were nearly touching. He slid his right hand toward hers. Perhaps danger was a turn-on for him.

In response, she pulled back her hand and sat up straighter. Taking notice, he nodded and did the same. She then watched as a complex parade of emotions played out on his face—interest, doubt, worry, a touch of fear, followed at last by longing, perhaps for her but probably more so for that handsome retainer, with the prospect of a bigger payoff down the road.

"I will need to give more thought to all of this."

"Of course."

"But I think that for the moment I can at least agree in principle to your proposal for regular consultation. With a retainer."

"Certainly."

"Provided that you, personally, will be handling the relationship."

Ah, so there was the first catch. Not only because it signaled that he might want something more from her than money, but also because her time here would be limited. Her long-range plan was to turn over the handling of Matas to a later arrival who would become his case officer, someone who, in turn, might want to handle Matas through a local intermediary or cutout. But those details could wait until after the hook was set.

"Absolutely," she said. "My preference as well."

"Shall we meet again, then, to discuss it further? And to clarify any loose ends."

"Of course."

He nodded. She could tell that he now believed he was firmly in control of this relationship, which was exactly what she wanted him to think. Then he glanced to the right, and his eyes lit up. He called out in greeting to a trim fellow in a black shirt, sleeves rolled to the elbow, who was passing briskly near the bar.

"Dimitri!"

The man turned and, after a fleeting glance of appraisal, answered with a smile that seemed especially calibrated for a man of Matas's high standing. He changed course toward their table, maintaining his smile the entire way. He was dressed in black from head to toe, well groomed and alert, with the somewhat careworn look of a bohemian nearing his sixties.

"You will forgive me for not having noticed you sooner, Sandor. And who is your lovely business guest this afternoon?"

"Cheryl Tucker, of Ellington, Buncombe. Cheryl, this is Dimitri Kolch, the proprietor of the Green Devil. A man who knows everyone. Or everyone but you, apparently!"

They shared a laugh, which gave her and Kolch a chance to appraise each other. He struck her as the sort of fellow who could sum up most of his customers fairly accurately after only a few moments of observation.

"Ellington, Buncombe," he said. "Didn't your people run that rollout campaign for Blatsk Telekom a few years back? The one that had all of us whistling that stupid jingle, which I suppose means it was effective."

"Yes, that was us."

"I don't remember you being here for that."

"I came on board about a year ago, but that tune is still high on our playlist, although I doubt anyone else here could've named the vendor. You're pretty plugged in."

"One has to be, in my profession."

Then he winked, and for the slightest moment she wondered if he had just relayed a hidden message. She then decided that, no, he was just one of those savvy bar owners who always kept his eyes and ears open and, from time to time, found ways to profit from his awareness.

"And how long will you be staying with us?" he asked, unerringly alighting upon the one question she hadn't wanted Matas to ask.

"As long as it takes," she said.

"Ah, flexibility. A valuable skill. A pleasure to meet you. And as always, Sandor, an honor to have you in my establishment."

He patted Matas on the shoulder and headed for the back, vanishing into the darkness of the rear room.

"Dimitri is a wonder. He has better stock tips than my so-called financial advisers, I can attest to that as well."

Matas checked his watch and frowned.

"Damn. It's later than I thought. Normally I would propose that we resume our discussions as early as this evening. But I'm afraid I have a prior commitment."

"You could always cancel."

"If it were with anyone other than the president, I would."

"You're seeing President Horvatz this evening? Impressive."

He flapped a hand as if it were no big deal.

"Some dinner he is hosting. Our minister was supposed to attend, but he is escorting a Chinese trade delegation, so I'm going in his place." Then, with a gleam in his eye, "Apparently the special guest is someone from the entertainment world in your own country."

"Really? Would I know the name?"

"Ah, I think that you would!" He laughed. "But everyone in attendance has been sworn to secrecy. Play your cards in the correct manner, and perhaps I can tell you later."

"Then let's make sure there is a later."

"Tomorrow, then? For dinner?"

"Or how about lunch?"

His smile was a little forced, but he nodded.

"Perfect. I know just the place. My treat again, of course."

All in all, not a bad first meeting. With any luck, by tomorrow afternoon she'd have a full account of how Hal Knight's welcoming dinner had gone, and she wouldn't even need a report from Knight to get it. Whatever role Matas ended up filling, he was at least going to be helpful in the near term, as long as she didn't scare him off. He was already an unwitting asset of the Central Intelligence Agency, and sometimes those were the best kind.

Matas again checked his watch. Obviously, this dinner invitation was more important than he was willing to let on. Good, because that probably meant he'd pay close attention to whatever transpired and would be full of news tomorrow.

They said their goodbyes. On his way out, Matas was again waylaid by the Brit at the bar, who this time intercepted him by the door, as if having calibrated his departure to coincide with Matas's. Ian, that's what Matas had called him. She still couldn't come up with a last name.

Lauren asked for the check, feeling like the Agency had already gotten its money's worth.

Chapter 20

———≈———

W as he supposed to be funny tonight? Would they expect jokes, remarks, maybe even some sort of monologue? At the moment, those were Hal's biggest worries, because in this weird new life of his, any crowd was potentially carnivorous, a beast that had to be placated more than entertained.

Surely cocktail chatter would take care of the first hour or so. There would no doubt be a few stilted introductions to endure—meeting the president, maybe his wife, a few friends and supporters. This would require handshakes and small talk, with a drink or two to ease the way forward. Being deferential seemed like the soundest survival strategy for that part.

Once everyone was seated for dinner, he figured he'd only have to engage with whoever sat to his right, his left, and directly across, unless of course they put him up on a stage at one of those long tables that faced outward to the rest of the room, like Jesus and the Apostles in every painting you've ever seen of the Last Supper. If so, maybe he'd make a little halo out of a napkin as a gag. Then he remembered Chris saying that Bolrovia was a fairly religious country, with a lot of Catholics. They celebrated obscure saint's days and even had pilgrimage sites where people lined up in hopes of miracles. He scratched the halo idea.

It was the after-dinner hour that loomed as the most worrisome. He imagined the president standing to deliver some welcoming remarks before turning over the mike to him—but for what? Words of gratitude? A ten-minute bit to warm up the crowd for the rest of the week? Or, counterintuitively, maybe a subdued show of humility that would bore them to tears. Yes, Hal could still be witty when necessary—scathingly so, the skill which had served him so well in his improv days. But put him into almost any large gathering where there wasn't a script, and his preference was to watch and listen. It was one way he gathered much of his material: by being a careful observer.

This reticence had come as a surprise to nearly everyone he'd met during his six months on Capitol Hill. Aides, lobbyists, petitioners, and fellow members had always seemed to expect a performance from him, which they showed with a conversational deference that had almost always led to awkward silences and shortened interactions. During his first committee hearings, nearly everyone in attendance had leaned forward in mirthful anticipation whenever it was his turn to speak or ask questions. They were nearly always disappointed.

Hal hoped Pavel Lukov would have some advice for him during their ride to the palace. Or maybe the best way to stop worrying was to concentrate on his spying duties. Instead of being alert to conversational openings that might lead to punch lines, focus on memorizing names and faces and watching the dynamics between the guests. Who had the president's ear? Who didn't? When they lowered their voices, what did they talk about?

Hal was due to meet Lukov in the lobby in another twenty minutes. It was certainly preferable to how Sarič had done it, coming up to poke around his room. It still bothered him that Sarič had asked so pointedly about the black notebook. Hal wondered how long it would be before some minion came up here to search the place—opening drawers, checking the pockets of his clothes. Although they already knew what was hanging in his closet, since they'd picked out all his clothes. That, in turn, made Hal wonder what might *already* be in the pockets, so he spent the next few minutes checking, and feeling along seams, before deciding he had better get dressed.

He surveyed the generous array of wardrobe possibilities. Maybe he should have asked the hotel concierge to rent him a dinner jacket. Then the voice of Shirley Halston piped up from over his left shoulder.

"If they'd wanted you to wear a tux, they'd have given you a tux. Use your noodle, Hal."

"Right. So you think this is casual, then?"

"Is this the fanciest gig you'll do all week?"

"Probably."

"Then pick out the fanciest items from what they gave you, duh. I hope this is jet lag."

"Yeah, well. It's a lot of things, as you know. But thank you, Shirley."

There was a suit, as it turned out: a light gray Calvin Klein with a sleek cut and narrow lapels—just the way he liked them. And of course it was a perfect fit. There was only a single tie. It was red with little gold emblems, which he assumed were symbols of Bolrovia—so that was another decision made. He vacillated for a moment between a white shirt and a blue one before choosing white, and by the time he'd knotted the tie it was nearly time for him to go.

He took a final glance at the mirror.

"Knock 'em dead, Wonder Boy."

"Poor choice of words, Shirley."

"Exactly why I picked 'em, to keep you on your toes. Speaking of which, don't forget your notebook, Mr. Super Spy."

He stuffed it into his pocket, along with a pencil. Then he grabbed his key card and departed.

The moment he stepped off the elevator downstairs he spotted Lukov pacing by the front desk. Lukov smiled in apparent relief.

"Hope you didn't think I'd blow this off."

"No, no, it's just . . . Good to see you. The car is waiting." He turned to go.

"Wait. There's something on your lapel."

Lukov stopped, looked down, then sighed in exasperation. He brushed away some crumbs, then wiped his fingers on his pants. Hal tried to imagine Sarič ever being this flustered or showing up with crumbs on his jacket. Not a chance. Bloodstains, maybe, to send a message. Lukov seemed a little bit in over his head—another reason to like him, since Hal felt the same way.

"Don't worry, Pavel. I won't misbehave."

Lukov smiled but seemed unconvinced.

"Yes, well, about that."

"Misbehaving?"

"No. But, well, I don't know if anyone has yet told you, but you should know that our president, even though he is a big fan of jokes, and especially of your jokes, he nonetheless, well . . ."

"Stop. I know where you're going with this."

"You do?"

"You were about to tell me that Horvatz can't take a joke."

"I'm not sure I would put it that way, but—"

"No, I get it. I've met tons of people like that, and they've all been rich and they've all been powerful. Thin skin comes with the territory. But thanks, it's useful to know."

They exited into the cool evening. A long black car—a stretch version of Sarič's Mercedes but without the extra antennae—awaited at the curb, and they were soon underway.

"How was your massage?" Lukov asked. "Was it . . . relaxing?"

Hal watched Lukov carefully. Did he really not know?

"That was canceled."

"You didn't want it?"

"It wasn't my decision. Your security guy did it. Sarič."

Lukov's brow furrowed.

"But it was his idea."

"He came up to my room."

"*Sarič?*" Lukov looked disconcerted. "Why?"

"To personally welcome me, he said. Although I got the idea what he really wanted to do was snoop around."

"Yes, well . . . he can be like that."

Lukov looked out the window, avoiding Hal's stare. Hal wondered if he should mention the visit to the cellblock and how Sarič had threatened him. Maybe he'd get some sympathy, or even a promise to look into it. Unless Lukov and Sarič were working in tandem—some sort of Good Cop/Bad Cop arrangement—so Hal kept his mouth shut.

A moment of awkward silence passed. The car turned onto a grand boulevard lined by statues and a memorial to some long-past war.

"I, uh, have a small favor to ask," Lukov said. "An autograph, for the grandson of a friend. If you don't mind."

"No problem."

Lukov handed him a pen and a sheet of paper.

"The boy's name is Kirov. He wants you to write, 'To Kirov, my biggest fan.'"

Hal double-checked the spelling of the name, then dutifully wrote the message, signed his name, and added the date. Maybe that would actually increase its value if any details of his mission ever emerged.

"Thank you," Lukov said, before tucking it away.

"Do you have kids?"

"Yes. A boy and a girl." Then, as if he might have misread the question, "But they are too young to be fans yet. Tomas is just five, and Ava, well—"

"No, no. I was just curious."

"Right. Thank you for asking. And you?"

"What?"

"Children?"

"No. Not a Dad. Not even married."

"Sorry. I should have already known that."

"It's not important. Look, about this evening, could I ask your advice on something?"

"Certainly."

"Will I be expected to make any kind of speech? Or do any kind of performance?"

"Oh, no. This will be very low-key. There is no particular program or format. You will meet the president, there will be a dinner, he may speak for a bit, and that is all. The big show that he has requested will be two nights from now. Whatever you decide to say or do that night will be up to you, of course. Maybe an hour's worth of, how would you call it, material?"

"Yes, material. An hour, sure. But nothing tonight, you're positive?"

"Not that I've heard."

It seemed painfully clear that Lukov was as hazy on the details as he was. Or maybe the Bolrovians had assembled this gig as hastily as the Agency had thrown together theirs. Two rival governments, clumsily employing the same disgraced comic. Wasted resources on both sides of the Atlantic.

The car pulled up to a gated entrance at the head of a long, curving driveway that led to a grandiose five-story palace built of white marble blocks. Two guards in red cockaded hats and blue nineteenth-century uniforms waved them through, and the Mercedes rumbled across the cobblestones toward the entrance. It was a huge neoclassical building. Ionic columns stretched from end to end on the ground floor, spanning a width of twenty windows. In the middle, marble steps tapered upward to a massive doorway where two more guards stood at attention. They held rifles affixed with gleaming bayonets. Engraved in the slab of marble above the entrance was a long line of Roman numerals, which Hal deciphered to mean that the palace had been built in 1810.

"Nice office," he said.

Lukov smiled sheepishly.

"You'd be surprised how quickly you get used to it."

Hal watched him closely.

"Something tells me you don't really feel that way."

This drew a wider smile.

"Maybe you're right. I still find it a little incredible to be working here."

Hal climbed out of the car. It was like arriving at a manor house in one of those British costume dramas, except in those scenes all the servants lined up in full livery to greet important visitors. The only person waiting for them, apart from the sentries, was a chiseled fellow in a buzz cut and a dark suit who stood at the top of the stairs. His jacket had a slight bulge, probably from a sidearm deadlier than either of the guards' rifles.

The man nodded as they climbed the steps toward him.

"The president is waiting."

He turned and led them through the entrance across a vast marble floor. The walls of the lobby were hung with massive tapestries. Arranged below them were ornate Biedermeier chairs, roped off so that no one would sit in them.

Their footsteps echoed loudly as they headed left into a short corridor, which opened onto a grand hall or ballroom where a long table had been set for about forty guests. Corinthian columns with gilded capitals lined both sides of the room. Between the columns on the left were tall windows with red velvet curtains. On the right was a table that had been set up to serve as a bar, although no one was yet on duty. Overhead, the high ceiling was a dazzle of colorful murals and scrolled gold-leaf plaster.

But Hal's attention was almost immediately drawn to the far end, where a man who he quickly recognized as Nikolai Horvatz stood in a gray suit, hands clasped at his waist, waiting. He was grinning like, well, a fan. A photographer, the one who'd been at the airport, hovered nearby, poised to shoot.

Lukov cleared his throat and wordlessly led Hal past the bar toward Horvatz. Hal decided it was best to smile back as he approached. Then he nodded, which broadened the grin on Horvatz's face.

Lukov again cleared his throat as they halted a few feet away from the president. His voice quavered slightly as he spoke.

"Mr. Hal Knight, it is my honor and privilege to introduce you to His Excellency, our President Nikolai Horvatz."

"An honor to meet you, Mr. President."

Hal resisted a silly urge to curtsy, a gag that would have been wholly inappropriate. Instead, he held out his right hand, which Horvatz grasped firmly, his flesh warm and dry. They shook like the oldest of friends, and before Horvatz released his grip he said, in a booming voice and impeccable English, "Really? Is this all there is, Little Man?"

Lukov went pale and his mouth dropped open, but Hal recognized the line right away. It was from one of his movies, *She's Faking It!*, so he seamlessly responded in kind, hamming it up for all he was worth.

"Well, it's certainly more than *you're* used to getting, Little Miss Perfect!"

The two men, still locked in a handshake, erupted in laughter, Hal's as much in relief as in mirth. Only then did Lukov exhale, as he finally realized what the two men were up to, even if he seemed to have no clue as to what it meant. Out of context, the line wasn't all that funny. Or even in context, Hal supposed. Yet here he was, exalted by a president who had seized upon it as the perfect icebreaker.

"I have been waiting all day to say that to you," Horvatz said. "My adviser Wally had told me not to risk it, but I was sure you would know what to say."

"Obviously we're on the same wavelength, sir."

"Please. None of this 'sir' business. Call me Nikolai."

"Call me Hal."

He took stock of the man. Every photograph had depicted someone who looked a little smug, a little haughty, with a hint of softness or even sloth. Up close, you got quite a different impression. Horvatz emanated vitality, a magnetism that he also communicated with his grip, his voice, but mostly with his eyes, which were alert, probing. If you liked him, or were currently in his favor, you probably drew energy from it. If you were on the outs, you'd shrink from it.

Lukov seemed deeply relieved that things were going so well, and Hal felt the same. Even if the other guests had never heard a single one of his jokes, they'd probably take their cues on how to react from Horvatz, who seemed gleeful to be in Hal's presence.

Then, two men in suits loomed up suddenly at Horvatz's right shoulder, and the evening immediately grew more complicated. The first fellow seemed friendly enough, smiling as if already caught up in the boss's mood. The second was Branko Sarič. Horvatz turned toward them to make the introductions.

"Gentlemen, you must meet tonight's guest of honor, Mr. Hal Knight. Hal, these are perhaps my two most important advisers."

Hal noted the use of the word "perhaps." A certain notorious studio executive had often employed the word the same way—to give notice that your current praiseworthy status was conditional, based entirely on whatever you'd done for him lately.

"This is Wally Wallek, my chief political adviser."

"Ah, the fellow who didn't think I'd recognize a setup line from Bolrovia's greatest straight man. Fortunately, your boss nailed it, or you might have been right."

Wallek laughed and took the jab in stride. As a political adviser, he was doubtless accustomed to playing the role of straight man, lobbing up easy material to Horvatz the way an NBA point guard tossed alley-oops to a superstar.

"I am still catching up on your body of work, but I've been greatly impressed by what I've seen so far."

Horvatz then turned to Sarič, who had remained a step back, as if seeking a shadow to duck into.

"And this is my chief of internal security, Branko Sarič, who is in charge of ensuring your security and, more important, your *privacy* throughout your stay. Although I gather you two have already met?"

"Yes. Mr. Sarič took me on a very interesting tour earlier today."

This seemed to be news to Horvatz, who arched his eyebrows in surprise.

"Oh, yes? To the Saint Astrik Bridge, perhaps?"

"This was a lesser-known attraction, which I gather only VIPs get to see. A little confining, perhaps, but quite worthwhile."

"Ah, well, that is good to hear."

Horvatz cut a sidelong glance at Sarič, whose expression had gone from sullen to—was this even possible?—a bit pink, making him seem a little off balance. He was on the verge of responding when Horvatz spoke again.

"Ah. And here come our other guests. Let the celebration begin!"

Several dozen more people, most of them men, were now pouring into the room through the same entrance Hal had used, which made him wonder where they'd been hiding all this time. Following in their wake were waiters carrying trays of appetizers, hors d'oeuvres, and glasses of Champagne. Horvatz spoke again, this time raising his voice to be heard over the rising hubbub.

"Please, everyone, help yourself to a drink, and then come to meet our honored guest!" Then, in a lowered voice to Hal, "You must also have a drink. Perhaps Pavel here can fetch you one before the line becomes too long!"

"Absolutely, sir," Lukov said. "What would you like?"

Wine would have been the safest option, a glass that he could nurse, sip by sip, until it was time to be seated. But a sidelong glance at Sarič, who was glaring at him with an intensity that was almost comic, made him change his mind.

"A whiskey. On the rocks. Any brand will do."

Lukov nodded and drifted toward the bar.

Horvatz had now turned away to consult in lowered tones with Wally, so Hal again sought out Sarič, but the security chief had already melted into the crowd. People were already lining up at the bar. Others were headed his way. Most were breaking off into various knots and factions, as people always did at gatherings like this.

Hal decided it was time to begin working the room. He would make the rounds, talk to as many people as he could. He would gather up names, titles, and faces, which he would later log into the little black notebook, which now rested in his pocket with the snug comfort of a firearm.

He would also watch how Sarič worked the room, and would take special notice of any apparent allies or confidants.

Oddly, he was excited by the whole idea. Having Horvatz on his side certainly helped with that. Because who would ever have the balls to jail or torture the president's favorite funnyman? Who knows, he might even learn to enjoy this.

Lukov arrived with his drink.

"Thank you." Hal noticed that the young man hadn't gotten one for himself. Still on edge, perhaps.

He downed a healthy gulp, then saw two men and a woman coming toward him, three abreast, all of them eyeing him tentatively, as if seeking permission to approach. He smiled and nodded, beckoning them forward. It was time to get to work.

Chapter 21

———— ≈ ————

Pavel avoided every drink, canapé, and hors d'oeuvre pushed his way during the cocktail hour, opting instead for a single bottle of water. He had to remain calm, steady, and alert. Yet, by the time he took his seat at the long table—three spots down from the guest of honor, and within listening range of the president—he was already suffering from indigestion.

The signs of trouble had become evident shortly after he'd slipped away from Hal Knight as the other guests began surrounding the comedian. By then Pavel had seen Knight in action long enough to realize the man could fend for himself. Hell, he had even managed to disarm Branko Sarič, if only for a moment, although Pavel was still puzzling over what sort of "tour" Knight had been referring to. Maybe it was another inside joke from one of his movies, although Sarič hadn't looked at all amused.

Pavel had then checked the crowd for any sign of the American (or Russian, or whoever he was) who Old Rudi had spotted earlier accompanying Sarič toward the rear of the palace. Nobody looked at all like him, which was fine with Pavel. One less item to worry about.

Then Wally Wallek had sidled up on Pavel's left. He'd been smiling—a good sign, since Wally usually wore a poker face. And the drink in his hand was nearly empty, which meant he already felt comfortable enough to let his hair down.

"Going very smoothly, Pavel. Nice work."

"Thank you. I was sure I was going to fuck it up."

Wally laughed and patted him on the shoulder.

"Let me get you a real drink. You've earned it."

It was tempting, but Pavel wasn't yet willing to risk it, so he shook his head.

"Maybe later."

"You're a careful man, Pavel."

"You should have seen me earlier. All day long I've been worried I'd do something stupid, like call for the wrong car and driver. Or show up terribly late, like Kelenič, and then you'd fire me as well. So I'm glad you're pleased. That helps more than any drink."

He turned to tap his bottle of water against Wally's glass as a sort of toast, but Wally was no longer smiling. Instead he looked puzzled, even troubled.

"You think it was *me* who fired Kelenič? For tardiness? I mean, I know that was the cover story, but . . ."

His words drifted off into the din of laughter and clinking glasses.

"Cover story?"

Wally shook his head, frowning. He glanced to either side, then leaned closer to Pavel and lowered his voice.

"Kelenič was arrested, Pavel. Early one morning at his house, before the sun was even up. I'm betting that, by now, half the people in this room know that."

Pavel was alarmed.

"Arrested? For what?"

"Some sort of security breach. He was, well . . . he was *spying* on us, Pavel. Or so Sarič believes. He laid out his case to the president, all the evidence he'd collected, and apparently that was enough. The only good thing is that so far they've kept it out of the press. It's one reason Nikolai has given Sarič so much, well . . . *extra room* to operate in recent weeks. In case there are others."

"Others? Spying for who?"

Wally shrugged.

"Sarič hasn't said. Not to me, anyway. But the logical guess would be the Americans. Them or the British."

"Where did they take him?"

Wally shook his head.

"No one seems to know, and no one is willing to ask. It's as if he never existed. I can't even say for sure that he's alive."

Pavel swallowed the last of his water. The plastic bottle crumpled in his tightening grip. Wally's head swiveled abruptly left, and Pavel turned to see Sarič briskly crossing the room on the far side, heading toward a knot of three men in animated conversation. Even at this event he was wearing his stupid orange water bottle. They followed his progress the way a pair of photographers might watch a lion closing in on a herd of wildebeests. All three men stiffened at his arrival, although their mouths kept moving.

"Do you think he's after one of them?" Pavel asked.

"Definitely not Surber, he's just the president's golfing buddy, runs a retail chain. The other two are political up-and-comers—Gleb Liebman at Defense, Sandor Matas at Commerce. Maybe he's just poking around, probing for weak spots."

The three men began nodding as one, their eyes on Sarič as he spoke. Then he parted. They didn't resume their conversation until he was out of earshot, and even then they gathered more closely, almost a huddle.

Now, seated at the dinner table half an hour later, Pavel felt his empty stomach doing somersaults, although at least he no longer had any doubt as to why there was a black box in the heating duct of his house, intercepting signals. Extra room to operate, indeed. And apparently even the president was okay with such actions. Sarič and his people were probably scrutinizing everyone who worked in the palace.

In his continuing preoccupation with Sarič—who, mercifully, was seated at the far end of the table—Pavel barely registered any of the repartee that seemed to be passing between Hal Knight, the president, and the other nearby guests. Even when he did pick up on a word or two or some laughter, much of it was related to films or comedy routines that Pavel had never seen. Good. At least that aspect of the evening remained on a safe track, and whenever he glanced toward the president, Horvatz was beaming. Knight looked comfortable as well. After emptying his whiskey he had switched to wine, and seemed to be taking it slowly.

The only downbeat moment occurred after Horvatz offered some brief remarks, in English, just as the waiters began pouring coffee. The president rose to his feet and pinged a wineglass with a knife, like the toastmaster at a wedding reception. He spoke with genuine warmth of Knight's ability to make him laugh and of how valuable Knight's movies had been in helping him master English. For some of the guests whose English wasn't as good as his, he occasionally paused to repeat his observations in Bolrovian. He then announced that Knight would be giving a show two days from now. Everyone present would be invited, and there would be other special guests as well.

It was at that point that things got a little tricky. With a glint of mischief, Horvatz said that the additional guests would include "several prominent Americans, whose identity will be revealed in due course."

He then switched to Bolrovian and added, "All I will say for now about that is that I believe the evening will mark the beginning of a new and special venture, with a spirit of deepest cooperation between this country and a select group of important friends abroad."

By then, Hal Knight's benign smile had vanished, giving way to an expression of mild panic. Horvatz, who never would have risen so high without being able to read an audience, noticed immediately.

"I hasten to add," he said, switching back to English with a nod toward Knight, "that these Americans will also be sworn to secrecy, just as everyone here has been. They, too, will not be allowed to bring their phones into the room or reveal the identity of our very special guest. As many of you know, Mr. Knight here has already endured far too much unwanted and undeserved scrutiny, and we will not be a party to subjecting him to more."

Knight nodded in response, although you could tell he and everyone else were already wondering who these mystery Americans were. As was Pavel. Why had no one told him? Surely, Wally must've known. But when Pavel looked his way, Wally's brow was furrowed and he was watching Horvatz intently. Sarič's face was stony, unreadable. Could this have something to do with the visitor Old Rudi had spotted?

Pavel also hadn't known, until just now, that tonight's guests hadn't been allowed to bring their phones into the ballroom. Had this been another edict from Sarič? Pavel still had his, but he was apparently one of the few who did. Had the others been told to leave their phones at home, or in their cars? Or had they instead been ordered to hand in their devices before entry? If so, then it was easy to imagine Sarič's people in some back room right now, monkeying with all of them while everyone ate and drank and laughed.

Horvatz completed his remarks, the guests applauded, and people began standing. Some drifted toward the exit. It was over, and Pavel still had his job. When he stood, his shirt was glued to his back by perspiration. He exhaled deeply with immense relief, then walked around the table toward Knight.

"I'm sure the car is waiting out front, so we can go whenever you like. If you're not ready to return to the hotel, the driver will be happy to take you wherever you'd like to go."

"What time is it?"

"About ten thirty. Plenty of places will still be open, if you'd like."

"Tell you the truth, I'm kind of done in. Between the jet lag and the drinks and having to perform, even if it was only for an audience of one, well . . ."

"I understand. But it went well, I can assure you of that. It was obvious that the president enjoyed your company. So thank you."

"I enjoyed his. Thanks for making this so easy. But do you know anything about these Americans who are coming?"

"I'm sorry. That was news to me as well. I can ask around, if you'd like."

"Sure." Hal smiled tightly. "Thank you."

"I need a quick trip to the men's room, if you don't mind. Then we'll go."

Pavel excused himself into the hallway, where he ducked into the door for the washroom. He was halfway to the urinals when he heard the door open behind him, followed by footsteps. A sidelong glance showed that it was Sarič, who stooped to pick up one of those rubber wedges that janitors use to hold open the door during cleaning. But Sarič jammed it beneath the door to hold it shut. They were locked in. Pavel, who felt as if he didn't dare move, much less unzip his trousers, watched as Sarič quickly checked all three stalls to make sure they were empty.

Then, still without a word, Sarič stepped over to a sink, where he unscrewed the cap of his orange water bottle, pulled out some sort of filter attachment with a plunger, and refilled the bottle. Pavel, who needed badly to pee, fidgeted as he watched this odd ritual. After filling the bottle, Sarič reinserted the filter plunger and pushed it to the bottom, the same way you made coffee with a French press.

Sarič screwed the top back on and eyed Pavel carefully.

"I suppose you think this is a foolish indulgence. I know that's what others say."

"No. Not at all."

"They have the same attitude toward a lot of security precautions. 'Oh, that's harmless, why bother.' Of course, they said that about Kelenič as well."

Sarič set the bottle onto the rim of the sink and faced Pavel from ten feet away, like a sheriff in an American western. Pavel crossed his feet and tried to hold it in, his bladder feeling like a water balloon that might burst at any moment.

"So, what do you think?" Sarič asked.

Pavel cleared his throat.

"About what?"

"The evening. And our American guest. The way he comported himself."

"I think it went as well as could be expected. The president seemed to enjoy his company."

"Yes, I think that is correct. In that sense, it was a success."

"I'm glad to know that."

"I don't like him."

"Mr. Knight?"

"He's an actor. They're paid to fool us."

"He's really more of a comedian."

"Even worse. Watch. By the end of the week, he'll have us laughing at ourselves. When people start doing that, they miss things. Important things."

"Yes, well . . . maybe we could use a few laughs."

"Fine, then. Laugh your way through the entire week. But don't lose your focus, because you have a role to play, a job to do. For me."

Sarič closed the distance between them and clamped a hand on Pavel's shoulder, the grip uncomfortably firm. Pavel had to shift his feet to hold his balance, even as he continued to concentrate on not peeing in his pants.

"I know that you are supposed to be his escort for certain events, but I am expanding your orders. You will accompany him everywhere, each day he is here. From breakfast onward, you will observe and listen to all he does, all he says. You will be a constant presence, his minder."

"I doubt he wants a minder. Besides, I have other duties this week. For the president."

"I have cleared this with him. You will follow my instructions."

"He knows you're having me spy on his favorite funnyman?"

"He knows you will always be there for Hal Knight's protection. And ours."

"Maybe I should take this up directly with the president."

The grip tightened.

"You are of course free to do as you choose, just as your predecessor was."

Pavel had no answer to that, other than to shift his feet again and tighten the muscles in his groin.

"You will carry out these duties with professional detachment. You will earn his trust, of course, but you will not become his friend or social companion. You will only be his shadow, and our shield. Others will assist you in these duties, including me at certain times."

"What others? Assist me how?"

"Those details are not important. All you need to know is that at the conclusion of each day, and only after you are certain that he has returned for good to the security of his quarters, you will contact me, no matter what the hour, to deliver a full report. Beginning this evening. And if you do not, then you can be sure that I will be in touch with you. Are we clear on this?"

"Yes."

"And when I call, you will answer. Not like this afternoon, when you ignored me."

"The battery went dead."

Sarič smiled, as if to say that didn't even merit a reply. Then, after a hard thwack on the shoulder, he turned, walked to the door, kicked away the wedge, and disappeared into the corridor.

Pavel drew a deep breath and exhaled slowly. Catching a glimpse of himself in the mirrors, he was dismayed to see the pale, drained face of a castaway, a lone man adrift on an angry sea.

He stepped shakily to the urinal, unzipped, and waited.

Five seconds passed, then twenty.

He couldn't produce a single drop.

Chapter 22

Hal wasn't lying when he told Pavel he had enjoyed the president's company. Was it wrong that he even kind of liked Nikolai Horvatz? The man obviously had his faults, but face-to-face he was engaging, even warm. His impressive command of English was especially pleasing, since Hal's movies had apparently played such an important role on that front. Horvatz had also tactfully avoided any mention of Hal's recent "troubles"—as another guest had awkwardly called them—which was a relief. This was the sort of public evening Hal had assumed he would never experience again, and he had enjoyed it. For that alone, he owed Horvatz his gratitude.

Okay, sure, the man's political views were reprehensible. But if people as far apart on the ideological spectrum as Hal Knight and Nikolai Horvatz could make nice for even a few hours on neutral ground, then maybe others who were similarly divided in these fractious times could do the same, or at the very least learn to be a little more civil with one another.

Which, of course, was complete and utter bullshit, like some empty utterance for the cameras at a congressional hearing, as Hal knew the instant the thought crossed his mind. It then occurred to him that his warm feelings for Horvatz were a symptom of one of his greatest weaknesses—the ease with which he had always been snowed and manipulated by adulation. And look at where that had led him.

Early in his stand-up career, Hal's material had been kind of edgy, even innovative. Or so the reviews had said. But whenever he played college campuses, or any venue where younger males tended to turn out, his biggest—and cheapest—laughs were always for his rawer, cruder material, stuff about desperate guys who just wanted to get laid and would gladly turn themselves into fools to do so.

So he began tailoring his act more to their tastes, and as his crowds grew larger the trend accelerated, which in turn drew more of this like-minded clientele. Without their support, he never would've gotten financial backing for his first film, which they had turned out in droves to see. And in Hal's second film he had continued to adjust accordingly, with more hormonal slapstick, complete with boob jokes, dick jokes, and just about anything that might make a pubescent fifteen-year-old boy laugh.

By then he was playing huge arenas and had landed a one-hour special on Comedy Central, and by the time his third movie, *Barefoot and Pregnant,* reached the screen to become his biggest hit, he was catering almost exclusively to the sorts of young men who spent most of their weekends at underage-drinking parties, fraternity keggers, or tailgating before football games. Or so Hal believed, in his own cynically disdainful way, which was probably also off the mark. Because whenever he actually met his fans, they seemed so filled with joy and innocent awe that he couldn't help but like them. And for all their transgressions of taste and judgment, hell, they were in their teens, and every bit as clueless and ill-informed as he had been at that age. So at least *they* had an excuse.

That had troubled Hal, especially as he'd watched the careers of colleagues who'd remained true to their originality wane and then wither. He knew he'd succeeded partly by selling out. But if the world operated in such a cynical way, why not push the envelope even further? So that's what he'd done, in his scripts and also in his behavior. And, ultimately, he also did so by running for Congress, a decision which had abruptly come about when the aging incumbent in his House district had dropped dead only months before his reelection primary.

Local party officials, desperate for a quick replacement, had appealed to him for an emergency run. Flattered, he had readily accepted, figuring that, at worst, he'd get some new material and broader publicity. A part of him had also wondered whether a seat in Congress might be his path back to full adulthood. It had felt like an escape, a chance to remake himself as someone more like the man he'd once been.

By then, plenty of Hal's earliest fans had aged into the electorate, and in a six-candidate field he had captured enough of the primary vote to win the nomination. There had been little time for campaigning, but the events had been easy—yet another series of shows with scripts to follow and autographs to sign afterward. Because the district was a Democratic stronghold, he easily won in November. But in the midst of all that, he had one last film to finish, *She Really Won't,* a contractual obligation which he had set out to fulfill the following summer, after Congress went on recess.

He was aware of the lingering implications of the #MeToo movement, of course, although by that time some of its fury had abated, or at least had disappeared from the daily headlines, thanks in part to the interventions of Covid and the traumatic 2020 presidential election.

Subconsciously, Hal may have also been convinced that, by being a member of Congress, his leftward political views would inoculate him against the damages of any stray inappropriate remarks, or against the occasional allegations of sexism that some critics—most of them women—had lodged against his films. Because, hey, how much did any of that matter, as long as he remained reliably pro-choice, anti-Trump, and so on? Plus, he knew how regretful some liberals still were for having precipitously chased off Senator Al Franken over transgressions that, in retrospect, seemed trivial.

So, by the time his Day of Disaster rolled around, Hal had almost perfectly primed himself to commit a heedless act of stupidity. And that's exactly what he did, on a hot July afternoon in New Mexico, on the set of his never-to-be-released comedy *She Really Won't.*

The precipitating moment was an afternoon argument over the script with the film's female lead, Mariette Garth.

Mariette was one of those actors who needed an excess of pampering. Her contract specified that a daily snack basket be delivered to her room, and that its contents must include a Starkrimson pear (*never* Red Anjou), a packet of locally sourced oatcakes, a Pierre Marcolini chocolate bar, and a one-liter bottle of Svalbarði, a Norwegian "iceberg" mineral water that went for $185 a pop. Her bedsheets had to have a thread count of at least 800 in Egyptian cotton, no one on the set was allowed to wear LA Lakers gear (something to do with Kobe, apparently), and the only car she would allow herself to be driven in was a Faraday FF 91 electric limo—to preserve the planet, of course.

Such behavior was not uncommon among her breed—that of the up-and-coming talent, the Next Big Thing. But the bigger problem was that she didn't want to be there. Having signed the contract four months earlier, just as her star was rising, she had since become convinced that she was being underpaid for a lesser role in a vehicle which would likely sell millions of tickets but would leave most viewers barely remembering her part in it. Because, well, that was almost always the case with the female lead in a Hal Knight comedy.

By the time her scene was ready for shooting that afternoon, Hal had already had some testy moments. That morning he had taken aside a male co-star, Sid Winkle, to lash into him for having arrived on the set not only hungover but thoroughly unprepared to deliver his lines. This had led to eleven retakes, and Hal had only accepted the final one because they were about to encroach on the lunch hour, and under union rules the crew was due a break, especially in the intense heat of the Southwest, which was sapping Hal's strength as well.

So, after changing out of his sweaty clothes, and with a light shooting schedule set for the afternoon, Hal had given everyone an extra hour for lunch. He had then met Jess for a bite at a café that had become their local favorite, where he had immediately ordered the featured drink, an exotic cocktail the color of a New Mexico sunset. He had drained it in about twenty seconds through a big red straw. The waitress, seeing it, had promptly alighted at their table.

"Another?"

"Sounds perfect."

Jess had frowned in disapproval.

"You sure that's a good idea?"

"This afternoon's so easy they could do it in their sleep. Two short scenes and the only thing important is the dialogue. Hell, they don't even need to hit their marks."

"Still, you seem kind of stressed."

The waitress set down the second drink.

"That's why I need two of these."

"But you know how you get when you mix alcohol and stress."

"Like I said, a stress-free afternoon. These will make me as tame as a javelina."

"Javelinas are nasty. Besides, I saw the bartender mixing one of those. They're stronger than you think."

"What I *think* is that I may need a third."

And so, to prove his point, he'd had another.

The trouble began in the first take, when Mariette refused to utter the scene's third line. Instead, she held up her right hand and took a step toward him, saying, "I just can't say that."

Hal, jolted out of his stupor by this act of insubordination, had frowned and said, "Can't or won't?"

"Both. It's nothing that any woman would ever say, not in this situation."

"But you're not playing just any woman. You're playing Callista, and this is her line, and she needs to say it if the rest of the scene is going to work."

Mariette shook her head and moved a step closer.

"It's not plausible. It's not realistic. No one will buy it, least of all me."

"Mariette, look around you. This is a Hollywood movie. It's a Hal Knight comedy. Nothing about it is *supposed* to be realistic. Just say the fucking line."

"Sorry. It doesn't work for me, because it doesn't work for the character."

"For fuck's sake, *mumble* it if you want. You can even just lip-synch the goddamn words for all I care and we'll dub it later with a voice actor who will probably make it sound better—excuse me, more *realistic*—than you ever could."

"Do that and I'll sue for breach of contract."

He was about to reply with something pathetically trite, like *"Do that and I'll see that you never work in this town again,"* but even in his semi-addled state he knew that wouldn't sell, not given her current status. Or maybe it was that, in the corner of his eye, he saw Jess, script in hand, lowering her head and cringing in embarrassment, either for him, for Mariette, or for this entire venture, and at some deep level it shamed him, then infuriated him. So instead he got right up in Mariette's face, surprising her so much that she took a step backward.

The instant she gave ground, he felt further empowered, so he struck quickly while he had the advantage—towering over her with voice raised, face reddening.

"Mariette, you're not here to fucking think. You're here to act, and if the script calls for you to be a submissive bimbo with the brains of a flea and the tits and ass of a stripper, then you'll by god play one or be in breach of *your* contract."

Her mouth dropped open, but no words emerged, which emboldened him further.

"Do you think you got this part because of your subtlety, your technique? No, you got it because of those." He nodded at her breasts. "And because of that." He slapped sideways at her rump. There were gasps behind him, perhaps even one from Jess, but by then he had become an unstoppable force, like a character written into the script. "So you're going to say these lines as they're fucking written. And if I want you to say them while your male lead is standing in front of you drooling like a moron, or even with his dick hanging out, then you'll damn well do it. Understand?"

And at that point Hal had unzipped and rezipped his trousers—quickly, like a flasher, and in a way that made it unclear whether he had ever actually exposed his dick—although it was certainly open to that interpretation to everyone who later viewed the video shot by the crew member, a fellow who had begun filming surreptitiously with his phone the moment Mariette first refused to do her line.

A horrified Mariette had then numbly delivered the line before walking off the set in tears. Hal, feeling stupidly triumphant, but also with a sense of uneasy foreboding, had immediately sought out Jess, only to discover that she, too, had departed.

The next morning he had adjusted the few remaining scenes so that they could be shot without Mariette, and that night he had returned to his home near LA. The video went online around noon the following day, although the confrontation which led to his outburst had been edited out, meaning the scene began with his words "Mariette, you're not here to fucking think" and ended with her tearful departure. By six o'clock eastern time that evening, millions had watched, shared, and reposted it across any and all possible platforms. Many viewers claimed they could see his dick. Others said it was just his fingers on the zipper, which still others took to be a hilarious verdict on the undersized nature of his package. And now, here he was in Bolrovia, already falling for the same kind of adulation that had led him to such a fine and memorable moment.

Hal blinked, as if emerging from a daze. The effects of wine and jet lag bore down like a heavy blanket. He wanted to sit, but that would only invite attention, maybe even concern, and at the moment he was blessedly unattended. Horvatz and his retinue had just departed, and nearly everyone else had filtered away to collect their coats and head home.

Hal looked around for Lukov, who seemed to have disappeared. Then he glanced at the sheet of paper in his right hand. Horvatz had given it to him only moments ago, after summoning an aide who had produced it from a document case just as the party was breaking up.

It was some sort of bogus award—a fake parchment certificate with a gold-leaf "Seal of Bolrovia" and a proclamation inscribed in English and Bolrovian which said that he, Hal Knight, was now in possession of a full and unlimited Pass of Entry to the Nation of Bolrovia, and all sights and attractions that it had to offer, and that, furthermore, no facility or institution or place of business would be closed to him for the duration of his stay. As Horvatz had given it to him, the president had laid a hand on Hal's right arm and explained that this document granted him free entry to any museum, restaurant, club, historic shrine, or national park. Or any other sort of place he cared to think of. No exceptions, and no reservations required.

"Just show them this, and they will know you are my personal guest."

Hal had to stifle a laugh. It had felt like something you'd get after speaking to the local Kiwanis or Chamber of Commerce. A Key to the City, a well-meant but largely symbolic honor which you would drop into a drawer—or a trash can—the moment you got home.

Instead he had nodded solemnly and said, "Thank you, Mr. President. I'll cherish this."

Still, the childlike eagerness with which Horvatz had bestowed it had been kind of endearing. And, yes, it was not lost on Hal that, had he been a refugee from Syria or an asylum seeker from the Balkans or even a nobody from Sherman Oaks, he would have received a kick in the pants instead of a welcoming embrace. But the gesture had left him with a warm glow. Yes, he was still a sucker for any and all brands of worship.

"Mr. Knight!"

He turned. Lukov at last, looking a bit pale as he approached from across the room. The poor fellow was probably as relieved as Hal to have the evening over and done. But each man in his own way had passed the test, and Hal now wanted nothing more than to shut the heavy curtains of his hotel room and curl up beneath the sheets. He would crash as deeply as possible into the oblivion of sleep, even though jet lag would inevitably awaken him in the middle of the night.

"What's that you're holding?" Lukov asked.

"Oh, this." He laughed awkwardly. "Some Key to the City type thing. You know, nice but meaningless. But Nick—uh, I'm sorry—the president took me aside and gave it to me as everybody was leaving."

Lukov glanced around nervously, like he was looking for someone.

"Was Sarič here when that happened?"

"That asshole? Hell, no. He'd have swapped it out for a Get-Into-Jail card for one of those basement cells of his."

Lukov looked puzzled by the remark, but Hal didn't care to fill him in on the background.

"Those are actually kind of a big deal. Hang on to it. And do *not* let Sarič know you have one."

"Really?"

Hal examined it again, as if he might have missed some important wording in the fine print.

Lukov then explained how, yes, these things had once been throw-away items, just as Hal suspected. But a couple years ago, after Horvatz had given one to a rather svelte and sexy concert pianist, she had tried to use it to avoid waiting in line at Le Roxy, Blatsk's most popular disco, only to be refused and even mocked by the bouncer. In a huff, she had taken her grievance to a local TV station, which ran a piece on the snub, prompting an affronted Horvatz to issue an official statement proclaiming that any future bearer of one of these certificates would have a presidential guarantee of entry and goodwill that must be honored at any location nationwide. It had made news all over Bolrovia.

This, in turn, had gotten Sarič so bent out of shape that he kept close tabs on the two honored guests who had received them in the meantime. In each case he had quietly taken aside the recipient and offered to "safe-guard" the document until their departure. Both had readily complied, partly because they had no idea of the value of the item, partly because they'd sensed that Sarič's proposal was more than a friendly suggestion.

"So, you see? One pissed-off pianist, and now these things are worth their weight in gold. And you're sure Sarič didn't see this happen?"

"Positive."

"Hide it, then. Now. And keep it safe."

Hal folded it lengthwise as Lukov winced, but it still wouldn't fit in the inside pocket of his jacket. So he folded it again, and then a third time. You could hear the crinkle of the gold-leaf seal, and Lukov lowered his head as if to officially disavow this act of desecration. But it was now small enough for Hal to slip between the pages of his black notebook, which he quickly tucked back into the rear pocket of his trousers.

By then, the room was nearly empty. Blessedly, there was still no sign of Sarič.

Their car was waiting out front. Neither man said much on the way back, and when they reached the Esplanade, Lukov escorted Hal to the elevators but didn't follow him upstairs.

Hal barely had enough energy to undress, and even the ghost of Shirley Halston couldn't rouse herself long enough to scold him for tossing his clothes to the floor. His final waking thought was to wonder if he should get out of bed to take his notebook and the certificate out of the pocket of his rumpled trousers.

Five hours later he opened his eyes, not really rested but wide awake. Jet lag, right on schedule. The lights of the city danced in a blur of reds and whites up on his ceiling, which alarmed him for a moment until he remembered he hadn't shut the curtains. The bedside clock said 4:08. All was quiet.

For weeks he had been seeking the balm of solitude. Now that he finally had it, it felt more like abandonment, a deep emptiness in a room far from home—or, worse, in a city where he would be watched and stalked by secretive means. At least with the paparazzi and the mobs of social media, you could see the threat coming. For all he knew, even now someone in that building where Sarič worked was seated at a desk with headphones on, listening to Hal breathe in the dark.

Would they also be listening if he got out the black notebook and began scribbling his observations from this evening? It was probably what he should do, if he was ever going to be of any value as a spy. But he would have to use the coded language the CIA people had taught him, and at the moment he was too damn tired to keep all of that straight.

He reached over to the bedside table and switched on a lamp. Better. The Roth was there, bookmarked to the passage he'd consulted earlier. He picked it up, opened it to another page at random, and his heart lurched as he saw darkened purple stains in the margins—berry juice, from the berries he and Jess had picked at the edge of an open field years ago, not long after they'd met. There were also a few small dried blue petals from some flower they'd picked that day. He had taken the book with him on a picnic somewhere along the coastal highway, just him and

Jess in the California sun, on a grassy bluff with a view of the Pacific. This was the other reason—the one he always kept to himself—that he kept the book with him like a talisman. Those petals and berry stains carried her mark, or at least the indelible evidence of their happiest times together. He gently shut the book and set it back onto the bedside table, taking care not to damage or spill any of the dried petals.

The memory put another thought in his head, one which he knew right away was unwise. All the more reason to act on it immediately, before he lost his nerve. Hal slid out of bed, stepped around his fallen clothes, and retrieved his laptop from the knapsack. The Plan Z pills rattled below as he rezipped the compartment. He set a fat pillow against the headboard, got back into bed, and opened the laptop for the first time in days.

He logged on to the hotel's Wi-Fi network, which was probably about as secure as a henhouse without walls. Then he opened the email server, typed in Jess's address, and began composing a message. The warnings of the CIA people shouted inside his head: *Don't write anything on an electronic device that you don't want them to see.*

Fine. Let Sarič's people think whatever they wanted. Maybe even Susan, or whoever she really was, would also be reading this by the time the sun was up. And if all of them wanted to conclude he was a careless, lovesick fool, that was also fine.

Besides, when two people knew each other as well as he and Jess did, there was always a sort of secret language available, a vocabulary of private moments which no one else would be able to decipher. Or so he told himself as he typed away for nearly an hour, confident but careful, driven by a sudden boldness that endured until the instant he hit the send button and heard that little *whoosh* that meant the message was now available not only to Jess, but to anyone else with the technological means to intercept it.

Oh, shit. Well, that was stupid.

Then, on second thought:

Good. I'm right in character. Fuck 'em.

Chapter 23

———～———

Jess Miller seemed to be eating dinner later every day. Some nights she skipped it altogether, only to wake up so ravenous the next morning that she would crack three eggs into a pan, make some toast, and slice a banana into a bowl of yogurt, needing every bite plus a pot of coffee to answer the cravings of an empty stomach.

Tonight, since it was already after eight o'clock, she decided to pillage the fridge for whatever was available. She'd eaten a leftover burrito the night before, so that option was gone. And she was sick to death of salad, or her recent version of it—wilted lettuce tossed with overripe cherry tomatoes and, if she was lucky, a few shreds of leftover chicken.

Maybe tonight she'd cook an omelet. Add some cheese, even bacon if it hadn't gone bad. Not the healthiest way to plan your main meal, but at least it meant she was busy again, with plenty of work to do and more requests coming in by the day—some out of pity, perhaps, but others because, well, she was damn good at it.

Jess was a script doctor, a writer who could take even the flabbiest prose and dialogue and sharpen them into scenes that would gleam with dollar signs at your next pitch meeting. This was how she and Hal had met, when, on a friend's recommendation, Hal had turned to her for help after several studios had rejected the script for his first film.

She had tuned in right away to what made Hal's humor work, and she immediately helped focus his dialogue, tighten his pacing. Their chemistry, both personally and professionally, had been apparent from the beginning, and the relationship had flourished with each successive film.

Unlike many others, she had also detected, deeper within his work, his capability for a more sophisticated level of humor—subtly embedded items that took root in your mind and produced hilarious payoffs later, but only if you were paying attention. Although, admittedly, such items had appeared less frequently in each further project, mostly because viewers and, more to the point, studio executives had never particularly liked or even noticed them.

Had she been complicit, then, in the gradual cheapening of his humor, as one box office hit led to another and his young audience began demanding more of the same? Perhaps, but she hadn't been complicit in his tipsy lunches, which she'd always warned him against, and she certainly hadn't aided or abetted his dismissive attitude toward his leading ladies, his financial backers, and sometimes even his fans.

In fact, here and there she had injected her own voice into their work, often by refining or supplementing the dialogue and character descriptions of their female roles. In engineering those changes she wrote the sort of lines that even Mariette Garth would have probably found to her liking. But when the script notes came back from on high, those were almost invariably among the items that the executives wanted to cut, and Hal obliged them without a fight.

Now, thank god, requests for her services were again filling her inbox and making her phone buzz. It was confirmation that, although Hal Knight's ship had gone down, hers remained afloat, even if they'd long been known as a team. And if returning to full employment meant that she missed a few meals, or ate them later than recommended, that seemed like a small price to pay. Granted, on her current project the producer had asked her to use a pen name. "Just until some of the clouds have had time to blow away," she'd said. But the pay wasn't any less.

Besides, the harder and later Jess worked, the less time she had to dwell on the whole big mess with Hal, who, as far as she was concerned, had died and left the planet. Or so she told herself whenever any thought of him crossed her mind. He was gone because he had destroyed himself. That part of her life was over.

Still, it might be nice just once to eat dinner before dark. Or at least early enough to grab some takeout from one of those spots down by the sea, maybe after strolling the promenade among all the tourists intent on either spotting a celebrity or overspending for some item at one of the high-end shops, even though, with only a ten-minute drive, they would have been passing through a tent village populated by thousands of the homeless.

She stood from her desk and glanced out the window. Fully dark, but at one corner her view allowed a narrow glimpse of the Pacific. Hal's place, a few blocks away, had a far better view, of course, but, well, he had made more money and been higher up the food chain.

Jess was about to head for the kitchen when she heard the little beep from her iMac that sounded whenever an email arrived. The chances were fifty-fifty it was spam, despite her filter, but the director she was working with on this latest project was also known to put in late hours, so she decided she'd better check.

It was from Hal Knight.

"Shit."

She quickly slid the mouse until the cursor arrow rested atop the little garbage can icon on the inbox task bar. Jess sighed, but she didn't click. Not yet.

"Oh, Hal. Enough."

It was the first time she had heard her own voice in hours, and she was appalled at how tired and desolate it sounded. Hal had already written her six letters. They sat in a neat pile on the far end of her desk, unopened, postmarked from various locations across the country. Knowing him, she figured he'd been hoping that the extra effort involved in sending lengthy handwritten pleas—and they were almost certainly lengthy, judging by the fatness of the envelopes and the extra postage—might convince her to at least hear him out.

Only three days ago, as if he were finally running out of steam, she'd received a postcard from some island called Vieques. On its front was a sunny scene of a white beach and a turquoise sea. Her first reaction had been mild surprise that anyone still sent postcards. Especially Hal, since anyone would be able to read it. But she had refused to read that as well. It now sat atop the pile of letters, picture side up.

Since she had been old enough to read, Jess had come across loads of books and movies in which an aggrieved or pissed-off woman had refused to open letters from an ex-lover. Not once had she been convinced. Did they seriously expect you to believe that your curiosity wouldn't get the best of you; that you would simply *ignore* a message from someone who had once been the most important person in your life? In the immortal words of Mariette Garth, "It's not plausible. It's not realistic."

Yet there they were, all of Hal's letters, still sealed. Barely even touched. Nor could she bring herself to throw them away, which was almost as absurd. Either read the damn things or toss them. Better still, take them down to the beach one night and set them aflame, a miniature bonfire for his misguided passions, a ceremonial marking of his passage into her past. But with the arrival of each one, she had meekly laid it atop the others, as if they were bills she'd eventually get around to paying.

And now, here was an email, as if Hal had given up on the outdated tactics of a spurned Victorian swain and had boldly decided to attempt instantaneous contact. It made his presence feel oddly close, as if she could hear him breathing in the next room, his slender fingers poised above a keyboard. Perhaps this was the push she needed to finally take action.

Jess eased the mouse left and slid the arrow onto the line for the message. She clicked.

The screen filled with his words. She averted her eyes, as if from a blinding flash, and then slid the arrow back over to the little garbage can. For several seconds her index finger rested atop the mouse, Jess playing the role of Roman emperor in the Colosseum while a hushed crowd awaited her verdict. Kill it or read it?

She exhaled slowly, slid the arrow back over to the text, and began to read.

Unavoidably, Hal's voice entered her head as she scrolled down the page. He was no longer in the next room; he was here, speaking every word from right over her shoulder.

She continued anyway.

Chapter 24

———≋———

Dickson Fordyce was the kind of boss who only called with bad news. It was his idea of being supportive. So when his number showed up on Lauren's encrypted phone only moments after she'd set out on an early morning run, she figured that her day—and maybe the entire week—was ruined.

It was six a.m., and she hadn't even had time to break a sweat when the phone began to vibrate against her rump in the rear pocket of her running shorts. She stopped halfway down a narrow lane less than two blocks from the hotel, where the only other people out and about were a baker hosing down his front walkway and a drunk trying to make it home before sunrise. Fordyce began speaking before she could even put the phone to her ear.

"Hate to tell you this, especially at this hour, but our new client is already off the leash."

At first, she thought he might be referring to her newly recruited source, Sandor Matas, which would be disheartening but bearable.

"How so?"

"A little while ago he contacted his closest associate by email with a long and fairly revealing message, which included an invitation to join him."

Nope, he meant Hal Knight, and thanks to a predetermined code she knew that "closest associate" was a reference to Jess Miller. But it was the words "fairly revealing" that were more troubling, because any email of Hal's was probably already being scrutinized by Sarič's minions at the Interior Ministry.

She turned away from the baker, who directed his hose in the opposite direction as a nod to her need for privacy at this quiet hour before the city had fully awakened.

"I see."

She continued walking.

"Obviously it's an unexpected complication. Maybe to the point where our offer to him is no longer viable."

"That bad?"

"I'll let you make that call."

Meaning that, from here on out, any failure would rest on her shoulders, not his.

When Lauren had first joined the Agency, she'd thought of its employees, especially those working in clandestine operations, as almost superhuman beings, an elite corps of secret warriors. And while the Agency was indeed highly selective, weeding out a high percentage of applicants and trainees, experience soon taught her that, as with any large institution employing thousands, it, too, had embedded layers of mediocrities and failures, people who not only would never measure up, but would be promoted while doing so. And, yes, sometimes she would have to answer to them.

She wondered if Fordyce was calling from the office. It was midnight in Langley, so probably not. He was generally a nine-to-five man, even when in charge of an overseas operation. She had never been to his home in Northern Virginia, but knew people who had, and from their descriptions, plus the persona he had crafted for himself, she pictured him standing before a crackling fireplace while some sort of retriever—a Chesapeake or a golden—snoozed on the hearth. Framed British hunting prints hung from every wall. A tartan wool blanket was draped on an overstuffed couch. His pipe was lit, and he was holding a snifter of brandy poured from a cut-glass decanter on an oak sideboard that had been in the family for at least two hundred years. If there was such a thing as a tweed bathrobe, he was wearing one. His meek and submissive second wife—a younger and sexier facsimile of the first one—was already tucked away for the night in their four-poster upstairs with one of those cozy mystery novels—*Death Comes on Cat's Paws* or some such title—next to her on the nightstand, still bookmarked at the page she'd reached two weeks earlier.

Or maybe Lauren was being uncharitable. Although just before replying she did hear a popping noise that sounded exactly like the snap of a burning log.

"Any indication the associate has accepted his offer?"

"No, but it's only been about an hour."

That meant Hal had been awake at five a.m. Had he stayed out on the town until then? If so, how heavily had he been drinking, and what sort of loose and reckless talk might he have engaged in among all those Bolrovians, including the president and, possibly, Branko Sarič? Already she was too agitated to finish her run, which would throw her off balance for the remainder of the morning. What she needed instead was a quick shower and a large coffee, and not the thin, watery stuff from room service. But first she had to get Fordyce off the line, which would happen faster if she let him do most of the talking. She turned the corner into an even narrower lane, where a skinny cat was chasing a bigger cat past a dripping downspout. On a nearby wall was a poster advertising a tent circus that seemed to belong to a bygone era.

A vague image of sad clowns and defanged lions crossed her mind as Fordyce continued.

"Of course, given the delicate nature of our relationship with this client, I'll also be apprising Marie of this development."

"Marie" was ostensibly a reference to Marie Ellington, lead partner of Lauren's cover employer. But the person he really meant was Tina Merritt, two rungs up the ladder from Fordyce, and one of only five deputy directors at the Agency. On this matter he was reporting directly to her.

This, too, was a Fordyce managerial trademark—notifying his superiors the moment any subordinate ran into trouble—which allowed him to serve immediate notice that it certainly wasn't the result of anything *he'd* done.

Lauren had met Merritt only once, briefly, at a dreary cocktail reception the previous winter in the Agency's executive dining room, on the seventh floor of the headquarters building. Merritt had just been promoted into the job. Her reputation was for being levelheaded but risk-averse, meaning Lauren might need to employ a little salesmanship to keep this op alive. Provided, of course, that it hadn't just become unsalvageable. She hated salesmanship, unless it was the kind she had employed on Sandor Matas yesterday afternoon.

"The other complicating factor, of course, is that I'm sure by now his message is already getting some close study in other quarters. So the sooner you can decipher its deeper meanings for Marie and me, the sooner you'll be able to determine the nature of our response."

"I'll give it a look."

"Sending it now. Following the usual protocols, of course."

"Of course."

Given the advanced nature of their security precautions—end-to-end double encryption for both their phones—they probably hadn't needed to speak in such guarded terms. But a little extra care never hurt, especially when your adversary was so technologically savvy.

Fordyce ended the call. She reached the end of the next block, spotted a bench just ahead in a small, charming park, and strolled over to take a seat. A creaking noise made her look up, but it was just an empty swing set swaying in the early breeze.

She opened her inbox and there it was, Hal Knight's overnight message to Jess Miller. Out of habit, Lauren bent over as if to shield the message from any prying eyes, and she began to read.

My dearest Jess,

Sometime soon, perhaps even in the next day or so, you will almost certainly learn of my current whereabouts, either by reading it online or via one of those horrible cable news channels, so I will preemptively tell you myself, followed by an explanation, as a prelude to an invitation.

I am in Bolrovia, as the personal guest of the president, Nikolai Horvatz.

Stop! Don't kill this message just yet, even though I know that would be my own inclination if our roles were reversed. I beg of you to please hear me out, if only because, given my current disconsolate and somewhat lost state of mind, begging feels like the only activity I'm worthy of at the moment.

Yes, I know this will be a disappointment to you—surprise, surprise—so for the moment I'll spare you any detailed elaborations on the warm hospitality that has been extended to me since my arrival, except to say that, despite our obvious political differences, he has been a kind and accepting host.

So, why did I come? Why did I accept this invitation? I suppose that the utter lack of anything else to do was one reason. My need for some sort of hospitable human contact was another. And, yes, deep in my darkened soul I am sure that the prospect of unconditional acceptance, and even adulation, motivated me as well. I am of course well aware of the haunted and distasteful places that those unhealthy impulses often lead me to. But I doubt I shall be here more than a week, and by then the inevitable backlash in the States will almost certainly be strong enough to prevent me from ever doing something like this again.

I suppose that another reason I am here is that I am pulling a Leo Holloman, so to speak, even though I am doing so only due to a recent case of the creeps. Completely unbidden, I assure you, but it was an invitation earnestly extended, so I am trying to respond in kind, or as earnestly as I know how. Tonight they threw a welcoming dinner for me, a whole lot of guests seated around a long and elaborately set table. The president sat at my side. He quoted some of our oldest lines back at me, which of course made me think of you. You would have laughed at me tonight, but for all the wrong reasons. I was mannerly and well behaved. I drank abstemiously and returned the warmth of my host. I decided that, as his guest, I should not display or even mention our political differences, and if that makes me an amoral opportunist, well, I suppose that is at least a small step up from my current status as retrograde pariah, an evolution from Neanderthal to merely feckless. So be it.

Now I will finally come to the point of this unsolicited message: my invitation for you to join me here in Blatsk, mostly so that I might maintain a suitable degree of self-control for the remainder of my stay. I am still a leaky and unstable vessel for whom you are my keel, my ballast, my better half. I have not yet informed my hosts of this invitation, but I am sure that the Bolrovians would be happy to have you as long as they realize that your presence will make their special guest more agreeable and accommodating. And, well, who knows, maybe you can also help bolster my resolve with regard to this recent case of the creeps, just as you always did whenever Leo was the issue in question.

So there you have it, in terms as clear as I can manage under my current circumstances. You would of course have your own separate hotel room, here at the rather splendid Esplanade, and if there is one matter for which you needn't do any reading between the lines, it is *this one: I am still in love with you and, as always, need you, even though I do not expect you to reciprocate either emotion. What I am hoping for is mere companionship. So, please, do consider joining me, even though I suspect that, judging from your silence to date, you haven't yet read even a single one of my letters (although I'm betting you also haven't thrown them away, not even that silly postcard).*

If you decide not to come, which I know is likely, or even if you decide not to reply, also likely, please do try to at least acknowledge in some way that you've read it, so that I'll know you're aware of the real reason I'm here—my version, not everyone else's.

With much love and longing and regret,
Yours,
Hal

P.S. Even though I have almost completely avoided the internet and have cut off all ties to social media, I HAVE been online just enough to read of your recruitment onto a couple of new film projects, and for that I am deeply relieved and grateful. If a visit here would jeopardize any of those in any way, shape, or form, then by all means DO NOT COME.

He was a lovelorn fool. It was actually kind of sweet, in a pathetic way. Unexpectedly so. But it was also stupid, which affirmed her earlier assessment that, at some level where things really mattered, Hal Knight was a dolt. Selfish, too, a wounded little boy seeking the company of someone who, if she came, would instantly be in harm's way. Although maybe that was a little harsh. He was a civilian who had agreed to work for them—for *her*—with no strings attached, so of course he'd be feeling overwhelmed, even abandoned. Besides, dolt or not, he was her dolt now. Although if he didn't file something to them within the next twenty-four hours, maybe it would indeed be time to pull the plug and just concentrate on getting him out of here in one piece.

She read the email again, slowly this time. Certainly he hadn't said anything that would offend the Bolrovians or their president, apart from the fleeting reference to "our obvious political differences." The problem was that damned paragraph with the cryptic references to "pulling a Leo Holloman"—whoever that was—and to Hal's "case of the creeps." It seemed obvious to Lauren that Hal was trying to tell Jess what he was really up to here, and if Lauren could see that, then surely Sarič and his minions would as well.

The question was whether they'd be able to decipher the references. Maybe Hal and Jess had been close enough that they had developed their own private lexicon over time—catchphrases and inside jokes, sly little remarks that they could exchange at parties or among colleagues so that, without a nod or a wink, they could secretly communicate deeper meanings. In which case, maybe his message would be indecipherable for anyone but Hal and Jess. On the other hand, Sarič had a team of researchers and decryption specialists who by now were probably already searching the darkest corners of the internet for any and all references to Leo Holloman.

Lauren did a quick Google search of her own. The name surfaced immediately. Holloman was a Hollywood producer, a wealthy backer of films and TV projects. But even if he had bankrolled some of Knight's films, which seemed likely, how would a mention of his name signal that Hal was a spy?

She contemplated trying to send Hal a message instructing him to never again take this kind of risk. But Sarič would be watching him more closely than ever now. Maybe Quint or Malone could take a closer look at Hal at some point during the day while he was out and about, to try to assess his state of mind, his stability, his recklessness.

On the other hand, the email's clarity of thought, its lack of typos, and even the occasional grace of its language made her doubt that he had written it in a drunken haze. Hal was becoming more complicated than she'd bargained for, which might be disastrous, but might also—if he lasted long enough—work to their advantage.

This told her she wasn't yet ready to shut down the op. And if that decision gave Fordyce further leverage to blame her later, so be it. Either way, for Lauren this was the second unexpected complication in as many days.

The first one was the chatty Brit named Ian who she'd seen and heard at the Green Devil the day before. His full name—Ian Farkas—had finally come to her several hours after she'd watched him speaking to her new asset, Sandor Matas.

Her only previous encounter with Farkas had come five years earlier, when she'd been observing a crowd of angry demonstrators outside the Chinese embassy in Brussels. Most of the demonstrators had been in their twenties, so he had stood out then as well. Like Lauren, he had seemed to be there to watch rather than participate. A male colleague of Lauren's had pointed him out.

"Now there's someone to keep an eye on if he ever pops up again," he'd said.

"Who's he work for?"

"Himself, supposedly. Private security contractor. Risk assessment, logistics, or so he tells anyone who asks."

"You think he's one of us?"

"He certainly used to be, or so they say, but nobody seems to know who employed him."

"What were the leading theories?"

"MI-6, MI-5, the South Africans. Mossad."

She'd laughed.

"Why is Mossad always the fallback whenever someone doesn't know what they're talking about? Should I be worried about him?"

"Only if you start seeing him a lot. Even then, I guess it depends on who his client is."

But they had never again crossed paths, until now, and from early indications his current role was much more out in the open—that of gadfly and glad-hander, buying drinks and handing out cards. Maybe he was only here to drum up trade. Blatsk was the sort of compact capital city that lent itself well to that kind of approach, and the Green Devil was just the right sort of location.

She had wondered whether she should mention him to Fordyce, but now she decided against it. He probably wouldn't even know the name, so why bother, especially if it made Fordyce even more fretful.

Lauren read the copy of Hal's message a final time, scanning it carefully for any buried meaning she might have missed before. Then she killed it. But all through her shower, her breakfast, and into her third cup of coffee, the words of that one cryptic paragraph continued to crawl around inside her head.

Chapter 25

H al figured it was time to earn his keep as a spy, even if no one was
paying him. In fact, working for free probably made him a chump.
Fine, then. A pay scale to match his espionage talents. Because in the
full light of day he knew his email to Jess had been a terrible idea. If
Bolrovia's security apparatus had people who could perfectly match his
wardrobe, wouldn't they also be able to figure out what he'd been trying
to tell her? And, not that Jess would ever come, but should he have even
invited her to take on the same risks he was facing?

He'd slept late, well past ten. He had then ordered a room service
breakfast and, while eating his eggs and toast, tried to atone for his
impulsiveness by composing a coded dispatch for his CIA handlers.
Vowing that this one wouldn't end up in the toilet, he filled three pages
front and back, removed them from the black notebook, folded them
inside a Bolrovian five-euro note, and slipped the wad into his pants
pocket. In the dispatch he also posed a question: Who were these Americans that the president had mentioned, and would their presence at
tomorrow night's show compromise his mission? He didn't necessarily
expect an answer, but he wanted to put the idea in their heads.

By the time he headed downstairs, it was nearly eleven thirty, meaning the Interior Ministry would have already had more than six hours
to study his email. Maybe a contingent of armed men would be waiting in the lobby to greet him. But as the elevator doors opened, he saw
only Pavel Lukov, seated on a couch fifty feet away, looking bored and
disheveled as he glanced at his watch. On the table in front of him were
three empty coffee cups.

"Shit."

Hal slowly backed into the elevator before Lukov could spot him.

"Can't I get even a single morning alone?" he muttered to himself.

Shirley Halston whispered into his ear. *"How 'bout a wardrobe change? Disguise yourself and give him the slip?"*

"You saw that closet. Everything in there is a hundred percent me. Unless you brought a gorilla costume."

"On your own, sweetheart."

Two men in business suits boarded just as the doors were sliding shut. Hal punched the button for the third floor. He hopped off and paused to reorient himself before heading down a long hallway toward the back of the building. Eventually he reached an exit door for a stairwell, where he descended to the basement and opened a fire door onto a cobblestone alley. Just across it was the back wall of another building. To his right was the hotel's freight entrance, a loading dock with a couple of laundry hampers perched in the opening. He then noticed a security camera mounted on the opposite wall, aimed right at him. He resisted an urge to smile and wave, then headed up the alley to his right. When he reached the street that passed in front of the hotel, he briskly turned left toward the main square. No one emerged from the hotel to follow him.

In keeping with Susan's advice, he had left behind his phone, so he stopped a block later to get out the small tourist map that the hotel had given him at check-in. His notebook was in his rear pocket, the coded dispatch in his left pocket.

How long had it been since he had functioned at such an analog level? Even on Vieques he had relied on his phone and the internet for booking rooms, finding restaurants, checking the weather, making payments. But there was something refreshing about being reduced to the basics of pencil and paper, a bit of cash, and his own imagination, all while traveling on foot and emanating no signal that could be used to track him. Hal was adrift in the heart of a vibrant city, momentarily free from the news cycle, social media, texts, email, cookies, passcodes, hackers, tracking software, and—he hoped—Branko Sarič and his wired-up security minions. Even so, he paused in the middle of the next block to check the reflection in a storefront window to make sure he was still in the clear.

A few minutes later he merged into the crowd of the main square, which felt a bit like plunging into a bracing current, a river of people who might take him anywhere, nameless and unnoticed. Not as relaxing as an empty beach on Vieques, perhaps, but still quite liberating.

Hal's contact, or "mailman" as Susan had described him, was a food vendor in an alley near the Presidential Palace, a young man who served a local specialty called haluski from a chrome cart with a bright yellow umbrella. What Susan hadn't mentioned in her description was that the fellow's cart was one of seven in the alley, offering items that ranged from banh mi to chimney cakes, although the yellow umbrella certainly made the haluski cart stand out.

The protocol for delivering his dispatches was simple enough, but he reviewed the steps in his head as he approached so that he wouldn't screw it up, especially the opening line, which would set everything in motion.

The young man looked up expectantly as Hal approached, tongs and serving spoon at the ready. He was supposed to know what Hal looked like, but there was no hint of recognition in his features, probably as instructed. Hal delivered the line.

"This looks like a treat I once had in Poland."

The young man responded with the requisite reply.

"Haluski is popular in many places."

"What do you recommend?"

"The wrap is my best seller."

"Sounds great."

"How many?"

This was when Hal was supposed to tell him how many replacement pages he needed for his notebook.

"I'm hungry enough for three, but I'd better just limit it to one."

"Certainly, sir. Ten euros."

Hal handed over the cash. He then reached for the wadded five-euro note with its three enfolded pages of notes, which he dropped into a large aluminum can with a taped label saying "TIPS" in red letters.

"Thank you, sir."

The vendor bent to his work, hands out of sight behind the top of his cart. A few seconds later he handed over the haluski wrap, bundled in greaseproof paper which presumably also held three replacement sheets of A6 paper for Hal's notebook.

As Hal turned to go, he spotted a musician, a busker playing a portable keyboard toward the end of the alley, maybe thirty yards further on. He, too, had a tip jar, and damned if it wasn't the CIA guy who had called himself Chris back on Vieques.

Hal briefly considered walking by to drop some money in his jar, just to let Chris know he'd spotted him. Then he wondered if all spies had to resist the urge to be smart-asses and show-offs. Doubtful. Or not the ones who lived the longest. But it was reassuring to see him there, looking for all the world like a vagabond musician playing his way across Europe. It was about then that Hal caught a tantalizing whiff of smoke from another cart—a warm pastry smell, probably from the old guy selling chimney cakes. Maybe next time.

He carried the wrap to a bench near the main square, set in the shadows of a nearby building and out of sight of the food vendors. He took out the three spare pages, popped them into his notebook, and then, as a reward, bit into the haluski. Tasty. But he wasn't all that hungry after his big breakfast, so he ate only half and rewrapped the rest for later. He then decided that it would be rude, and probably stupid, to keep Pavel Lukov waiting all day in the hotel lobby, so he hustled back toward the hotel, only to find that the fire door in the alley was locked from the inside.

He would have to use the main entrance. Maybe if he moved fast enough he could slip unnoticed past Pavel, then double back after reaching the elevators. But he had barely made it to the front desk when Pavel called out from across the lobby.

"Mr. Knight!"

Hal turned. There was now a fourth empty coffee cup on Pavel's table. Hal felt a little shameful, mostly because of the crestfallen look on Pavel's face.

"Hi there, Pavel. How long have you been waiting?"

Pavel checked his watch.

"Five hours."

"You're joking, right? I only headed out about an hour ago. For breakfast." He held out the remains of the wrap. "Haluski. Not bad."

"Haluski for *breakfast*?"

"Okay, then. Brunch. Had a little trouble sleeping last night, so I was a little late getting started."

"I can't believe I missed you."

"Don't be so hard on yourself. Like I said, it was only about an hour ago. If I'd seen you, I would've said hello."

Pavel eyed him skeptically, head tilted, which made Hal think he was laying it on too thick. Or maybe they were both so new and so bad at this game that they were the perfect couple. If there was any one person here he wanted to be able to trust, it was Pavel Lukov. But that meant he would have to earn Pavel's trust in return, a realization that brought on a sudden burst of candor.

"Look, here's the truth of it. I came downstairs about an hour ago and spotted you the second I got off the elevator, and, well, I guess I simply couldn't stand the idea of not being able to just take a walk on my own. So I went back upstairs, found a stairwell in the back, and went for a walk and a bite to eat. Okay? I hope I didn't get you in trouble or anything."

"Were there any security cameras near the back door?"

"Yes." He decided not to tell him about almost waving.

Pavel grimaced.

"Then would you mind terribly if I made up something, like, I don't know, that I paid someone to tip me off if you left by the back and then followed you anyway?"

"But what if they check the lobby cameras to see what you were up to?"

He thought about it for a moment.

"Yes, you're right. It's probably better if I say nothing about any of this. Pretend you didn't tell me."

"So you're reporting on all my movements?"

Pavel exhaled loudly, looked down at his feet, then nodded.

"To our best pal?"

"You can say his name. I'm not miked."

"As far as you know, anyway."

Pavel glanced to either side of him, as if momentarily alarmed by the idea. Then they both broke into laughter, and just as quickly went silent because, well, what if he *was* miked? Christ, what a way to live.

"So how 'bout this," Hal offered. "I just ate, but now that it's already afternoon, I wouldn't mind another walk, and maybe after all that coffee you'd like some lunch."

"Yes, that would be good."

"Then let's grab something and take it to some pretty spot, like maybe a park, where we can spread out and just kind of chill for a while. Then we can figure out what to do for the rest of the day."

Pavel, who seemed relieved by the idea, nodded. Without a further word they headed for the door.

Chapter 26

Quint began packing up his keyboard not long after Hal departed. He waited until the vendor Egon cleared out his tip jar before approaching the man to buy his own haluski, which came wrapped with the pages of Hal's dispatch inside. Then he left the alley. Later he would transcribe the dispatch into an encrypted text, which he would send to Lauren, who would, in turn, forward it to Langley.

He had walked about two blocks when his phone rang. Probably one of his bandmates, to badger him yet again about lining up some bookings. Between his trip to Vieques and his busking, which was always a handy way to do some surveillance in a public setting, their calendar was pretty vacant, and his sax player, bass player, and drummer weren't happy about it.

But this was a number he didn't recognize, so he answered warily.

"Yeah?"

An accented male voice spoke in English, "Do you not speak our language?"

Quint replied in Bolrovian.

"Some, but not great."

He was actually pretty fluent, but he didn't want everyone to know that.

"English is fine. I was just curious. Besides, I am mostly interested in your talents as a musician, because I would like to book your band."

"And this is?"

"Dimitri Kolch. I'm proprietor of—"

"Shit, man, everybody knows who Dimitri Kolch is. Is this for a gig at the Green Devil?"

"Yes."

"Well, damn, that would be big for us. Have you heard us before?"

"No, but your trio comes highly recommended from a friend."

"Quartet, actually. Who's the friend?"

"Quartet. Of course. I'll confess that the pay isn't the greatest, but we do encourage tips, and it's good exposure to a lot of people who matter. So, if you think you might be interested . . ."

"Damn right I'm interested. What dates did you have in mind?"

"Well, that's the catch, as you Americans say. This is a little short notice, because we've had a cancellation. Tomorrow night, if you can make it. Two sets. Then on Saturday we're doing karaoke early, but that's usually over by nine or so, so your band could do a set afterward."

"I gotta run this by my mates, but I'm sure they'll jump at it. So unless you hear from me in the next hour, let's say that it's on. Oh, and what's the amount?"

Kolch quoted a number that was higher than Quint expected.

"Sounds good. What time?"

"For tomorrow, do you think you can get started by seven thirty?"

"Sure."

"The real action will be later. There's a big event nearby that will be ending around ten, and I'm guessing we'll get a lot of the spillover afterward."

"Great. And like I said, if this isn't a go, I'll know pretty soon. Otherwise, see you then."

In speaking to Kolch, Quint had been so fired up in his role as band manager that he could barely contain his enthusiasm. The moment he hung up he began wondering about it from his perspective as a spy.

The Green Devil? Really? Their humble quartet could lay down some nice licks, but up to now their biggest booking had been a one-hour slot on the secondary stage at the annual Hops Festival the previous fall. Usually they worked smaller clubs.

Recommended by a friend, Kolch had said, but he had not offered a name, even when asked. Given the Green Devil's clientele, that could mean just about anybody, including someone from the Bolrovian government, an idea that put him on edge, especially if it was someone from the Interior Ministry.

Was his cover blown? Was this a tactic to isolate him, a way to keep an eye on him during the night hours while he helped get a new and important operation underway? It could even be a setup for an easy and very public arrest.

He could still say no, of course. But if word ever got back to his bandmates—and it would, because that's how things worked in Blatsk, which in some ways often felt like a small town—then he would soon be looking for another set of partners. It had taken him months to put his band together, and the four of them hit it off pretty well, even if Daniko, their drummer, wasn't exactly the best.

So yeah, he'd take the gig. But he had better let Lauren know as soon as he'd forwarded Hal Knight's dispatch, because at a joint like the Green Devil even she might walk through the door, and none of them ever liked unwanted surprises.

Chapter 27

———≈———

Something was already going wrong with Sandor Matas. First, he had called to cancel their lunch, saying he'd rather meet instead at a small private art gallery, The Androlux, a place she'd never heard of and wasn't even on the tourist maps. Even for that appointment he had arrived twenty minutes late, and from the moment he came through the door, checking his flanks and glancing over his shoulder, he looked uncomfortable.

"Ah, there you are," he said, spotting her by the front desk, where the solitary attendant sat quietly by a stack of photocopied exhibit catalogs and a poster promoting upcoming events. The current offering of the Androlux was a collection of paintings by asylum seekers and residents of internment camps. The gallery was located several miles from the city center, in a decidedly untrendy neighborhood, and Lauren's cabdriver had nearly gotten lost on the way.

"I hadn't pegged you as a fan of refugee art," Lauren said in greeting.

"I'm not. Nor is anyone I know."

"I see."

The restaurant he had chosen was wildly popular among government types, but the odds of being spotted here by someone in his circles were practically nil. Something had spooked him.

The woman at the desk, who still hadn't said a word, swiveled an open guest book toward them and offered a pen.

"Don't sign that," Matas said.

"I wasn't planning to."

He took one of the catalog sheets, nodded to the woman with a queasy smile, and headed toward the back.

"Let's go in," he said, and with another rearward glance he steered

Lauren through a doorway into a room where the walls were lined with about a dozen paintings. He exhaled deeply and began to relax once it became apparent that the woman up front had left them on their own.

Lauren did a quick survey of the paintings. Most were abstract, but that didn't obscure their disturbing nature, a vivid conveyance of fear, horror, abandonment. The most prevalent tones were blacks and reds, and the one painting rendered in more calming blues and greens turned out to be, on closer inspection, dotted with debris that seemed to represent drowned bodies tossed by an unforgiving sea.

"Before we talk business," Lauren said, "tell me about the big dinner last night, the one with the super-secret special guest. And don't worry, I won't even ask his name."

She spoke in a lowered voice, but the room's high ceiling still made her words almost echo.

"Oh, him? Yes, well. He didn't have much to say, actually. Apparently, he's going to give a show for all of us tomorrow night. Apparently, he's kind of crude and uses slang that a lot of us won't know." Then he paused, as if something had just occurred to him. "Maybe that's why the president has added all those Americans to the guest list."

"Americans? The president said that?"

"Yes. I hoped for a moment he meant people like you. Business guests. But apparently this bunch is more political, part of some special venture. That's a big secret, too, supposedly. But my boss will be going that night instead of me. Just as well."

Matas then folded and unfolded the catalog sheet, as if needing some way to occupy his hands. He glanced toward the door as if worried someone else might walk in, and by then Lauren was also distracted. Because who the hell were these incoming Americans? She had received no word or warning from anyone in Langley about a contingent of visitors from the United States, official or otherwise. And while their presence would certainly not make Hal Knight happy, the bigger problem was the tricky position that she, Quint, Malone, and their whole effort here would be put in. Because, as a rule—by law, in fact—Americans were off limits as intelligence targets for the CIA, even when they were abroad.

There were exceptions, of course, although most of those required the Agency to seek prior approval from the Justice Department, a complication which always risked leaks and delays. Short of that, there were a few ways you could fudge things in your activities and official reports to protect yourself against any wrongdoing, or at least gloss it over.

But that sort of finesse would become exponentially more difficult if these Americans were "more political," as Matas had just said, especially if they were the type who Horvatz was already known to associate with, due to his favorable coverage in American right-wing media—the very sort of people who would loudly scream about the intrusions of the "Deep State" at the slightest whiff of any interest by a U.S. intelligence organization. And if this made Lauren antsy, that would go double for Dickson Fordyce.

"And you say the president didn't mention any names?"

Matas looked up with a start. The catalog sheet slipped from his fingers and oscillated to the floor.

"Pardon? Names, you said?"

"Of these American guests."

"No. No one seems to know who they are. Well, except for Wally Wallek, but he wasn't saying."

He reached down to pick up the sheet.

"Sandor, is something wrong?"

"Yes. Or no, I don't think so. Not yet. But maybe for a while we should, well, keep things a little quieter."

"I'm fine with that. But what makes you say that?"

"Last night, during the cocktail reception." He blew out his cheeks, like he was remembering a bad moment.

"Yes?"

"Three of us were having a perfectly nice chat, and then the security chief, this fellow from Interior, came up to us."

As before, he did not mention Sarič by name.

"I see."

"And, well, you might say that he put us on notice, all of us."

"About what?"

"Our drinking, for one thing, which struck us as rather silly and moralistic. He cautioned us to not imbibe—and that was the word he used, in Bolrovian—to not 'imbibe to excess,' at the risk of 'loosening our tongues' in the presence of the night's special guest. A comedian, no less! A man who tells raunchy jokes! Can you believe it? And then to make it worse he told us that everyone at our level of government would soon undergo a strenuous—also his word—security review. Phone records, banking records, everything. All of us!"

"And that's when you got to feel smart about opening that account in Switzerland."

"Yes, thank god for the Swiss. But, well, it did make me wonder. Maybe I would be better served by . . ." His voice trailed off.

"By what?"

"Well, by sending him a report about these meetings I have had with you. In the interest of full disclosure. And as a matter of state business, of course. Just so there will be no undue suspicion."

Lauren smiled her sweetest smile and said, "I see. Well, if it's full disclosure you want, then I'm afraid I'd also have to oblige him."

"What do you mean?"

"Well, to report these contacts from my end of things. Including our discussion of financial terms."

"Is that level of reporting strictly necessary?"

"Not if yours isn't."

"I see."

There was a long pause. He looked away, and again folded the catalog sheet.

"Look," Lauren continued, "if this security chief is your main worry with regard to your business as a public servant, then how about if we treat our dealings from here on out more as a matter of private and personal business? Nothing official, meaning nothing to report, since we'll be meeting more as friends rather than as client and contractor. As you said yourself, we're not even part of a contractual agreement at this point, even though I hope that will certainly come later."

"Yes. Yes, I like that idea." He actually smiled. "Friends. Of course."

"Platonic friends."

His smile dimmed a bit.

"Are you married?" he asked.

"What does that have to do with anything? Are you?"

Then a look of alarm passed across his features. He lowered his voice.

"Look, you're not, well, working for someone *else* while you're here, are you? Someone other than Ellington, Buncombe, I mean."

Lauren frowned as if deeply disappointed in him.

"Whatever could have possibly given you that idea?"

"I don't know. Maybe because, well . . ." He went a little pale.

"Ellington, Buncombe would fire me immediately if there was even a whiff of that kind of double-dealing. I'm appalled that you'd even jump to a conclusion like that. In fact, given our current arrangement, this probably isn't something we should even speak of in jest, don't you agree?"

"Yes. You are right, of course."

"Good. But let's stay in touch, if only to justify those retainer payments, which my employer—Ellington, Buncombe, and only Ellington, Buncombe—is quite happy to keep making."

Matas nodded quickly, wanting to believe all of it. She named a time and place for them to meet a week later. He again nodded but did not say a word. As they passed by the desk on the way out, Matas slipped the folded catalog sheet into his pocket.

"Is that really a good idea?" Lauren asked.

He frowned, not understanding the question at first, but then his eyes widened and he quickly reached into his pocket before dropping the evidence of his subversive taste in art into a trash can.

They went their separate ways. Lauren, pleased that she'd been able to evade his questions without having to lie—technically, anyway—was wondering which way to go to find a taxi when her phone buzzed. It was Quint.

"Yes?"

"I've gotten an unexpected booking request for our band."

He filled her in on the details. Lauren immediately thought back to that moment when Dimitri Kolch, proprietor of the Green Devil, had seemed to be trying to tell her something. Or not.

"I guess the big question is who this friend of his is."

"Yeah, but Kolch wouldn't say. I'm also about to send you our friend's first dispatch. He delivered it about an hour ago."

"Well, that's good news, at least."

"We'll see if you still think so after you've read it."

"Based on what I've already heard about that dinner, I'm guessing he mentions something about an incoming contingent of Americans."

"He does. This could get tricky. And the timing bothers me. I mean, really bothers me."

"Me, too, considering our employer's current state of disarray here."

"It's almost like a few mice decided to sneak in to play while the cat was away."

"Except that the cat's here."

"But they don't know that."

"Maybe we're overthinking it. This could've been in the works for a while. Either way, let me worry about what we can or can't do. If we need to make any adjustments, I'll let you know. In the meantime, maybe you should worry about why you're suddenly getting such a great gig."

"Is that a comment on our talent?"

"Well, you could use a new drummer."

"Tell me about it."

"How 'bout this? I'll drop by for your first set. That way, if anything bad goes down, I'll be there for you."

"To alert the embassy to my arrest, you mean?"

"Let's hope it doesn't come to that."

"And these Americans?"

"Our friend will probably want to avoid them as much as we do."

"Yeah, but will they want to avoid him?"

"Sounds like a legal loophole to me."

Quint responded with a low rumble of laughter, which told her he was certainly on board with exploiting any loopholes.

"I'll look for you tomorrow night."

"See you there."

Chapter 28

———≋———

Pavel and Hal ended up walking for more than an hour before they bought any food. It was a sunny, pleasant day, so Pavel took him through the oldest and twistiest lanes of the city center. They reached a promenade along the bank of the River Volty, which led by kiosks of artists and booksellers. Hal seemed to enjoy browsing and taking it easy, and Pavel enjoyed Hal's running commentary on the passing scene, punchy remarks laced with wit, curiosity, and even wisdom. He was good company. Jana might even like him, despite the way she'd felt about his movie.

Eventually they reached the green oasis of Labovka Park, the lungs of the city, with six hundred acres of trees, gardens, meadows, and walking paths. Pavel bought a sausage with sharp mustard from a sidewalk vendor, and they each got a foaming cup of pilsner before sitting on a bench with a view of a pond where ducks and turtles were keeping dozens of children entertained.

Pavel, who realized he was famished, bit into the juicy sausage with a sigh, smearing mustard on his cheek. Hal took a deep swallow of beer. Pavel was now comfortable enough with the American to feel like they didn't always have to be making conversation.

At the next bench over, an old man was feeding a few dozen pigeons, tossing pieces of a baguette onto the gravel as the birds fluttered and lunged, strutting in a way that Pavel had always thought made them look pompous. The old fellow wore a faded army coat. On the right sleeve was a fraying blue armband with a double-headed gold eagle.

Hal, nodding toward him, asked, "That patch on his coat, what's it mean?"

"He probably got that at the big reunion of old resistance fighters, quite a few years ago. The ones who fought the Nazis. My Poppy—he's my grandfather—he has one, too, although he put his away in a drawer."

"Your grandfather fought in the resistance?"

"When he was only fourteen. His whole family had been killed, so he ran off to the woods. The Javorska Forest, way up in the north."

"He must have some great old stories."

"None that he ever tells us."

"Ah. Not uncommon. The silence is how you can tell the real ones from the blowhards who are making it all up. How do all those old vets like your boss?"

"Most of them love him. The new nationalism. Bolrovia for Bolrovians and all that."

"What about your Poppy?"

Pavel chuckled.

"Now that is a subject where I wish he *would* remain silent."

Hal laughed along with him, but didn't wish to stray too deeply into the weeds of politics, lest Pavel reveal a side of himself that would ruin the moment. Pavel finished the sausage and tossed the wrapper into a nearby trash can.

"How was that?"

"Excellent. Bolrovian sausage is like a cross between bratwurst and kielbasa. You should try one."

"That and one of those chimney cakes."

"I know just the place. We'll go tomorrow. Or today if you want."

"That haluski filled me up pretty good."

Pavel again wondered about where Hal might have really gone when he'd slipped out the back of the hotel that morning. He had yet to decide if he would report it to Sarič. No sooner had that thought crossed his mind than Hal asked, "This Sarič guy, how well do you know him?"

"Why?"

"Well, he certainly seems to have done a lot of research on me. But it's not like I can really do the same about him, so . . ."

"Mostly what I know is what I hear from others."

"And?"

Pavel shrugged, uncertain as to how much he should reveal. But maybe full disclosure—only to a point, of course—would help keep Hal from doing something that might get them both in trouble.

"Well, for someone who is so enamored of technology and always having the latest gizmos, he is very old-fashioned. Goes to church every week. Two boys and a girl. Believes that his wife shouldn't work. Doesn't smoke. And only drinks when it is required by his job, for official toasts, that kind of thing."

"Yeah, he was sticking to water whenever I saw him last night. Although I could say the same about you."

Pavel blushed.

"With me it was nerves. Sometimes I feel like Sarič is watching me as closely as you. And, well . . ."

"Go on."

"He has a talent for making those who displease him, well, *disappear*. My predecessor, for one. Or so I was told, quite recently." Hal's mouth dropped open, but he didn't reply. Pavel decided maybe he'd gone a bit overboard, even though he'd spoken the truth. "You know, I once saw Sarič out in the wild, so to speak. In this park, in fact, down on the playing fields. I wasn't yet on his radar because I was working for some backbencher."

"But you knew who he was?"

"Oh, everyone knows who Branko Sarič is. His picture is never in the papers or on TV, but people always point him out when he's at some official function so you won't do anything stupid. But this was on a fall afternoon. He was watching his son's football match. Clapping, cheering, the usual. The boys were young, maybe ten years old, and one of them made this remarkable shot—a real laser, like something you'd see from a kid twice his age—but instead of reaching the goal it hit Sarič's poor son in the side of the head."

"Ouch."

"Everyone got very quiet, and his boy came running off the field, crying loudly."

"Uh-oh."

"Yes, I thought the same thing. I have seen so many idiot fathers who would have screamed at him. 'Stop crying! Get your ass back out there!' But Branko was very sweet. He got down on his knees, talked to him softly, gave him a big hug, and then kissed him on the forehead. It was a little unnerving, really."

"Like finding out that Dracula grows orchids."

"Exactly! Which reminds me, I am told he wears a crucifix, although I have not seen it. He must keep it hidden beneath his shirt."

"He should do the same with that stupid water bottle."

They shared a laugh.

"Part of his obsession with purity. It's like a badge for him, especially when he's in a crowd of drinkers."

"Is he also one of those assholes who always has his hand out, asking for more?"

"No. He has his government Mercedes, sure, but that's for the bells and whistles. His command center, he calls it. Money is not his thing. He lives in a modest house, isn't a big spender. His aspirations are different. You've met Wally Wallek, yes?"

"Now there's a fellow who I'll bet knows how to play all the angles." Pavel smiled.

"You read him well. Wally says that Branko's greatest dream is to have a CCTV camera on every corner of Blatsk, like in London, and then eventually nationwide, in every village and on every country lane. So, if he likes, he can choose whoever he wants and monitor them sunrise to sunset, cradle to grave. That's where *his* euros go—not into his pocket but his empire."

They watched the old veteran toss the last of his baguette to the pigeons before rising with some difficulty and strolling away.

"What about you?" Pavel asked. "A believer?"

"Lost my faith ages ago. And certainly nothing has come along since to make me get it back."

Pavel wondered about the ramifications of the latter remark. He had read the story of Hal's well-publicized fall from grace, of course, but hadn't asked him about it, and certainly wouldn't do so now.

"We should go," Pavel said. "I am guessing you may need some extra time to prepare for your show tomorrow night. I can arrange for a rehearsal space, if you want?"

"Prepare? Rehearse? Hell, the kind of routines this crowd, especially your president, will probably want are things I could do in my sleep. With some of this old material, I could stop in the middle of a line and the crowd would finish it for me. It's like comedy comfort food. If he's hoping for new stuff, I'm afraid he'll be out of luck."

"I'm sure that will please him."

"I was thinking that afterward I'd open things up to some questions.

From him, from the crowd. That way, at least I can end it on a fresh note."

"Yes, good."

"Any subjects to avoid, apart from politics? He's pretty plugged in to Western culture, right?"

"Yes and no. Music, for example. Not his thing. Never has been."

"Really? That's pretty much our number-one export. Soul, rock and roll, jazz, R&B."

"Apparently he was not all that into rock and roll when he was young. Not even the Beatles. You could mention five different song titles and he wouldn't know a single one. Oh—and, well . . ."

"What?"

Pavel grimaced, as if it was too embarrassing to say.

"He's not really a fan of anything by black people."

"You're fucking kidding, right?"

"Afraid not."

"Does it ever bother you, working for a guy like that?"

"It really bothers Jana, my wife."

"That wasn't what I asked."

Pavel looked away, then exhaled loudly.

"It was too good of a job to pass up."

"I can see that. Still."

"I know. And the things he says sometimes . . ." Pavel shook his head.

"Well, all of this is good to know. So thanks."

They watched the ducks and children for a while. Then Pavel looked over at Hal, who seemed lost in thought. Pavel wondered what it must be like to endure such a public humiliation, to know that your career was basically over at the age of forty-seven. Small kindnesses probably became more important than ever.

"You know, tomorrow evening before the show, why don't you come over to my house for a home-cooked meal of Bolrovian food. We can go straight to the palace from there."

"All the better to keep me from straying off the leash, huh?" But Hal said it with a grin.

"Of course! And Jana is curious about you, so there's that as well. But maybe you'd rather spend some of your downtime in somebody's home, instead of the hotel. And, well, it would allow me to spend some time at home as well."

"Oh, sure. Sorry. Having to escort me around at all hours must be pretty hard on your home life. Yeah, that would be great."

"Any ideas about tonight? Anywhere in particular you'd like to go?"

"A bar would be nice. One with some character, where we can also get a bite to eat, maybe even hear some music."

"I know just the place."

Chapter 29

———≋———

Shortly after noon Pacific time, Jess Miller strolled into Salt's Cure, a block north of Santa Monica Boulevard, for a business lunch with a longtime friend and her most reliable current patron, who happened to be the same person. Belinda Locke waved to her from a table toward the back.

Belinda had picked the meeting place, saying she wanted to come here for the famous oatmeal cakes, which were indeed pretty wonderful as long as you didn't mind paying seven bucks for a side of bacon or ten for fries. But Jess was grateful her friend had chosen such a popular spot. It was the clearest signal yet that she was being welcomed back into the good graces of People Who Mattered.

They'd known each other since their earliest days out here. Jess was from Raleigh, North Carolina; Belinda from Nashville. Both had sanded the edges off their accents and brought their flexible Sunbelt sensibilities west in their twenties, in hopes of creating the sorts of shows and movies they had grown up watching. Or maybe even something better. They had met while waiting in the order line at a Mexican joint on Pico Boulevard just as workers from the health department swarmed past them to shut the place down for rodent infestation—exactly the sort of bonding experience you'd expect among piecework artists surviving on pizza, ramen, and cheap takeout.

Belinda was now a showrunner for a limited series that had just been green-lighted by HBO for production next spring, her third such project over the past five years. And while she and Jess didn't get together as often as in their leaner days, Belinda had been the first colleague to offer her work in the wake of Hal's disaster. As word of that assignment had seeped out, a second job had followed, and then feelers for others. Jess owed her, and now she felt as if, with this lunch, Belinda was taking the next big step to bring her back out into the open.

The only drawback to working for Belinda was her insistence on exhaustive research, in the interest of what she called "artistic authenticity." For this show, for example, based on a novel about a female pilot in the 1920s, she had insisted that Jess and the other two writers enroll in flying lessons. Whenever she set something in a foreign country, you had to have traveled there yourself within the past few years. If you hadn't, she made you take a refresher tour before she'd let you anywhere near the project.

They hugged in greeting and slid into their sleek chairs, facing each other across the table. It was such a cheerful place, with its blond wood and full sunlight. Not long after they placed their orders, Belinda's words brightened the mood further.

"I was just looking over your latest pages last night. Your work is great, although that's no surprise, so the first thing I wanted to tell you is that you really don't need to stick with the pen name. Unless you want to, of course."

"Oh. Wow! You're sure you're ready to do that? I mean, I know *I* am, but . . ."

"Yes, Jess. I'm certain. I know our initial arrangement was for a pseudonym, but, hey, I think it has now become clear that you were the single best thing about his movies, his work. He failed in spite of your help."

"Hal, you mean."

"Well, of course."

Belinda looked around a bit uncomfortably, and the message was clear. It was one thing to be seen with Jess, quite another to be overheard discussing You-Know-Who.

"I heard from him yesterday."

"Oh, god."

"Yeah. It was a letter. Or an email, but a long one. He was kind of pouring his heart out."

"Glad to know he has one. Sorry. I know you two were close, but still."

"He's overseas." Jess didn't feel like she should reveal where, given the circumstances.

"Good. The further away, the better, don't you think?"

"Sure. But it was weird, his letter."

"Is that really surprising?"

"No. Not that way. More like, well . . . Look, this is something you can't tell anyone, okay? But I have to tell *somebody* because it's so odd that in some ways I think it can't possibly be true."

Their food arrived, but by then Jess had Belinda's full attention. And even though Jess realized she was now on precarious ground, she *had* to talk about it, if only as a means of testing her own reaction, because she was still somewhat amazed by the implications of what Hal had seemed to be trying to tell her.

The moment she'd read that he was in Bolrovia, she remembered the brief stir that had ensued on social media when the country's president, Nikolai Whatshisname, had invited Hal to be his personal guest. Had Hal fallen for that? Apparently so, and Jess had been tempted to stop reading then and there. What a perfect match: a crypto-fascist strongman and a disgraced boorish funnyman—like two thirteen-year-old boys having a sleepover after being expelled for looking up a girl's dress. Maybe they'd find the key to Dad's liquor cabinet or his cache of dirty magazines.

Nonetheless, she had continued reading, even after wincing at his initial allusion to his pathetic need for adulation. From that point she'd fully expected him to begin wallowing in self-pity. Instead, the words of his next paragraph had hooked her in an entirely unexpected way.

I suppose that another reason I am here is that I am pulling a Leo Holloman, so to speak, even though I am doing so only due to a recent case of the creeps. Completely unbidden, I assure you, but it was an invitation earnestly extended, so I am trying to respond in kind, or as earnestly as I know how.

Leo Holloman had been the main backer for the first of Hal's movies. He had also been a major pain in the ass, insisting on showing up on the set nearly every day to make sure things were being done to his exact specifications. He had even barged into a few writers' meetings, making such a pest of himself that Hal and Jess had developed a code, a secret language they could use whenever Holloman was around in order to make edits and production changes without him knowing it. "The way spies do it," Hal had said. Their use of this private code soon carried over into other situations—pitch meetings, press conferences, casting calls—a tactic they both began referring to, only between themselves, as "pulling a Leo Holloman."

Seeing those words pop up in this email told Jess she was about to receive a coded message and also that, for whatever reason, Hal felt he needed to communicate clandestinely. All of which became even clearer when, in the next sentence, he referred to "a recent case of the creeps."

This took her back several years to the time of a joint project in which, for about three weeks, they'd toyed with the idea of writing a spy comedy, in which Hal had decided that all the CIA characters would be referred to as "Creeps." He'd liked the term—his own alternative to spy slang such as "spooks," "snoops," and "secret agents"—so much that they had decided to title the film "A Case of the Creeps." They wrote a treatment, sketched a few lead characters, and roughed out half a dozen scenes before deciding they really didn't know where to take the plot next, or even where the film should be set. So they never pitched it, not to a single soul. The whole thing had then gone into a drawer, and if Jess were to spend a few hours she might even be able to find it.

All of that, plus his reference to an unbidden invitation, earnestly extended, led to an immediate conclusion that Hal had become some sort of spy. She told herself this was crazy. She then decided he was only playing with her, having some fun at her expense. Then she went online, Googled the recent news from Bolrovia, and right away found a few obscure but recent stories about the deportation of several American diplomats from Blatsk on allegations of spying, allegations which a State Department spokesman had vehemently denied.

She read the email again, and this time she was sure of it. When she had awakened this morning, she had felt more certain than ever. And now, here she was with her old friend Belinda, the one person who might understand.

"Tell me, then," Belinda was now saying. "What was so weird about it?"

"Well, you saw all those tweets a few weeks ago about Hal, right? From that leader in Eastern Europe?"

"Oh, god. How could you miss them? In Moldova or something?"

"Bolrovia."

"Right. Yeah, that was a hoot. But, well, I didn't have the heart to say anything about it to you. I knew you must have been, like, mortified."

"I was. And thank you. But, well . . . and *please*—you cannot say a word about this to anyone, okay? I mean, you have to promise me."

Belinda leaned closer.

"Okay. I promise."

"He went over there. He's there now. But that's not even the weird-est part."

Belinda was holding her breath, raptly attentive. Not even the sudden shout of "Oh, for fuck's sake, I ordered it rare!" from a famous director three tables away could divert her attention.

"I have this uncanny feeling that he might even have been invited to go over there to work for . . . Oh, god, this is going to sound *so* nuts."

"For who?"

"The CIA. Or somebody like that."

"No fucking way!" A few heads turned, including the famous direc-tor's. Jess leaned closer and whispered.

"Please! This has to stay secret."

"Sure. Sorry. But he *said* that?"

"No, that's the strangest part. It was sort of in code, like he knew other people might read it."

Then, lowering her voice further, Jess explained the context, the back-ground, and the special language they had once developed for dealing with the intrusive Leo Holloman, plus their aborted idea for a spy film. She also mentioned the recent news items about the deported spies.

In spelling it out like this for her friend, Jess realized how ludicrous it must sound, and for a moment she wondered if Hal had just managed to make her the butt of a colossal practical joke. But Belinda was neither laughing nor frowning. She looked quite serious, and her eyes were wide.

"Wow. I think you might be right." A pause, an incredulous shake of the head. "I think you *are* right."

"And it gets weirder. He then proceeded to invite me over there. To help me in his work, or that's what he implied."

"Oh. My. God. Are you going?"

"Fuck no. That would be insane. And we're finished."

"Oh, Jess, I dunno."

"What do you mean?"

"What do I *mean*? Well, think it through. I mean, like, if what you're saying is true, can you imagine the possibilities of what that must really be like? And you'd be able to witness it firsthand. *While it was happen-ing.* You may never have a greater chance in your professional life for achieving such a deep level of artistic authenticity—and, well, I'd *love* to work with you on whatever you came up with in the aftermath."

Jess's first reaction was to kick herself for not having seen this coming. Material this good would never be allowed to simply sit unused, not in the world that Belinda and Jess lived and worked in. The only surprise was that Belinda had latched on to this aspect of it so quickly.

"No. I couldn't. I mean . . . I just couldn't."

Belinda seemed to realize she'd crossed a line of decorum a little ahead of schedule.

"Of course not." She took Jess's hand. "You're absolutely right. But still . . ."

Belinda couldn't keep a smile from creeping onto her face, and Jess imagined she could see the wheels already turning inside her friend's head.

"Like I said, you cannot breathe a word of this to anyone. I mean, yes, I'm done with him, completely so, but I wouldn't want him to, well, *die* because of something I said or did."

"Oh my god, you think it's that serious?"

"Belinda, *really*? It's not a movie he's making. It's, well . . ." She again lowered her voice to a whisper. "He's a spy. And spies are shot. Or worse."

"Or maybe just expelled. Like those diplomats you mentioned."

"No. We can't risk that. *I* can't risk that."

"Presuming you're right about all this."

"And I might not be. But you cannot tell a soul. I'm serious."

"Of course. But, god, what an opportunity."

"Yes, well."

"But you're right. About the need to keep it quiet. I get that. And, you know, it kind of makes me rethink what I was saying earlier. Because I guess I hadn't realized until just now how raw all this must still be for you. And for a lot of other people, too, probably. So maybe I should trust your instincts more than mine. About going fully public, I mean."

"You mean with the pen name?"

"Yeah. Maybe it's still too soon."

Belinda then glanced around at the other tables, as if she were suddenly considering fleeing the restaurant. But she didn't. Nor did she ask the waiter for the check when he breezed past them a moment later. She instead spread a dollop of molasses cinnamon butter onto her oatcakes, poured a luxurious helping of syrup, and began to eat, chewing slowly and with relish.

That's when Jess added it all up and saw what Belinda had really just done and, worse, what she now needed to do to correct her mistake. Her friend had given notice that, in the transactional economy they both lived and worked in, Jess would need to buy her silence, preferably by cutting her in on this splendidly juicy story and wherever it might lead. Otherwise, Jess felt quite sure that by day's end, or certainly no later than tomorrow, bits and pieces of this story would begin drifting into the public domain, where, under the right circumstances, they might quickly metastasize into something viral.

Poor Hal.

Had Jess really just thought that? She supposed so. And that, too, was due to his email. Because, for all the intrigue and interest he'd stirred with his cryptic references, the item which had sunk its hooks deepest into Jess had been his final little flourish:

P.S. Even though I have almost completely avoided the internet and have cut off all ties to social media, I HAVE been online just enough to read of your recruitment onto a couple of new film projects, and for that I am deeply relieved and grateful. If a visit here would jeopardize any of those in any way, shape, or form, then by all means DO NOT COME.

It hit her hard because, for a change, Hal had showed his regard for someone other than himself, even from the pits of what must be a fairly deep well of misery and humiliation. And now, thanks to her carelessness, Hal's secret—one which might be potent enough to do him great harm—had been set loose into the information marketplace of Hollywood.

So, she then haltingly made what she would later think of as her pitch, an offering she hoped would be sufficient to buy Belinda's silence, even if it meant that Jess would now have to, at the very least, go through the motions of planning a trip to Bolrovia.

"Okay, then, Belinda. How about this? How about if I at least check a few flight schedules. And then, after a day or two, I'll get in touch with Hal to suggest that I might be willing to go over there. If only to try to shake out a little more info from his end."

Belinda put down the next bite of her oatmeal cake and nodded emphatically.

"If I *do* decide to go, then, depending on what Hal is willing to tell me, maybe you and I can start roughing out a treatment. That way, you'd be in on this from the beginning. But not by doing anything reckless, and with the strict understanding that *none* of this can go beyond the two of us until we've moved it further along."

"Ooh. Yes, I like that. All of it."

So that part was taken care of, at least. This gave her about a day to think up what she should say to Hal in her reply, which she would try to send tomorrow night, meaning he probably wouldn't see it until the morning after next. So that was two days of time she would buy for him. In the meantime, as a further delaying tactic, tonight she would look up the available flights and send Belinda a prospective itinerary. All of this would probably be sufficient to hold her at bay for at least three more days. By then, maybe Hal would be safely out of Bolrovia.

If not? She wasn't yet ready to contemplate that possibility. Because she certainly had no intention of actually going there.

Chapter 30

———≋———

Hal liked the Green Devil from the moment he walked in. Maybe it was the hint of woodsmoke in the air, which felt warm and cozy after coming in from what had turned into a fairly chilly night for late September. Maybe it was the immediate sense he got that this was a gathering place for both the powerful and the folks from the neighborhood. In other words, the kind of bar you almost never found in LA, where a joint like this would have been crawling with autograph seekers or people with their phones out, eager to film anyone they even vaguely recognized from a large or small screen.

He also liked its pleasant hubbub of conversation and laughter, which at the moment was being dominated by the voice of a fellow holding court at the end of the bar with a rapt audience of three, all of whom appeared to be local, even though he was speaking English in a British accent. He looked to be about Hal's age, late forties, in a business suit that was impeccably cut, although his tie was loosened. His movements and gestures were those of someone with an easy, graceful confidence in a crowd. You might even have called him dashing, and he spoke in the rhythms and cadences of the seasoned raconteur. Hal eased closer to listen in.

"So, the East India Company, you see. That would be the perfect model for achieving world peace today." He said it while swinging his full beer glass in a wide arc for emphasis, as if to encompass the globe, yet without spilling a drop. "Private armies, that's the way to do it, each of them representing the common interests of all the major multinationals. That way, your cause extends beyond borders, beyond cultures, beyond color or religion or any of the nationalistic shit that usually divides us."

"Hear, hear!" said one of the locals, clanking his glass to the speaker's.

Pavel sidled up on Hal's right.

"What would you like to drink?"

Hal was on the verge of asking for a dirty martini, then decided that was a pose he would gladly discard—a bygone part of his island phase, as he already thought of his time on Vieques.

"You're the local. Pick something."

"A beer, then?"

"Sure."

Pavel then frowned and reached into his pocket for a rather odd-looking phone, one which Hal hadn't yet noticed him using. It was buzzing vigorously.

"Sorry. I have to take this."

Pavel headed for the relative peace and quiet of the outdoors. Hal was perfectly fine with being left untethered for a few moments. It was even a relief. He liked the man, but he liked freedom even better. He again tuned in to the vocal Brit, who was still talking up his Big Idea.

"And I don't care if it's paid for with dollars, euros, yen, yuan, or even crypto. That part will take care of itself. Just give me the common value and we'll take it from there. As long as every country, or at least every important leader, gets a piece of the action, then no one will be able to knock it off course."

It was a wacky idea and deeply flawed, but Hal certainly enjoyed the delivery, the presentation. The fellow was a born salesman. Then the man's eyes alighted on Hal and the brightness of his gaze increased by a few hundred lumens.

"Hey, I know you!"

Hal's heart sank. Another public unveiling. Then the jokes would begin, the mob would gather. His stomach curled into a protective knot, like a small furry animal preparing to be seized and devoured.

"You're the, uh . . ."

Hal readied himself for a rapid retreat.

". . . the guy who's the next big thing over at the palace, right? Hal Knight? Welcome, man. Welcome. What's your poison? As you can see, I'm buying."

"How 'bout a beer?"

"Perfect choice, old son. The local pils. You know, the first time I ever came to this country—and this was ages ago, maybe a decade after the

Iron Curtain came down—I was driving out in the country at dusk and saw all these students walking home from the fields with their empty lunch buckets at their sides. They'd been picking hops, doing their duty for the local farmers so Bolrovia could make one of its finest exports. Like something medieval but also very communal. It was beautiful, man."

He then turned toward the bartender, who was already smiling at the man's story, towel on his shoulder. The bartender turned toward Hal.

"Don't listen to a word he says about our beers. He's from the UK, where they think beer is supposed to be the temperature of piss."

"Well, yes, Kika, but this fellow is from America, where they think beer should be as cold as the balls on a warlock. So how 'bout if you fill up a half liter of pils for Mr. Hal Knight, soon to be the toast of the town."

Oh, dear. Hal wasn't sure he liked the sound of that. Then, as if reading his uncertainty, the fellow leaned closer on his bar stool and lowered his voice.

"Or maybe just the toast of this little corner of the Green Devil, if that's your preference."

"Yes. A lower profile would be nice."

"Certainly," he said, lightly touching his shoulder and then handing him a large glass of beer, which seemed to have materialized from nowhere. "However you want it, my friend. Discretion is a smart byword around here, especially lately. So don't mind an old loudmouth like me."

"What's your game here?" Hal asked, because with skills like his, surely he was in town for some kind of hustle, legal or otherwise. "Or just your name, maybe, if discretion is still on the menu."

"Farkas, Ian Farkas. But, yes, I do have a game. Here." He produced a business card from the palm of his hand as magically as he had produced the beer. Hal read the words aloud.

"'International Security Consultant.' No wonder you're an admirer of the East India Company and its private army. Are you here to raise one yourself?"

Farkas laughed amiably.

"I don't raise them. I just find clients for them. And this little town, believe it or not, has become quite the crossing point for, well, people who might be in the market for that sort of thing."

"Multinationals?"

"And countries that don't want to dirty their name by sending in the flag. Privatizing is a growth industry in their world. I suspect you may not wholly approve of that."

"Doesn't matter anymore what I approve of."

"Yes, well. The less said about all of that, the better."

"My sentiments exactly."

"So are you here on your own, or part of the vanguard?"

"The vanguard?"

"Of all those Americans people are talking about."

Interesting that this fellow had already plugged in to that. It made Hal wonder why his CIA pals hadn't forewarned him. Or maybe they hadn't known, which would be a little unsettling.

"Definitely not part of the vanguard. In fact, I know nothing about them, including who they are, why they're coming, or even *when* they're coming."

"Oh, but they're here! In this bar, I mean. Two of them, anyway. That's why I was wondering if all of you might be traveling together."

Farkas had nodded toward the far corner as he'd delivered that news, but Hal didn't really want to look in their direction. Because if he saw them, they might see him, and he wasn't yet ready for that.

"I suspect you'll know their faces as easily as they'll know yours," he said, tuning in immediately to Hal's biggest worry. "No idea who the rest of them will be."

"In that case, maybe you could save me the trouble of looking."

"Well, Baxter Frederickson, for one."

"*That* asshole?"

Farkas grinned.

"Obviously, opinions vary, especially at the palace, where I'm told he's a longtime favorite. But, yes, *that* asshole."

Hal couldn't resist a quick glance, and he recognized the man right away. Baxter Frederickson was a TV pundit whose specialty was rousing the masses, the more ignorant the better. His viewership was alarmingly large—the "Baxterites," so called for their loyalty and their daily feeding frenzies on his chum of half-truths, distortions, and outright lies. Or that was Hal's view, anyway.

"So is he here on his own dime, or did Fox send him?"

Farkas did a double take.

"Oh, my. Is that a serious question?"

"Did I say something wrong?"

"Are you really not aware of their little parting of the ways? All that fallout from some lawsuit, and now his new media venture, his piratical act of defiance?"

"Seriously? Fox fired him?"

"You *are* out of the loop."

"Only for the past two months because, well, you know the story. But, yeah, I disconnected from just about everything. TV, social media, all of it."

"Two months is practically a decade by previous standards of the news cycle, old son. Entire trends have come and gone since you slipped into radio silence. Radio silence—now there's a quaint term you'll never find on TikTok. But, yes, Frederickson and Fox parted ways about three weeks ago. And now he's the standard-bearer for Wolf, another beast altogether."

"Wolf?"

"Frederickson's answer to Fox. His very own network, populated by other defectors and renegades. They've taken the Baxterites with them, and their hope is that Wolf will become an even fiercer and nimbler beast of prey than Fox. If early ratings are any indicator—which, as we both know, is the only indicator advertisers care about—it's working."

"Great. Just what the world needs. Who's with him?"

"That anorexic blonde who used to work in the White House. She does commentary now. Supposedly she and Baxter are kind of an item."

"Katie Carlin?"

"Yes, that's the name."

"Nutjob. Why are they even here?"

"The prevailing wisdom is that they're setting up another overseas P-PAC convention, like the one they did with Orbán in Hungary, complete with seminars like 'Western Civilization Under Siege' and 'Trust in God, Not in George Soros.'"

P-PAC was the Patriot Political Action Committee. It had contributed heavily to Hal's campaign opponent, but some of its standard-bearers had also cheered rather loudly while watching video clips of his meltdown tirade—*for* Hal, not against him. Hardly surprising.

"Sounds pretty boring," Hal said.

"Indeed it does. Which is why everyone thinks they're really here for something else. Because supposedly they've come with money to burn, and not just for buying a few rounds at the Green Devil."

"Where do you hear all this shit?"

Farkas laughed into his drink, and, in lieu of a reply, took another swallow. Hal had nearly finished his first round and now needed to pee. He checked to see if Pavel had returned, then set his empty glass on the bar and turned back toward Farkas.

"Need a quick trip to the gents', as your people say. Tell Kika I'd like a refill, and it's my round this time." He held out a credit card, but Farkas waved it away.

"Nonsense. But in compensation, perhaps you could wander past our illustrious visitors on the way to the loo. Maybe you'll pick up a thread I can use."

"Or maybe I'd rather step on a rattlesnake."

Hal set off for the men's room. But the room was now more crowded than when he'd come in, forcing him further right, which took him closer to where the Americans stood chatting with a few locals. Then, as if the whole thing had been choreographed by Farkas, he was pushed further in their direction by a waiter making his way toward the bar from the kitchen with a tray of food. And at that point Hal *did* hear a stray line, partly because it was uttered by Katie Carlin, whose voice emanated at a pitch and frequency engineered to be heard over almost any level of commotion.

"Well, considering the amount we're kicking in, a tour is the least they can do for us."

Hal glanced in her direction just as she turned to scan the room, so he abruptly turned his head to avoid being seen. He certainly didn't want to engage either Katie Carlin or Baxter Frederickson in conversation. Being recognized by them at tomorrow night's show was going to be bad enough. If they saw him here, they might make some dumb post about it on social media, or even snap his picture. He kept his head down until he reached the back room, where the crowd was sparser.

Then, just ahead, emerging from the door of the men's room, Hal spotted another American who he also recognized right away, a big fellow who was still zipping his trousers as he walked toward the bar. He was not a TV personality or pundit, and Hal doubted that most Bolrovians would recognize him. But for anyone who had anything to do with American politics—even a congressman who had barely managed six months in office—he was instantly familiar.

It was Reece Newsome, the political consultant. Pale, pasty, slovenly, and unshaven, a malleable blob of flesh shaped mostly by the cut of a very fine suit which seemed to have been built to contain rather than clothe him. On television he had always looked equally disheveled, but somehow the cameras had also made him look more powerfully built. In person, the greater impression was one of softness. In fact, had he looked any softer, you could have spread him onto a sandwich, one which you would have immediately tossed in the trash.

Fortunately, Hal managed to avoid his somewhat drunken gaze. Grateful for having run the gauntlet without recognition, Hal now needed more badly than ever to pee. But he was already wondering if his luck would hold out on his return trip to the bar.

Chapter 31

Pavel, still out on the street in the night chill, was finally nearing the end of his call from Branko Sarič, who had phoned to demand his daily report on Hal Knight, which he'd wanted here and now even though Pavel had already explained that the day was still in progress and that they had just entered the Green Devil.

"Keep him out of trouble there. And if he starts telling jokes about the president, I want to know immediately, no matter what the hour."

"He's been very respectful throughout the day."

"Make sure he continues to do so."

Pavel had already decided that he would not mention Hal getting loose from him for an hour or so that morning, and he quickly brought up the subject of the invitation he'd extended to Hal for dinner at his home tomorrow evening.

"Good. Smart move, Lukov."

Yes, especially if that black box was empowered to do more than intercept his wireless signals. Or maybe there was more hardware stashed away in some other nook or cranny.

After listening to Pavel's heavily sanitized rehash of their long conversation in Labovka Park, Sarič interrupted with a request.

"I am glad to hear you are growing closer, because I need you to ask him about a few things. The first is a man named Leo Holloman. He was a financial backer for some of Knight's films. Find a way to bring him up in the conversation, to see what he says."

"How?"

"Say that you read about him on the internet. I don't care how, but pay close attention to his answer, even if it does not seem important. Find out what this man Holloman means to him."

"Okay." He already felt uncomfortable about the whole idea.

"Two, at some point, I need for you to use the phrase 'a case of the creeps.' Tell him you are still learning American slang and want to know if you are using it correctly."

"This is all going to be very awkward."

"I don't care. This is important information. You don't need to know why, but you *must* ask these things, even if it makes you feel stupid. Do you understand?"

Sarič then circled back to the first part of Pavel's report.

"So you say he did not even emerge from his room until early afternoon?"

Oh, shit. Did Sarič know? Had he posted someone else at the hotel to check up on his work?

"Yes. That is what I said."

"I would like you to make sure that is not the case for him two days from now. Not tomorrow morning, but the day after. He needs to be out of his room between the hours of ten and eleven a.m. Can you manage that?"

"I guess I could invite him somewhere."

"Make sure that you do."

So they were going to search his room, then. Or maybe adjust some device that wasn't working properly. It all felt so tawdry and unbecoming. He felt embarrassed for his country.

"Sure. Okay."

Now he needed a beer, so it was a relief to step back into the warm bar, although he experienced a brief moment of panic when he was unable to locate Hal right away. Then he spotted the man toward the back of the main room, where he appeared to have been cornered by a thin, bleached-blond woman who was practically spilling out the front of a silky gold blouse, mostly because she had undone the top three buttons. Behind her, a tall and fairly handsome fellow, who looked instantly familiar even though his name didn't immediately come to mind, seemed to be eyeing Hal and the woman with some irritation, as if he might be a bit jealous.

Pavel decided he'd better get over there before ordering a beer, in case preemptive action was needed, so he pushed through the crowd. Fortunately, Hal seemed relieved to see him.

"Ah, Pavel. This is a, um, media personality from the United States, Katie Carlin, who, well, I know you used to be with Fox, but . . ."

"Wolf," she said. "Wolf News. I'm a commentator. I also used to work in the White House."

"Pavel Lukov," he said, nodding.

"Pavel is chief administrative aide to President Horvatz," Hal said, which impressed her so much that she edged away from Hal to turn her full focus on him, a move that released a gust of perfume that nearly floored him.

"And I'm Baxter Frederickson." It was the tall fellow. Pavel instantly recognized the name, mostly because he had helped arrange several remote television interviews of the president by working with one of Frederickson's producers.

Frederickson slipped an arm around Carlin's thin shoulders, as if to reclaim possession of her from Hal, which told Pavel he had made the right move by coming at once. Although Hal, if anything, looked relieved to have been cut loose.

Then a bloated fellow badly in need of a shave, also speaking English in an American accent, loomed up on Frederickson's right and began speaking into the taller man's ear, which altered the dynamic of the group enough to further lower the tension.

Hal, who didn't look the least bit eager to say hello to the new arrival, or even acknowledge his existence, instead turned away so that he was again facing Carlin. He seemed to be at a loss for words, so Pavel picked up the slack.

"Will you be at the show tomorrow night?" he asked Carlin.

"Oh, we wouldn't miss it. Wally invited us."

"Ah. Of course. Politics are more in his line than mine. I'm afraid I haven't been involved with any of the logistics for your visit."

"Probably because it's top secret," she said, in a very chirpy way, but with enough of an edge to make it feel like more than a joke.

"Really?" Hal said, perking up considerably.

"Well, the headliner will be the P-PAC convention, which we're setting up for next May. But that's a no-brainer. We're obviously birds of a feather with this administration. Brothers in arms and all that."

"Of course," Hal said. "And the rest?"

She placed a hand on his chest and eased closer, breathing her answer into his face in what she probably thought was a confidential tone, although it was still loud enough for Pavel to overhear.

"Even if you were *extremely* nice to me, I doubt I'd tell you that. Besides, we've already been warned about you."

"Warned?"

"By Branko Sarič, who I gather isn't much of a fan."

"So I've gathered as well."

"Not that you should worry much. Seems to think mostly you're a bit of a bore. Drinking beer in the park and visiting food carts."

Hal seemed taken aback, and Pavel was as well. How had Sarič already known that, since Pavel hadn't reported it until a moment ago.

"But he did say we should avoid you. So here I am, of course, a known connoisseur of forbidden fruit. Although our little contingent *is* hoping to keep a low profile here. And I'm guessing you're hoping for the same, right?"

"Yes, as a matter of fact."

"Good. No pictures, then, right?"

"Deal."

"Nice to know we already have some common ground." She eased closer again. "And since we're keeping things so private, maybe if you *are* nicer, I'll be able to share more about what we're up to."

"Ah, well." Hal looked uneasy. "There's always a price, isn't there?"

Carlin frowned, as if wondering if it was a joke, although she eventually decided to laugh. Hal nodded toward the bar.

"Well, it's been a pleasure, Katie. And very stimulating. But I have another round awaiting me at the bar." Then, turning to Pavel, "And let's get you one as well."

He pointedly did not offer to do the same for Carlin. Instead he took Pavel's elbow and steered him through a thicket of new arrivals toward the bar. Once they were out of earshot of the Americans, he spoke into Pavel's ear.

"You know, this is a great place, but some of the company's not really to my liking, so maybe we should make a night of it."

"Yes, I agree."

They bypassed the bar and headed out into the night.

Chapter 32

Next morning, earlier than he would have liked, the trim, tanned American staying in the cheaper hotel took a call from overseas. Same person that he had talked to before, and his caller got straight to the point.

"That complication we talked about? It's reached a new level. He has already made contact with at least three of our people."

"What do you mean by 'contact'?"

"Visual and aural."

"Well, hell, sure he has. And you know what? Six of them have been invited to some show he's giving tonight. So that's going to be further 'visual and aural' contact, and our people might even be the ones to instigate it. He's famous. Or infamous, anyway. Not much we can do about it unless you want to issue some sort of 'off-limits' policy."

"Hell, tell these people not to do something and it's the first thing they'll want to try before breakfast. Who made the decision to invite them to this show of his?"

"The man himself. It didn't come from the security side; you can be damn sure of that. Our contact is as antsy about the possibility of cross-pollination as you are. But short of me escorting them personally, there isn't a hell of a lot we can do. Not until this silly-ass command performance is over and done."

"Then maybe keep a closer eye on him in the meantime. You said you know his hotel, right?"

"The Esplanade. It's where they're all staying."

"There you go. He probably hasn't even gotten out of bed."

"Our contact already has someone on him."

"And we've seen how well that's working. Humor me."

"I can give it a few hours, tops."

"Fine, then. It's just . . ."

"What?"

"This . . . cross-pollination, as you called it. What if it, I dunno, creates some kind of hybrid?"

The answer was obvious, but maybe it would be useful to spell it out for him, because far too often people like him didn't even want to know.

"Well, if what we get is a bed of roses, then we just stand back, take a photo, and admire the beauty. If, on the other hand, we get some kind of noxious weed . . ." He let the words hang for a second. "That's what herbicide is for. And last I checked, there's no EPA here to tell me what I can and can't spray. Feel better now?"

"As long as you use it judiciously."

"I'll use as much as the job needs."

"Maybe it won't come to that."

"And maybe it will. Which is why you tasked me with—how did you put it before?—'a full range of options.'"

"No need to repeat my words back at me, as if you're keeping some sort of record."

"You know that's not how I work. But if you really want to help, it's not like you're without resources here, given where you're sitting every day."

His caller responded icily.

"The less said about my current vantage point, the better. The whole reason I hired you is to keep everything outside."

"Point taken."

They hung up without a further word.

Chapter 33

Hal decided while drinking his room service coffee that he would deliver his next dispatch while in the company of Pavel Lukov, even though he was now more nervous than ever about the first delivery. Katie Carlin's throwaway remark about Sarič mentioning food carts had made him wonder if Pavel was his only minder. Maybe a second one was lurking even deeper in the shadows. Or maybe Hal had become one of those moving dots on the tracking screen in Sarič's Mercedes.

If so, then having Pavel along might actually discourage the need for a second set of eyes. And now that Hal was better acquainted with the lay of the land at the drop site, he figured it would be easy enough to distract Pavel long enough to make a second delivery.

He had written the dispatch the night before, four pages front and back with details of the Americans he'd met, including Katie Carlin's cryptic remark about a bigger project secretly in the works. Maybe she was blowing smoke—it wouldn't be the first time, based on what Hal remembered of her performances in the White House press room—but he figured it was worth passing along, especially since the highest levels of the Bolrovian government seemed to be involved.

The morning's down note was that Jess still hadn't answered his email. He had considered writing her again, if only to withdraw his ill-advised invitation, but had decided that one security breach was quite enough.

Pavel, having learned his lesson the day before after spending a ridiculous amount of money on hotel coffee, was waiting downstairs at an empty table in the lobby.

"Ah. My personal escort, waiting patiently as always."

"Good morning, Hal. Are we still on for this evening? Jana is quite excited to be having you as our guest."

"Yes. Looking forward to it."

"Where to now? It's a little early for a museum, but maybe if we have a coffee first?"

"Sure. Any place you'd recommend for afterward?"

"A lot of Americans seem to like the House of Terror."

"The House of *what?*"

"Terror."

Hal could guess easily what that was all about, but the image that flashed in his mind was of those cells in the basement of the Interior Ministry.

"Do they actually charge you for that experience?"

"It's about our history under Hitler, then the Soviets. But it ends in victory, of course."

"Of course."

"I can tell you're not interested."

"Or maybe I'm just wondering why they think the terror ended in, what, 1990?"

Pavel looked around nervously.

"It's okay, Pavel, you're not miked."

The young man broke into a smile.

"Okay, then. No terror. Maybe just food and a walk and, later, the National Museum, yes?"

"Or even a beer."

They headed out to find coffee for Pavel. Then they began to wander.

An hour later they crossed the River Volty into a charming gallery district, where Hal resisted the urge to buy a hand-painted ceramic inkwell for Jess, mostly because he knew it would end up on his own desk after she sent it back to him. He then decided it was time to deliver his dispatch.

"You know, there's this great alley of food carts where I got the haluski yesterday, right off the main square, and I was thinking we might go back there for lunch."

"Oh, yes. Near the palace. I can see it out my office window."

"Really?"

"Yes. Whenever I look, it makes me hungry, so I try not to look too often."

The idea that his mail drops were so readily visible from the palace made him wonder why his handlers had picked it. The more he learned about this job, the more it felt like a rush job.

On the way there, Pavel cleared his throat, as if he were about to say something awkward, or rehearsed.

"I did some reading online last night about your career."

"Nothing that included reviews, I hope."

"What? No." He cleared his throat again. "One of the stories mentioned one of your early backers. Leo Holloman? It made me wonder how you were able to find people like that, and what made him so special?"

Hal had to withhold a laugh. But he was glad for the question. Even though it meant Sarič's people were definitely reading his emails, it also meant they must be stumped, so they'd asked Pavel to inquire on their behalf. Good. He'd send them down a few blind alleys.

"Ah, you really *have* been digging deeper. Well, Leo's a producer. Without his backing, I never would have made a single movie. A lot of people think he's an asshole, a controlling son of a bitch. But it's his generosity that always comes to mind for me, because deep down that's what Leo is all about. Being generous."

He glanced over at Pavel, who was nodding, listening carefully.

"In fact, sometimes, when I'm feeling especially magnanimous—do you know this word, 'magnanimous'?"

"Uh, sort of."

"It means generous, or even forgiving. So, anyway, whenever I feel that way, I might say to a friend of mine that we should 'pull a Leo Holloman,' meaning do a favor for someone. Like the one I'm doing for your president by putting on a show. I'm pulling a Leo Holloman. Sounds dumb, I guess, but . . . well."

"No, no. It makes perfect sense. Thanks."

"Anytime."

A few blocks later, while crossing the main square, Pavel got to the next item on what must have been Branko Sarič's checklist for that morning.

"Spending time with you really helps with my slang, but there's a phrase I heard last night in the bar from one of those Americans that I wasn't familiar with."

"Try me."

"'A case of the creeps.'"

Hal didn't even try to hide his amusement this time. Pavel was a worse spy than him, probably because his heart wasn't in it. Or maybe he was just a bad liar, which certainly wasn't a strike against him, although it made Hal wonder how long the young man would last in his current job.

"Well, I can't answer for whoever you heard saying it last night, but that's what I always say when I'm starting to get cold feet about something."

"Cold feet?"

"Reluctance. I had a little bit of that just before I came to Blatsk. You know, by wondering if I was really doing the right thing."

"Sure. And how do you feel now?"

"Like I'm having a lot more fun than I thought I would. Even now, in talking to you."

Pavel frowned, as if knowing he'd been played. A bad liar, yes, but certainly not stupid.

"Sorry," Pavel said, "but he asked me to ask you. I don't even know why."

"Because he's been reading my emails to my girlfriend, that's why."

Or ex-girlfriend. And it was only one email, which she hadn't even answered. And suddenly it wasn't such a fun day anymore.

When they reached the alley, Hal saw that Chris was again busking with his keyboard over to the left. At the moment he was emulating the sound of a Hammond B3 while laying down a pretty great rendition of "Green Onions." Pavel detoured over to drop a few coins into Chris's tip jar. Hal lagged behind, uncomfortable with their proximity.

"What's the matter?" Pavel asked. "You don't like his music? He's good, don't you think?"

Hal checked Pavel's face for any sign that he knew more than he was letting on. A moment ago Pavel had seemed like such a hopeless dissembler. Now Hal wondered if *he* was the one being played.

"Yes. He's quite good."

Pavel's attention was then diverted by a vendor, the old guy who sold chimney cakes.

"Young Pavel! I have news for you!"

"Be right back," Pavel said, which conveniently allowed Hal to slip away to the haluski cart with its yellow umbrella, where the vendor had already spotted him and was waiting expectantly.

"Welcome back, sir. How hungry are you today?"

"Oh, hungry enough for four! But just one, please."

"Certainly, sir."

Hal dropped his little bundle of secrets into the tip jar, then waited for the vendor to wrap the haluski, which he dropped into a plastic bag. When Hal turned around, he saw with relief that Pavel was still in conversation with the guy selling chimney cakes. Nor did anyone else seem to be watching.

Chapter 34

———≈———

Old Rudi lowered his voice.

He had begun their conversation, as he often did, by asking after Pavel's father and grandfather. Now he was telling Pavel what he had learned about the big fellow they had seen the other day with Branko Sarič.

"I have seen him twice more. Both times coming from the back of the palace. No one claims to know him, but everyone seems to think he is American, and both times he was gone quickly, like a cloud of mist."

"He might be part of this visiting contingent that Wally is handling. It seems to be mostly TV stars. Newspeople."

Rudi shrugged.

"I don't know so much about American TV stars. Except for your friend, of course." He nodded toward Hal. "And even with him, it is only because of my grandson. Thank you again for the autograph. Kirov was very happy."

"Would you like me to introduce you?"

"No, no." He waved his tongs as if to ward off that possibility.

"I'm sure he wouldn't mind."

"No."

"What's wrong?"

"Your friend. He tips that filthy foreigner."

"What?"

"Yesterday, he put money in stupid Egon's tip jar, and today, just now, he did it again!"

"Maybe he likes haluski."

"And maybe he is an overspending Hollywood show-off. It's not just coins, it's a bill! With euros that means it is at least a fiver, and he is only buying a wrap, which costs ten. What kind of idiot tips fifty percent?"

Maybe he's just pulling a Leo Holloman, Pavel thought, which made him blush anew over having asked his idiotic questions. Then Old Rudi went quiet and forced a weak smile, because Hal had just arrived, holding his bag of haluski. Pavel decided to introduce them anyway.

"Pleasure to meet you, sir," Hal said. "And I have to say, those chimney cakes look delicious."

"They are," Pavel said. "I've been eating them since I was old enough to walk."

"What's the best way to get them?"

"With cinnamon sugar. No contest."

"Then that's what I'll have."

Rudi, who'd maintained a sullen silence up to then, quickly got to work. He brushed a final coating of butter onto one of the cakes and sprinkled on more cinnamon sugar. After one last rotation above the spit, he removed the rod from its holder and slid the pastry onto a paper plate.

"Four euro," he said, handing the pastry to Hal.

Hal paid with a five-euro note, which Rudi accepted and then held aloft, hesitating, as if uncertain whether to hand back a euro coin in change. He glanced at Hal, and then at Pavel, until Hal, finally sensing what was afoot, spoke in a rush.

"Oh. Keep it! And thank you."

Rudi couldn't hide his scowl. Fortunately Hal had already turned away. The old man grumbled quietly in Bolrovian, although Pavel heard it clearly enough.

"You see? For me, only twenty percent."

"Twenty-five, Rudi. Twenty-five."

Then Rudi's eyes lit up as he spotted something over Pavel's shoulder. He spoke in a rushed whisper.

"There's your man again! The big American!"

Pavel turned. It was indeed the same fellow as before, on the move halfway down the alley before disappearing into a narrow passage that practically no one ever used.

"You see?" Rudi said, snapping his fingers. "Gone. Like mist."

His wasn't the only vanishing act. Pavel now noticed that the musician, the black man who'd been playing "Green Onions," had also disappeared, although his keyboard and tip jar were still in place, looking abandoned and unguarded.

Hal, thanks to his chimney cake, seemed oblivious to all these comings and goings. He chewed slowly with a look of deep satisfaction while flakes of pastry fluttered to the ground like cinders from a fire.

Chapter 35

Lauren had just received a text confirming the completion of a bank deposit when Quint called for a second time in as many days. This is how it always seemed to go when you hurried an op into existence. You ended up dealing with one complication after another.

At least the deposit had gone through—a tidy sum into the Zurich account of Sandor Matas, to set the hook more deeply. She was out walking as she answered, so she kept moving to thwart any possible eavesdroppers.

"Yes?"

"I've just seen a ghost."

"Did it have a name?"

"Skip Kretzer. Used to be with us. I did a training session with him maybe six years ago, me and about a dozen others. Heard he went private a couple years ago. Contract employer, but we're not always the client."

"Think he's working for the American mystery guests?"

"Could be. But about five minutes ago he was taking a long, hard look at our boy as he made his mail drop."

"Shit."

"Yeah."

"Do you think he figured it out?"

"Hard to say. The drop looked pretty smooth to me, but I'm biased."

"We knew that location was risky when we set it up, and that Egon was a little green."

"Fucking Leo Garvin. Half the people I worked with have either been locked up or have gone into hiding."

"This Kretzer, how long had he been following our guy?"

"Hard to say. After the drop he took off in another direction. I decided to shadow him a while, but I could only stay with it a few blocks. Didn't want to risk drawing his attention and, well . . ."

"Yes?"

"Couldn't leave my keyboard unguarded. Not with our big gig coming up tonight."

"Understood. What else do you know about him?"

"The quiet type. Likes sticking to the shadows, but happy to get physical when needed."

"Who used to run him from our shop?"

"Latin American desk. Phil Lacey, I think."

"Who now heads the Central Europe desk, right down the hall from Fordyce."

"Anything more you want me to do about him?"

"That would probably be Malone's department. You sure he didn't make you?"

"Hell, he barely noticed me even in that class we had. Only time he ever said a word to me was some crack about how I better be ready to swat a lot of flies in Zambia."

"Charming. If you see him again, try to get a picture."

"Got one today. I'll send it. Oh, and I just transcribed our friend's latest. Our boss is going to flip out."

"That bad?"

"Those mystery guests are already here, and our boy met them face-to-face. He cites three of them by name. Names you'll know. Exactly the kind of people who could get us into some really deep trouble."

"Shit."

"Yeah."

"Thanks. Good work. See you tonight."

She paused and waited for the photo to arrive. She'd also need to take a careful look at Hal's new dispatch before forwarding it to Langley. Just as she'd expected, Dickson Fordyce had reacted with disapproval even to Hal's vague references to the unnamed American visitors in his first report. Fordyce had responded with a brief, testy email overnight, which she'd opened while taking her first sip of coffee.

If you'd like for all of us to be hauled before the Attorney General and, in doing so, place the balls of the Director of Intelligence firmly between the AG's teeth, then please have our client continue on his current path into harm's way. Or, alternately, shorten his leash.

Was Fordyce overreacting? Of course. Did that matter? Hard to say. The photo of Kretzer arrived.

He was a big fellow with a nice suit, suggesting he wasn't just here to deal with street-level contacts. And he certainly stood out as American, even though Lauren couldn't have told you precisely why. After enough years working overseas, it was a skill you acquired, spotting nationality by appearance alone. It wasn't foolproof, but it was accurate often enough to tell her when someone wasn't even trying to blend in with the locals. If Kretzer had been here to do that, or to tail Hal full-time, he would have looked and dressed differently.

Skip Kretzer. The name wasn't familiar, but the face was, vaguely. Perhaps she had seen him in the hallways of Langley wearing a green security badge, the color they handed out to the privateers. If he was here on a contract job, she supposed he might even be freelancing for the Bolrovians. Then she read Hal's dispatch and was somewhat appalled by the high profile of the visitors. They'd certainly be the type to complain loudly and publicly at the first hint of CIA scrutiny. And if Kretzer was part of their contingent, he'd probably sniff out Hal's secret role before they would.

She debated whether to pass along Kretzer's name to Fordyce, who would be in enough of a tizzy about Hal's interest in the other Americans. Nonetheless, she was intrigued by Hal's report, especially the tantalizing bit about how the visitors seemed to be cooperating on some secret venture with the Bolrovians.

Shorten his leash? Lauren's inclination was to unclip it and let Hal run. Toward that end, she decided to hold off on forwarding his latest dispatch for as long as possible, preferably after midnight tonight. With any luck, Fordyce would put in his usual nine-to-five and, even with the time difference, wouldn't see it until tomorrow morning. By then, maybe Hal would have found out something with a solid enough link to Bolrovian misbehavior to justify it as a legitimate line of inquiry. She would also tell Fordyce about Kretzer. Yes, it would upset him, but the man was a potential danger to their operative, and maybe Fordyce could actually do something to help.

There was also the matter of Quint's scheduled show tonight. It was shaping up to be a tricky evening, with the potential convergence of a lot of interested parties. She decided to get to the Green Devil early for the best possible seat.

Chapter 36

Hal returned to the Esplanade around four p.m., in need of a shower and some downtime before dinner at Pavel's and the big evening at the palace. After spending most of the previous two months alone, he was a little surprised at how exhausting it was to constantly be in someone else's company.

The first thing he did after reaching his room was to check his email. Still no answer from Jess.

Not a surprise, really, but he had made the mistake of allowing himself to hope. He reached for the complimentary bottle of water that he'd opened that morning after drinking his coffee and took a few more swallows.

He then paused before shutting his laptop. He wondered if the presence of those three prominent Americans—Frederickson, Carlin, and Newsome—had yet created any sort of splash online. Doubtful, if they were as interested in secrecy as Carlin had implied. But would all three of them be able to keep from drawing attention to themselves for more than a day or two?

A search of social media would have answered the question in an instant, but Hal still felt such an aversion to that universe that he decided to instead do a quick Google News search for each of their names.

Nothing.

He then grabbed the remote and turned on the television. The hotel's limited selection of American cable channels included Fox News and CNN International. Hal endured six minutes of the former before switching in exasperation to CNN, which also quickly wore him down. He was about to shut it off when the anchor said, "And now, for an update on that developing story in Bolrovia, we take you to our correspondent Derrick Chaffee."

Hal's pulse quickened. But it was soon apparent that the story in question was a crisis at Bolrovia's southern border, where more than twelve thousand refugees were now encamped just inside the country after having come up through Europe from Syria via the Balkans.

"Conditions here are wretched," Chaffee said, "as pressure grows for the Horvatz government to deal with this sudden influx from the south."

It indeed looked bad, especially when a spokesman for an aid agency appeared on screen to say that local authorities had blocked his organization's shipment of provisions from reaching the encampment.

How uplifting, he thought. With a sigh, he shut off the TV and tossed aside the remote. He took off his socks and shoes, reopened the water bottle, drained the last of it, and tossed the empty to the floor. Then he stretched out on the bed, while wishing it was eight hours later so that the show would be over and he could climb beneath the sheets to sleep.

For now a nap would have to do, but when he rolled onto his side a glance at the Roth paperback on the bedside table made him immediately sit back up, staring at the book. It was exactly where he'd left it, but next to it was a small blue dried petal, which could only have fallen from its pages if someone else had opened it.

Someone had searched his room.

Not surprising, perhaps, but Hal was nonetheless irritated. He got up, checked the closet, the dresser drawers, then the bathroom. Everything seemed to be in its place, although he wasn't sure he'd even notice if something was missing.

His small backpack was still on the floor by the closet, right where he'd left it.

"Shit," he said, wondering with a sudden sense of alarm if they'd checked the small zippered pocket near the top.

Hal checked inside. The pill canister was still there, thank god. He picked it up, gave it a shake, and heard the reassuring rattle. Or maybe not so reassuring. He shook the bottle again. It didn't sound right, so, after struggling for a moment with the childproof cap, he looked inside.

There were three capsules where there should have been five. Why five, when one was supposedly lethal? No idea, but that was the number of pills that his friend, the supposed expert in exotic pharmaceuticals, had provided to him. And now two of them were gone.

He checked the floor in a panic, hoping that maybe the intruders had just spilled a few. Nothing. His attention was then drawn to the empty water bottle, which prompted a thought which nearly made him wretch. He had opened the bottle this morning, meaning anyone could have easily broken open the capsules to mix the contents into the water. He then remembered his friend's description of the pills. Odorless and tasteless.

He was frantic now. Should he stick a finger down his throat and vomit into the toilet? No, it was already too late. The pills supposedly worked in less than a minute. Unless dissolving them in water delayed the impact. Hal paced the floor, nearly hyperventilating now, wondering wildly if he would collapse at any moment. He sat back down on the bed, trying to control his breathing. Surely by now something would have happened. His breathing slowed, and after another few seconds he decided that the danger had passed. As usual, he was being an idiot. Or maybe not, because those missing pills could lead to all sorts of trouble.

Maybe Sarič's people would test them, find out what they were, and then throw him into one of those basement cells, pegging him for an assassin. Or maybe they'd use them to kill someone else, and frame him for murder.

Either way, he was fucked.

He now questioned his entire rationale for acquiring the pills. Had he seriously ever thought that he might really kill himself? Or had this been yet another act of vanity, playing the role of victim to its logical extreme? And look at where that had gotten him—two lethal pills were now loose among a cast of characters he neither trusted nor understood.

He took the plastic canister into the bathroom and flushed the remaining three capsules down the toilet. He then put the empty canister in his pocket, vowing to toss it into the first trash can he saw out on the street.

To calm down, he took a long shower. He then stood before his open closet. Maybe he should dress like a refugee to make a statement to his host and to those other Americans. But he'd look pretty stupid walking over to Pavel's house that way, and he doubted anyone would get what he was trying to say.

No, he would instead do what he always did. Play to his audience, go for the easy laughs.

Scarcely thinking, he reached for a bright knit shirt. Shirley spoke before he could remove it from the hanger.

"What are we trying to say here, Hal? Lounge lizard does Vegas? If your dignity's feeling wounded, that's not going to fix it."

"Right."

"Pretend you're playing Carnegie Hall. Like that'll ever happen."

He reached for a white shirt and the suit. Then the tie.

"Skip the tie tonight. Performer's prerogative."

"Right again, Shirley."

"As always."

By the time he was dressed and had located the outline he'd scribbled earlier of the routines he planned to perform, it was time to leave for dinner. Pavel, for a change, had decided to trust him to walk unescorted from the hotel to his house. Hal consulted the tourist map. Pavel had marked the site of his home with an "X." It was in the heart of what the map called "the historic Prospekt Quarter," on the corner of Jalovna Street and the Boulevard of Heroes.

Hal folded away his notes and the map, patted his pocket to check for the empty pill canister, and headed for the elevators.

Chapter 37

———≈———

With Hal Knight due any moment, Pavel rushed to stuff the take-out boxes from Gertmann's into the garbage can by the kitchen sink while Jana plowed past him with the vacuum cleaner at full tilt. He spoke over the roar of the machine.

"We can't let him see these! I told him it would be home-cooked!"

"On an hour's notice? Think again. Besides, Gertmann's is home cooking, just not *this* home. Move your feet."

Pavel stepped nimbly out of the way, but in doing so stepped on his son's small wooden train engine, which, by rolling quickly forward, nearly dropped him onto his ass.

"Tomas! Pick up your train set!"

There was a pounding of tiny footsteps. Tomas appeared at the kitchen door holding a clutch of small plastic dinosaurs against his chest with both hands. He dropped them to the floor in a scatter of orange and blue, then picked up the train engine and ran with it from the room.

Jana switched off the vacuum.

"Well, that worked well." She stooped to gather up the dinosaurs. "Tomas! Leave your train and come get your reptiles!"

Across the kitchen, Pavel reached for a cracker from a tray of beautifully arranged hors d'oeuvres.

"Don't!" Jana said. "It looks perfect as it is. There are more in the box if you're hungry."

"Shit. I think I just threw that box away."

He put the cracker back onto the tray. Jana dropped the dinosaurs into the bread drawer, slammed it shut, and then nudged the cracker until it was sitting exactly where it had been before.

"I made the mistake of looking up what he did to get into such trouble over there."

Not on our home desktop, I hope. That was Pavel's first thought, but all he said was, "Yes, I looked it up, too. A few weeks ago."

"He's not going to talk like that around here, I hope."

"No, no. He's been very well behaved. A gentleman, even."

"Oh, yes? And how many women has he been around at these events of yours so far? Young women, I mean."

Pavel considered the question. The audience at his introductory dinner had been mostly male. The women in attendance had mostly been older and more matronly. The only female he could think of who might have been much of a temptation was the skinny American who'd been flirting with him at the Green Devil, and Hal had seemed to handle that okay.

"Not many," he answered. "But I've heard your old university friends say far worse, if I remember correctly. All those guys you knew from the rowing club?"

"Yes, well, everyone talked like that then. Not that I ever liked it. But today? And with everyone out there ready to turn their phones on the minute anybody starts acting like a jerk?"

"He won't be like that here. I promise."

She nodded, but didn't seem convinced. The doorbell rang. He was here.

Chapter 38

Hal swallowed the last bite of a tasty dumpling and set his fork down on an empty plate. He was stuffed, having also polished off pan-seared potatoes, a ragout of lamb, and a red cabbage dish that was a bit like sauerkraut, only better.

Pavel's wife, Jana, had treated him kindly, and both of Pavel's children had behaved splendidly. Tomas was now on the floor playing with a toy train. Little Ava had nodded off in her high chair, chin smeared orange by pureed carrots.

"Thank you for such a wonderful meal, Jana. Everything was delicious."

"Please. It's takeout."

"She's joking," Pavel said.

"I'm not. I'll show you the boxes. I can't cook for shit. Is that the best way to say it in English?"

Hal burst into laughter.

"Yes. You said it perfectly."

"It's okay to curse in English around the children. They don't speak it yet. But in Bolrovian I am as pure as the snow. Around here, anyway. It's Pavel who is not so careful. But he works for an asshole, so I'd be cursing all the time when I got home, too."

Hal laughed again, even louder this time.

"Do I sense a political rift here, a house divided?" Pavel reddened but looked more worried than embarrassed. "It's okay, Pavel. Your secrets are safe with me."

But they weren't really, of course, which produced a twinge of guilt as Hal contemplated the degree to which his work might damage this young man and his family.

He was gratified they had made him feel so welcome. Hal could have had a life like this, too, he supposed. A wife, children, a comfy home base that might have tethered him more firmly to reason and humility. Would he have been as successful if he had lived that way? On the other hand, without that success, would he have ever fallen so precipitously? Odd to feel nostalgic for a life that never happened. Or maybe he was just missing Jess, who had also opted out of this safer sort of existence.

Jana began clearing the table. When Hal rose to help, she shooed him back into his seat. After she disappeared into the kitchen, Hal turned toward Pavel and lowered his voice.

"By the way, I think Sarič's people must have searched my room while I was out today."

"What?" Pavel looked truly shocked. "*Today?* No, I am quite sure he would not have done that."

"Well, he did. Or someone did, anyway."

"No, seriously. I mean, I'm not saying he wouldn't ever, but, well . . ."

Pavel looked around, wondering for the umpteenth time during the past several days—ever since he'd found the black box in the heating duct—whether his house might also be bugged. He got up, strolled to a stereo console on a side table, and flipped on a radio station before returning to the table, where he pulled his chair closer to Hal and leaned forward until their noses were practically touching.

"Look, it's like this . . ."

He then told Hal about the instructions Sarič had given him over the phone the night before—to make sure Hal was out of his room during a specific window of time *tomorrow,* but not today.

"And I can't imagine he would have changed that without checking with me first."

"So you've known that since last night and didn't tell me?" Hal, getting into the paranoid spirit of the moment without being asked, whispered as he spoke.

Pavel looked down at the floor.

"Yes. Sorry."

"Well, I guess it means something that you're telling me now. But if that's true, then who was up in my room today?"

"Did they take anything?"

"Um, well . . . yes."

"Then maybe it was thieves. You should report it!"

"It was nothing important."

"Still."

Pavel looked like he was about to push the point when suddenly there was a furious pounding at the front door. His eyes widened as he turned toward the sound.

"Who is it?" Hal asked.

Pavel stood, his face pale with worry.

"I don't know. Most people use the doorbell. Wait here."

The pounding resumed. The clatter of dishes and cutlery in the kitchen had stopped, leaving only the radio voice of a newscaster who was going on and on about the refugee crisis at the southern border. Ava remained asleep in her high chair, but Tomas had gone still on the floor and he, too, was staring toward the front door.

Hal heard the door open and he braced himself for the thudding of boots, the clatter of weapons and utility belts. Instead, he heard the voice of an older man, strong but a little scratchy. The man was speaking Bolrovian, so Hal still had no idea what was happening.

It was left to Tomas to supply the answer. Beaming, he bolted to his feet, dropped his toy train, and broke into a run toward the front of the house while happily shouting, "Poppy! Poppy!"

Chapter 39

Leave it to Poppy to show up at the worst possible time. And he was already talking nonsense, babbling about his need to drop off a new ladder he had just bought.

"There is no room at Anton's apartment, and if I leave it on the truck overnight someone will steal it. You know how it is where he lives."

"You should've called me first. You could have come for dinner."

"I have no phone. You know this."

"Then use Anton's, or a phone box."

"A phone box? They have taken them all away!"

He was right about that, of course, and Pavel probably should have been expecting Poppy after his father had forewarned him only a day ago.

It happened this way every fall. Poppy would show up unannounced, usually around dusk on some evening in late September, citing some pretext like the ladder or needing to borrow something. But he would never stay overnight in the heart of the city, for reasons which only he seemed to fathom, opting instead to lodge with an old friend, Anton Brod, who lived in a gray 1950s high-rise in one of the city's bleakest outermost suburbs.

Poppy's old truck was parked at the curb, steam seeping from underneath the hood. It was a lumbering old Bedford flatbed, dark green, a massive 1980 model. Strapped on the bed was a ten-foot aluminum stepladder which would have probably fit easily into Anton's apartment.

"Let me help you with that."

"No, no. I can bring it up."

"Stay and say hello to Jana and your grandchildren, Poppy. Stay and talk to our guest."

"Your guest?" His face clouded over with suspicion. Pavel rested a hand on his shoulder.

"He's American. You might have to speak a little English. Be nice to him."

Pavel clomped down the stairway. In his wake he heard the joyous cries of Tomas and the gruff laughter of his Poppy, and knew without turning that the old man had lifted the boy into the air. Someday soon he would no longer be able to do that. Jana loved Poppy as well. He wondered what Hal would make of him.

Pavel unstrapped the ladder and awkwardly hauled it up the steps, where, having forgotten his keys, he had to push the doorbell for Jana to let him in.

"Don't you need to get moving?" she said, holding the door open.

"Shit, you're right. Try to keep him here until I'm back."

"Yes, good luck with that. Especially when he hears where you're going."

He set down the ladder on the floor of the hallway, lengthwise, then he and Jana joined everyone in the living room. Poppy sat in an easy chair, with Tomas on his lap. But for the moment the old man was engaged in halting conversation with Hal, who sat catty-corner on the couch. Poppy turned to Pavel and, in Bolrovian, said, "This man is a guest? Of the palace fool?"

"Of the president. Yes, Poppy."

Hal laughed, apparently having detected Poppy's disapproval of Horvatz. Poppy rounded on him gruffly.

"Easy for him to laugh. Not so much for us who live here."

Pavel translated that for Hal.

"Well, yes. But that's my job, to make people laugh. It's the only reason I was invited."

When Pavel translated that, Poppy seemed a little puzzled, so Pavel explained it further.

"He's a comedian, Poppy. Someone who tells jokes, makes funny movies. Or used to."

Poppy thought it over for a moment, then nodded.

"Good. If someone can make him laugh, then maybe he'll forget about tormenting the rest of us for a while."

Pavel was about to translate that when he saw Hal checking the time and realized how late it was.

"We had better get going."

Hal nodded but didn't look at all frazzled or in a rush. The mark of a professional, he supposed. Anytime Pavel had to make a speech or any other sort of public appearance, he was always a nervous wreck for hours beforehand.

Poppy stood to say goodbye, but now he was frowning.

"So you are going there, then, for the evening. To pay court to that jackass."

"It's my job to pay court. Sorry. But please stay with us tonight. It would make all of us so happy."

"No, no. This location is not safe."

"Poppy, I work for the government."

"My point exactly."

It was the same sort of thing he said every year, but for Pavel the irony was that this year he may well have been correct.

"But soon it will be dark, and that long drive out to Anton's is tiring."

"I have done it a dozen times."

"What if that old truck of yours breaks down at such a late hour?"

"Then I will sleep in the cab and wait till morning."

"Do you need any help tomorrow in gathering your supplies?"

He waved off the idea.

"My needs are simple. The firewood is already chopped and stacked. I will be buying a new handle for the well pump and a lot of provisions. I can easily manage on my own."

Say what you will about Poppy's biases and delusions—and Pavel's father always said plenty on both those fronts—at the age of ninety-four he was still a tough old survivor. When he finally left this world, it would probably be by some sudden means. An aneurysm, a falling tree, an oncoming tractor trailer on some narrow rural road. But he would never simply waste away, or maybe that was Pavel's wishful thinking, because it was certainly something he never wanted to witness—his Poppy bedridden and incoherent, barely there at all.

"But what of *your* needs, Pavel? Are you attending to them properly?"

"I have all I need, Poppy. I'm doing well."

"So I see. You know, during the war I knew people like you, and also during Soviet times. Good people, friends even, but people who played along in order to 'do well,' as you say. Mostly because they were certain that the future would only hold more of the same."

"I know you don't like my boss, but—"

"Please, let me finish. You made the choice to take this job. Fine. I am sure it pays well. I ask only that you be aware of what you have become a part of."

"I'm aware, Poppy. And I'm doing what I can."

"Okay. But when the next choice comes—and there will be one, there always is—which direction will you go then?"

In farewell Pavel stepped forward to hug him, something that Poppy never let Pavel's father do, or even any of Pavel's three older sisters, who Poppy almost never saw. In spite of everything, Pavel remained his favorite, even if, at the moment, Pavel felt totally undeserving of that status.

"Give a message to your boss for me, will you?"

"Certainly, Poppy."

"Drop dead."

"I'll try to remember that."

Chapter 40

Hal took a seat at his place of honor up on the dais, near the center of a long table that had been set up in the style of one of those godawful celebrity roasts that he'd watched on cable reruns as a kid. The ones featuring TV and Hollywood talents well past their prime, like Don Rickles, Sammy Davis Jr., and that guy who always played a drunk, Foster Brooks—the same tired crew and their same boozy and suggestive insults, year after year, with the audience always laughing hysterically. And now Hal was the washed-up talent on display, and his master of ceremonies was the President of Bolrovia.

He spotted the visiting Americans seated together in the audience—six of them in a row, although he only recognized the three he had encountered the night before. Even dressed in a suit, Reece Newsome looked like he had just come off a five-day bender, and he was one of the few males in attendance, apart from Hal, who wasn't wearing a tie.

Hal glanced at his notes and began to concentrate. He was on the verge of slipping into the pre-performance trance he liked to achieve before any live show when he was distracted by a man rushing toward the dais from over to his right.

He looked up in time to see Branko Sarič intercept the man at the far end. The fellow spoke quickly into Sarič's ear. Sarič, dressed as always in a black turtleneck and gray jacket, then nodded and grimly waved the man through. The fellow came down the table until he reached President Horvatz, who at the moment had his back turned to Hal and was speaking to someone two seats away. Horvatz looked up as the fellow halted before him, breathless.

"Da?" Horvatz asked.

The man launched into a stream of Bolrovian. There was urgency in his words.

Hal turned toward Pavel, who was seated to his immediate left.

"Is everything okay? What are they saying?"

Pavel, already listening closely, translated as the exchange proceeded.

"It's Olli Dolnov, with the Ministry of Human Resources. He's saying the situation at the border encampment has become untenable. Do you know of this?"

"Yes, I saw it on the news."

"He says seven aid organizations are demanding entry. The president says to refuse them, that we will deal with the problem ourselves. Then Olli said it may take up to thirty-six hours to marshal the necessary supplies."

Pavel waited a few seconds, listening as the words grew more heated. Hal turned back toward the conversation. He watched with fascination the emotions playing out on Olli's face and in his body language as Horvatz spoke rapidly, but with no evidence of any heat or anger. Olli's rigid posture began to go slack, as if the air were leaving his body. The expression on his face went from eager alertness to consternation, and then shock, even horror. But when Horvatz was done, all Olli did was nod and say, somewhat shakily, "Da, Mizster Prezident." Then he left the dais, strolling past Sarič without even a glance.

Hal turned toward Pavel to see that he had lowered his head. When the young man looked up, he was ashen. Hal leaned closer and whispered.

"What just happened?"

There was now anger in Pavel's eyes.

"Do you really want to know?"

"Yes."

"The president said he has ordered an armored brigade to the border. They are waiting only ten miles away. An hour from now, after aid workers and news media have been cleared from the area, the brigade will move in to put an end to the encampment."

"What about the people there? Aren't there something like twelve thousand?"

"They will be pushed back across the border. The tents will be . . ." Pavel paused, swallowing with difficulty. "They will be flattened."

"But what if there are people who can't get out? Children, the old, the sick. What will happen to them?"

Pavel looked him straight in the eye.

"Olli asked the same. The orders are for the tents to be flattened. That is all the president would say."

Hal glanced over his shoulder. Horvatz was again talking to someone in the next seat, and he sounded cordial, relaxed. What struck Hal now about the exchange he had just witnessed was the president's delivery—his words had come rapidly but calmly, and with no hint of fire, as if he'd been explaining to a dolt exactly where to place glue traps for an infestation of mice.

He turned back around to ask Pavel another question when a hand clamped warmly onto his shoulder, in the manner of a friend. Hal turned to see a smiling Horvatz.

"I am sorry for that interruption. It was a matter of state, nothing that will interrupt or impede our proceedings here tonight."

Horvatz said it with a note of genuine concern, like the host of a dinner party apologizing for the tantrum of a spoiled child or the unwanted attentions of the family dog.

"Yes, well . . ."

Hal glanced down at his notes, which were now crumpled and damp with sweat. Horvatz spoke again.

"So, then. Are you ready for an entertaining evening, my friend? I will confess that I have been looking forward to this for months, and you will never know how grateful I am that you have agreed to do it. Shall we begin?"

His smile was charming, even boyish.

"Yes, sir." Hal's voice felt unsteady, uncertain. "Let's get things rolling."

Horvatz nodded, stood, and stepped toward the lectern in the middle of the dais.

Hal swallowed a lump of bile and looked again at his handwritten notes. But all he could think about were the rows of those miserable white tents he had seen earlier on CNN, except now he imagined them collapsing beneath the treads of tanks, like blades of grass leveled by a mower, while screams and cries for help were drowned out by the rumble of diesel engines, the clattering of the treads.

He then realized that Horvatz had just spoken his name, the voice amplified by the microphone, and now the crowd was applauding. Some people were even rising to their feet, although none of the six Americans. Horvatz had extended an arm in his direction, his cue to begin.

Hal stood and pushed back his chair. He glanced at Pavel, who looked down at his plate. Then he wiped his hands on his trousers, picked up his notes, and stepped to the lectern.

Someone had thoughtfully filled a glass with water and placed it by the microphone, and Hal reflexively raised it to his lips for a swallow as the applause continued. Then he thought of the missing pills, and in rapid succession glanced at the glass, at Sarič, and at the crowd. Surely the man wouldn't murder the president's jester at his own gala? He set the glass down anyway, careful not to spill a drop, and then looked out at the crowd as everyone went quiet. He wondered what the hell they must be thinking of all this, and if any of them had overheard what had just been ordered, or if any of them would have even cared. Then, as always, the urgency of performing somehow took over, although his opening remarks were completely unplanned.

"Well, thank you for that, everyone. And thank you, too, Mr. President, for your generous words and your warm Bolrovian hospitality, which is in such evidence tonight for all the world to see."

The president smiled up at him, nodding his appreciation.

"But maybe I could get a drink up here, so that we can achieve the full Vegas effect of this evening? Could the bartender oblige me with a double whiskey, perhaps?" Before he'd even finished the sentence, he'd noticed two men in white jackets springing into action behind the bar, which was in the same place as it had been the other night.

"Ah, there we are, perfect," he said, as one of them hustled across the room and handed it up to him.

"Let it never be said that your country doesn't know how to treat visitors." He took an immediate swallow, which roared down his throat, and he then held the glass aloft. "To Bolrovian hospitality. It's been so overwhelming that I'm practically flattened."

The crowd applauded warmly. The president was now beaming.

Hal then got down to the rather desultory business of performing his routines. He knew the material so well by now—even the items he hadn't performed in years—that he could have done it from a sickbed. The words and inflections came to him as readily as catechisms to a monk. And although it certainly wasn't his most inspired presentation, not by a long shot, the president and the relatively small percentage of others who were familiar with the material reacted just as he'd told Pavel they would.

Some were so readily anticipating the key lines that they began laughing before the words were out of his mouth. As for the rest of the crowd, most were so eager to laugh along with whatever their president liked that, by the end, he was getting a full-throated roar for each punch line, and he finished to a thunderous round of applause. The toadyism was as addictive as it was toxic, and Hal imbibed it in tandem with his double whiskey.

Toward the end he asked for a refill, and the crowd laughed obligingly. He played it the way Dean Martin used to, making a prop out of the alcohol, even as it was fueling a small fire in the back of his mind, where his improv skills were already in overdrive, wondering what sort of new material he might bring to bear before the evening was over. A glance at Pavel told Hal that his new friend—were they really friends, or just allies in their captivity?—might well be the only person in the room who had understood his earlier double entendres, because the poor young man looked deeply worried, as if he already knew what Hal was planning to do next.

After the applause died down, Hal told the crowd that he would take questions from one and all. Then, turning toward Horvatz, he offered the setup line that he had been planning since he first rose to his feet.

"And I certainly hope, Mr. President, that you will have a question for me. But let's save that for a moment and get started out there among the rest of you, so please don't be shy. Yes! You out there, toward the back."

The questions, as he could have predicted, were softballs. Routine stuff like where he got his ideas, who his influences were, and what sort of comedy he liked himself. No one asked about his downfall, of course—they would not have dared in front of the president—and none referred even tangentially to Hal's current status as an outcast from his own country.

Then, having decided the time was right, Hal looked back at Horvatz and said, "And now, Mr. President, I think it's your turn."

The president stood. He, too, was accustomed to performing before an audience, and he didn't need a microphone to project his words throughout the room.

"Yes, Mr. Knight. Or should I just call you Hal?"

"Please do, sir."

"Well, then, Hal, in one of your previous answers you suggested that you might write this event into your life story someday. Is this a work we can actually expect? Because I, for one, would certainly read it, or anything else you might choose to write. A novel, even. Would you ever write one of those, perhaps?"

"Ah, I see. Yes, very good question."

Then, with a spark of malice set aflame by another swallow of whiskey, his improv brain sprang into action, marshaling everything he knew about Horvatz—all his weaknesses, blind spots, and insecurities—to plot out his answer. The man didn't know a damn thing about the pop music of his youth, for instance—not even the Beatles. In recalling that, Hal saw his opening, and seized it in a flash.

"Well, as a matter of fact, Mr. President—and maybe you could even call this news—I have been scribbling at the beginnings of something. And, yes, it's more on the lines of fiction than memoir. A novel, just as you said."

Hal noticed that now even the contingent of Americans seemed to be leaning forward in their seats. The president spoke again.

"What sort of novel?"

Exactly the follow-up question he'd hoped for. The lyrics of the Beatles' song "Paperback Writer" came to him as if they'd been typed onto a page in his mind.

"Well . . ." Hal paused for dramatic effect. "It's the dirty story of a dirty man." Another pause, two beats. "And his clinging wife doesn't understand." He paused again. If Horvatz was going to recognize the lines, then surely he would do so now. Instead, true to his reputation, the man who hated to be mocked or made fun of or exposed as a fool simply nodded, smiling idiotically as Hal lured him deeper into the role of unwitting straight man.

"Yes? Please, tell us more."

"Their son is working for the *Daily Mail,* and it's a steady job, but he wants to be, well . . ."

"Yes? Tell us!"

Hal saw that several of the Americans were chuckling, although most of the Bolrovians looked restless, edgy, well knowing how badly their president hated to be the butt of a joke. Hal was exhilarated. He continued to follow the lyrics of the song.

"A paperback writer."

"I see," Horvatz said. "A little confusing, perhaps, but how far along are you?"

"Oh, a thousand pages, give or take a few. But I'll be writing more in a week or two."

"A *thousand*? Splendid!"

A few people who didn't know better applauded. For the rest, this was no longer a bit of joking around; it was an act of public humiliation that had surpassed the limits of decorum. One elegantly dressed woman had put her hands to her face in horror. Then one of the Americans stood. Reece Newsome, of course, perhaps the only person here tonight who was boorish enough to break into an exchange between the president and the night's honored guest, which was fine with Hal, because it made Newsome complicit in this act of comic vengeance.

Swaying a bit, drink in hand, Newsome's eyes gleamed maliciously as he shouted toward the front, joining in on the joke by seizing upon another of the song's lyrics.

"Is this book of yours perhaps based on a novel by a man named Lear?"

"Why, yes! As a matter of fact, your portliness, it *is*." Then, turning back toward Horvatz, "And if you really like it, Mr. President, you can have the rights. I'm sure it could make a *million* for you overnight."

By now even the other Americans had gone silent. The only people still smiling were a few tone-deaf Bolrovians. Sarič was stone-faced, but in a blank way that hinted that he, too, wasn't yet in on the joke. Poor Pavel, however, seemed to be trying to bury his face in the table. And that's when Hal belatedly began to perceive that the cost of this buffoonery might well exceed the bill he was willing to pay, and that the damage could extend to others in his orbit. He decided to deescalate immediately and wrap things up as quickly as possible.

"But mostly, Mr. President, what I'd like to do now is thank you for this evening. Not only for honoring me with this event, but by also being such a good sport, and even letting me poke a little fun at you, which I assure you is a rare quality in any man of your stature."

So there it was. Hal had managed not only to spoof the man in front of his most loyal followers; in the end he had abased himself as well, and had done so in the presence of those Americans whose very existence he abhorred.

Horvatz was still smiling, although now he also looked a little puzzled, and was probably wondering how Hal could have made fun of him without him noticing. Fortunately, he did not ask for clarification. Instead, he brought the evening to a close.

"Mr. Hal Knight, ladies and gentlemen. Thank you, Hal, for an enchanting evening."

The president clapped. Everyone else followed suit, none more loudly than those members of the audience who, moments earlier, had looked so mortified, Pavel among them, as if they were retroactively trying to drown out everything that had just transpired.

Chapter 41

Pavel, feeling drained and betrayed, wondered how long it would be before someone told the president that his favorite funnyman had just humiliated him in front of his cabinet, his top supporters, and his American guests.

Hal had been angry, and Pavel understood why. But *this*?

Making it worse was that Pavel had unwittingly showed Hal the target and had then supplied the weapon, first by telling him the president couldn't take ridicule, then by describing the blind spots in the president's cultural education. If Pavel were a samurai, he would now be obligated to commit seppuku, right here on the dais.

Instead, he collected himself and went to fetch Hal from the knot of six admirers who were now asking for his autograph and telling him how much they had enjoyed the show. All of them were men and women currently seeking favor with the president, and were no doubt hoping Horvatz would take note of this show of homage. Pavel guessed that most of them hadn't even understood most of the humor, and he allowed himself a brief moment of mirth as he imagined how they'd feel about those autographs once the truth emerged.

He walked up behind Hal and took him by the arm, not caring at all if he was interrupting.

"We're leaving."

Hal, to his credit, looked sheepish as he turned around. He ducked his head in apparent shame and said, too low for his admirers to hear, "How long before someone tells the emperor he wasn't wearing any clothes?"

"I recommend we not stay long enough to find out. Maybe by the time he sees you next he will have gotten over it, but I wouldn't count on it."

"So you think that's a possibility, though? That he'll get over it?"

"I don't know him well enough to say. I've only been working for him a few weeks. But his reputation?" Pavel shook his head.

"Right. Then maybe we should get a drink."

"Or maybe you shouldn't have started drinking at all."

"Yeah, there's that, too. But if tomorrow's going to be hell, I should at least be prepared to start the day with a hangover. I do have some experience with falls from grace, you know."

And that's when it occurred to Pavel that, no matter how careless and reckless his friend—and, yes, he now thought of this strange man as something of a friend—had been tonight, he had done so while knowing he would be alienating maybe his last powerful friend on the planet.

"Fine, then. But maybe a quieter location tonight. This is going to be the talk of the town at the Green Devil."

"Right." Then Hal stopped and tilted his head. "Unless."

"What?"

"Maybe if I go there I could at least start planting the seeds of a cover story."

"The damage is done. Don't make it worse."

"No, hear me out. I can tell everyone who will listen what a good sport he was. I could even start spreading the word that he was in on it from the beginning and handled all his lines perfectly. Nicky Horvatz, world's best straight man. What do you think?"

"It will never work. And stop saying 'Nicky' before someone else hears. He hates that name."

"Okay. But maybe trying will be enough. As long as he hears about it later."

Probably not. Although maybe Pavel should at least let Hal give it a shot. But before he could answer, they were surrounded and swarmed by the Americans and about a dozen Bolrovians—a big, sloppy bunch of revelers ready to party.

"We're heading to the Green Devil," one of them shouted, "and you're leading the way!"

"Sounds like a plan!" Hal replied, trying to sound jolly.

The group engulfed them like a wave and swept them out onto the palace grounds on a loud and drunken tide.

Chapter 42

The boozy procession moved through the narrow streets like an assault vehicle, clearing everything in its path. Each time Hal tried to sink back into the pack, they bumped him forward, their anointed leader. As they exited the palace, he'd started talking up the cover story by loudly saying what a great sport the president had been to play along with his gag, although Reece Newsome had immediately knocked it down.

"Nice try, Hal," Reece had shouted above the hubbub. "But at least you're covering your ass on this one better than you did with Mariette Garth."

"Covering his *balls,* you mean," someone else had chimed in.

Now, as they tunneled down a narrow lane, a young woman wearing a backpack rounded a corner toward them just as they were reaching a choke point where a repair crew had cordoned off half the lane with bright orange barriers and a tarp that covered a hole. Someone would have to give way.

Hal stopped. The woman stopped. *Go home,* he wanted to warn her. *Turn back and seek shelter from all this forced hilarity.* Then he looked into her eyes and saw a flash of recognition, followed by an instant, visceral dislike. She was American, probably a student studying abroad, and she knew who he was. Great. And he saw by the movement of her eyes that she had already taken the measure of his following. She spoke in a low voice that only he could hear.

"The Pied Piper, leading his rats."

A decent line, so he nodded.

"Look, I just . . ."

"Move it, bitch!" It was shouted by a man just behind him, and who-

ever it was now jostled Hal forward, even as the young woman edged closer until their noses were practically touching. Hal spoke in a low, urgent tone, as rapidly as he could: "Look, I know you hate me, but these people are fucking crazy and might do anything, so if—"

"*I said move it, you fucking bitch!*" This time the shout came from just behind his right ear. It was deafening. The man's enraged spittle flecked Hal's cheek and the weight of his body pressed Hal forward. If Hal didn't manage to hold his ground, there would be an onslaught, and the young woman might be crushed in the surge.

She must have sensed that as well, because she suddenly made a nimble step backward, then pivoted smartly before rushing around the corner she'd emerged from, just as Hal was propelled forward by the shouting man and everyone to his rear.

A cheer went up from the crowd as the vanquished young woman disappeared up the alley, yet even then the loud fellow continued his obscene tirade against her. Hal was swept along in the mob's triumphal progress, barely keeping his balance on the uneven pavement.

Glancing over his shoulder, he now saw several Bolrovians holding aloft the glowing screens of phones, filming it all. It was all he could do to keep from retching onto the cobbles.

Chapter 43

Quint's band, bad drummer and all, was already playing in the back room by the time Lauren reached the Green Devil. The place was only half full, and most of the customers were still near the bar up front. Taking her drink into the back would have shown more solidarity with Quint, but she would have stood out too much for comfort.

She wondered how Hal's show had gone and whether he would have anything significant to report. It probably wouldn't be long until some of the attendees began to arrive. If Sarič's people were planning to make any sort of arrest, that's when they would strike, for maximum impact.

A loud voice from over by the bar caught her attention, but this fellow was speaking Bolrovian, not English. No sign tonight of Ian Farkas. The thought crossed her mind that he might somehow be in league with Kretzer, but they seemed an unlikely pairing—a loud charmer who sought attention; a quiet thug who preferred ambush. Then again, opposites attract.

Just about then the door opened. There was a gust of laughter and voices as people piled in. You could tell by their clothes that they had been at the palace, and they just kept coming. Lauren then spotted two of the Americans Hal had mentioned in his reports—Baxter Frederickson, the TV blowhard, and Reece Newsome, the political fixer. Then came the blond head of Katie Carlin. Even Lauren's casual surveillance of them would probably be enough to make Fordyce fidget and fume. All the more reason to keep watching them.

Most of the others seemed to be Bolrovians, although it was clear by their energy and the patterns of conversation that everyone had walked over here together. There was an edgy air of raw jubilation about them, like that of hunters arriving home from the kill.

Finally, as practically the last one to enter, there was Hal, looking overwhelmed, or maybe just tired. He was followed closely by a beleaguered Pavel Lukov, who shut the door behind him.

The room now felt a little overcrowded, but Lauren wanted to make sure that Quint remained a free man for at least another few minutes now that things were coming to a simmer. She drifted toward the back room as the crowd swelled near the bar. To complete the scene—and make it even more stifling—in walked Branko Sarič. The bartender, no fool, noticed him right away and asked his pleasure. To Lauren's surprise, he actually ordered a drink. She noticed some garish orange object hitched to his waist, and for a moment wondered bizarrely if it might be a colostomy bag. But, no, it was only a water bottle.

She watched his reflection in the mirror behind the bar. He had ordered red wine, and his first sip was tiny, that of a cat lapping at milk. He seemed to have arrived without any henchmen—a good sign for Quint—and he hadn't given even a glance toward the band, which by now you could barely hear above the din of voices. Instead, he gravitated toward Frederickson and Newsome, and it soon became apparent to Lauren that Sarič was here to socialize.

Witnessing so many figures of interest all in one place gave her an odd sensation of claustrophobia, of operational jeopardy. Wait long enough and maybe even Sandor Matas would stroll in. Without a further glance at anyone, she headed for the door.

Chapter 44

———————≈———————

When Hal first spotted Chris and his band in the back, and then saw his handler, Susan, drinking by herself in a far corner up front, his first reaction was to wonder if an emergency had arisen and they were about to bundle him out of here on some sort of rescue exfiltration.

Had word already spread of his little joke at the president's expense? But neither made a move in his direction, or even acted as if they recognized him. Lauren then departed, and he was surprised to feel a little let down. Given what had just transpired out on the streets, an emergency exit might have been the one thing that could have cheered him up, if only by affirming he was worth the trouble.

He needed a drink, another stiff one. But before he could reach the bar, Katie Carlin was at his side, taking his arm, squeezing it. A cloud of her perfume enveloped him like a fogbank.

"You were magnificent."

He shrugged. This was the kind of flattery you routinely got in Hollywood and on Capitol Hill, and it almost always came from people who wanted something.

"All of it was pretty old material."

"No. I meant just a minute ago, confronting that bitch out on the street. Even Baxter was impressed."

"Whoa, now. That wasn't me yelling all that shit."

She frowned, then broke into a knowing smile.

"Oh, I see. Already in damage control. Relax. She had it coming, and you're among friends now."

Just what he didn't want to hear. Boffo reviews from the worst possible audience.

"Look. Whatever that was out there, it just kind of happened."

"Yes, that's what all the greats say. The best part is that you made it all look so easy. You're a natural."

Fine. Let her believe whatever she wanted. Not that the truth was ever a major concern of Katie Carlin's. Feeling queasy, Hal detached her from his arm.

"I think I'll get a drink now."

"By all means. You've earned it."

He stepped toward the bar and raised up on his tiptoes to try to signal for a drink. The bartender—Kika, wasn't it?—was swamped at the moment, but not at all flustered. Hal caught his eye long enough to mouth the words "Double whiskey, neat."

Kika nodded, and within seconds a glass tumbler with a slosh of amber was being handed through the crowd. Hal held aloft a folded bit of cash, but Kika shook his head and mouthed, "On the house," which made Hal wonder who was paying. Susan? Chris? The proprietor? Or maybe even, lost somewhere in the mob, that Ian Farkas fellow, although he was nowhere in sight.

Hal decided to listen to Chris's band, but he had taken only a few steps toward the back when he was again waylaid by Katie Carlin, who again took his arm. It was clear he wouldn't escape anytime soon, and the idea of spreading a cover story on Pavel's behalf already seemed dead on arrival, especially after Reece Newsome had so deftly shot it down. He looked around for Pavel but couldn't find him. After two days of wishing he could give Pavel the slip, Hal now felt desperate for the man's company.

"That was the perfect end to one helluva day," Carlin said.

"Yes. Quite a finish."

Hal decided to give it five minutes. Then he'd shake her off again by saying he had to pee. The idea made him remember her remark from the night before, the one he'd overheard while walking to the men's room. And that, in turn, reminded him of why he was even here, so he halfheartedly decided to do a little spying.

"What made it such a great day for you? Apart from my show, of course. Did you get your money's worth on that big tour?"

She looked surprised.

"How'd you know about that?"

"Baxter was talking about it earlier." A lie, of the sort that tended to work in both Hollywood and on Capitol Hill on the easily duped.

"Then I guess that part's no secret." She reached down and squeezed his thigh. Obviously, her mind was on other things.

"A cooperative venture between you guys and the Bolrovians, right? Or that's how Baxter made it sound." An educated guess, but her shrug told him he hadn't completely missed the mark.

"Only if that's how you'd describe something where one side is pretty much picking up the whole tab."

"Sounds like you think you're getting a raw deal."

"You'd think so, too, if you knew the price tag. Still, they were pretty convincing. And, well, the potential of the whole thing kind of blew me away."

Now he was intrigued, in spite of her closeness, in spite of another squeeze by her right hand, this one even further up his thigh, one which then turned into more of an upward stroke. His heightened curiosity—was he close to learning something important?—lent a small sexual thrill to the moment, or maybe it was also that she had reached his crotch, where he was surprised and somewhat horrified to discover that he now had an erection.

"I'm trying to think of a joke I could make about a mike drop," she said, easing closer and turning her grip into a squeeze, "but I can't quite get a handle on it."

"That line will probably do for now," he said. "But is that all you're going to tell me about this tour?"

"Depends on how much time we spend time together. And how receptive you are."

"Ah, well . . ." He nodded, not yet sure what he was willing to say, much less do, in response to that.

"I mean, even I barely got in to see it, and only because of those two assholes."

She nodded over to the left, where Hal now saw, with a mild sense of alarm, that Baxter Fredrickson and Reece Newsome were both deep in conversation with a very somber-looking Branko Sarič—now when had *he* entered the bar?—and who, for a change, actually had a real drink in his hand, even though it was red wine in a stem glass, while everyone else was guzzling whiskey or beer. The effect was oddly effete for a fellow as stern as him.

Someone then jostled up on Carlin's left, a local oaf who must have recognized her, and with a starry-eyed gaze the man began asking about her TV career. She showed her annoyance with a plastered-on smile, then launched into an obligatory response about hard work and talent. Hal took the opportunity to slip away, even as she held on to his arm a second too long.

He gave her a nod, as if to say, *"Later,"* and she smiled back. He weaved through the crowd until he had moved up just behind Sarič's left shoulder. Under normal circumstances, a man as wary as Sarič would have immediately taken notice, but Hal could see by the shine of his eyes that the wine was already making an impact. That was the problem with abstainers when they occasionally dipped into the well. It went straight to their heads. By now, Newsome had moved off and Sarič was speaking mano a mano with Baxter Frederickson. Hal sidled closer to listen.

"The biggest problem with the Cold War was that no one ever bothered to explore what we all had in common," Sarič said. "But now, with the rise of radical Islam and, in your country, all the nonsense you call wokeness, the contrast to all the things that you and I hold sacred has become even more apparent."

"Yes, absolutely," Frederickson said.

Had this been occurring on television, Hal would have already switched it off. Instead, he ducked his head, sipped his whiskey, and kept listening, because Sarič was far from finished.

"The one thing that Soviet propaganda always got right about your country was the part about race and crime and permissiveness. And that's *still* true. So, instead of trying to mix everyone and act like it's harmonious, maybe we should go our separate ways, yes? For the good of all!"

"But the moment you suggest something like that," Frederickson said, "they call you a racist or say you're against 'diversity.'" He formed quote marks with his fingers and gave that little smirk that had somehow endeared him to millions.

"Of course," Sarič said. "Only because they want to tear down the solidarity among all of us who are Christian and white. Or swamp us with refugees, with unwanted immigration."

"Absolutely."

"And all of you people who have come here this week know this. And you see the same kind of thinking with Nikolai Horvatz. So, while I do not drink much, for this I will raise a toast. To our fight against the common enemy."

He raised his wineglass and tapped it daintily against Frederickson's tumbler of whiskey. Hal eased his own glass into the scrum, startling Sarič, whose smile immediately fell into a scowl. Nothing pissed off a professional eavesdropper as much as being eavesdropped on.

"Wise words from a wise man," Hal said. He then smiled, as if daring Sarič to smile back. But it was Frederickson who responded.

"You know, when I first saw your little show had been added to our schedule, I groaned. Another goddamn hypocritical liberal Democrat. But that little performance I just saw from you out there on the streets—" He shook his head in seeming admiration. "Man, that was perfect, the way you handled that bitch."

Hal flushed in spite of himself. Did *everyone* think he was the guy who had yelled at her and gone off on a tirade? Dismaying, but possibly helpful, although maybe from here on out these kinds of people would be his sole clientele, his only audience. Hal Knight, patron saint of comedy for the Baxterites. He tried to remember the last time he had seen a truly funny right-wing American comedian. Dennis Miller, maybe, for about ten minutes. Otherwise, nada.

But Frederickson was still talking.

"That took some real guts, man. Especially considering all the shit you've already been through. So, yes, let's raise our glasses to the common good. C'mon, Branko, you, too."

Sarič reluctantly raised his glass but did not touch it to Hal's. Frederickson kept talking.

"You know, even before you came around to reason, I loved *Barefoot and Pregnant*. My wife, Becky, did, too. We even took our kids."

"Oh, yeah? How old were they?"

"My boy was eleven at the time, my daughter thirteen."

Hal was appalled by the idea of anyone taking their young daughter to see that film, and he imagined Jess standing to his left giving him a sidelong I-told-you-so look.

"Well, my films are not for everybody, you know."

"Oh, don't let those pussy leftist reviewers beat you down. And look at what they've done to you now, right? Purged your entire body of work. And your crime was what? Your real one, I mean. Not that one outburst, because that's not what they were really punishing you for—I hope you realize that."

"Well, I mean . . ."

"I'm serious." Then, turning toward Sarič, "You've heard what they did to this guy, didn't you?"

Sarič nodded grimly but said nothing.

"They took one slipup and used it to hammer you for all the rest of your work."

"It was a pretty big slipup."

"Debatable. But even if we concede that point, what they were really nailing you for is your comedy, the things you've always done to make us laugh, which they hate because it reminds them that, not so many years ago, *they* were laughing at it, too. So fuck them."

Hal needed all his willpower to maintain a fixed smile to the end of Frederickson's sermonette, which was doubly obnoxious for sounding rehearsed, like something he might have once read from a teleprompter. Sarič, at least, had seemed to be speaking from the heart, even if it was a cold and shriveled one. But the most painful part of Frederickson's spiel had been that last bit—about humor which was no longer funny. Painful because it was true. In the past several years, quite a few of his friends, and Jess's as well, had confided to her—but never to him—that they'd stumbled upon one of his earlier films on cable and, after having settled in to enjoy it anew, had instead ended up cringing and then turning the thing off, finding themselves aghast at lines and gags which, ten or fifteen or even twenty years earlier, had made them laugh uproariously.

To now hear Baxter Frederickson citing this phenomenon, but from the opposite point of view, was even more troubling, because it appealed to Hal's angry and aggrieved side. Wallow too long in this kind of affirmation and he might even begin to believe it—*You're okay; it's everyone else who's the problem.*

"Yeah, well," he replied halfheartedly. "You know Hollywood. Not exactly filled with courageous people."

"You're goddamn right about that."

Sarič, Hal now noticed, seemed to flinch every time Frederickson said "goddamn," which only made Hal want to say it over and over.

Katie Carlin then joined them. Hal could tell that Sarič was even more put off, perhaps by her slit skirt, or her voice, or maybe the idea that a woman, a lesser being, could just waltz right up and join their conversation as an equal. That was Hal's theory, and he was sticking to it. But when he next turned in Sarič's direction, the man had vanished.

Chapter 45

—————≈—————

Pavel was a bit shocked to see Sarič accept a second glass of wine. Either he was trying to fit in with his American visitors or he was in a celebratory mood. Maybe both, although he wore the same severe expression as always.

Pavel had pretty much given up on the idea of reining in Hal for the remainder of the evening, unless the man decided to wander off into the streets. As long as he remained here, most of his words would at least be cloaked by the din. Although he did tense up when he saw Hal enter Sarič's orbit, where he remained for a disconcertingly long time. On the other hand, maybe Hal had used his proximity to spread his cover story. Not that Pavel had any realistic hopes that it would work. With any luck, Sarič, tone-deaf when it came to irony, was still clueless about the whole thing.

Pavel would have liked to go into the back to listen to the quartet that was playing. Up here near the door, he could barely hear it. But on his one trip to the men's room he was somewhat surprised to see the keyboard player who'd been busking near Old Rudi's food cart. Blatsk was such a small town sometimes, and the provincial attitude of his boss was making it feel even smaller. Or maybe Pavel was starting to think like his Poppy, a dangerous idea for a man in his position.

Pavel breathed easier when he saw Sarič depart a half hour later. The man's wineglass was still half full when he set it down on the bar on his way to the exit. Sarič then paused at the door for a long swig of his ultra-pure water, as if to rinse away this entire experience.

Maybe now would be a good time to coax Hal back to the Esplanade. Pavel had watched him polish off two double whiskeys since arriving, and the crowd was beginning to thin. Then he saw Hal emerge from a knot of people with that skinny American woman, Katie something, clinging to him as tightly as the skin on a plum. They went out the door into the night.

Pavel waited for a few seconds, then followed. He heard her voice as soon as he stepped into the street. They were heading right, back toward the hotel, weaving slightly due either to drink or to the fierce way she was holding on to him.

Pavel followed at what he hoped was a prudent distance, feeling like one of those tawdry private investigators who photographs illicit couples through telephoto lenses. They were two unmarried, consenting adults, yet Pavel couldn't help but feel a little queasy about the whole thing on Hal's behalf, especially when, a block later, they briefly ducked into the darkened alcove of a storefront. When they emerged a minute or two later, Hal was rearranging his trousers and she was smoothing her skirt.

Pavel trailed them all the way to the hotel, where, from just outside the revolving doors, he watched them cross the lobby together toward the elevators. He didn't have the stomach to go any further, much less to watch the numbers light up above the elevator doors in order to see which floor they wound up on. At that point, he no longer wanted to know.

Chapter 46

Overnight, a low fog crept into the center of Blatsk from the west, threading its way up the River Volty and down the city's narrow lanes like gray snakes swallowing everything in their path. For most early risers this was cause for gloom, but for Hal, who against all odds had bounded onto the streets at dawn, it was a magical experience, a way of walking on the clouds in spite of a hangover that had been throbbing at his temples from the moment he'd awakened—quite alone and unencumbered—in his room at the Esplanade.

A double espresso from a yawning barista quickly took care of that problem. Besides, Hal was too excited to let a headache stand in the way of such a fine and promising morning. And by the time he had stopped off at a café for a huge breakfast and a second coffee, the fog had lifted, the city had come fully awake, and the only remaining cloud on his horizon was the memory of the nasty confrontation the night before on the way to the Green Devil, when his unwanted following had sent that poor young woman scurrying away for her life. Unfortunate, to put it mildly, but when he had checked the internet just before bed—his first major foray into social media in two months—no one had posted any videos.

What he *had* seen online at that late hour, and the main reason for his upbeat mood, was an email reply from Jess. She was coming! Or check that—she was actually only *thinking* about coming, but she had already gone to the trouble of checking flight schedules and had even asked what sort of timing would work best with his schedule.

I might also want you to book me a room, she had written. *A separate room, of course. While I'd like to offer you moral support, that will be the extent of my involvement with you.*

He was okay with that. He would also have been okay with a refusal. At this point, any answer at all from Jess was progress, something he could build on.

She had then written, *In the meantime, maybe you could give me a clearer idea of what you're really up to over there,* a remark that he had thought was a little reckless, given his circumstances. But at least she hadn't said anything coy that might have alluded to secrecy or spying or even Leo Holloman.

Opening her email in his fairly boozy state the night before had felt like an immediate vindication for the way he had, moments earlier, resisted the temptations of Katie Carlin. Was this what spying was really all about, then? Maintaining control, even of your libido, as you peeled away secrets from someone who was trying to peel away your clothes? He liked to think that at some deeper level he had simply refused to wind up in bed with someone so dreadfully soulless.

The irony was that Hal had gotten most of what he'd wanted from Carlin during their walk back to the hotel, when she had begun talking—in between gropes and grabs—about their big tour. Its main attraction had been a new data center called The Hub. Reece Newsome had apparently come up with the name.

"So that's the item with the big price tag?" Hal had asked. "But why would you guys agree to foot the bill? I mean, I know Baxter's loaded, but—"

She had laughed at his question.

"What, you think we're chumps? C'mon, you were part of this political racket, at least for a while. Have you already forgotten about dark money?"

"Ah. Of course. Which keeps everything off the books."

"And if you're a big donor looking to get creative, what would you rather pay for—some nobody in your local House primary or an innovation like this, which could be a game changer." Then her eyes got a dusky, faraway look. "Dark money. I get kinda hot just thinking about it."

And at that point, halfway between the Green Devil and the Esplanade, she had pulled him into the shadows of a storefront alcove, where she had pried loose his belt buckle while Hal unbuttoned more information.

"This money talk really *does* get you going. All that hardware at The Hub must cost plenty."

"Speaking of hardware."

She had slipped a hand down his trousers, but she hadn't stopped talking.

"It's not the hardware that's expensive. It's the talent. A lot of it's imported, straight from Center Sixteen."

"We should move on to someplace more comfortable," Hal had said, although he was already wondering what Center Sixteen could be.

"I'm all for that."

She had pulled him back onto the lighted sidewalk before he could rezip his trousers.

"It's not far from here," she'd said, dangling that bit of information with a coy smile. "The location is downright cheeky."

"Hiding in plain sight, you mean?" A guess, but since Hal had recently been an expert at hiding in plain sight, it seemed like a good one.

"More like that it's right behind an Apple Store." She'd laughed. "Nothing like sticking one up Steve Jobs's ass into the bargain, right?"

"Except he's dead."

"Who?"

"Steve Jobs."

"No way!"

"Yeah. Years ago."

"Well, still. The symbolism alone."

Her sexual attentions had peaked in the hotel elevator, where she had again unzipped him. But when the elevator bell had pinged to announce their arrival at her floor—she was on six, his room was on four—it had pinged in Hal's head like a tiny wake-up call, and when he had looked into her eyes he realized that he wasn't the only one angling for something other than sex. How convenient for Hal to have come along, as such an apparently easy mark, at a time when she seemed to be trying so hard to piss off Baxter Frederickson, or just get his full attention.

That thought had occurred to him as she'd slid a hand southward. By then, the elevator doors had opened. When they began to shut, Hal thrust a foot out to stop them.

"Nicely done," she'd said. "Shall we continue to my room for a more horizontal position?"

He had then disengaged slightly to dart a glance down the hallway, in case anyone was out there to witness their sloppy arrival, with his trousers already drooping to the top of his hips.

"Horizontal sounds good," he said.

"Seems to me you're pretty vertical, which is also good." She stroked the head of his penis.

"Yes, well . . ." He tried to ignore the shiver of pleasure. He needed a quick way out of this, so he managed a bit of improv.

"There is one further obligation that I have to attend to first, as long as you can wait."

She frowned but kept her hand in place. Hal had to again poke his foot out to stop the elevator doors from shutting.

"I'm scheduled to meet a local TV crew downstairs."

"At *this* hour?"

"In ten minutes. For some *Blatsk After Dark* show. I was going to tell you in the lobby, but, well, the prospect of the ride up was too good to miss."

"Oh, I can give you a ride all right, and it'll take you a lot higher than this elevator."

Her grip turned into a squeeze.

"Ah . . . yes, I can imagine that quite clearly. But this interview will be brief. So how 'bout if I rebook for takeoff in, what do you say, half an hour?"

She seemed mildly disappointed. But if anyone knew the importance of interviews and media exposure, even when in direct competition with sexual conquest, it was Katie Carlin. So she went with the flow.

"Absolutely. And if it runs long . . ." She gave him another squeeze. "The interview, I mean, then later is fine, too. The runway will be open all night. Room 634."

Hal jammed his foot out again to stop the shutting doors.

"And, uh, there won't be any other, well, jets ahead of me on the taxiway?"

"Air Baxter has been temporarily grounded."

"Ah. Hope he at least gets to redeem his frequent-flier miles."

And with that lame little joke, which had registered on her face with a slight frown, Hal had nudged her into the hallway just before the doors finally closed. He then hitched up his trousers and rode all the way to the lobby, in case she was watching the progression of lighted numbers back on her floor. (He had doubted she would, but he supposed this was the sort of attention to detail that was expected of a spy.) Then he had headed back upstairs to his room, where Jess's email awaited him.

Even now, having already showered and walked and eaten a full breakfast, Hal thought he could detect a hint of Katie Carlin's perfume wafting from his pores. He then began planning out his day, because the first order of business would be to find the data center, The Hub, a task that had become even more urgent after he had Googled "Center 16" before leaving his room.

The top hit, or at least the most intriguing one, was an item from a Washington think tank about a notorious cyber-operations center of that name that was run by the FSB, Russia's Federal Security Service. It was renowned for its ability to hack, penetrate, and spear-phish its way into protected data systems and email accounts worldwide, including, most famously, those of some prominent American Democrats and, more alarmingly, a few U.S. state elections systems and their voter registration rolls. It also spread disinformation, created bot farms, and set up fake websites.

Hal had then searched for the location of the nearest Apple Store, hoping that there weren't too many. There was only one, two blocks off the main square. In fact, it was the only Apple Store in all of Eastern Europe, with the closest other location being in Dresden. He had enlarged the map, zooming closer until it revealed the shape and configuration of the buildings on that block, as well as the names of the most prominent tenants.

It had quickly become apparent that there was indeed an unnamed occupant in the rear section of the building where the Apple Store was located. This space ran the length of the block and backed onto a rear alley, which was probably where you entered. It was only about a fifteen-minute walk from the hotel.

He decided to include all this information in his next report to the CIA, which he proceeded to write while he ate breakfast and sipped his coffee, filling four more pages front and back. Then he folded the pages of his report into a five-euro note and stuffed it in his pocket for later delivery to the haluski stand, which wouldn't open for several more hours.

By the time he got back to the hotel, it was nearly nine a.m., but Pavel hadn't yet arrived. While that felt liberating, he had already decided that being accompanied by a ranking presidential aide might work to his advantage in his efforts to get a closer look at The Hub. Far less chance of being arrested, too. He also decided he would need to go back up to his room to get his phone. Taking it with him would violate one of his main rules, but he might be able to snap some photos.

Hal decided to wait in the lobby for Pavel until noon. If Pavel didn't show by then, Hal would call him. He took a seat on a couch with a view of the elevators but also of the street out front. If Katie Carlin appeared, he would slip out of sight to avoid an embarrassing confrontation.

He was eager to get going. Outside, the sun was now shining, and the sidewalk crowds looked vital and full of energy. Hal hadn't felt this upbeat since, well, You-Know-What had happened.

He smiled. Yes, it was a good day, and it was only going to get better.

Chapter 47

Several hours later, and a few floors above where Hal still sat, Lauren's phone buzzed. She'd been waiting all morning for Fordyce to call. By now he would have read Hal's second dispatch, even though she had held off on sending it until well after midnight—or around seven p.m. Langley time. He also would have seen her additional inquiry about why Skip Kretzer, a former CIA fieldman who now worked freelance, was hovering at the periphery of their op.

Fordyce's voice was cold and abrupt. He sounded pissed off, and this time he seemed to be calling from Langley, even though it was barely six a.m. over there.

"Are you somewhere we can talk?"

"Yes. My room."

"We're recalling you, effective immediately. You're to tell both of your people there on the ground to stand down. You've overstepped your parameters, and so has the client. And this is straight from . . ." He paused, nearly saying Tina Merritt's name. "This is straight from Marie."

"Look, I see the dangers as clearly as anyone, but maybe there's actually something we need to know about these activities. And it's clear that foreign nationals are involved."

"This isn't just from me. Or even from Marie." He could only be referring to the director. "When an op starts running off the rails to this degree, it triggers consultations with selective other parties. And the client's most recent information definitely snagged that trip wire."

She noted his use of the plural with regard to "selective other parties."

"What other parties, besides the obvious one?" The name Phil Lacey—Kretzer's old boss, and Fordyce's office neighbor—was on the tip of her tongue, but she withheld it.

"That's above your clearance."

"What about my other contact?" Sandor Matas, she meant.

"He'll keep, especially now that he's already being paid. The bottom line here is that the client has moved onto forbidden ground, so you're standing down and so is he. That aspect of your op is finished. Clean up any loose ends and get the hell out, preferably by this evening. When the ground cools, we can start thinking about reentry."

"I'm not leaving until the client is safely out."

"He made his own bed. Your only role now is to cut him loose and give yourself some immediate distance. Send word that you're leaving, and he can play it as he chooses."

"We're throwing him to the wolves?"

"Any reason to believe they're even circling?"

"Well, we already know that one is. I gave you his name."

"We're not getting involved in a matter between two private American citizens. So unless you think he's endangered by some of their people—"

Sarič, he meant.

"We have to assume he is. It also depends on what might have happened in the interim, and until he files his next dispatch, we're blind on that."

"And will remain so, by my order. He lost his focus. That's on him. And maybe you as well."

"Yes, well, that will make a nice line for your final report. But you know how failure always tends to percolate upward. All the more reason you had better let me ensure a safe exit for the client."

She let him stew on that for a moment. He was probably trying to imagine how lurid the headlines would be if a disgraced Hollywood figure and former congressman died in a foreign land on his watch.

"I'll book him a flight, then. For tonight. I'll send you the details, and you can forward them with his notice of severance. If he decides to stay put, that's on him."

"I'm remaining in place until he's out. Book my flight for tomorrow morning, and I'll see that he's gone by then."

Another pause, followed by a sigh.

"Okay, then. Tomorrow morning. But he's solely your responsibility now."

"Fine."

"Oh, and there's one other complication we could both do without. The client's girlfriend. Or ex-girlfriend."

"What about her?"

"She replied to his email. Apparently, she's actually considering his offer, although she hasn't yet booked any travel."

Lauren was floored. She wondered what must have changed in their dynamic to bring this about.

"Send it to me."

"Just did. And I'll have those flight arrangements within the hour."

So there it was. The op was in ruins, and she had only a few hours to get word to Hal that he had been cut adrift, a victim of nothing more than his own curiosity, of poking his nose into forbidden places—in other words, of actually being a pretty decent spy.

Lauren wondered who else had been involved in this decision. Had Phil Lacey managed to pick up in the corridors what was going on with Hal? Or maybe, if he was running Kretzer without Agency authorization, he had picked up a tip from that direction and acted preemptively to shut down a threat to his own off-the-books activities? If so, that would be a far bigger scandal than spying illegally on a few famous Americans. But Fordyce seemed to be too intent on covering his own ass to notice, or even care.

In any event, her most urgent need was to get word to Hal in a way that wouldn't endanger him further, and then make sure he safely left the country. All of that would become far more complicated if, in the meantime, Jess Miller hopped on an incoming plane. Although Lauren's worries on that front abated as soon as she read Miller's email, which made it clear that her arrival wasn't imminent.

With no knowledge yet of what Hal had been up to overnight, she was already operating at a disadvantage. It was time to call in some reinforcements. Quint would be needed, but he might not be enough. She picked up her phone and punched in the number for Malone.

Chapter 48

By the time Hal called, Pavel had been at his office since eight a.m., coordinating damage control with a very irritated Wally Wallek. News of the "Paperback Writer" gag was burning its way across social media like a flash fire. In Bolrovia, it had already overtaken the story about the ruthless military operation at the border.

The worst item so far had been an online post on *Politika*, a site run by opposition media figures who'd splashed it atop their main page with the headline "The Fool on the Hill: President's Favorite Comic Turns His Ignorance of the Beatles into the Night's Best Punch Line."

Fortunately, no one had filmed Hal's show, mostly because Sarič had again collected everyone's phones at the door. But plenty of people who had witnessed it seemed to be talking—anonymously, anyway.

Pavel's spin was the one Hal had suggested—that the president had been notified in advance and had played along perfectly. So far, the only takers were media outlets sympathetic to the president, but since his friends controlled most of the major papers and TV networks, Pavel was actually making progress.

The web page for BolroTel, the network with the country's largest viewership, had posted an online headline an hour earlier which read, "The Joke Was on Him . . . by Design: President Horvatz Deftly Plays the Straight Man."

Wally, who by midmorning had been muttering that the whole mess was unsalvageable, had popped into Pavel's office only moments earlier to give him a beaming thumbs-up:

"Nice work. Keep it going, Pavel."

"Maybe. But how are we going to sell it to *him*?" Meaning the president.

Wally smiled wickedly.

"I just saw him. Fortunately, he wasn't even paying much attention—you know how he avoids the opposition sites—until the BolroTel piece ran. I told him the whole thing was actually a well-timed smoke screen, designed to divert international attention from the actions he'd ordered at the border. I said it was your idea, that you dreamed it up right there on the spot. You'll get all the credit."

"Or all the blame."

"Still. In a weird way, it's working." Wally shook his head, marveling at the strangeness of it all. "Every time I think I've figured out what makes news," he said, "some shit like this comes along, and suddenly three hundred dead bodies at the border don't matter anymore."

"Three *hundred?*" The bottom fell out of Pavel's stomach. Wally nodded grimly.

"But nobody has that yet, and you sure as hell didn't hear it from me. We're trying to keep all the aid workers out of there until the bodies can be moved. So keep fanning the fires on this thing and talking about what a good sport the president is. I'll handle him."

"Sure."

Pavel went back to his desk, needing to sit down after that news. *Three hundred bodies.* Yes, Pavel was certainly doing important work here, for his country and for the world, by helping divert attention from that. He imagined his Poppy shaking his head in disgust.

Pavel's phone buzzed. He couldn't bear the thought of talking to yet another reporter or opinion maker right now. Or maybe he just didn't trust himself to say the right thing. Then he saw that it was Hal.

"Hal, where are you? Shit, what time is it?"

"Just after noon. Don't worry, I'm still in the lobby, but I'm definitely ready to roll. How soon can you get here?"

In a way, this summons was a relief. Now he could stop lying for a while.

"Is half an hour good?"

"Sure. And hey, is everything, well, going okay? After last night, I mean. I can issue some kind of official statement, if you think that will help."

Five minutes ago Pavel would've gladly accepted the offer. Now he no longer gave a shit.

"Don't bother. See you soon."

Chapter 49

———————≋———————

Hal came up with his plan of action for the afternoon while waiting for Pavel. The safest approach would've been to head first to the food carts to drop off his latest dispatch, but his eagerness to make a run at The Hub overcame his sense of caution. For all he knew, an angry Horvatz might soon order further limits on his movements. A pissed-off Katie Carlin might also be able to stir up some trouble.

"Where to?" Pavel asked. He looked a bit harried, which made Hal feel a little guilty.

"Let's take a walk," Hal said. "There's a place I've been meaning to check out."

"Did you change your mind about the House of Terror?"

"This is along the same lines, but a little newer."

"What's it called?"

"The Hub."

Pavel frowned.

"It's a museum?"

"You'll see. C'mon."

Hal led the way, but after a few blocks Pavel seemed restless.

"Are you sure you're not lost?" He got out his phone. "I'll look it up for you. The Hub, you said?"

"No. We're there. It's just ahead, behind the Apple Store."

"*Behind* it? In the alley?"

"Yes."

Hal was already moving toward the left side of the building, where a narrow passage led toward the alley in the back. Pavel ran a few steps to catch up.

"Is it a bar?"

"No."

"Some kind of private club?"

"No, but you're getting warmer."

Hal turned right into the alley and then stopped. An armed guard sat in a folding chair by an unmarked steel door. Another chair sat empty. Two security cameras were mounted overhead, and a couple of unfinished wooden booths, or sentry stations, stood to either side of the door, indicating just how new the facility must be. But for the moment it was guarded by only one man, who now stood, alert. Pavel jostled up from behind, then gasped as he saw the lay of the land. He lowered his voice to a whisper.

"What is this place?"

Hal could already see there were no windows along the back wall. The guard still had not spoken, but he had leveled the gun at him.

"It's some kind of data center. The other Americans have been here, so I thought I'd take a look."

"What kind of gun is he pointing at us?"

"I think it's an AK-47."

Hal smiled and raised his hands to show he meant no harm, then inched forward.

"Halt!" the guard said. Hal did so.

"It's okay. We're with that group of Americans that came yesterday. We just didn't have time to come with them."

The guard frowned. He replied in a burst of Bolrovian and took two steps closer. Pavel translated nervously.

"He is telling us to slowly back away and leave the alley."

"Tell him what I just said."

Pavel sighed with exasperation but spoke to the guard, who shook his head and replied curtly.

"He says we must go."

"Tell him who you are."

"*What?*"

"Don't you have some kind of ID that shows where you work and who you work for?"

"Yes, but . . ."

"And I've got this."

Hal reached inside his jacket for the folded entry certificate in his lapel pocket. The guard reacted in alarm, barking out a command. With an alarming clatter, he chambered a round into his weapon and leveled it at Hal's chest.

"He says to back away! Now!"

"Okay, but show him this."

"No! We should leave."

"Look," Hal said, waving the paper like a white flag and hoping the guard might at least understand that one word of English.

The guard lowered his weapon ever so slightly, then tilted his head, peering with interest at the fake parchment and its gold seal. After a pause, he motioned for Hal to step forward, although the gun barrel was still at waist level, and when Pavel also moved forward, he again shouted, "Halt!"

Hal inched closer, sliding his feet to keep from alarming the fellow further. He stretched his arm out, holding the document close enough for the guard to read it.

It took a few moments—Hal doubted this fellow did much reading—but after a perusal in which the guard's lips moved as he scanned, his features softened and he nodded. He then motioned Pavel forward, and when he next spoke his voice was calmer.

Pavel answered, also nodding. He got out his wallet and showed his Presidential Palace ID. Hal twice heard the words "Prezident Horvatz," and both times the guard nodded. His gun was now at his side, the barrel pointing at the ground.

The guard then spoke briefly, as if outlining a series of instructions.

"Da, da," Pavel said. He turned toward Hal.

"He says we may enter, but once we're inside we must immediately ask to see the security chief. We are not allowed to go any further into the facility without an escort."

"Good enough for me."

The guard pressed a button and stood before a camera. A voice blared over the speaker, and he answered it. Then a buzzer sounded, and the guard opened the door to let them in.

There was a small entryway with a coat closet and a few storage lockers, but even from there you could see a large room just ahead to the right, where several workers sat before large monitors, working at keyboards with headphones on.

"I guess this is where we wait," Pavel said.

The door had already shut behind them, and no one had yet

approached, so Hal decided to move closer to snap a few photos before they were kicked out. He pulled out his phone and stepped quickly forward until he reached the entrance.

"No, Hal. Wait!"

But Hal had already reached the entryway, and his view was of a vast open floor plan with at least fifty desks and monitors, all of them in use.

He quickly took a few photos and then began filming a video, sweeping his phone from left to right to capture the full panorama. Pavel rushed up behind him, whispering, "Stop! Stop!"

Hal was giddy, triumphant. He was the dumb innocent American abroad and, like so many before him, cocksure that his nationality and his status would make him immune to any serious consequences, even though, unknown to him, he was now directly in the gunsight of another guard, who had leveled his weapon from across the room.

"Halt!" the second guard shouted.

The cry brought an immediate hush over the clatter and clamor of the workers, all of whom now looked up from their desks to gawk at Hal and the guard. A few of them dropped to the floor from their chairs, covering their heads with their hands.

Hal slowly lowered his phone, dropped it into his pocket, and shouted into the sudden silence. .

"I'm with the visiting Republicans, the Wolf TV guys. The, uh, P-PAC guys."

It didn't sound at all convincing, even to Hal. The guard marched forward, gun leveled. He chambered a round as he approached, just as the other guard had done, only this fellow seemed more resolute and determined. He approached along a narrow aisle between desks without once averting his eyes, and he didn't stop until the barrel was pressing against Hal's sternum. Pavel was just behind him, not moving a muscle.

And that's when Hal finally awakened to the idea that "immune" didn't mean bulletproof, and that, in a finely balanced moment like this, something as trivial as a twitching muscle or a slight error in judgment—by him, or by the guard, who, for all Hal knew, had spent half his life waiting for a pretext to blow someone away—could result in, well, death. Yes, there was something worse than dying onstage or online, and this was it. His throat constricted, his mouth went dry. Why did wisdom, especially for him, always seem to arrive belatedly?

Then another voice called out from the far side of the room, this time in accented English.

"You two! You are under arrest! Bring them this way."

The man who had called out wore a suit and tie. Presumably he was the head of security, the fellow they were supposed to wait for by the door. He stood with his hands on his hips, staring, seemingly enraged.

He led them into a corridor, with Hal following, then Pavel, and then the armed guard. On their right they passed an open doorway to an office, where another fellow in a suit didn't even look up from his terminal, and then an open doorway on the left, where, this time, the fellow did look up. Behind him he heard Pavel gasp and call out a name.

"Maksim!"

Hal glanced over his shoulder to see the guard shove Pavel forward with the barrel of his gun. The security chief shouted angrily.

"Quiet! You are forbidden to speak to anyone here!"

The jostling stopped as they reached an open doorway on the right. The security chief directed them and the guard inside. It was a window-less cubicle with three plastic chairs and a bare table with two pairs of handcuffs attached. The air smelled like sweat and cigarette smoke. The door shut behind them.

The security chief began punching a number into his phone. He nodded at the guard and shouted, "Empty your pockets, both of you! Put everything on the table."

Hal thought immediately of the four pages of handwritten coded notes, folded inside a five-euro note in his right pocket. So much for the idea that he had learned to play the spy game by paying attention to detail.

Pavel had already pulled out his wallet, phone, and keys, but Hal was so stunned and panicky that he hadn't even reached into his pockets.

The security chief looked up from his phone, which was burbling with the ringtones of an outgoing call.

"I said to empty your pockets. Now!"

The gun barrel nudged him from behind. Hal reached first for his wallet while he desperately tried to come up with a plausible explanation for the notes. But no amount of improv skills could save him now. This was a major fuckup, a beginner's error, and now he would pay for it.

Chapter 50

A sense of impending doom lowered itself to the base of Pavel's stomach with the weight of a thousand dumplings from Gertmann's. How had this happened? Why had he allowed Hal to talk him into entering this strange place? Should he call Sarič to get them out of this mess, or would that only make things worse? And what *was* this place, anyway? A data center, Hal had called it, The Hub. But when they had come through the door, he had heard more voices speaking Russian than Bolrovian. Already he felt like he knew more than was good for him, which in turn made him wonder why Hal had been so determined to get inside.

At the moment his biggest concern was the barrel of the Kalashnikov, which was poking into Hal's back as the rattled man fumbled for his wallet and phone.

Then the door opened behind them. To Pavel's immense relief, it was his geeky friend, Maksim Polikon, who—thank god—must have heard Pavel call out as they'd passed his office.

"Ladislaw, what the hell is going on here?"

"This is not your business, Polikon. There has been a security breach."

"I am the director; everything here is my business. And why have you detained a ranking presidential aide?"

The question seemed to throw Ladislaw off balance. When a voice chirped on his phone in answer to his call, he glanced at the screen, raised it to his face, and said, "Sorry. Misdial."

He then looked at Maksim as if uncertain what to do next. Hal had stopped emptying his pockets and was dropping his phone back into his pants. Only his wallet was on the table.

"I know you have priority in security matters, Ladislaw, but if you'd like to report a breach on your watch, I can expedite the process with a direct call to Vice Minister Sarič on my secure phone." Maksim raised his phone into the air. It looked just like the encrypted one Sarič had foisted on Pavel. "Just say the word and I will initiate the process."

Maksim paused to let the full import of his words bloom in Ladislaw's imagination. Even Pavel could imagine what this "process" might signify—forms to fill out, embarrassing questions to answer, perhaps a formal review to navigate. Maksim lowered his phone and spoke again.

"Or, if you prefer, I can speak to the ministry later on a more informal basis. Without any paperwork, while allowing you to maintain a clean slate."

"You said he's a presidential aide?"

"The president's chief administrative aide, yes." Then, turning toward Pavel, "You do have your ID, Mr. Lukov, yes?"

Pavel nodded and, for the second time in the past few minutes, handed over his ID.

Ladislaw took a quick look and was handing it back when Hal spoke up.

"Should I show him this as well?"

Ladislaw groaned the moment he saw the white sheet of fake parchment with the gold seal.

"Oh, fuck. One of *those*? You're that American funnyman, aren't you. Is this whole thing some kind of fucking prank?"

"He is a presidential guest," Pavel said. "Mr. Hal Knight."

It was obvious from Ladislaw's expression that the name meant little to him, but clearly he had seen the news about a visiting comedian. He sighed loudly and turned to Maksim.

"I'll give you ten minutes with them, Polikon, but not a second more. Handle them as you see fit. But afterward I will need a full report from you. *In writing*. For my files only."

The latter words told Pavel that, for the moment, Sarič would not be notified, which was a victory unto itself. Maksim smiled tightly, but Pavel could tell from his eyes that Ladislaw had regained the upper hand. Putting this episode into Ladislaw's files would give the security chief leverage going forward, especially if anything negative ever resulted from this breach.

But for the moment, at least, he had yielded the field of battle. Ladislaw and the guard departed. Hal snatched his wallet off the table and Pavel gathered up his own things.

Maksim unloaded the moment the door was shut, in an angry burst of Bolrovian.

"What the fuck are you doing here, Pavel? Are you trying to get the two of you killed?! Not to mention me!"

"So this is the new job you were talking about?"

"Yes. This is the job. Figurehead local supervisor to a bunch of FSB hackers." Then, with a nervous glance at Hal, "And please tell me that this blundering asshole doesn't speak Bolrovian."

"He doesn't. He tells jokes for a living." Although by then it must have occurred to both of them that the letters "FSB" sounded the same in either language.

"Yeah, well, this is quite the belly laugh, and the joke is on both of us."

"What do people do here?"

"I've already said too much, and you've already seen too much. And now I am going to have to find some way to get you both out of here without Ladislaw seeing, before he changes his mind. So let's get moving. And please, Pavel, keep your stupid overeager friend out of trouble for the remainder of his stay."

"Of course, Maksim. Of course."

Instead of heading back the way they'd come, Maksim led them further down the hallway to an unmarked steel door. He took out a key, unlocked it, then opened it onto an empty hallway that ran perpendicular to the one they'd exited, along an expanse of painted brick that Pavel guessed was the rear wall of the Apple Store.

Maksim, standing with his foot wedged in the jamb to keep the steel door open, pointed right, toward the far end of the hallway.

"Go to the end and use the fire exit. No alarm will sound. And wherever you're going next, maybe you'd better take a roundabout way, if you catch my meaning."

"Yes, Maksim. And thank you."

Maksim frowned, shook his head, and disappeared back behind the steel door, which closed with a loud, echoing bang. Pavel turned to see that Hal had his phone out and was scrolling through the photos he'd taken.

"Are you insane? Let's go!"

They hurried down the hallway, shoved the bar to open the fire door, and emerged back into sunlight. They rushed toward the front of the Apple Store and headed right. Pavel and Hal both kept looking over their shoulders, but no one seemed to be following them. Not yet, anyway.

Twenty minutes later, after randomly turning left and right down several side streets, they emerged onto King Viktor Square, where they quickly lost themselves amid the usual crowds of tourists.

Only then did Pavel breathe easier.

Chapter 51

Hal's sense of relief following their narrow escape lasted only as long as it took Pavel and him, in their roundabout way, to reach the alley with the food carts. As they turned the final corner, he instantly saw that something was amiss. All seven carts were there, along with the yellow umbrella. But the haluski vendor was gone, and so was his tip jar. Hal tried not to overreact, which wasn't easy when less than an hour ago he'd been held at gunpoint. Maybe his mailman was on a bathroom break and had taken the jar with him for safekeeping.

But there was an edgy vibe among the other vendors. Several were talking to each other in lowered voices, and the old guy selling chimney cakes waved Pavel over the moment he saw them. He spoke rapidly, while pointing with his tongs toward the yellow umbrella.

"What's he saying?"

"The haluski vendor was arrested. Rudi says the police came and took him away."

Rudi kept talking.

"They threw him into a van and drove it straight across King Viktor Square."

"Why? Why'd they arrest him?"

Another exchange between Pavel and Rudi followed.

"He doesn't know, but he said it wasn't the regular police. Their uniforms were different. He thinks maybe it was the border patrol."

Or Sarič's people. And why would they take his tip jar as well?

Hal wondered what he should do with his dispatch, wadded in his pocket like stolen goods. He looked over to where Chris had been busking the day before, but a local guitarist was now there, singing a Bolrovian folk tune.

"You don't look so good," Pavel said.

"Let's head back to the Esplanade."

"Maksim seemed to think it was safer to keep moving."

"As if they don't know where I'm staying."

"Or where I live." Pavel sounded ticked off, and Hal couldn't blame him. Dragging him into the data center had made them both toxic. But the sight of the vacated haluski cart made him feel vulnerable here, so he turned toward the hotel, and Pavel followed.

The mouth of the alley was obstructed by three approaching construction workers in tool belts and yellow hard hats. One was balancing a long stepladder on his shoulder like a battering ram. As Hal tried to ease past them, the guy holding the ladder turned to speak to his colleagues, which swung the ladder toward them. Hal tried to duck out of the way, but a glancing blow knocked him to the ground.

"Shit!" he heard the man shout. "I am so fucking sorry, man. Didn't even see you coming." His English was American, and the voice was familiar, putting Hal on alert as the guy rushed over to help Hal to his feet.

"You okay, man? Sorry, but my Bolrovian's pretty lousy."

Hal looked up into the face of Sal, the other CIA guy from Vieques, the one who supposedly worked here as a construction foreman. His grip, firm and strong, lifted Hal to his feet.

"Not a problem," Hal said. "I'm American."

"Ah, well, at least this won't turn into an international incident, right? Dumbass American clocks local. Hey, don't I know you?"

Hal was confused. Shouldn't they be pretending they *didn't* know each other?

"Uh, I don't think so."

"Sure, you're that comedian, Hal Knight." He turned to his colleagues. "This is that guy who the president invited over." Then, turning back toward Hal, "Hey, man, okay if I get a picture?"

There had to be a point to this, so Hal played along.

"Sure. Seems like a fair trade for knocking me on my ass."

Sal laughed a little too hard, then handed his phone to Pavel to take the shot. Pavel looked inquiringly at Hal, who nodded. Sal posed to the left, throwing his right arm around Hal's shoulder, but not before stuffing something into the back pocket of his trousers.

Pavel took the photo, then handed back the phone.

"Thanks, man. And sorry."

"No problem."

Sal picked up the ladder and the three men continued on their way.

"What an idiot!" Pavel said, glancing over his shoulder. He shook his head, then laughed. "Some people, yes?"

For all Hal knew, Sal was trying to warn him against returning to the hotel, so he figured he had better read the message as soon as possible.

"Anywhere around here where I could take a leak?" Hal asked.

Pavel pointed just ahead to the right, where people were seated at outdoor tables in front of the Shamrock, one of those touristy Irish pubs that you saw in every major city in Europe. Hal headed for the door at double time.

"Be right out," he said over his shoulder.

It was as dim inside as a November afternoon in Dublin, which was probably why most of the customers were outdoors. The barman directed him to the back, across a floor covered with peanut shells. The men's room had only a single stall by a tiny sink, so Hal latched the door of the stall and unfolded Sal's message, which was handwritten in pencil. The words hit him harder than the ladder had: *Folding our tents. Get out. AA6821. 22:00.*

So it was over, then, just like that—even though his latest dispatch was still undelivered and he now had all those photos of The Hub, as well as a firsthand report of everything he'd seen and heard, including an unmistakable mention of the FSB by the facility's director, a local fellow named Maksim who had struck him as someone in over his head.

And apparently, despite all of Susan's earlier promises about "exfiltra-tion" if things got dicey, he was now expected to get out of the country on his own. He assumed that the letters and numbers in the message were a reference to an outgoing flight, probably American Airlines, at 22:00, meaning ten p.m. But that was more than five hours away, leav-ing plenty of time for Branko Sarič to snatch him, which seemed likely now that his mailman had been arrested and his CIA handlers were shutting down the op.

He was furious, and also confused. Why close up shop now, just when he was making progress? And why cut him adrift without even throw-ing him a rope to pull him to safety? Unless his carelessness had put his CIA colleagues in danger as well. For all he knew, Susan and Chris had already been locked into a couple of those basement cells.

Where to next, then?

Even if no one was waiting for him at the Esplanade, surely they'd intercept him at the airport. They might even be looking for him out on the streets, and since he was carrying his phone he'd be pretty easy to find. Plus, he was now in possession of plenty of incriminating material—the note, his dispatch, the photos and video on his phone.

Hal tore up the first two items and flushed the shreds down the toilet. He considered smashing his phone on the rim of the toilet and then submerging it in the bowl. But he didn't want to destroy the photos, not after nearly paying for them with his life. Surely there was some way to get this information into the right hands.

He decided to send copies of the photos to his own email account, and also to Jess's, and then delete them. But as he opened his email account, he realized that this, too, was a foolhardy idea, especially if Sarič's people were intercepting his emails. Maybe the best option was just to get moving again. He was about to close his inbox when he saw that a new message from Jess had arrived only an hour ago. Excited, even a little giddy, he opened it.

Her message was brutally brief:

Travel plans canceled. Just like you. Below she'd provided a hyperlink.

Hal felt like he'd been punched in the stomach. He clicked on the link and was treated to a TikTok video of the confrontation the night before with the young American woman in the narrow alley. Whoever had recorded it had gotten a perfect shot of her face, contorted by righteous anger. Worse, Hal's mouth was moving in almost perfect sync with the angry shouted words of the vile fellow who had pushed him from behind. A professional dubbing technician could not have managed it better. Hal knew what he'd *really* said, of course, but there was no way to explain all that now, and no one would believe him anyway. Hell, even Carlin and Frederickson had thought he'd said all this shit, and they'd been there.

The video had been posted two hours earlier. There were already more than twelve thousand views and two thousand comments. Hal stooped over the bowl and heaved, but nothing came up. He turned off his phone, unlocked the stall, and splashed his face at the sink. He stared into the smudged mirror. The poor lighting gave his skin the pale sheen of boiled cabbage.

He had nothing now. Nothing but those photos, the video, and his own eyewitness account of all he'd seen and heard. He could still do them great damage, but only if he made it out of here tonight. Then what? More trips to lonely bolt holes so that other unreconstructed assholes could seek the aid and comfort of his oldest and stalest jokes? He was a failure, a walking joke who was helping provide PR cover for a genocidal creep.

With a sudden overboil of rage he smashed the heel of his palm against the mirror, which sent a lightning bolt of cracks across its surface. Then he shoved through the door, crunched across the peanut shells, and stepped into the sunlight. Pavel was waiting beyond the outdoor tables. As Hal passed the last one, he snatched up a full mug of beer from a tray that a waiter had just set down and he kept on walking.

"Hey, what are you doing?" Pavel said.

Hal guzzled the beer as he went, not caring if anyone saw him. Then he dropped the empty mug into a garbage can. A block later, as they passed another outdoor café, he snatched a second drink, this one from the table of a woman who had turned to speak to a friend. Whiskey this time, gone in seconds. He set the glass on a window ledge and wiped his mouth on his sleeve.

"This isn't the way to the hotel," Pavel said. He sounded baffled, even alarmed.

"I don't give a shit."

"What's happened to you? Where are we going?"

"Anywhere but where we are. Just keep moving."

Pavel nodded but didn't say another word. It was all he could do to keep pace.

Chapter 52

Lauren had just begun packing for her flight the following morning when Quint called. The last thing she needed was more bad news, but what else could it possibly be?

"Yes?"

"Just thought you should know, I'm at the Green Devil setting up for my next gig, and Hal Knight is here."

"Well, at least now we know where he is. Malone delivered his severance message, but that was hours ago. What's he doing?"

"Looks kinda shit-faced, tell you the truth. And not at all like a guy who's planning on making a flight out of here in another three hours. No bags or anything, and he sent that Lukov kid off into a corner like a whipped puppy."

"If all else fails, we can throw him in a cab and take him to the airport ourselves."

"If he lasts that long. He's got that look about him, like he might be about to do something stupid."

"What do you mean?"

"Well, for one thing, it's karaoke night."

"So *that's* what I'm hearing. Good god, is someone doing 'Bohemian Rhapsody'?"

"Yeah, and a few minutes ago Hal went over to speak to the guy running the music machine. The guy nodded and wrote something down, like maybe he was adding Hal to the lineup."

"For *karaoke*?"

"That's what it looked like. Then Hal went off into a corner with a double whiskey, and all he's done since is scribble in his little black notebook, right out in the open."

"You're right. This isn't good."

"Now he's got his phone out, which he isn't even supposed to be carrying. And if our postman is already squealing, well . . ."

"He didn't know enough to hurt us. Or not for a while. And you're sure Hal hadn't dropped off a message before they snatched the tip jar?"

"Positive. It's a pretty thin silver lining, but yeah."

"Keep an eye on him. And if it gets worse—"

"Shit."

"What?"

"Branko Sarič just walked in with two of his goons. He's giving Hal the look."

"What's Hal doing?"

"Hasn't even looked up from his phone."

There was a pause. Lauren could now hear a woman screeching out the opening lines of "Dancing Queen." She sounded like she was being waterboarded.

"Sarič is deploying them around the room. Now he's quizzing Lukov, who looks like he's about to shit his pants. Fuck, and I just got a better look at one of the goons. It's Skip Kretzer."

"I'm coming over. Start planning some contingencies."

"Will do."

She rushed from the room, leaving her suitcase open on the bed. The moment she reached the lobby, her phone pinged with a text. It was from Hal Knight. Her first reaction was to wonder how he'd even gotten the number. Then she remembered giving it to him on Vieques in case of emergency. Meaning he, too, must know by now that things were getting pretty dire. Why, then, was he getting drunk and signing up for karaoke?

The text was a little incoherent, but its contents were sobering, enough so to make her stop halfway to the revolving doors and read it a second time. The message was filled with rich and intriguing material, and much of it seemed to be from firsthand observation.

Then a batch of photos arrived, along with a brief video. The latter was of particular interest, not only because it appeared to show the interior of "The Hub," as Hal had described it in his text, but also because some of the voices in the audio were clearly speaking Russian. The short scene ended with quite the exclamation mark, the sight of a gun barrel pointing directly at the camera.

In the brief time it took Lauren to digest how monumentally important all of this might be, she also realized why Hal must be feeling so hopeless. He'd been abandoned in the wild just as he'd stumbled upon something huge, and now the wolves really *were* circling.

Lauren gathered up the photos and his message into a new file, punched in a few more commands, then continued, quickening her pace.

Chapter 53

Hal would no longer listen to reason. That much had become clear to Pavel as soon as they'd entered the Green Devil, where they had eventually arrived after several wayward hours of itinerant drinking and petty theft. Hal had taken one look at the sign out front advertising karaoke night and, with a sudden light in his eyes, had said, "I'm doing this. But first I've got to write something. Bring me a double whiskey and leave me the fuck alone."

Pavel hadn't liked the sound of that, but he'd obliged Hal anyway by placing his order at the bar and delivering the glass. And now, as if things couldn't get any worse, Branko Sarič had arrived with one of his henchmen, plus the tall American.

Sarič stepped toward Pavel and clamped a hand on his shoulder.

"How long has he been here?"

Pavel checked his watch.

"Maybe half an hour?"

"How many drinks?"

"Hard to say. This is the fourth bar we've stopped in. Or passed." It wasn't worth mentioning the stolen drinks along the way. Then, as he noticed Sarič eyeing his beer glass, half full, he raised it slightly and said, "My first."

Sarič narrowed his eyes as if he didn't believe it for even a moment. Then, as if to exhibit his moral superiority, he unclipped the orange water bottle from his belt and took a long swig.

He then turned to watch Hal, staring for a solid minute without interruption, arms folded, as if willing Hal to look up from his work and notice him. But Hal kept working, except now he was tapping at his phone. He paused only once, to reach for his whiskey glass, which was nearly empty.

Finally Sarič seemed to tire of this standoff in which only he was participating. He unfolded his arms, again clamped a hand on Pavel's shoulder, and spoke roughly into his ear.

"I am stepping outside to attend to other arrangements, but only for a few minutes. Keep him here until I return. An order, not a request. If something happens while I am out, you will coordinate with that man over there to bring the situation under control."

Sarič gestured toward the tall American.

"Who is he?"

"Do you understand me?"

"Yes."

Sarič nodded and headed for the door. Hal still did not look up, not even for a glance.

Chapter 54

By the time Sarič departed, Quint was working on a few contingencies, as Lauren had put it. The first order of business was to get a better feel for the lay of the land, so he approached the Green Devil's proprietor, Dimitri Kolch, who stood next to the karaoke stage, watching as the young woman who'd been singing "Dancing Queen" curtsied to acknowledge a tepid round of applause.

"Got a second?"

Kolch nodded. Quint leaned closer to be heard above the noise.

"Something I need to know before we play our set. Kind of a safety quirk of our bass player's, who had a bad experience at some gig a long time ago. I think it was a fire, but he doesn't really talk about it."

"And?"

"Well, I know I should've asked sooner, but I need a rundown of all your exits and entries, to set his mind at ease. Fire doors, stairways, passages. He always feels better if he knows all that in advance."

Kolch took a step back, as if to take a better look at Quint. There was a quizzical expression on his face, with the hint of a smile.

"Come with me."

He led Quint downstairs to a small office tucked behind the basement bar. No windows, eight by eight, with a cluttered desk. Kolch slid behind the desk into a creaking chair. On the wall behind him was a whiteboard calendar where he'd written all the upcoming events.

Quint saw the name of his band in the slot for last night, with an arrow that ran straight through to tonight. The name of another—and better-known—band had been crossed out. Quint wondered yet again how his guys had merited such special treatment. Maybe, as Kolch had said, the other act had canceled. But he could've sworn he'd heard that the other band was playing tonight at a smaller and less lucrative venue.

"Fire doors and exits, you said."

"Yeah."

Kolch shook his head, smiling wryly. He unlocked a drawer and pulled out a white letter-size envelope, which he handed across the desk to Quint. It was sealed and unmarked.

"What's this?"

"I do not know. But when the friend who recommended you gave me your number, he also gave me this. He said to give it to you if you asked any questions about, as he put it, ingress and egress issues. At the time I thought it was one of the most absurd things I had ever heard. Obviously, I was wrong."

He smiled with amused fascination as Quint tore open the envelope. Two pages were folded inside. The first was a detailed diagram of the upstairs floor plan, with all doorways, emergency exits, and stairways clearly marked. Some had handwritten annotations in English, but with the kind of lettering Europeans used. The second page was a diagram of the basement level, which was even more complex, and certainly more interesting. It was exactly what he needed.

He looked over at Kolch, who was studying him closely.

"It's just a—"

"No, no. I do *not* want to know what it is. And I'm guessing that you, better than me, will understand why."

"This friend of yours—"

"Requested that I not reveal his name. I try to accommodate my friends' requests. My performers' requests as well."

"Thanks, man."

"Oh, and perhaps if you could do me one favor."

"Sure."

"Whatever that is, could you make sure it isn't still on the premises at the end of the evening?"

"Must've read my mind."

They went back upstairs, with Kolch leading the way. Quint arrived just in time to see Sarič reentering the bar. A minute or two later, Lauren walked in. He tried to get her attention, but her eyes were already on Hal, who had stood from his table in the far corner and was now walking somewhat unsteadily toward the stage. It was showtime.

Chapter 55

It was quite the tableau. In all her years as a spy, Lauren had never witnessed a scene so heavily populated with significant players. Was this how it always went when you worked with a professional performer? Did their flair for the dramatic include an innate sense of choreography? Although she'd rarely seen anyone who looked as oblivious and unheedful of his perilous surroundings as Hal Knight did just now.

On further inspection, her assessment was even more dire. Hal wasn't oblivious; he was defeated. He had given up. She had seen this before in the field: the vacant, unconcerned look of an operative who had become resigned to the prospect of imminent calamity. While Lauren hadn't always liked her agents and assets, she hadn't yet lost a single one of them, and wasn't about to do so now. Not without a fight.

She quickly made her way to the back room, standing only a few feet from Quint. By then she'd noticed that the proprietor, Dimitri Kolch, seemed quite engrossed with what was transpiring. He stood by the stage, watching intently as Hal reached the microphone and began peering at a sheaf of handwritten notes. It was a little horrifying to see Hal openly displaying pages from his notebook, but, well, that whole message system was shot to hell, so why not? By now most of the clientele from the bar and from downstairs had also made its way into the back, drawn by the news that Hal Knight would be offering the evening's final karaoke number. But even he couldn't command everyone's attention once Branko Sarič entered from up front. The restless crowd went eerily quiet. People made room for him, as if he were emitting a force field, and it was clear to everyone that his only focus was Hal.

Taking advantage of this moment of uneasy distraction, Quint sidled over to Lauren and passed her a note, which she glanced at right away. She nodded back in acknowledgment of its message. Up on the stage, Hal took the mike from its cradle and, old pro that he was, casually scanned the room.

"Well, hell, looks like the gang's all here! All my friends and all my enemies. Kinda perfect, really." Considering how much he'd had to drink, his words were remarkably crisp and clear. "Okay, then! Is everyone ready for some laughs?"

"Yes!" the crowd answered as one, loudly and boisterously, as if spoiling for mischief.

"Well, that's a shame, really, because this is going to be more of a confessional. My very own pity party. But I hope that first you'll indulge me in the luxury of a little introduction for the number I'm about to do."

There was a hubbub of puzzled chatter, of people turning to each other and wondering what was up. Shrugs, nervous laughter. Or maybe this was just misdirection, part of his shtick, a clever lead-in to some great punch line. He talked right over them.

"When I was a kid, my mom used to do two things to help her make it through the day. One of them was drink." He mimed holding a glass aloft. "So cheers, everybody."

There were a few shouts of "Cheers!" in reply. Sarič's frown deepened.

"The other thing she did was play show tunes on our old stereo. Vinyl soundtrack LPs that she'd had since the sixties. *Brigadoon, The Sound of Music, The King and I, West Side Story*—all of that shit. It drove me bananas, but as a by-product I learned every last word by osmosis, and the number that I'm about to sing, but with my very own lyrics, is from an old movie called *Paint Your Wagon*. Hated that one, too, especially the signature track, a godawful song about how the wind was a woman and her name was Mariah. So, for your enlightenment, and possibly your torture, here we go. Maestro?"

He nodded to the man running the machine, who cued up the song. Lauren immediately recognized the tune. Then Hal began to sing.

Here in Blatsk they've got a name for me and rain and fire,
The rain is Sarič, the fire is Nick, and they call this man Pariah.
Pariah thought he was a star, with jokes and dollars flying,

But now he makes a cringing sound like a stand-up comic dying.
Pariah, Pariah. They call this man Pariah.

The crowd teetered for a moment between silence and wide-eyed shock, then settled on uneasy laughter. No one dared to even glance at Sarič, whose gaze of withering contempt remained steady as Hal launched into his second verse.

Before I knew Pariah's fate, I laughed at wails and whining,
I had a girl and she had me and the sun was always shining.
And then one day I left my girl, I left her far behind me,
Pariah blew her love away and now there's no one here beside me.
Pariah, Pariah. They call this man Pariah.

By now there was no more laughter. Some of the patrons were looking around, as if seeking cues for how to react. The ones nearest Sarič had edged away further, so that he now stood on an island of open space, although over in the margins Kretzer was grinning in amused acknowledgment of Hal's chutzpah. Lauren's worries multiplied. How deeply would Hal sing his way into his secrets, or even *their* secrets? He launched into his final verse, his voice stronger than ever.

Here in Blatsk they've cut a deal with Yankee lowlife shadies,
They bulldoze tents while a spooky gent watches all from his
  Mercedes.
Yes, I'm bankrupt, a grasping man, with no star left to guide me,
Pariah blew his love away when I needed her beside me.
Pariah, Pariah. They call this man Pariah.

The music faded to silence. A few more daring souls looked pointedly at Sarič, whose face was now red in fury. Someone coughed, and it was enough to make people flinch. Hal had not merely bombed, he had baffled, a funnyman's greatest crime. No matter. With a rumble of static and a blare of feedback he settled the microphone back into its cradle. As if in pity, some people began clapping weakly. Then Dimitri Kolch stepped nimbly onstage and leaned into the mike.

"Put your hands together, everyone, for that intriguing interpretation by Mr. Hal Knight!"

As if relieved to be told how to react, just about everyone—with a single notable exception—erupted into applause. By then, Lauren and Quint were already edging toward Hal.

The applause died away.

Things then began to move very fast.

Chapter 56

Having pulled himself together for his musical finale, a spent and fairly drunk Hal was quickly overwhelmed by the tumult that followed.

The first thing he noticed was Chris, rushing at him from the left, with Susan close in his wake and a befuddled-looking Pavel seemingly trapped between them. Further back, a grim Branko Sarič was nodding toward his underlings as he began trying to shove his way forward through people who were streaming back toward the bar.

"Let's go, man, let's go!" Chris shouted into his ear. Hal, moving as if in one of those dreams where your legs are filled with lead, felt himself propelled toward the wall behind the karaoke machine, where, as if by magic, a door suddenly opened.

Glancing over his shoulder, he saw that Sarič and his people were still caught up in the crush. The rising din of the crowd was then punctuated by the voice of Dimitri Kolch, whose jovial words sounded above them all.

"Mr. Sarič! What a pleasure to have you back in my establishment yet again!"

"You must move out of my way!"

"Pardon?"

"*Move!* It is a matter of national security!"

"Of course. I am so sorry!"

By the end of this exchange, Chris had shoved Hal through the opening, and he could feel the press of other bodies behind them. Hal teetered at the top of a landing, reeling a bit as he peered down into the dimness of a steep wooden stairway, which then went black as the door slammed shut behind them. Susan and Pavel were bunched against him, with Chris at his side, and for a moment it felt like they were all about to topple in a heap down the stairs.

Chris lifted him off his feet and half-carried, half-manhandled him to the bottom. Somehow, they ended up safely at the entrance to a gloomy corridor lit eerily by a red overhead bulb. It was chilly and damp down here, which had a sobering effect. Hal steadied himself.

"Keep going!" Chris said. "This way—now!"

They quickly turned right and then left into another subterranean hallway. This one had an arched brick ceiling dripping with moisture.

"Watch your step, it's slippery," Chris said. By now some of Hal's wits and coordination had returned. They'd gone about twenty feet and were approaching a steel door on the right when a loud crashing noise sounded from above.

"They've broken through!" Susan shouted.

"We're good," Chris answered. "This is the way back up. It locks from the other side."

The four of them rushed through the open door. There was a sound of footsteps pounding down the stairwell, but it was snuffed out as Chris shut the door behind them and threw down a bar to secure it.

They now stood in a darkened hallway, much like the other one, with arched brickwork overhead and a wet, gritty floor. The only light came from Chris's phone. Chris lowered his voice to a whisper.

"That tunnel we were just in continues for another quarter mile. They'll probably keep going, and there are at least three more doors, and none of them leads this way. So keep it quiet, and let's go."

Muffled shouts rose in volume from the other side of the door, then receded. Water dripped onto Hal's neck, and he shivered as a droplet crawled down his back.

They continued for what must have been at least two city blocks before they reached an old, rusted steel stairwell, leading upward. The elevation must have been lower here, because they had to climb two full flights before reaching another steel door, which opened onto the ground floor of a parking deck.

Pavel, who hadn't said a word since they'd gone down the first stairway, spoke up as he peered toward the opening onto the street.

"I think we're on Prelovan Street. If we go left out the front, there's a tram stop at the next corner for the 6 and 11 lines."

Susan spoke to Hal and Pavel.

"You two, head toward the street and stay ready to roll. I need a quick word with Quint."

"Quint?" Hal said. "I thought . . . oh, right. Of course."

Hal and Pavel took off toward the street. Pavel looked over at him with an expression of confusion, then anger.

"So you know him? The keyboard player?"

Hal nodded.

"Who are these people?"

"It's a long and complicated story."

Poor Pavel. He was no doubt wondering what the hell he'd gotten himself mixed up in. Even explaining what he had done up to now was going to be difficult, if not impossible, and from here on out things were only likely to get more complicated and dangerous.

Hal heard Chris—or Quint, as he'd just learned—conferring with Susan in the shadows behind them, their voices fading as Hal and Pavel neared the street. He should cut Pavel loose, urge him to stay behind. This wasn't his fight.

Chapter 57

———— ≈ ————

Lauren hurriedly briefed Quint on what Hal had found out, the evidence he had provided, and how he had sent it.

"No wonder they closed in," Quint replied. "It also explains what Kretzer has been up to. Running interference for all those fuckers."

"And if Phil Lacey is illegally running Kretzer—"

"Then we're in deeper shit than I thought. And thanks to the mess Garvin made, there's not a single safe house in Blatsk that hasn't been compromised, so it's not like we've got somewhere to lay low."

"Get him out of the city as fast as possible."

"What about you?" Quint asked.

"I'm asking Fordyce to leave me in place."

"And if he says no?"

"I'll find another way. So leave some breadcrumbs for me, through Malone or some other way. You know the options."

"Will do. But without authorizations won't we be, well . . ."

"A little shorthanded?"

"Yes."

"Completely. But I have some ideas on that front as well. Go. Now."

Quint nodded and ran toward Hal and Pavel. They were just moving out of sight when Lauren's phone buzzed with an incoming call, not from Fordyce but from a blocked number, meaning it could be just about anyone—even Branko Sarič, she supposed. Hal's call had almost certainly compromised her phone. She should probably get rid of it as soon as possible.

Finally, it stopped buzzing. Hal, Pavel, and Quint went left on Prelovan Street. Lauren set off in the opposite direction. She had a lot to do, with little time left to do it.

Chapter 58

———— ≈ ————

The keyboard player, who Pavel now knew was apparently named Quint, reappeared out of the darkness. He was alone.

Hal, standing next to Pavel, said, "Where's Susan?"

"Wait," Pavel said. "You know her, too?"

"Yeah, well. They're . . ."

"We're part of his security detail," Quint said. "He hired us privately, and, as you can see, our services were needed."

Did Pavel believe that? No. Did it matter? Yes, especially if he was now in league with a foreign government, perhaps even the CIA. His predecessor, Kelenič, had already been arrested for spying, and maybe Pavel would be next.

"Hey, man," Quint said. "Your local knowledge would really be a plus in getting us out of here, but if you want to split, I'm cool with that. Make up your mind now, though, 'cause it's go time."

Pavel nodded but kept walking alongside them down the street. He was still reeling from the last few minutes. Those dark and damp underground corridors had especially freaked him out. Up to now he had never been convinced that such places really existed—a whole network of tunnels beneath the city center, or so it was said. He had only read about them, or maybe he'd overheard Poppy talking about them, or his father. They'd supposedly been built in medieval times, then were augmented and reinforced during the war, to help hide and supply members of the resistance. In traversing them just now he had eerily sensed his Poppy at his side, a far younger version, running for his life. The chill of the place was still on his skin.

They headed for the tram stop. Pavel followed out of inertia but was in turmoil over what to do next. The stop was a junction for two lines, one running north–south, the other east–west. Pavel could already hear the groan and whine of a southbound Number 11 tram approaching from a few blocks away.

"Pavel, it's okay," Hal said. "We can look after ourselves. Take off."

"Where will you go?"

"Somewhere on a tram," Quint said. "But only after Hal throws his phone onto this one, to give 'em something to track. Then we'll take the next one. Beyond that? No idea, and if you're not coming then I don't want to tell you—and believe me, you don't want to know."

"Right. Of course."

He thought again of Poppy, who must have faced these same kinds of choices so long ago. But Poppy had been young and alone, his family dead. Pavel had a wife, two children. What would he tell them about all of this, not just tonight, but years later? Provided he lived that long.

The tram rumbled into view, brakes squealing as it neared the platform.

"Get your phone ready, Hal," Quint said.

The tram stopped. The doors levered open. There were only a few passengers in the car. Hal stepped aboard and slid his phone beneath a seat. A woman sitting nearby looked up, then returned her attention to her own phone as Hal hopped back down to the street. Pavel supposed that now was the time to say goodbye, to turn and walk away or even run, and then do his best to salvage his job, his life. He gripped his phone tightly. A chime sounded on the tram as a crackly amplified voice warned that the doors were about to shut. There was a hiss of hydraulics, followed by a creak of hinges as the doors began to close.

Pavel, as if hypnotized, tossed his phone underhanded. It sailed through the narrowing aperture just before the doors clamped shut. There was a tightness high in his throat, and for a few seconds he thought he might gag. As the tram pulled away, he experienced a wild impulse to run after it. But he held his ground, and the moment passed.

Hal's mouth was agape, speechless—which made Pavel want to laugh, if only to break the tension. Instead, he drew a deep breath and said, "I can always take off later, or say you forced me at gunpoint. But first we need to catch an eastbound Number 6. I think I know where we should go next."

"Where?" Quint said.

"You'll see."

Seconds later they heard the rumble of an eastbound Number 6. When the doors opened, Pavel noticed Quint giving Hal a look, as if to ask if this young man could be trusted. Hal supplied the answer.

"Lead the way, Pavel."

They boarded without a further word.

Chapter 59

———— ≋ ————

Five blocks away, and still heading in the opposite direction, Lauren was on the phone to Fordyce, her last call before she planned to dispose of her phone. In a rational world, all she'd need to do to extend her stay would be to tell him what Hal had discovered. Given the current dynamics, that was too risky, especially if whatever she told Fordyce was likely to be passed along to Phil Lacey, either by carelessness or by design. Fordyce didn't strike her as being nearly bold or independent enough to be part of a scheme like the one they'd uncovered, but he was certainly prone to gossiping with his hallway neighbors.

"Bad news," she said, the moment he answered. "The client is in the wind, and half of Bolrovian internal security seems to be after him."

She heard him sigh.

"That's unfortunate. Stay out of it."

"And if he reaches out to us?"

"Make sure you're not available. Tomorrow morning you're leaving anyway."

"I'm canceling my flight. I need to remain in place until this is resolved."

"No to all of that. If anything, you should be putting more distance between you. Clearly he's become a liability, and clearly it's due to his own actions."

"Actions on our behalf."

"This has never been official, or not by our usual rules. You know that."

"There's paperwork. You insisted on it, and he signed it."

"I'm sure you've heard the expression 'not worth the paper it's printed on.'"

It was hopeless, just as she'd known it would be. But there were other ways of doing things, especially once your supervisor began emphasizing how "unofficial" every aspect of this operation had now become, and it was time to pivot in that direction.

"I should also tell you that this number has been compromised."

"How so?"

"The client contacted me directly earlier this evening. It was his emergency number."

Another sigh, longer than the first one. Apparently, Fordyce hated losing good equipment more than he hated losing assets.

"Follow the usual protocol, then. And make sure you're on that flight."

"No."

"*No?* You're disobeying a direct order?"

"I'm suggesting we amend it to make it more to your liking. If it's distance you want, why have me wait until morning? Unless you'd prefer to have that detail emerge in a postmortem. There's a flight to Munich in an hour and a half. If I hustle, I can make it."

"Then by all means do so." He sounded deeply relieved, which only pissed her off more. "Stay overnight near the Munich airport, and I'll book you on an a.m. connection to Dulles."

"No to that as well. If I'm going to hang our client out to dry, then you owe me some time off, preferably while I'm still on the continent."

"In Munich?"

"Florence. I can take an overnight train, and I already have a hotel in mind. The Continentale. It's right on the Arno."

There was a smug chuckle from his end.

"Leveraging an imperiled client for a few days in the Tuscan sun. You're even colder than I thought. Fine, then. I'll book it for you. And once you're there, use your company card for meals, for everything. I suppose I owe you that as well."

"Not to mention, you'll be able to keep track of exactly where I am and what I'm doing."

"Or maybe I just know how to show a girl a good time."

She squeezed her phone and answered as neutrally as possible.

"I promise not to break the bank."

"That's never been my worry where you're concerned."

Then, after a short pause, punctuated by the clatter of a keyboard, he said, "Okay. I've got the hotel's website up. Very tasteful, if a bit pricey.

Not that keeping you out of any further trouble isn't worth it. How many nights?"

"Three should do it."

"Oh, make it four. I'll book you for a Thursday return to Dulles."

"Fair enough."

After disconnecting, she looked for someplace to dispose of her phone. But first she would need to destroy it, or at least try. All the while she continued down the sidewalk. There was little time to spare if she was going to make that flight.

She spotted a row of stone bollards linked by a chain along the curb of the next block just ahead. The tops of the bollards were pointed. That would do just fine. She was only a few steps away when her phone buzzed, one final signal before she shut it down.

It was again a blocked number, maybe the same caller as before. She raised the phone above the spearpoint of the first bollard, poised to smash it down as it buzzed again. Then her curiosity won out. Even if it was Sarič, she'd at least know that he was on to her, and that she would need to change plans.

"Yes?"

"I'd like to offer my assistance. I'm guessing you're needing some about now."

It took a second, but she recognized the voice, or at least the British accent, the gregarious tone. The prudent action would be to disconnect. But so many other things about this op had already been unorthodox, and from here on out she would be terribly outnumbered and working from well beyond the edge of propriety, even by her employer's loose standards. So she kept talking even as she walked at double time.

"How did you get this number?"

"Mutual acquaintance. One of your lunch companions."

He had to mean Sandor Matas.

"Disappointing, but not surprising. Why should I trust you?"

"Mutual adversaries?"

"Anything more?"

"Isn't that enough?"

"Depends on who you're working for."

"Surely we've both been around long enough to not play that game."

"What are you offering?"

"Finally, the winning question."

Then he told her. Lauren, still not convinced, replied that her phone was about to permanently go out of service. She then asked for his number and said she would reply in the morning.

"By then it may be too late."

"Sorry, best I can do under the circumstances."

He gave her the number, which she committed to memory. She disconnected without a further word.

A block later, she settled for a stone wall as the best available anvil. It took three emphatic strikes before the phone came apart. She gathered up the pieces, tossed them into the next three sewer grates, rounded a corner, and hailed a taxi for the airport.

Her plan was in motion. Better still, she now had a potential ally. Or, equally plausible, an enemy posing as a friend. She would know soon enough either way.

Chapter 60

———≈———

Forty minutes after boarding the tram, the three of them stepped off the platform onto a dystopian landscape of bleak high-rises, poking into the night sky from an asphalt plain like massive gray stalagmites.

"You sure this is the right stop?" Hal said.

"Yes," Pavel said. "But we have to hurry. We may already be too late."

They headed right at a brisk walk, Pavel in the lead, Quint backing them up.

"What is this place?" Hal said.

"Novi Blatsk. Built right after the war."

"Who are we looking for?" Quint asked.

"My grandfather."

"Your Poppy?" Hal said.

"He stayed out here last night with a friend. Unless he has already left."

Two blocks later they rounded a corner. Pavel stopped and exhaled in relief.

"He's there! That truck, just ahead."

It was the big Bedford from the night before, but now, in addition to the new stepladder, it was piled with bags and boxes of supplies, a load of winter provisions lashed down by a chaotic webbing of yellow nylon rope.

Poppy and another man roughly his age were still tying knots and securing items as the threesome approached. He looked up in surprise and stiffly stepped down from the flatbed.

"Why are you here, Pavel? Is something wrong?"

"The next choice came along. I made it. Now I have to get these men somewhere safe. So if you have room . . ."

Poppy held his gaze on Pavel a moment longer before embracing him and pounding his back. He hugged him so tightly that Pavel could feel the beating of his heart, but when Poppy let go and backed away, Pavel saw that his face was somber. The old man eyed Hal and Quint, sizing them up.

"It will be a tight fit, but these old Bedfords have a big cab."

"When can we leave?"

Poppy looked at his friend.

"Anton, how close?"

"Two more knots."

He turned back toward Pavel.

"Does your family know?"

Pavel shook his head.

"I had to get rid of my phone. But if there's time, maybe I could call from Anton's apartment. Unless he has a cell phone."

"He doesn't. But I think you misunderstood my question. You don't *want* them to know. It's better that way, Pavel. Better for them."

"Right. Of course."

"You can still stay here if you want. I will take your friends."

He was tempted. Maybe he had done all he could do for Hal and Quint. Maybe having one more person along would only slow them down. And he hated the idea of his family worrying once he failed to turn up and, worse, their being questioned by the authorities in his absence.

But without him along, who would interpret when things got complicated? Poppy's English wasn't that great. And after Poppy had embraced him so fiercely just now, as if finally welcoming him to the fight, could he now simply withdraw?

"No. They need me. Let's go."

His grandfather nodded. Anton hopped down from the flatbed and gave a thumbs-up. They were ready to roll.

———

Three hours later, everyone in the truck was asleep except for him and Poppy, who had stubbornly remained at the wheel the entire way, refusing all offers of relief.

"What do you think I'd be doing if you and your friends hadn't come along, letting go of the wheel so it would steer itself?"

"Poppy, you're ninety-four."

"And I didn't get to this age by falling asleep on a blind curve. So shut up."

Pavel had accompanied him on this drive many times as a boy, and two times since Poppy had moved out here for good. It was always fascinating to see the change that came over him as the road began to climb into the hills and trees. The muscles of his face slackened; his hands relaxed on the steering wheel. This was his homeland.

The Javorska Forest was a geographical anomaly. Its dense woods and craggy terrain lay astride a vast plain which ran westward toward Germany and eastward toward Russia, making it a natural roadblock to invading foreign armies or, as had more often been the case, a refuge of last resort for the remnants of routed home forces, a place to make a final stand. Enemies entered at their peril, a pattern that dated all the way back to the era of King Viktor IV, who had turned back the Mongol hordes only by luring them into the Javorska Forest, where he had defeated them piecemeal. It is where Poppy had fled at the age of fourteen to join resistance fighters in 1943, not emerging until the Germans finally retreated, two years later. And now, for anyone eager to disappear, it had the added advantage of having almost zero cell phone coverage.

Poppy almost never talked about his wartime experiences. Most of what Pavel knew about them had come secondhand, from histories he'd read or televised interviews with other aging veterans—tales of daring raids by small bands of men who struck quickly and then disappeared into the birches and pine boughs, hiding in snowdrifts or the folds of the hills, shivering in thin coats which at least allowed them to travel more lightly than the better-clad Germans. For food they had dug up roots, scraped bark from trees. They had skinned and eaten any creatures they could catch or kill—rodents and songbirds caught in snares and traps and then clubbed to death because bullets had to be saved for shooting Germans.

In some ways Poppy had never recovered. It wasn't due only to the hardship or his wounds. (Pavel had seen the scars on his grandfather's back only once, red corded strips like rolled bacon, exposed at a lakeshore one summer when Poppy had stripped down for a swim on a day when the water was too cold for everyone else.) It owed itself more to the deep disappointment of the postwar years, when the Germans had been immediately replaced by the Russians, who had loaded almost as many people onto outbound boxcars as the Nazis. Only the destinations had changed. Poppy's bitterness over all that had then hardened when his wife was killed by a stray bullet during the uprising of 1958. From then on, he had fought back in his own quiet way, and by building his dacha deep into these woods.

Pavel watched his grandfather drive. The bony hands were not as steady as they'd once been, but they still managed to handle the truck, with its skewed suspension and worn-out shocks. Poppy then spoke without turning his head.

"Do you still remember the way to the dacha?"

It was a test, not a request for assistance. Poppy had never written the directions, and refused to let anyone else do so.

"Yes. I think so."

"*Think* so? Not good enough. Tell me."

"Well, the first turn is coming up in about . . . three kilometers?"

"Good. Landmark?"

"Smotrich. The village with the red cowshed at the far edge of town. Red for left, so that's the direction we take. But it's the third left after the shed."

"Yes."

"Then there are all those curves before we pass the clearing with the old windmill, which means it's one more kilometer until we take a right turn. But it's tricky, because there are four or five other dirt roads before the one we'll want. I'll know it when I see it."

"How? What is the landmark? These forest paths are a maze. One wrong turn and you might not come out for days."

Pavel struggled for a moment. He was positive he would recognize the correct turnoff, but now he was having trouble remembering why. Then it came to him.

"The game warden's hut. You can see it through the trees, just off to the left before the turn."

"Then what?"

"We cross a stream on an iron bridge. Then there are all those forks."

"How many?"

It took him a few seconds.

"Three. We go right, then left, then right."

"You're almost there. But you can still end up lost or even stranded up at the northern border if you're not careful."

"From there . . . from there I look for the double boulders. At the fourth turnoff. No, fifth, where we go right again. After that, it's only two klicks. We'll see Petaro's cabin, then take the next right to yours."

"Good!"

Pavel noticed that Quint was awake now, and listening closely. The man had surprised him a few times earlier in the drive by speaking fairly good Bolrovian, so he probably understood everything they were saying. Pavel caught his eye, and Quint nodded.

A few years back Poppy probably would have noted this silent exchange, and might even have remarked on it, perhaps in disapproval. But no one retains all their sharpness at ninety-four, not even Poppy, because he almost certainly would not have knowingly spoken his next words in front of a stranger.

"It is best if you never forget any of that, not with the way things are in this country now," Poppy said. "Perhaps we will yet make a resistance fighter of you." Then he grunted with something approximating mirth, the closest he ever came to laughter.

A few minutes later they rolled into Smotrich, a huddle of a few dozen homes and a small general store with gas pumps out front. It, too, was dark, but Poppy wheeled into the gravel lot.

"I need a few more things," he said.

"It looks closed."

"It is, but Harko knows the sound of my truck. He'll open for me."

Sure enough, a light came on as Poppy was climbing out of the cab. Pavel watched his grandfather walk stiffly toward the door after his three hours at the wheel. He worried they were demanding too much of him, and putting him in danger. Quint spoke up, whispering to keep from waking Hal, who was leaning against the passenger door, snoring softly.

"Those directions you just read back to your Poppy. Mind saying 'em again for me?" He had his phone out. "I've barely got any bars as it is, so this might be the last chance to send a text."

"Who's it for?"

"Do you really want to know?"

Pavel sighed, and wondered yet again about what he'd gotten involved in.

"And this town is called Smotrich, right?"

"Yes," Pavel said. He then recited the rest. By the time Poppy emerged from the store with a full bag of supplies, Quint had put away his phone and the cab was again quiet.

Poppy unscrewed the cap on a bottle of Coke, took a long swallow, and set the bottle between his legs as they got back underway.

"This all feels very familiar to me," Poppy said. "These kinds of movements at night, with the pressure building behind you, from someone in pursuit."

For a moment Pavel thought his grandfather might be about to launch into a story from his wartime days, finally opening up after years of silence. But the tires thrummed, the headlights tunneled deeper into the trees, and Poppy's eyes again took on their fixed look of quiet determination.

Chapter 61

The elevator was broken, of course, so Skip Kretzer took the stairs, climbing eleven floors to his destination. He was east of the city, only a few blocks from where, ten hours earlier, and unknown to him, Poppy's truck had headed off into the night. Sunrise was still half an hour away, but there was already enough light to see that a few of these towers had been recently renovated and were now painted in bright primary colors. Even drab brutalism could come back into vogue when the price was right, he supposed. Although not Igmar Yolvan's building, which still wore the tired look of the early 1950s.

Kretzer paced himself on the way up so that he wouldn't be out of breath when Yolvan first saw him. The apartment was toward the end of a long corridor. The man was supposedly an early riser, and, sure enough, Kretzer heard the sound of a television as he approached the door—canned laughter with Bolrovian dialogue. He waited a few seconds to make sure no one poked their head out of any of the neighboring apartments; then he knocked sharply, four times. The volume of the TV dropped almost instantly. There was a tremor in the slab floor from the plod of footsteps.

He didn't speak Bolrovian, and he knew that Yolvan's English was terrible. But Yolvan had been a Cold Warrior, which meant they would have Russian in common, a skill which, for Kretzer, had recently been regaining its value.

When he sensed the presence of an eye on the other side of the peephole (because an old counterintelligence chief would never have simply opened the door at the sound of a knock), Kretzer stepped back to give Yolvan a better look. Then, in the best Russian he could manage, he said, "Greetings, comrade. I am an American, but I am here in an official capacity."

Then he spread his arms, palms outward, while showing a manila file folder in his right hand. For good measure, he opened his coat to show that there were no suspicious bulges, although a fat white envelope was poking from an inside pocket. There were plenty of other hiding places for weapons, of course—ankle holsters, back pockets. He might even have propped a long gun just out of sight in the hallway. But Kretzer hoped that his gesture of openness would carry the day.

After a few seconds he heard the jingle and clank of chains and locks, like the clatter of hardware when someone was unlocking a prison cell. The door creaked open to reveal a man roughly his height but much thinner, even bony, yet with a potbelly bulging the front of a white shirt tucked into dark gray slacks. Yolvan wore house slippers. He smelled like toothpaste, and his stiff white hair was uncombed. But his eyes were sharp and alert.

Yolvan's look of appraisal was every bit as careful and comprehensive as Kretzer's. Then he spoke, also in Russian.

"Who sent you?"

"I'd prefer not to say just yet."

"Then it must have been that bastard Branko Sarič."

Kretzer smiled to reward the correct guess.

"In that case I will need a drink, even at this hour. Come in. Sit."

He waved Kretzer through the door and gestured to a sagging couch that was catty-corner to a big armchair that faced the television and was draped with a wool blanket. Kretzer settled gingerly onto the couch, trying not to disturb the layers of dust on the cushions. Yolvan shoved the armchair around until it faced the couch. He tossed the blanket to the floor and switched off the TV. Then he walked toward the opening of a small galley kitchen.

The apartment was a mess. Newspapers and books were splayed in disarray on the floor and coffee table. The thin green carpeting was stained and spattered in so many places that it might have been a Jackson Pollock. The room's only window was covered with a yellowing sheet of plastic, presumably for insulation, although the upper right corner had peeled away like a translucent tongue. Lined up along the sill was a battlefield jumble of dead bugs—flies, moths, a beetle—in varying states of decomposition. Kretzer thought he could detect their essence in his nostrils, with an underlying bouquet of skillet grease and damp newsprint. Oddly, there was no hint of cigarette smoke, and there were no ashtrays. He heard the clink of glasses and a gurgle of liquid. Yolvan called out from the kitchen.

"You'll drink with me."

"I'd prefer not."

"Then you'll leave."

"Make mine a double."

Yolvan emerged from the kitchen with a tray. Set atop it were two glass tumblers half filled with some sort of amber whiskey, plus a floral china plate with almonds, black olives, and a few stubs of wilted celery. Yolvan set the tray on a pile of newspapers on the coffee table, which left it slightly atilt. He popped an almond in his mouth, then raised a glass.

"To our health!" He knocked back his first swallow of the young day.

Kretzer picked up his glass and eyed the brown liquid.

"No vodka?"

"This was the cheapest thing on offer. Irish whiskey, made in Poland. On a pension, you stop being choosy."

Kretzer took an exploratory swallow. He drew in his lips at the taste, but the burn on the way down wasn't so bad, and its antibacterial powers were certainly welcome.

Yolvan got down to business.

"I don't expect you to tell me your real name, but I do need to see some credentials."

Kretzer handed over a folded sheet of paper that had been tucked behind the fat envelope in his jacket. Yolvan opened it on the coffee table. At the top was the embossed letterhead of the Interior Ministry. Below was a brief message in Bolrovian, with Sarič's signature at the bottom. Kretzer had no idea what it said, but he had urged Sarič to offer, at the very least, a measure of humility.

Yolvan read it, refolded it, and set it aside beyond Kretzer's reach.

"You can make a call, if you'd like," Kretzer said.

"No need." He eyed Kretzer for a moment longer. "So you know my story, then?"

Kretzer nodded.

"Former chief of CI." Counterintelligence, in other words, the business of rooting out enemy spies. "You initiated a recent operation against the Americans. Highly successful, I might add. Then you took early retirement."

"Ah. Sarič's version. And I'm sure he also used words like 'past his prime' and 'couldn't adapt,' even though I had just rolled up an entire network run by that drunk Leo Garvin. In appreciation, Branko exiled me to Archives and replaced me with one of his young technocrats. So I quit."

"If it's any consolation, he now seems to be aware of the value of what he threw away. That's why he sent me."

Yolvan offered the hint of a smile.

"So he has fucked up, has he? I am guessing he has lost some needle in his big haystack of microphones, embedded chips, and intrusive software."

"Something like that."

"Is there a name for this missing needle?"

"Hal Knight. An American. Someone you probably won't know, and someone with no history here or any connection to the games that you and I have always played."

"So he is a civilian, not a spook."

"But an agent all the same. That seems clear now. And we're pretty sure he's on the run with an aide to the president, Pavel Lukov. It's all in here."

Kretzer dropped the file folder on the table. Yolvan immediately opened it, and his eyes lit up at the sight of documents, names, numbers, and photographs. He nodded at a photo of Lukov.

"A local. Always a good starting point, but it will still take time."

"How long?"

"Given his high profile, probably hours rather than days, but only if I have the proper manpower. I'm guessing that Branko's arsenal of ingenious little devices has been of only minimal help, or you would not even be here."

"Less than minimal. Last night he tracked both their phones to a tram terminal south of Blatsk. Both were, of course, unaccompanied by their owners."

Yolvan got a nice chuckle out of that, which was the main reason Kretzer had told him.

"He says you'll have whoever you need at your disposal."

"Will I now? And what will Branko and you be doing?"

"Going where you tell us to go, based on your findings."

He nodded, thought it over for a minute.

"And when this is over, what will I have then? Because it will have to be more than just a pat on the back or one of his silly medals. And I am certainly not seeking a job."

Kretzer had anticipated this moment, even if Sarič initially had not. He took the fat envelope out of his jacket and handed it over. It wasn't sealed.

"Count it, then keep it. You'll get another one, same amount, on successful completion of the operation."

Yolvan counted it and seemed pleased. He set it aside as well.

"I will need three people. My own, not his. I'll be able to reach all of them within the next half hour, and each will welcome the opportunity. But they, too, will require compensation." He nodded at the envelope. "Same amount, but divided three ways."

"Okay."

"You are authorized to say that?"

"I am authorized for a lot of things."

"And who are you working for? Besides Branko."

"That's above your current pay grade, even if we count your completion bonus. Let's just say that this is a cooperative venture between public and private interests."

"I see."

He reopened the folder and glanced at a few items. Then he frowned.

"This is all quite fascinating, of course, but it raises a rather obvious question. I have heard nothing on my television this morning about either of these two men you are seeking. If it is so vital that they be caught, why not raise a general alarm? Show their photos, declare them to be enemies of the state, and let the public do some of our work for us?"

Kretzer smiled. This was one of his favorite parts of the whole mess.

"Apparently, certain sensitivities are involved. Is that the correct word in Russian? Sensitivities?"

"Yes, a handy one from the good old days of the Chekists."

"The American is somewhat famous. And he is here as a special guest of the president."

Yolvan grinned.

"I see. Am I to gather, then, that the president does not yet even know this fellow has gone missing?"

"That's correct."

"And what about the local." He glanced again at the contents of the folder. "His *chief administrative aide*? In the wake of the arrest of Kelenič, no less. Yes, I am beginning to see why Branko would prefer to keep all of this quiet."

"There are also other American special guests currently in the country, and no one wants them to know what is happening as well."

Yolvan began to chuckle.

"I am guessing that these . . . sensitivities, as you said, have limited the amount of personnel that Branko feels he can comfortably deploy."

"It has. He is trying to keep everything as low profile as possible. At the airports and rail stations he's mostly relying on his recent installation of facial-recognition software."

"Well, at least one of his expensive new toys is proving useful."

"Your people will need to proceed in a somewhat less obtrusive manner as well."

"Of course. It won't be the first time they've had to operate that way. But I don't expect it to slow us down."

"Good to know."

"Then let us begin."

Kretzer stood to leave. Yolvan didn't bother to rise, or even bid him farewell.

Instead, he got out his phone, which looked as obsolete as everything else in the apartment. And within half an hour, just as he'd promised, he and three other like-minded fellows were already out on the streets, working as quietly as possible as they began tracking down their first leads.

Chapter 62

Hal awakened shortly before dawn on a lumpy couch that smelled of woodsmoke and mildew. His head hurt, his mouth was dry, and he badly needed to pee, but he had slept deeply.

They had arrived in the dark, with only a flashlight and the glow of Quint's phone to show the way, so he was now getting his first good look at what Pavel had called his Poppy's dacha. "Rustic" was an understatement. It was a single-room cabin, about sixteen-by-sixteen feet, with plank walls, plank flooring, and a cast-iron stove smack in the middle atop a slab of stone. The stove's chimney pipe rose straight up through a vaulted ceiling. The fire had gone out overnight, but Hal could see embers glowing through the smudged front window.

The sleeping arrangements were tight. Poppy was on the bottom level of a roughhewn double bunk that he'd built into the back corner on the opposite side, with Pavel on top. Quint, who had fashioned a bedroll out of a quilt and some blankets, had slept on the floor on the other side of the stove, but now the blankets were rolled aside and he was gone.

Hal sat up. To his right, behind the couch, a pale light shone through one of the room's two small windows. He could see little more than dense, dripping evergreens. He was still wearing his clothes from the day before and he'd kept his socks on for warmth, but his shoes were over by the stove.

Moving quietly, he rolled off the couch, then sat on the floor to put on his shoes. Back in the corner bunk, Poppy raised his head, his breath vaporing like smoke into the chill of the room. The old man narrowed his eyes in apparent suspicion. Hal offered a halfhearted wave, then stood and headed for the door, where several jackets hung from pegs. He grabbed one on his way out.

The dacha was on a small plateau amid rolling wooded hills. A layer of morning mist coated the ground, and the birds were already in full song. To the left was a path leading to an outhouse, a narrow wooden closet which, to Hal, looked tailor-made for bugs and snakes, not to mention the stench, so instead he walked over to a big spruce and unzipped his trousers. Never before had he felt so remote. Pavel had said last night that there was no cell coverage out here, and in peering through the trees Hal could see no sign of any other human habitation. Although he supposed that wouldn't stop Sarič from eventually finding him, a thought that made him antsy to get moving. The northern border was supposedly a three-hour drive from here. With any luck he'd be safely across it by noon.

He was finishing up when the snap of a twig made him wheel around while his dick was still half out of his trousers. It was Quint, emerging from the trees to his left.

"Isn't that what got you in trouble to begin with?"

Hal zipped up.

"Jesus. You 'bout gave me a heart attack."

"Sorry. The good news is that it's pretty quiet around here, the whole perimeter. Not an easy place to sneak up on somebody, unless they're peeing on a tree."

"So what's the plan? Head straight for the border?"

Quint shook his head.

"We'd be flying blind. There are five northbound routes from here, with three possible crossings. For all we know, Sarič has all of them covered. And with no cell service, we've got no way of checking. I gotta fix that."

"How?"

"There are two cabins within about a mile of here. Pavel said one belongs to a guy named Petaro, kind of a hermit like his Poppy. He's got juice, but no landline. The other one looks like a summer place that's locked up for the winter, but there's a phone line running to it, so I'm thinking that's our best bet."

"You'll break in?"

"Yeah."

"How long do you think we have?"

"Hard to say, but at some point the cavalry should arrive."

"Sal?"

Quint shook his head.

"He's busy working logistics. Lauren."

Hal frowned, then figured it out.

"Susan, you mean?"

"Shit. I guess by the time this is over you'll know all our names."

"Who's Sal, then?"

"Malone."

"Well, I'm glad we finally got all that shit straight, although he kind of looks like a Sal. What do we do now, then?"

"You should get some breakfast."

"What about you?"

He pulled a half-eaten scrap of bread from a coat pocket.

"Already ate. And I've got more work to do."

Then he nodded and set off. Within seconds he had disappeared into the trees, and Hal couldn't hear even a whisper of his movements.

He reentered the dacha to the smell of fresh-ground coffee. Pavel was chopping something on a worktable in the back, and Poppy was turning the handle of a scrolled brass coffee grinder. The woodstove was burning hot again, flames visible through the glass. The two Lukov men seemed to be in the middle of a contentious conversation, but Pavel looked over at him long enough to nod in greeting.

"Is everything okay?" Hal asked. "I'd certainly understand if he's wanting to get rid of me."

Pavel laughed.

"No. I was just telling him that, if he wanted, I could pay someone to string a wire out here so he wouldn't have to do everything by hand. Old Petaro's place is only four hundred meters away, and it would be easy to extend the line."

Poppy gave him a dark look while continuing to crank the handle.

"I take it he's opposed."

"He said, 'Sure, string some wire out to my house, then all they'll have to do to find me is follow the line.' He said that's how Nazi officers always gave away their location during the war. They needed their comforts, so the first thing they did at any new command center was wire it up. He said they might as well have painted a big sign, 'Officers Live Here.'"

"Maybe he's got a point. Even now."

"Maybe." Then, after a brief pause, "Where's Quint?"

"He's hoping to get into that nearest summer house, to use the phone."

Poppy, who was trying to follow at least the gist of their conversation, grumbled again to Pavel.

"What's he saying?"

"He doesn't want to make trouble for his neighbors, even the assholes who only come for the summer."

"I can understand that."

"He says you should go north. He will ask Petaro to drive you."

"I'm fine with that, but Quint thinks I should wait until we know more about the situation on the roads. That's one reason he needs a phone."

Pavel translated that for Poppy, who listened patiently, nodded, and calmly spoke a few words in reply.

"He understands. He said he knows what it's like to stumble into a trap."

Poppy then put down the coffee grinder, turned to Hal, and in halting English said, "I know also this. Wait too long, they come. Always, they come. You sit? You die."

All of which would be bad enough if Hal were the only one doing the sitting. But there were four of them at risk, including Pavel's grandfather, who had no stake in this. Maybe Hal should set off on his own. Make his way through the woods to a road, then stick out his thumb and hope for the best. If the net closed, then it closed. At least then he'd be the only catch. He'd already unloaded all the useful information he'd managed to gather, but there was nothing much waiting for him on the other side of the border. Freedom, yes, but to do what or go where?

For years now Hal had lived the life of someone whose needs had always been catered to by others—as a filmmaker, a Hollywood figure, a congressman. Maybe it was time that stopped.

"Coffee's ready," Pavel said, approaching with a mug, a look of concern on his face. "Here. You look like you need it."

He had that right. Hal nodded in gratitude, but said nothing in reply.

Chapter 63

It was early morning in Florence, and the picture window in Lauren's room offered just the sort of charming view that hotels love to put on websites and in travel brochures. To the left, the Arno River glittered in low sunlight. Looming above it was the Ponte Vecchio, the medieval stone bridge covered by an arcaded row of jewelry shops.

Lauren had her back turned to all that.

Having arrived from the train station only a few minutes ago, she was focused instead on a black ripstop nylon shoulder bag, the one that carried her laptop. Using a pair of scissors commandeered from the front desk, she reached inside to slit open the bottom panel from end to end. In doing so, she opened a shallow hideaway chamber, with a second layer of nylon just below.

Fitted snugly inside was a stiff membrane, impervious to the prying rays of airport security sensors, folded lengthwise. She carefully slid it out, set it on the bed, and tore off two bands of tape that were holding the fold in place.

The flaps fell open to reveal a U.S. passport, a New Jersey driver's license, and two charge cards, all bearing the name Carol Jean Lanier. Years earlier, a veteran colleague had advised Lauren to privately obtain documentation for at least one off-the-books identity, not as a license to misbehave, but as a fallback in case your other identities were ever compromised by an in-house security breach. But it was certainly a handy item for misbehavior as well.

The photos in the passport and on the driver's license showed her with shorter, darker hair. Lauren carried the passport and scissors into the bathroom, where, after studying the photo, she began snipping at her light brown locks. Five minutes later she opened a box of hair dye she'd bought at the airport. The directions said it would take only twenty minutes, but previous experience had taught her to beware of such easy promises, so she had allowed for up to an hour. That's how much time remained before she was supposed to meet an old friend, Sarah Wallace, on the hotel's rooftop terrace for breakfast.

Sarah, who she had known since college, was an art history major who had come here on a fellowship more than a decade ago, then had fallen in love, gotten a job, and divorced her husband. Six years ago she had begun writing mysteries set in Tuscany, and they'd become popular enough that she now lived in a refurbished hilltop villa in an olive grove thirty miles away.

In college everyone had always remarked on how much they'd looked like each other—same build, same cheekbones, same way of carrying themselves—but it was their similar outlooks on life and its follies that had kept them in touch over the years. Sarah had long known that Lauren worked for some sort of secretive government agency, and she had been tactful enough to never pry too deeply about it.

Lauren had called her from the airport in Blatsk the night before while waiting for the flight to Munich to board. She had used a burner phone that she'd bought several days earlier for just this sort of contingency. The call had been something of a shot in the dark, with Lauren, perhaps unrealistically, hoping that the flexibility of Sarah's profession would allow her to participate in what she had in mind. If not, then she would have to come up with some other option.

"Sarah? It's Lauren."

"Oh, my, what a wonderful surprise! I hope you're about to tell me that you just happen to be in my neck of the woods."

"Not at the moment, but by early morning, yes. In Florence."

"You should have told me earlier!"

"This trip came up suddenly, so I hope you're not too busy for a visit."

"You know me, always ready for an adventure. My latest is going through copy edits, so as it happens I'm pretty footloose at the moment."

"Perfect, because I was hoping to meet for breakfast."

"Tomorrow?"

She sounded a bit taken aback.

"I know. It's short notice. But if you're up for it, there's even the proposition of a getaway weekend in it for you—or for you and a friend, even—as long as you don't mind all your expenses being paid in a rather swank and beautiful hotel."

Sarah laughed at this turn of events.

"Oh, dear. And I think *my* mind is too preoccupied with devious plots and subplots. You know, I've never pinned down exactly what you do for a living, but that makes this sound all the more intriguing. Breakfast, then. Good. And is it all right if I bring Alessandro?"

"Wasn't there a Steve last time we talked?"

"There was. I traded up from a Chevy to an Alfa Romeo."

Lauren laughed, while wondering what make of car would best describe the man she'd most recently been involved with. A Volvo, probably. Sturdy and dependable, but a little boring.

"Sure, bring him along. But maybe wait to introduce me until after we've had a chance to chat. And pack for four nights, if possible. Hope that's not a deal-breaker."

"Deal-breaker? Do you have any idea how slow it gets out here in the hills, with only olive trees and wild boars for company?"

"Oh, and you'll be staying under the name Cheryl Tucker, if that's okay."

"This gets better every second."

"Eight o'clock, okay?"

"Ouch. Can we make it a more sensible hour? You don't know how hard it is to get Alessandro out of bed sometimes."

"That sounds fairly sexy. But let's still say eight."

"Oh. Okay." Then, with a note of concern, "You're not in some kind of trouble, I hope?"

"No, no. It's someone else's trouble I'm concerned with, and all of that is transpiring far from Florence."

A slight pause, maybe a moment of doubt.

"Oh, what the hell. Sure. It will be great to catch up."

"Wonderful. I'll fill you in tomorrow on everything you need to know."

"'Need to know.' I used that exact phrase in my third book, uttered by a character not unlike you. She was a spy."

"Remind me to skip that one. I'll be at the Hotel Continentale, on the Arno. Come up to the rooftop terrace. Oh, and they just called my boarding group. I'd better get moving."

"See you soon!"

But instead of lining up to board, Lauren had sent three texts—one to Quint, one to Malone, and one to her most recently acquired ally—to give them her new number. Then, almost in desperation, she'd made one more call, this one to Los Angeles, where at the time it had been around midday.

And now, up on the top floor of the Continentale, Lauren stepped off the elevator just as Sarah Wallace was being seated at a table across the terrace. No one who might have been Alessandro was in sight, which was just as well.

Lauren noted with relief that, after her earlier cut-and-dye job, Sarah now looked more like the photo in her Cheryl Tucker passport than she did. And that, of course, was the photo the front desk of the Continentale had copied at check-in. Although when did any hotel or restaurant ever check those things anymore, especially once you were running a tab?

Sarah welcomed her warmly but seemed mildly taken aback that Lauren was carrying her overnight and shoulder bags, as if she already had a foot out the door. Twenty minutes later, Lauren handed over her room key card, her corporate charge card, and a sealed, addressed envelope containing several other items—the Cheryl Tucker passport among them—with instructions for Sarah to express mail them back to the United States three days from now.

Sarah frowned with concern.

"None of this is going to bring a black helicopter swooping down on my villa, I hope."

"The worst that could happen is that some auditor will visit my apartment in Alexandria."

Sarah tilted her head, thinking it through. Then, opting to get into the spirit of things, she laughed and spoke in a confiding tone.

"You do realize that this will all end up someday in one of my books."

"I'd expect nothing less. Just don't forget to write off for taxes whatever you spend on postage."

Five minutes later, Lauren exited the downstairs lobby and raised her hand to hail a cab.

Chapter 64

—————≈—————

As the pilot announced they were on final approach to land in Vienna, Jess Miller wondered for the twentieth time why she had agreed to do this. Then she remembered Belinda Locke's reaction, eighteen hours earlier—a whoop of manic joy at the loopy intrigue of it all, followed by a lot of jabber about how, if they were lucky, her trip would set off a burst of "creative synergy" that they could easily build on.

Jess was more focused on practicalities—how much energy she'd have for the long drive ahead, and whether she was really up for this. As for the possibility she might see Hal Knight face-to-face for the first time in months, well, that was something she wasn't yet ready to contemplate, even though he was the reason she was here.

The wheels touched down, and she got out her phone to see if there were any further instructions from the woman who had called her the day before. It had been one of the oddest conversations Jess had ever had.

"I hope I've reached Jess."

"Who's calling?"

"A friend of a friend. I'm in Bolrovia, and before you hang up, I know that what I'm about to tell you is going to sound totally ludicrous. What I'm about to ask you to do, even more so."

"If this is about Hal Knight, ludicrous wouldn't surprise me in the least. Who is this?"

"Call me Susan. I work for a government agency. And, yes, I know that must sound like a premise for one of your comedies, one that might even give you a case of the creeps, but I'm deadly serious, because even as I speak our mutual acquaintance is on the run from some rather rough and unsavory local authorities."

"Well, at least that time you didn't call him our mutual friend. But thanks to your choice of words, you now have my full attention."

"You should also know he's done some good work here. Valuable work, even, which has gotten him into some dangerous trouble, and I doubt that either you or I would feel comfortable with the idea of him simply disappearing."

Silence. Then, haltingly, "No. You're right. I wouldn't want that."

"Good. In that case, there are several things I need you to do for me, if you're willing, and I'd like you to write them down because it's important that you get them exactly right."

"Okay."

"Some of this is easy, and you can get started right away by sending a few emails. The rest is, well, more involved. Is your passport up-to-date?"

"I don't like where this is headed, but yes. It is."

Susan then told her what she wanted Jess to do. The directions were somewhat involved, and Jess had to ask her to slow down a few times so she could get every detail right.

"Okay if I ask a question?"

"As long as it's quick." Jess could hear noises in the background, which made it sound like Susan was in an airport.

"Doesn't your . . . organization have its own people to do these kinds of things?"

"Not on this job. I'm operating a bit off my leash, and I'm frankly outnumbered or I'd never even ask."

"I see. Still, it's hard to see how I can make much of a difference."

"Look, the larger truth here is that I need someone reasonably close at hand who Hal actually trusts, or at least cares for."

"Why?"

"His current state of mind. Last time I saw him, he looked like a man who was ready to give up. I need someone in place who he might actually listen to, who might even be able to get him off his ass when it's time to make a move, or follow my lead, or follow an order that he might otherwise choose to ignore. I know that person isn't me, and it's not either of my colleagues here. You're a voice he might heed, maybe the only one."

"Plus, even though you may not even like him, you don't like to lose, do you?"

"There's that, too. But I'm serious about the other stuff. Can you do it, then? More important, will you?"

And at that point, Jess had imagined Belinda egging her on—*"It's an opportunity, Jess. Take it!"*—while, in the background, she'd heard someone announcing a final call for boarding.

"Okay. Yes. I'll do it."

Now, as the door at the front of the plane opened onto the jetway and everyone around her began scrambling for their bags, Jess felt a flutter of excitement over what she was about to do. She also experienced a sense of foreboding as she contemplated the one possibility that bothered her even more than the idea of seeing Hal Knight live and in person—and that was the possibility of instead being asked to identify and retrieve his body.

A sudden, vivid image of Hal's pale, stripped corpse laid out on a chrome slab flashed in her mind's eye. His eyes were vacant and glazed, his chest gouged by gunshot wounds. For a fleeting moment, the stale air in the cabin smelled of formaldehyde and putrid flesh. Jess shivered, stood, then reached up into the overhead compartment for her bag.

Chapter 65

———— ≋ ————

In the tiny woodland village of Smotrich, Branko Sarič's Mercedes stood out like a luxury yacht in a bay of leaky rowboats. It had been sitting in the gravel parking lot of the town's one and only store since midafternoon, slowly collecting dust as lesser vehicles came and went, all of them parking timidly on the opposite side. Now, as the last of the daylight bled into the brooding darkness of the spruces, Skip Kretzer was beginning to wonder if they were ever going to get out of there.

He sat upon a low stone wall by a grove of trees at the edge of the lot, finishing his second bottle of Coke in the past hour. Sarič paced nearby, staring at the screen of his phone as the fluttery signal came and went.

"How 'bout if we go door-to-door?" Kretzer said. "Someone in this village is bound to know his truck, or even the man himself. At the very least they'll know which direction he generally heads. Who knows, we might even find somebody who's been there."

Sarič answered with a cold stare, followed by a lecture.

"No one in these woods has a sense of national duty. It has always been so. They are their own kingdom, loyal only to one another. Of course someone will know, but they will never tell us."

Kretzer shook his head and tossed aside the empty bottle.

"Should've sent Yolvan's people up here. They'd have gotten what we need in about ten minutes."

"They have expended their usefulness. We have the necessary leads. Now it is simply a matter of triangulating what we have learned."

"Triangulating." Kretzer snorted. "Maybe next time try cultivating some local sources."

Their manhunt, with Yolvan's help, had made rapid progress through-out the morning and early afternoon. Yolvan's people had spoken to

Pavel's father, wife, in-laws, and finally to Anton Brod, a friend of Pavel's grandfather. By then they were pretty certain everyone had gone north, to the dacha owned by Pavel's grandfather, Laszlo Lukov. The problem was that no one—not even Pavel's father, Lucien—knew the exact location of the dacha. Nor was it registered anywhere with an address. All anyone seemed to know was that it was on a nameless woodland track, one of hundreds that twisted through the Javorska Forest. They found a registration record for Laszlo's Bedford truck, but it was linked to an address in Blatsk, as were his driver's license and taxation records.

If Laszlo had been a customer of the nation's electrical grid, that would have made the search much easier. Displayed at the moment on Sarič's laptop was a giant map culled from power company records and satellite imagery and plotted with GPS coordinates. It showed where all such customers lived. It also showed at least two dozen small houses which *weren't* connected to the power grid, but they were spread across nearly four hundred square miles of rolling wooded countryside, mostly on unmarked roads. Even with unlimited resources, visiting all of them would take hours, maybe days. And because Sarič was trying to avoid the sort of embarrassing spectacle that a public manhunt for the president's most favorite recent guest would have created, he had limited his manpower to about thirty people, most of whom had been dispatched to border crossings and approach roads on Bolrovia's northern and western frontiers, the only logical exit points for anyone coming from the Javorska Forest.

Sarič and Kretzer might have tried poking around a little on their own in these woods, but Smotrich seemed to be the only spot with any cell service, and even it was spotty. So here they were, waiting for further information. And now Yolvan's people had been ordered to go back to all the sources they'd talked to earlier, this time armed with printouts that showed the same map that Sarič had on his laptop.

Kretzer fumed in silence. Then Sarič finally responded to his most recent criticism.

"Fine, then. If it is a local source you want, I am sure the proprietor of this store is as good as any. And he, at least, must rely on the state for permits, licenses, taxation. I will have a word."

He headed briskly for the door.

"His name is Harko."

Sarič stopped. He eyed Kretzer with suspicion.

"How do you know this?"

"I heard another customer call him that when I was buying a Coke."

"Were they discussing us?"

"Hell, I don't know what they were discussing. My Bolrovian's not that good."

Sarič nodded and continued inside. Kretzer, figuring that the interview with the shopkeeper might be more entertaining than staring into the pines, stood and followed him inside. He watched Sarič's body language with disdain as the security chief stepped toward the counter—rigid posture, face unsmiling: a man who wanted you to know that he was a figure of authority. In other words, exactly the wrong approach to take with the slow-moving fellow behind the counter, who probably knew most of his customers personally.

Kretzer's Bolrovian was indeed lousy, but he was able to pick out a few words and phrases while intuiting others from gestures and motions, like when Sarič pointed to the store's business license, posted by the cash register.

Security matter of national importance . . .
Your duty as a citizen . . .
Your licenses and permits . . .

None of those boded well for cooperation, and Harko responded just as Kretzer would have predicted—by folding his arms, nodding blankly, and saying nothing in reply. Then he shrugged and said words to the effect that he knew nothing about any of this, which caused Sarič to raise his voice and say something about a noisy Bedford truck. Harko nodded impassively, threw up his hands, and said something about lots of people up here having noisy trucks. Then he shrugged a final time and again folded his arms. Sarič banged through the door back into the parking lot.

Kretzer winked at the storekeeper, who nodded, deadpan. He then rejoined Sarič outside.

"The insolence of these people! When I receive the necessary budget for extending our network of public cameras, his will be the first establishment up here to be put under full-time surveillance. We'll post one on that pole right across the street. We'll see everyone who goes in and out of his shitty little store."

"You just don't understand, do you?"

"What do you mean?"

"Humint. It means 'human intelligence.'"

"I know what the hell it means."

"Then act like it. Christ, play the nice guy, or the visiting hunter, or the goddamn village idiot even, but don't waltz in there like a ministry high hat with that orange fucking water bottle strapped to your ass, acting like he owes you everything he knows."

"Very good. Expert advice from the man who only a week ago assured me that the way was free and clear to pursue our joint venture with our American guests with no chance of detection."

"Because it *was* free and clear, goddamn it! There was no way that drunken fuck Leo Garvin would have noticed a thing. Blame your president—he's the one who just *had* to invite his favorite fuckup, and now here we are chasing his ass through the woods."

Sarič scowled and looked away. He unclipped the water bottle and took a swig, draining it dry before he'd taken two swallows. This, too, seemed to piss him off. He unscrewed the cap, shook out the remaining drops, and strolled over to a nearby water pump by the low stone wall. It was the old-fashioned kind, with an iron lever that you had to work by hand. Beneath the spigot was a wooden tub filled with standing water, for catching the spillover.

Kretzer watched as Sarič repeated the ritual that he had already seen twice before—removing the plunger with its filter, then filling the bottle, except this time it was sloppy going, with the gushing water spilling down the sides of the bottle. Sarič then reinserted the plunger and slowly pushed the filter toward the bottom. When he was done, he screwed the cap back on, set the bottle on the stone wall, then pulled out a handkerchief to dry his hands.

"How come you never drink any right away?"

"I like to wait at least an hour, often longer. For greater purity, better taste."

"That's part of the instructions?"

Sarič shook his head.

"Personal preference."

More like superstition, Kretzer figured, but he withheld further comment, figuring that things were already rocky enough between them. The man was certainly a hoot. You'd have thought he was talking about an ice-cold beer or some rare vintage of wine. They were a poor match as travel companions, but at least with Sarič you weren't likely to get killed by doing something half-assed. The man did pay attention to detail, even if he and Kretzer sometimes disagreed over which details were more important.

Sarič got out his phone and frowned.

"I missed a call, probably while I was in the store. But the signal is still terrible."

"Best signal I've been able to get was across the road, about thirty yards down. Here, I'll show you."

Kretzer stood and gave him a pat on the back as he passed. It was probably better to mend fences, especially if they were going to be stuck here any longer. Nightfall was complete, and the prospect of yet another hour in Smotrich seemed gloomier than ever.

"Yes, it's much better here," Sarič said as they reached the spot, which was just down the street from the parking lot, with the trees blocking their view of the store. "Thank you."

Kretzer heard the call go through. Sarič listened for a while, nodding, then issued some orders. If Kretzer was translating correctly, he didn't like the sound of some of them. Sarič pocketed his phone and brought him up-to-date.

"Hal Knight's girlfriend has indeed arrived at the Vienna airport."

"You're shitting me."

"Visual confirmation, via security cam. You were wrong about those emails only being an attempt at misdirection."

"So it seems. I guess I didn't think she was that stupid."

"She has rented a car. Two hours ago she arrived at a town just across our western border, where she has checked into a hotel room. The signal from her phone shows she is still there waiting, and she has sent two further emails to notify him of her location and her readiness."

"Any response?"

"His account remains dormant. But I have redeployed some of my people to the western crossings and their approach roads."

"Won't that leave us a little thin on the ground on the northern routes? Maybe it's time to call in a little help from the district cops."

Sarič shook his head.

"They are no better than that gorilla behind the store counter. Thoroughly corrupted, all of them. And stupid enough that they would probably just shoot him on sight."

"Nothing wrong with that. And did I hear you correctly, emphasizing that you want him taken alive, him and his buddy Lukov?"

Sarič narrowed his eyes.

"You keep saying your Bolrovian is no good."

"So am I wrong, then?"

"It is my strong preference that they be taken alive, yes."

"Not mine. For a lot of people—you and me included—it's far better if those assholes are never heard from again."

"Of course. But only after they are interrogated. There is much to learn."

"Yeah? Seems pretty goddamn obvious who must have recruited him."

"That's not enough. I want names, contacts. Root and branch. And I will get it, all of it, by whatever means. Afterward? Yes, of course, nothing will be heard from them publicly. There will be no trials, no exchanges."

"Good. Finality is always cleaner."

Ten minutes later, they at last got the breakthrough they'd been waiting for. One of Yolvan's people had gone back to Pavel Lukov's father with a blowup of the satellite imagery for several sections of the Javorska Forest, which had showed the various cabins without electrical power. He had pointed to a small rooftop and had identified it, with reasonable certainty, as his father's dacha, based on the relative location of the outhouse, the well pump, and the driveway. He had also finally remembered the name of the nearest neighbor with electrical power. Petaro something or other, and when a Petaro Konar had then showed up as a customer of the power company with a cabin only a short distance away, that had confirmed it.

"It's no more than an hour from here, even on these shitty roads," Sarič said as he studied a GPS image on his phone. "We should get going."

"You don't want to call in a couple of your other guys to join us?"

"You said the Agency had recalled whoever they'd sent here to assist him, correct?"

"Yeah. That came straight from my guy in Langley. But that pal of

Lukov's grandfather, Anton Brod, said there was a fourth member of their party, some black guy."

"Who you said would probably also be recalled."

"'Probably' isn't your usual standard. He would make it two against four."

"But one of those four is a ninety-four-year-old man, one is a comic, and one is a desk jockey who shivers whenever I raise my voice. Besides, waiting for help would take at least another two hours, maybe longer."

"Your best argument yet. But this will be our last chance to reach anyone else. All we'll have going forward is GPS. The phone signal will be gone the moment we leave this village."

"There is no point in waiting further. We leave now."

Kretzer nodded, and they headed back toward the parking lot. They were halfway to the Mercedes when Sarič reached down toward his belt with a look of alarm.

"My water bottle."

He trotted over to the stone wall where he had set it down earlier and clipped it to his belt, while Kretzer tried not to smile.

They pulled out of the lot and headed in the direction indicated by the GPS. Fifty meters further along they passed a shuttered hut with rusting gas pumps out front, where, set back in the shadows and just out of sight, a Lada Granta of recent vintage, brown, with tinted windows, sat silently beneath the trees.

A few minutes later, with the entire village gone quiet, the Lada's engine cranked to life, but the headlights did not flicker on. The car pulled out of the lot, turning in the same direction as the Mercedes, and disappeared into the darkness.

Chapter 66

Lauren peered into the night from the passenger side of the Lada while wondering how Ian Farkas could even see where they were going. As her eyes adjusted to the dark, she saw the faint outline of the road in a dim wash of starlight. There was no moon out, and as they moved deeper into the forest even this much light would be hard to come by.

"What was that little jaunt through the trees all about?" she asked. "I didn't think you were going to make it back in time before they left."

"Just seizing a moment of opportunity for a few small but important errands. Besides, we're pretty sure we know where they're headed thanks to those directions of yours. Right?"

The ones that Quint had texted her the night before, he meant. She had shared them with Farkas earlier, and now she had them open on her phone.

"Yes. And we should be looking for a red cowshed. We'll take the third left turn after that."

"I think I see it." He flicked the headlights to make sure. Red indeed, but weathered and fading. A few minutes later they turned onto a dirt lane. From here on, there would be no more paved roads.

"'Small but important errands.' Is that really all you're going to tell me?"

Farkas glanced at her. She detected a slight smile by the glow of the dashboard light.

"If it's full disclosure you're after, fine, as long as it's a two-way street."

"Point taken."

She and Farkas had joined forces an hour after her flight had arrived from Florence. A local fellow had picked her up at the taxi stand and had driven her to a rendezvous point just north of Blatsk. She had been surprised by Farkas's shabby choice of cars, but now saw the logic of it. The Lada was six years old, dusty and dull, with a dented rear fender. The lettering on its license tags began with "JVK," the code for all cars registered in the Javorska district. It looked like it belonged up here. But Farkas's biggest selling point in luring her along for the ride was his professed ability to track Branko Sarič.

"It's that vainglorious command center, the Mercedes with all the bells and whistles, that makes it possible," Farkas had explained. "A high priest of surveillance technology, and he installs the ultimate Trojan horse in his own goddamn set of wheels. A few weeks ago I paid a very skilled local fellow to hack into its GPS system. Piece of cake, according to him. Something to do with the telematics and how the programming language functions. All I know is that it works for me like a homing beacon."

So here they were, having caught up to Sarič and Kretzer only an hour earlier by arriving in Smotrich, where they had tucked the Lada into a hiding place to await their next move. Lauren still wasn't sure why Farkas had a stake in this game or who he was working for, but she wasn't sharing her deeper secrets, either. It was a marriage of convenience, which would last only as long as their interests remained mutual. Her contribution to the alliance was the info she was receiving periodically from Malone and Quint.

"Who's this person you've sent up to the western border to draw away some of Sarič's people?" he asked now. "I gather it's not a professional, or they'd be doing more than just cooling their heels in a hotel room."

"Who says that's all they're doing?"

He thought that over for a moment.

"Ah, I see. Laying down a false trail with phone calls and emails, then ditching the phone in the room to go off on their own. Sound about right?"

"It's one possibility."

"But a civilian, yes? Local or American?"

"I'll trade you for a description of those small but important errands."

"Sweeten the offering and I might oblige you. Especially if it involves a taste of whatever Hal Knight managed to uncover. Based on his sudden need to take flight—and yours—I'm guessing it's fairly good stuff."

"I doubt you have anything of comparable value."

"Look, I've been in this country for months now, playing the erudite, money-grubbing fool at the Green Devil while I watched Branko Sarič roll up your employer's entire network. The whole time I've been wondering what sort of grandiose plan he was clearing the decks for, and now I suspect you've discovered it. So if you really want my help in securing your findings . . ."

"Phil Lacey seems to be involved. I can tell you that much."

Lauren figured it wouldn't hurt to put Lacey's name out there, especially if Fordyce tried to hush up everything later.

"I see."

"Do you really?"

"Yes. Especially if this is connected in any way to all these right wingers who've blown into town. From what I've heard about Lacey, maybe he sees whatever they're up to as his own personal episode of *The Apprentice,* his chance to become Director if the Big Orange Boss wins his way back into the White House."

Lauren had a queasy feeling that his hunch was correct.

"But this is all big picture stuff," Farkas said. "What did our friend Hal stumble onto?"

"Tell you what. Help me get my asset out of this alive and I'll be so generous you'll think it's Boxing Day. But for now, slow down. We've got another turn coming up."

"Yes, your majesty."

What they knew from Malone's work was that there was still no opening for escape at any of the border crossings to the north. But now that Sarič and Kretzer were back on the move, the time was approaching that Hal would need to set out anyway from the dacha. The problem with that contingency was that Quint's only means of communication was a landline that was a twenty-five-minute walk from the dacha, so he was only able to reach her once every hour. And now, since Lauren no longer had cell service, even that line of communication had gone dead. In her most recent contact she'd at least been able to relay the news that Sarič and Kretzer were lying in wait only an hour away, but she had no way of warning Quint that they were now on the move.

Even if Hal got away safely, Lauren had no idea yet what to do to help Pavel Lukov and his grandfather. She and Quint had discussed some possible ways of making their cooperation look coerced, but none of those ruses would work if Sarič caught them unawares.

"Are we still on track?" Farkas asked.

"Yes. Next turn is a little further."

"We're probably, what, half a mile behind them?"

"Something like that."

"I'm a little surprised he didn't wait for more of his men to come up."

"Hubris."

"He's certainly no stranger to that."

Farkas then braked sharply as some sort of large animal dashed across the road just ahead, followed by two more.

"What the hell was that?" he asked.

"Wild boar, I think."

"Those little flashes of white must've been tusks. Too bad we can't send it after the Mercedes."

"You know, you might at least tell me what London's interest is in an American comedian's visit to Bolrovia."

"Ask London yourself, provided they even know who I am. Then I'll get on the horn to Langley. I'm sure that, between the two of them, we'll be regaled with full and frank discussions of all relevant particulars."

She couldn't help but laugh.

"Speaking of communication," he said, "have we definitely lost our phone signal?"

"Yes. Quite a while ago."

He shook his head.

"We're playing by all the old rules again. Sarič must hate it. What's our next landmark?"

"An old windmill in a clearing."

He chuckled under his breath.

"Will there be little dwarves out front, dressed like miners?"

Half an hour later, they had to stop so Lauren could poke around in the trees in search of the next waypoint—a game warden's hut. Not long afterward they spotted the boulders marking the final turn. They were now only two kilometers from the dacha.

Farkas dropped the Lada into the lowest gear. They were moving at walking pace, and even the starlight was now blotted out by a canopy of spruces. Two red pinpricks of light flickered suddenly in the darkness at least a quarter mile ahead. Farkas stopped the car.

"Their brake lights," he said. "Even at this speed, we've nearly caught them. Cat and mouse from here on out."

"Which one are we? Kill the engine. Roll down your window."

The only sound at first was the whine of the power window as it lowered, then a thunk as it stopped. The forest was quiet. Any other night creatures in the area must have already retreated to avoid the two cars.

Then, barely discernible, Lauren heard the sound of a car engine, the purr of a Mercedes, followed by a crunch of gravel. Then nothing.

Farkas whispered.

"If we can hear them, then they'll sure as hell hear this rattly-ass Lada the moment we start her back up."

"We're close now. We'll go the rest of the way on foot. Turn off the dome light."

He nodded and did so before they gently unlatched the doors and got out. They saw a second flash of brake lights. Then the Mercedes also went silent. Lauren whispered.

"They're going on foot, too."

"Let's wait a moment, then, lest we stumble into them."

After thirty seconds of silence, Lauren decided she'd had enough.

"I'm going in. With or without you."

He nodded, and they slowly moved forward through the trees.

Chapter 67

———⪨———

Walking a woodland path in total darkness was a clarifying experience, Hal decided, especially when you were convinced that you might be frozen into place at almost any moment by a beam of blinding light so that some hidden sniper could blow you to pieces.

He was on his way back to the dacha after having just filled a bucket of water at the well, and he was moving strictly by feel. The soles of his shoes told him he was still on the path. Both of the dacha's windows had been covered with heavy blankets and duct tape, to make the place as invisible as possible, meaning that all Hal had to guide him was the muffled sound of voices from inside the cabin, twenty yards away.

From the trees off to his right, something thumped against the forest floor. A hoof, perhaps, or a fallen object. He stopped—alert, waiting—as the bucket handle bit into the curled fingers of his right hand. Some of the pumped water had splashed onto his shirt and trousers, which he had now been wearing for the past thirty-six hours, and he needed to blow his nose. He sniffled, turned toward the sound, and called out through the trees.

"Hello?" His voice sounded tentative, but far too loud. "Anyone out there?"

A rustle of underbrush told him that whatever it was had decided to move off. But by turning he had momentarily lost his orientation, so he slid his feet to make sure he was staying on the path. He was then startled by a metallic rattle, which at first he was certain must be someone chambering a round into a weapon. Instead it was the latch of the cabin door, which opened to spill a band of golden light onto the ground just ahead. Pavel's voice called out.

"Hal? Are you out there?"

"Coming around the corner. Keep the door open so I can see my way forward."

It had been a long and arduous day.

Hal and Pavel had fixed the roof, recaulked both windows, and chopped and stacked more firewood. They had tried to install a new iron handle on the well pump, but the connecting hardware was the wrong size. Meanwhile, Quint had left every hour to check for updates.

The moment they ran out of chores, Hal had become edgy, then morose. After brooding a while, he made up his mind to act on his own. He had burdened these people enough.

"I'm taking off," he told Pavel. "If I'm caught, then I'm caught. But I can't endanger you and your grandfather any longer."

Pavel looked at him like he was nuts.

"Do you really think it's that easy? That you're the only one who needs to keep running? While I do what? Wait here for Sarič?"

"Then how 'bout I stay, and you tie me up, like you've caught me. At least until Quint gets back. Or, if he's back in time, maybe we could tie up you guys so they'll think—"

"Stop! It's too late for any of that. Even if it wasn't, Poppy would never go along with it. For him, it is all about fighting the good fight."

Then Quint had returned with news that some of the security personnel posted at the northern border was now redeploying elsewhere, due to Lauren's use of a decoy along the western border.

"A decoy?" Hal asked.

"Jess Miller. Lauren wanted me to tell you that."

Hal needed a moment to absorb that.

"Jess is *here*? She came?"

"And if you make it out of here, we'll try to make sure she's the one who meets you on the other side."

For Hal, that had changed everything—his readiness, his mood, his willingness to follow any order. Poppy had then cooked a pot of hearty soup with root vegetables and cured venison, which they'd shared along with a bottle of homemade brandy as darkness had fallen. Then Quint had set off for what he vowed would be his final trip to the phone line, to try to get the latest possible update before he and Hal set out for the border.

Now, as Hal reentered the cabin, he saw Poppy unwrapping oilcloth from an ancient bolt-action rifle.

"What the hell is that?"

"A Mauser Karabiner," Pavel said. "He took it off a dead German during the war."

"It still works?"

"Most of the time. He killed a boar with it a few months ago."

Poppy opened a cardboard box of gleaming cartridges, each of them about two and a quarter inches long. He loaded five of them into the magazine, one by one. He motioned to Pavel, and then mimed various motions to demonstrate how to fire and reload the rifle.

"Have you ever used it before?" Hal asked.

"Once, when I was a boy. A very long time ago, to shoot at a rabbit. I missed."

There was a sullen abruptness to Pavel's manner, and Hal couldn't blame him.

Poppy then spoke in a rapid burst of Bolrovian. Pavel nodded grimly and reached for his jacket.

"What did he say? What are we doing?"

"He says it is time to deploy."

"Deploy?" Hal felt some of the air go out of his lungs.

"Until Quint is back. He said if all we do is wait in here, we will be easy prey if they come. He said to shut the lantern, go outside, and fan out in a line, the three of us."

They shut the valve on the lantern and watched the light die. Poppy got out a small flashlight and they trooped outdoors, huddling in front of the cabin. Poppy spoke as he cradled the rifle in his left arm while gesturing with his right hand, pointing in different directions with the beam of the flashlight. Pavel translated.

"He wants me to go left, over behind that tree. He wants you here, behind the woodpile, and not too far from the door. If any shooting starts, he says you should try to get back inside and hide under the bunk."

"Would that even do any good?"

"Probably not, but it might buy him enough time to get off a good shot, especially if they decide to rush the house."

It all sounded a bit delusional, but Hal stepped toward the woodpile. Next to it, propped by the door, was the iron pump handle. Hal grabbed it, if only to keep from feeling quite as helpless, then moved behind the shoulder-high pile of logs.

"And where will your Poppy be?"

"Over there." Pavel pointed to the Bedford truck. "He said the flatbed makes a good firing platform."

Poppy nodded, as if to confirm it. No sooner had he done so than there was the sound of crunching gravel from far up the driveway, and the faint whine of a car engine. Poppy immediately shut off his flashlight.

"Was that a car?" Hal whispered. He was peering over the firewood like a frontiersman in a log fort.

"Maybe it's Petaro, coming early."

"Then why'd he stop?"

Poppy stepped quietly toward his truck, but Hal and Pavel were momentarily locked in place as they peered into the darkness toward the source of the sound. Just as Hal was wondering if it had only been an animal, a voice called out in English through the trees from maybe a hundred yards away.

"Do not move, or we will shoot." It was Branko Sarič. "Two of us are going to approach, but there are others who are watching. They have nightscopes and will kill anyone who moves."

Hal had to resist an urge to bolt and run. Even then he wondered if he was doing the right thing by just standing there. Maybe being shot in the back would be preferable to whatever Sarič would have in store for him later.

Poppy, the only one of them with experience in this sort of thing, continued to move stealthily toward the flatbed of his truck, as if calling Sarič's bluff, which now didn't seem like such a bad idea, because Hal had already lost sight of the old man. Then, in the instant just before everything began to spin out of control, it occurred to Hal that maybe Poppy simply hadn't understood what had been said. In any event, Hal wasn't the only one who had noticed the old man's movements.

"You, with the gun. Halt!" Sarič called out.

The bright beam of a light shone suddenly from maybe fifty yards up the driveway. They must have been pointing it toward wherever they'd last heard movement, because Poppy was now fully illuminated. In the snapshot glare of the moment, he looked for all the world to Hal like a soldier from a bygone war—kneeling, resolute, the stock of the old rifle pressed against his shoulder, head tilted as he sighted down the barrel.

He was ready to fire.

Chapter 68

⁓

Lauren was walking slowly, picking her way forward through the dark-ness, when she heard a man's voice call out in warning from well ahead, although she couldn't make out the words. Farkas, from just over her left shoulder, whispered, "Sarič?"

"Let's pick it up!"

The voice called out again, another unintelligible command. Then there was a gunshot, and a faint cry of agony.

Lauren broke into a run, tripping almost right away but somehow maintaining her balance as she lunged forward, with Farkas right behind her. She was already calculating the distance and the odds that they would arrive in time to help. They were still at least a minute from the dacha, probably more, and they also had to worry about blundering into an ambush.

Up ahead through the trees, a flashlight beam was swinging back and forth like a beacon. There were more shouts, the sounds of movement. They were going to be too late. She knew it already. But she didn't stop running.

Chapter 69

⸺⸺≈⸺⸺

Hal felt as devastated as if he had been shot himself when he saw Pavel's Poppy cry out in pain and slump sideways. A moment earlier Poppy had pulled the trigger of his rifle, an action which had created only a metallic click and a puff of smoke. A misfire. He had then cursed and began working the bolt to eject the faulty cartridge when someone had fired at him from the trees, and now the old man was rolling in agony on the flatbed.

Pavel raced past Hal toward his grandfather, crying out in Bolrovian while Hal watched helplessly. The ghastly scene was illuminated by the bouncing beam of the bright flashlight as two men ran toward them out of the darkness. One was Sarič. The other was the big American, who Quint had called Kretzer.

"Don't touch that gun or we'll shoot you as well!" Sarič said. Both men held handguns, but Sarič also held the flashlight, meaning Kretzer must have fired the shot. Hal wondered how many more shooters were out there, drawing a bead on him and Pavel.

"Easy, Branko," Kretzer said. "Grab the rifle, then let him tend to his granddad. It'll keep him occupied." He turned toward Hal. "And you. Come out from behind that woodpile."

Hal stepped into the open, unable to even swallow.

"Drop whatever the fuck you're holding, or I'll blow your head off."

Hal hadn't even realized he was still gripping the pump handle in his right hand. He let it fall against the woodpile.

Sarič set the flashlight on the flatbed so that the beam now slanted upward, throwing long shadows from all of them. He tossed aside the rifle and unclipped his water bottle for a long, deep swig, as if savoring the spoils of his victory. Then he turned toward Hal.

"I will deal with you first. And when I'm done . . ."

Then he faltered, frowned. His eyes went very wide as the bottle slipped from his fingers and he clutched at his throat. Then, slowly, like a high-rise imploded by explosives, he toppled to the ground, where his body twitched violently, then went still.

Kretzer, while holding Hal at gunpoint, stared in amazement, as did Hal. Had someone fired a silenced shot from the trees? Was it a heart attack?

"What the fuck! *Branko?*"

Kretzer stepped toward him for a closer look. Hal, seizing the moment, reached back toward the woodpile and, in a single continuous motion, grabbed the pump handle and swung it like a heavy tennis racket toward Kretzer, who belatedly turned just as the length of iron smashed into his temple with the sound of a hammer striking a concrete block. The blow dropped him instantly, and he landed crosswise atop Sarič with a massive grunt. Both men were silent.

More footsteps were now pounding toward them from the trees. Hal wheeled around, clutching the pump handle like a caveman with a femur.

"Grab his gun!" Pavel shouted from the flatbed. "I've got the rifle!"

Hal pried it from Kretzer's hand and sank into a defensive crouch. It sounded like two people were coming. Then a woman's voice called out.

"It's me, Lauren! Don't shoot!"

She materialized into the surreal lighting as Hal watched in thrilled disbelief. A low moan issued from Kretzer, but he didn't move. Hal nonetheless moved farther away from him, doubting he'd be able to keep the man from overpowering him. Nor did he think he'd have the fortitude to shoot him, even if whacking him in the head had been satisfying.

A second person emerged from the dark. It was, incredibly, the jolly Brit from the Green Devil, Ian Farkas. And for a giddy and very disorienting moment, lit by the low-angle beam beneath the looming trees, Hal wondered if in reality he had just been shot and these images were the final wild imaginings of a brain going into shutdown.

"Tie him up!" Lauren said.

Her voice snapped him back to attention. Yes, this was really happening.

"Here," Hal said, handing Lauren the gun. "You might actually know what to do with it."

"Someone help us!" Pavel called out. "It's his shoulder. We have to get him bandaged before he bleeds to death."

The old man irritably croaked out a few words in Bolrovian, which seemed like a good sign. Then Hal remembered the box of medical supplies he had seen in the dacha, in the cabinet with the pots and pans.

"I'll get the first aid kit."

He ran inside, legs rubbery from the surge of adrenaline, his mind going in a dozen directions at once. Was it really going to be this easy? Or were more of Sarič's minions still out there? In which case, with Sarič's body now lying out front, unconscious and quite possibly dead, Hal was probably in more trouble than ever. And what the hell had happened to Sarič, anyway? Had Lauren shot him from the trees?

Hal found the first aid kit and grabbed a towel from the washbasin. By the time he was back outside, Farkas had rolled Kretzer onto his stomach, and was now tying the big man's hands behind his back. Lauren was checking Sarič's pulse. She shook her head in disbelief. Hal peered into the darkness, straining his eyes for any sign of movement.

But there was nothing. The trees were quiet. No one else was coming.

"Hurry!" Pavel said. "Bring it here!"

"Yes. Sorry."

Hal hustled over to the flatbed, where Poppy was now sitting up and cursing at something. The gun, Hal realized. The old fellow was cursing his old Mauser, the one he had taken off a dead German nearly eighty years ago, probably not far from here.

Chapter 70

Poppy's wound seemed to be superficial, despite all the blood, and the old man was now asking mistrustful questions about the newcomers as he sat on the flatbed of the Bedford, propped against the cab.

Kretzer was still out cold, but to Hal his big frame looked as menacing as ever, a wolf that had been tranquilized and trussed.

Quint had just rejoined them, out of breath from running through the woods after hearing the gunshot. He now stood in a circle with Hal, Lauren, Farkas, and Pavel around the body of Branko Sarič, who was indeed dead.

"I thought maybe one of you had shot him," Hal said.

"With what, a blowgun and a poison dart?" Lauren asked. "We're not even armed."

"But a poison dart, that's at least closer to the truth," Farkas said. It was his knowing tone as much as his words which made the others turn expectantly in his direction.

"Well?" Lauren said.

"It's not me you should be looking at," Farkas said. He turned toward Hal. "*That's* the fellow who plays so fast and loose with his pharmaceuticals."

Everyone turned toward Hal, whose mind was working so fast that he didn't even notice he now had everyone's attention. The missing pills. Plan Z.

"It was *you* who searched my hotel room," he said to Farkas. "Not Sarič."

Of course. The smiling spy who was always happy to buy you a drink, or maybe even spike it with something lethal. "But . . . how'd you poison him? Where'd you put the pills? In *that?*"

He nodded toward the orange water bottle, which lay on the ground at Sarič's side. Pavel stooped for a closer look.

"But that's impossible," Pavel said. "This thing filters out all known pathogens, as he always liked to say."

"Of course it does," Farkas said. "Unless you drop something in after he's already pushed down the plunger. I heard him say he likes to wait at least an hour before he drinks from a fresh batch, so my only worry was that he wouldn't get thirsty in time to help us."

"Your small but important errand," Lauren said.

"That plus a quick phone call to an old compadre."

She tilted her head, wondering who he meant, but Hal spoke again before Farkas could explain.

"So, I'm fucked, then. I mean, if they find it in his blood and trace it back to me."

"Oh, come now," Farkas said. "You don't think I'd prepare that poorly, do you? How many pills were missing when you first discovered it?"

"Two."

"Exactly." He then used a handkerchief to remove a small plastic bag from his right pocket. Inside it was the other pill. He walked over to Kretzer, who still hadn't stirred, and gently stuffed the bag into the man's right pocket.

"In a minute or two, I'll put a few of Kretzer's fingerprints on the bottle, to neaten things up." He checked his watch. "Then, in about half an hour, a detective inspector for the district police should be arriving to handle the rest. Although I'm guessing that Lauren and Quint won't want to linger for that portion of the postmortem."

"The police?" Pavel asked with alarm. "I can't be here for that. Or my Poppy, either. I should probably go wherever Hal is going, but only if you promise to help my family."

Farkas shook his head.

"You're the least of my worries, Pavel."

"Yes, I can see that." Pavel was seething, as angry as Hal had ever seen him, and he could hardly blame him.

"I think what he's trying to tell you," Lauren said gently, "is that you're going to be the hero in all this. Am I right, Ian? A hero of the state?"

Farkas smiled, enjoying his role of impresario far too much.

"The way I see it, Pavel—and the way I've already explained it to my old friend, Detective Inspector Orbal—is that this fellow Sarič was betraying his country by working with that fallen American over there in order to recruit Mr. Hal Knight to spy on the president's top people. But you, Pavel—yes, *you alone*—fought him off and spirited away Mr. Knight in the nick of time. And when their chase came to a bad end, here in the forest, the defeated Mr. Kretzer tried to cover his tracks by poisoning his co-conspirator."

"They'll never believe that."

"Oh, but they will. Inspector Orbal's experience in these sorts of rearrangements goes back to the latter days of the Cold War, in cooperation with an old colleague of mine who introduced us a few years back. Once I've briefed you and your Poppy on exactly what to tell him, he'll come to all the proper conclusions."

"But I will have to act as if all of this is true. I'm not sure I can pull it off."

Farkas turned to Hal.

"Mr. Knight, please tell your friend here what acting is all about. And how, even at its hammiest, it's often quite convincing as long as you have a willing and sympathetic audience."

"But this Detective Orbal, he doesn't even know me."

"You're correct. But about a year ago, Branko Sarič ordered a shakeup of the district's entire security apparatus. Detective Orbal's wife and eldest son both lost their jobs as a consequence, and Orbal was demoted from detective supervisor. Besides, do you think this will be the first time a policeman in this district has manipulated evidence to suit the needs of the moment? Ask your Poppy, he knows the score."

Farkas then explained it all in Bolrovian to Poppy, who nodded, seemingly not at all surprised. Poppy then said something to Pavel, who translated.

"Javorska justice, he says."

"There you are."

But, alas, it would not be an immaculate escape for Pavel, because Lauren then took him aside. She led him out of earshot, but from Pavel's forlorn expression Hal could make a pretty decent guess of what she must have been asking of him—further cooperation, in exchange for her help today. Pavel nodded gamely, but it was obvious his heart wasn't in it. Poor fellow. Handed off from one scheming spy to another.

Then he looked over at Poppy, who seemed to be in decent spirits. Although surely at his age he should be getting better care than this.

"Shouldn't we get Pavel's Poppy to a doctor?"

"It's already arranged," Lauren said. "There's a doctor in Smotrich. Quint's going to drive him in the Bedford."

"Maybe we should get Kretzer looked at, too, if he ever wakes up. I'm worried I might have fractured his skull."

She frowned uncomfortably and looked at the ground. When she looked back up at him, her eyes were full of concern.

"He's dead, Hal. I'm sorry."

"What?" Hal's chest went cold. "But I heard him moan after he hit the ground." He felt panicky, as if there might still be something he could do to reverse it. "I only hit him once. I thought . . ."

"It's okay. He would've killed you, you know. Quite happily, and you wouldn't have been his first. Not nearly."

Hal needed to sit down, but there was no place to do it, so instead he sank into a squat.

"Shit. I'm so sorry."

"Hal, look at me."

Lauren had stooped next to him so that they were face-to-face. "You did what you had to do at that moment. For your friend, for yourself. In some ways it may be the best thing you'll ever do."

"I'll never feel that way about it."

"Good. That's a good thing, too." She rested a hand on his shoulder. Then she stood, so he did as well, although he felt unsteady on his feet.

"You should get ready to roll. We're going to get you out of here as soon as we can. The neighbor, Petaro, will be coming over with his truck."

It took a few seconds for the words to sink in.

"Wait. I'm leaving *now?*"

"Not right away. You'll need to speak to the detective. As soon as he's done, Petaro will drive you north to the border. We'll have someone waiting for you there, and they'll put you on a flight home."

"Jess? That's what Quint said."

"Maybe. If she can make it to the crossing in time. Apparently Petaro doesn't speak any English, so it will be a pretty quiet drive."

"Good. I could use some quiet."

"You did good work, Hal."

"Yeah, so good that they pulled the plug on us."

"And I'm plugging us back in. Your photos, the video, your reports.

I've sent everything straight to the top. And if that isn't enough, then I'll send them somewhere else. Justice, the FBI. If necessary, I'll go public."

"That might not be too healthy for Pavel."

"I'll find a way to protect him, to put the blame on Sarič. And I'm pretty sure I know who Kretzer was working with inside the Agency. His phone will tell us for sure."

"Will you keep your job?"

"If I don't, then it's not worth keeping."

Hal nodded. Then he looked over at Kretzer's body, but a glimpse was all he could bear.

Chapter 71

By the time Detective Orbal had come and gone it was nearly midnight. By then, Pavel was reasonably convinced that this might actually work. Orbal's contempt for Sarič was palpable, and the detective had nodded with obvious relish as Pavel had spun his part of the tale.

Farkas had then taken him aside to offer further embellishments for use with journalists and security underlings over the next several days.

"There are always holes in these stories," he'd said. "Don't worry about them. Most people won't ever notice, and the ones who do will deal with them in the ways most advantageous to themselves. You and I will of course not be able to communicate directly from here on out, but if you ever need to reach me, leave a message with Dimitri Kolch."

Pavel did a double take.

"Are you serious?"

"He's a patriot in his own way. Your Poppy would call him a hero of the resistance."

Farkas had instructed Hal to write a farewell letter to President Horvatz in the pages of his black notebook, in which he apologized for his hasty but necessary exit, thanked him for his hospitality and good humor, and expressed his hopes that the president would be better served by his staff now that the duplicitous and disloyal Branko Sarič had been unmasked and vanquished.

The rumble of Petaro's truck was now approaching through the woods. Pavel turned to see Hal walking toward him.

"My ride is here. Farkas gave you the message I wrote, right? The one for your president?"

Pavel nodded.

"I hope you'll be able to forgive me for getting you into all this shit."

Then, as if to preempt Pavel from answering, he said, "And I hope Lauren didn't pressure you too hard to play her game. She won't rat you out if you refuse, I hope you know that."

"It's a moot point anyway. I plan to submit my resignation after a week or so, once everything settles down. I can't keep working for him in good conscience, and I'm sure that as a hero of the state I will have plenty of private opportunities."

Petaro's truck braked to a halt, and he called out from his open window.

"What's he saying?" Hal asked.

"He wants to get moving. Are you ready?"

Hal nodded and looked expectantly at Pavel, as if there was more that still needed to be said.

"Do you think you will ever come back here?"

"Fuck no. But you could always visit the States. Your whole family. I'd be happy to show you around."

"We'll think about it."

"Although you might not want to be seen in public with me."

"We'll think about that as well."

"Good. Tell Nicky for me that it's been real."

Pavel laughed and then shook his head, already marveling at what the next few days were likely to bring.

"My god, the lies I'm going to have to tell."

"But for all the right reasons. Your Poppy will be proud of you."

Hal stepped forward in a rush to give him an awkward hug. He then walked to the truck, where he turned, gave half a wave, and climbed in. Petaro, framed by the open window, yawned, not exactly a good sign before you were about to go on a long drive on darkened roads. He then fired up the engine with a blast of blue exhaust and drove away.

Pavel followed the progress of the red taillights until they winked out of sight.

Chapter 72

———≈———

Hal reached the border about an hour before first light. As promised, the last remnants of Branko Sarič's security patrols had all gone home—from this route, anyway—after being ordered home several hours earlier by the provincial police chief.

There were no checkpoints or customs booths because the neighboring state, like Bolrovia, belonged to the European Union. There *were* a few immigration police cars on the Bolrovian side, posted to make spot checks of incoming vehicles for human smugglers or fleeing refugees. But their job was to keep people out. Leaving was a breeze.

Petaro had come close to nodding off at the wheel several times during the previous two hours. He had stayed awake mostly by chain-smoking, so Hal had cracked open his window and wheezed his way along. Sleeping would have been impossible anyway, mostly because he was so keyed up by the prospect of who might be waiting for him. Surely it would be someone else.

The road ahead was clear as they approached the bridge over the small river which marked the border. Petaro nonetheless seemed uncomfortable with the idea of traveling any further with his potentially illicit passenger, so, when they were about fifty yards away, he pulled onto the shoulder beneath some pines and motioned with his hands that Hal should continue on foot. The poor old fellow looked exhausted, although he perked up considerably when Hal gave him the agreed-upon sum of cash for his troubles, probably enough to pay for all his winter supplies.

Hal felt vulnerable and exposed as he walked across the well-lit bridge. Not even the birds were up yet, and the only sound was his footsteps on the concrete walkway. He must have looked strange, a traveler crossing into another country without a single piece of luggage. But no one got out of any of the police cars parked nearby.

Looking ahead, to about fifty yards beyond the bridge, Hal felt his spirits lift as he saw Jess Miller leaning against a rental car in a parking lot by a small store. Then, for a moment, he was convinced it was only a look-alike. But no, it was her. He could tell by her pose, her posture, and the way she was holding a foam cup of coffee that had probably gone cold hours ago. He quickened his stride but didn't speak until he reached the parking lot.

"Sweet Baby Jesus. Of all people."

"Just doing my duty for my country."

"How long have you been here?"

"Only about an hour."

"Thank you."

"I spoke to Susan. She told me everything."

Susan, Lauren, what did it matter at this point? Hal nodded and suddenly felt the weight of all the events of the past few days collapse within him like some rickety old house that had finally fallen to pieces. He realized he needed to sit down.

"Hey, are you okay?"

"Just tired. And, well . . . my friend's grandfather. He saved our asses, then he got shot. Plus this other guy who was coming after us—I hit him in the head with something and, well . . ."

"Yeah, she told me that, too."

Then she hugged him, a bit tentatively, but far better than nothing.

"Thanks for that."

"For moral support only. Don't get any ideas."

"I won't."

He now felt a little awkward, but mostly he was grateful.

"Guess we should get rolling, then," she said. "Oh, and here's your airline ticket."

It was the old-fashioned kind, printed out and enclosed in a sleeve of blue paper.

"Are you on the same flight?"

"No. I'm headed to LA."

"And I'm not?"

"So I've been told."

He frowned, puzzled, and checked the ticket.

"Washington Dulles?"

"Susan said to tell you there would be a couple of guys waiting for you in customs. An official debriefing, she called it. It could take a few days, but apparently they will have already seen your reports and photos, and now they want to know everything. She said you'd think that was *good* news."

"Yeah. It probably is." Then, after a pause. "Or maybe not."

"What do you mean?"

"Well, in my very brief career as a congressman I learned that, in Washington, anything that seems to be a done deal immediately becomes null and void the moment your side loses an election."

"You're saying that a year from now someone might be able to make this all go away?"

"Yes."

"Meaning you just risked your life for nothing?"

"Possibly."

But Hal's more urgent worry was of a more personal nature, because he had already latched on to the comfortable idea of collapsing onto a seat next to Jess for a long transatlantic flight. All those hours in her company, even on a plane, would have given them time to talk, whether she was ready for it or not. And, perhaps, given enough time . . . No, the whole idea was absurd, and now it was also pointless because they'd be on separate flights. They would say goodbye at the airport, and that would be the end of it. He had better enjoy this while he could, and be thankful she had come at all.

"Oh, one other thing." She opened the passenger door and grabbed a plastic bag, which she tossed to him. "Here. You kinda stink, and Susan said you might need this."

There was a fresh T-shirt, socks, some boxers, and a pair of khakis in the bag. He went inside the store and used a restroom sink to wash up as best as he could. Then he put on the new clothes, which smelled like the plastic they'd come in. He started folding up the dirty items, then realized that they smelled like fear, like sweat, like Petaro's cigarette smoke. Worse, they smelled like death. He stuffed them into the garbage can, and even Shirley Halston didn't speak up in protest.

When he stepped back outside, Jess was waiting at the wheel with the engine idling.

They drove mostly in silence for the next hour or so, but nothing about it felt uncomfortable—for him, anyway—and they reached the end of the forest just as the sky was beginning to lighten in the east. Jess stopped in a small town to upgrade her coffee, so he got one as well, plus a day-old ham-and-cheese baguette wrapped in plastic, which tasted like the best thing he'd eaten in ages.

He began to relax. He again thought of Kretzer, and of Pavel's Poppy, the cost of it all. At ninety-four could you fully recover from a wound like that? And for what? Maybe Hal would learn more from whoever met him at Dulles. Or probably not, because chances were they wouldn't tell him a damn thing. They would ask lots of questions and offer zero answers, because that was how this business worked.

Jess looked over from the driver's seat, her face illuminated by the pale morning sky. It was exhausting to contemplate what lay ahead, and he must have sighed.

"Do you want to talk about it?"

He was about to decline her offer in favor of some sleep. Then he realized this might be his only chance to tell her his version of events. It might even be the last time they spoke. So instead he nodded.

"Yeah, I do."

He told her everything, from the moment they'd cornered him in the bar on Vieques to the moment he'd climbed into Petaro's truck for the ride to the border. Although he did skip his karaoke performance, if only to avoid reciting his maudlin lyrics. It took nearly an hour. Jess listened quietly, nodding now and then, her eyes offering consolation at all the right places. She then told him about her lunch with Belinda, and why that was the only reason she had originally decided to pretend she might come. He laughed at that part, disappointed but not really surprised. Then they ran out of words for a while.

Hal drifted off, his head drooping until his chin rested against his chest, then awakened with a start as the car braked sharply to avoid a wayward truck. He gasped in alarm and thrust his hands forward to protect himself, as if Kretzer were now swinging the iron pump handle at *his* head in front of the woodpile.

Jess reached over to touch his arm.

"It's okay. You're safe now."

He nodded, steadied his breathing, and leaned back against the headrest. For the next few miles he kept checking the side mirror and glancing over his shoulder for any sign of a black Mercedes in pursuit. A few minutes of silence passed as they began climbing in tight switchbacks up the side of a wooded mountain.

"I've been thinking about what Belinda wanted you to do."

"Yeah. Pretty shitty, huh?"

"You should do it. I'll help, but you do all the writing. And only you. I'll sign over the rights. You'll have to change the name of the country, of course, to keep that asshole Horvatz from suing you."

"Change it to what? Poland? Hungary?"

"Just make it up. Upper Slobovia or something, Americans won't know the difference. Oh, and change all the names, of course. And try to leave poor Pavel out of it completely, or make him a regime toady."

"Okay."

"As long as you don't make me out to be too much of a flaming asshole."

She snorted.

"C'mon, Hal. We've at least gotta keep it plausible."

They laughed about it together, which felt good.

"Okay, then, so I'm no Humphrey Bogart. Just don't turn me into Peter Lorre."

"Hell, you'd have to die if I did that, which would fuck up the ending."

"Oh, and you have to keep the karaoke scene."

"There's a *karaoke* scene?" She groaned.

"Trust me, you'll like it. And, well, if you could just leave out . . ."

"Yes. I will."

He thought again of Kretzer, and that final moan of his. A few seconds passed before she spoke again.

"You're sure you want me to do this?"

"Absolutely. It's the only way I have left of gaming the system. Hell, if the wrong people take over in twenty-twenty-four, it might be the only way the story ever gets out."

She nodded, and they were again silent until the car reached the top of the mountain, where, as they rounded a curve, the road opened onto a panoramic view. Hal pointed to a turnoff just ahead.

"Pull into that overlook. I gotta pee."

The only other vehicle in the turnout was a pickup hitched to a caravan trailer, with curtains drawn on the windows. Hal walked to some bushes at the opposite end, relieved himself, then headed back toward the car. Jess had strolled over to some big rocks at the edge of the slope and was up on her tiptoes, trying to check out the view. Out across the plains below, the sun was now rising above the horizon to their left. The view straight ahead was southward, back toward Bolrovia. From here Hal could just make out the undulating green edge of the Javorska Forest.

"Beautiful, isn't it?" he said.

"I can't see over the treetops."

"Here." He held out a hand to help boost her atop one of the rocks. She climbed up, then rested a hand on his shoulder to steady herself.

"Wow. Yeah, this is nice." Then, without turning to face him, "You know what all of this has made me realize? About you and me, I mean."

"What?"

He sought out her eyes, but she was still staring off into the south.

"That I didn't want you to die."

His hopes for some deeper renewal of their old connection plunged straight off the side of the mountain. But he laughed because, well, what else was there to do at this point?

"There you go, then. A tiny step, but better than no steps."

"And maybe the only step. Or maybe not. But I will say this. Your . . . downfall, collapse, whatever you want to call it, plus everything that happened to you over here. In some ways I think it's made you a better person. In other ways? Same old Hal."

"Probably. I can live with that. Guess I have to."

She hopped down from the rock. They walked back to the car, opened the front doors on both sides, and then stood for a moment looking at each other across the roof.

"One other thing," Jess said. "I still enjoy talking to you."

"Well, good. Because it's another two hours to the goddamn airport."

She smiled, but only briefly, and they got back into the car.

A Note About the Author

DAN FESPERMAN served as a foreign correspondent for *The Baltimore Sun*, based in Berlin. His coverage of the siege of Sarajevo led to his debut novel, *Lie in the Dark*, which won Britain's John Creasey Memorial Dagger Award for best first crime novel. Subsequent books have won the Ian Fleming Steel Dagger Award for best thriller, the Dashiell Hammett Prize from the International Association of Crime Writers, the Barry Award for best thriller, selection by *Oprah Daily* as one of their Favorite Books of the Year, and by *USA Today* as the year's best mystery/thriller novel. He lives just north of Baltimore.

A Note on the Type

This book was set in a modern adaptation of a type designed by the first William Caslon (1692–1766). The Caslon face, an artistic, easily read type, has enjoyed more than two centuries of popularity in our own country. It is of interest to note that the first copies of the Declaration of Independence and the first paper currency distributed to the citizens of the newborn nation were printed in this typeface.

Typeset by Scribe,
Philadelphia, Pennsylvania